continued . . .

Titles by Juliana Gray

A Strange Scottish Shore
A Most Extraordinary Pursuit
The Duke of Olympia Meets His Match
(novella)

Writing as Beatriz Williams

Along the Infinite Sea
Tiny Little Thing
The Secret Life of Violet Grant
A Hundred Summers
Overseas

A Strange
Scottish Shore

JULIANA GRAY

BERKLEY
New York

BERKLEY
An imprint of Penguin Random House LLC
375 Hudson Street, New York, New York 10014

Library of Congress Cataloging-in-Publication Data

Names: Gray, Juliana, 1972– author.
Title: A strange Scottish shore / Juliana Gray.
Description: First edition. | New York : Berkley, 2017.
Identifiers: LCCN 2017019954 (print) | LCCN 2017030070 (ebook) |
ISBN 9780698176492 (ebook) | ISBN 9780425277089 (softcover)
Subjects: | BISAC: FICTION / Romance / Historical. |
FICTION / Mystery & Detective / Historical. |
GSAFD: Romantic suspense fiction. | Historical fiction. | Mystery fiction.
Classification: LCC PS3607.R395 (ebook) |
LCC PS3607.R395 S77 2017 (print) | DDC 813/.6—dc23
LC record available at https://lccn.loc.gov/2017019954

First Edition: September 2017

Printed in the United States of America
1 3 5 7 9 10 8 6 4 2

Cover art © David Moore
Cover design by Sarah Oberrender
Book design by Kelly Lipovich

*To all those who have stood where history
was made and felt its echo.*

A Strange
Scottish Shore

There was a time of great prosperity, when riches were abundant upon the land and disease was rare, and even the poor did not starve, but lived unto old age. Still there was great unhappiness, for misery is the lot of mankind, and a certain Lady, whose husband's greed for treasure knew no limits, went one spring to the seaside with her servants and her only son, and swam in the nearby ocean every morning at dawn. Though the Lady knew great strength and skill in the sea, she wore always a thick, elastic suit to cover her legs and her arms, for this land lay in the far north of the country, and its waters were icy . . .

THE BOOK OF TIME, A. M. HAYWOOD (1921)

One

The man stood near the corner of the booking offices as I emerged from the ladies' waiting room, pretending to read a newspaper. He was dressed in the kind of comfortable suit of brown Harris tweed with which any fellow might clothe himself for a long train journey, except he wore it awkwardly, stiff and overly buttoned, like a schoolboy given his first grown-up jacket and trousers. His face I recognized. It was plain and wide, the pale skin hung upon a pair of broad cheekbones, and the hair underneath the tweed cap was a raucous ginger: a man I could never forget. I had first seen him in March, five months ago, upon the Greek island of Naxos.

For an instant, we met eyes. I say an instant, but it felt like a minute or more, so charged was the connection between us, and so deep the shock to my bones. He made no sign of recognition, except for having taken the trouble to transfix me at all, and once he accomplished this act, he folded the newspaper twice, tucked it under his arm, and walked off in the direction of the departure platform, where he disappeared into the thickening crowd.

According to the station clock, it was now forty-eight minutes past nine, and the Scottish express left King's Cross station promptly at ten. The air was grossly hot and smelled of coal smoke and human perspiration. At the end of the platform, an enormous green locomotive rumbled and boiled, working up a head of steam; the space between us was a carnival of passengers, porters, carts, conductors, and luggage, and somewhere inside it all lurked the man with the ginger hair.

My palm was damp inside its cotton glove. I renewed my grip on the handle of my valise—I have always carried my own luggage, whenever possible—and turned to the right, marching toward the first-class Pullman coach exactly midway down the platform. The conductor frowned slightly at my serviceable jacket and hat, at the valise in my hand. I held out my ticket. His face transformed. "Good morning, Miss Truelove," he said, "and might I trouble you to follow me?"

Thus we boarded the train.

I cast a final glance down the platform as I mounted the steps, but saw no flash of ginger beneath a brown tweed cap. It was not until I settled in my seat—in a private compartment reserved entirely for my use by my employer, the Duke of Olympia—that I caught sight of him again, walking slowly toward the locomotive, hands shoved in his pockets. I craned my neck until he passed out of view, and then I rushed from the compartment to stick my head from the door of the coach, balancing dangerously from the iron steps while shreds of steam drifted around me. Nearly all the passengers had boarded; the last tearful farewells were taking place, the swift embraces between lovers. For a second or two, a series of baggage carts obscured the man's back, until he emerged alone, the fringe of hair just visible at his collar, and swung suddenly to the left into a third-class carriage on the other side of the dining car.

The whistle screamed. The shouts of the conductors rang down the platform. I pulled myself back inside the coach, while the beat of my heart echoed above them all, spinning my blood, and somebody's hand came to rest on the sleeve of my jacket.

"Is something the matter, Miss Truelove?" asked the conductor. He was about fifty years old, and his face briefly resembled that of my dead father: kind and serious, bracketed by a handsome pair of muttonchops. I stared at him until the shrill whistle cried again, and the vision went away. The whiskers dissolved, the man's face reassembled into its plain, haggardly London self.

"Thank you for your concern," I said, "but I am quite all right."

⁓

I suppose I must have fallen asleep after I returned from the dining car at half past one o'clock, for when I opened my eyes, a woman had taken the seat across from me. A light Midlands mist drizzled against the window glass, and a note of roses had joined the damp odors of the train compartment. The newcomer was short and somewhat stout, wearing a blouse of fine white silk atop a plaid skirt, and a handsome black velvet jacket over all. Her hair was brown and shining, parted exactly down the middle, and her blue eyes frowned at me, as they usually did. The roses, I knew, belonged to her.

"It is most unseemly to fall asleep in a public conveyance, Miss Truelove," she told me.

I yawned and stretched. "Hardly a fair criticism, from a woman who has always had the good fortune to travel privately."

"A head of state cannot possibly travel on a public railway carriage."

"I beg leave to point out that you're doing exactly that, just now."

"Ah," said the Queen, looking wise, "but you don't believe I exist, do you? A figment of your imagination, as you call me."

I was too fatigued to engage in games of logic, so I turned my head to look out the window, where the middle of England presently unrolled in curves of dull, foggy green. "To what do I owe the favor of this audience?" I asked the Queen's reflection.

"Some time has passed since last we conversed—"

"And for those weeks of peace I am wholly grateful."

"Don't interrupt. I want a word with you."

"So I guessed." I stuck my hand by my hip, where it pressed against the side of the carriage, to assure myself that the leather portfolio was still tucked between the two. "I suppose I have misbehaved in some way? Disappointed you by thought or deed?"

"You already know how I feel about the matter of your employment with the Duke of Olympia. I believe I made that plain when you first took up his offer to direct this little institute of his—"

"The Haywood Institute is not small," I said. "Only men's minds are small."

"As it happens, however, I am not here to remonstrate with you about that particular folly, which is beyond our immediate hope of correction. I am here to warn you."

"Warn me. Of course." I turned to face her. "What dangers do you imagine for me this time?"

"In the first place, your rushing down to Scotland to begin with, when you were safely in residence at the duke's house in Belgrave Square, however unsuitable the manner of your employment."

"The duke has taken up an invitation to a shooting party in the north of Scotland, and requested my assistance urgently."

"That, above all, should have warned you off. Any urgent request on the duke's part is likely to prove unsuitable at best, and dangerous at worst. I don't see why he couldn't ask his private secretary to perform this task, since the fellow's already in his company."

"Because—as the duke's telegram informed me—he has discovered another one of his mysterious objects, and Mr. Miller, for all his *admirable* qualities, is not especially qualified to assist him in that kind of investigation."

"I don't see why not. I don't see why he should require a woman to perform this task, when she lacks the strength and judgment of a man."

"A quaint sentiment, from a woman who once reigned over half the globe."

The Queen lifted her chin and turned it to the window.

"Besides," I continued, "the investigation may involve some further exploration of the duke's particular talent, of which Mr. Miller is—as yet—wholly unaware."

The Queen fixed her hands upon her lap and said, "In the second place, you ought to be aware that there is a man lurking on this train who has followed you all the way from London."

"Yes, I know."

"You *know*? You seem remarkably unconcerned."

I shrugged my shoulders. "What can I do? I am untrained in the arts of spycraft. If the man continues on the service to Inverness, I shall simply report the matter to the duke, upon my arrival."

"Well!" said the Queen.

"If you wish to be of actual help, perhaps you can tell me which carriage he presently occupies."

"Number four," she said, with an air of reluctance.

"Interesting. He hasn't moved any closer. I suppose that means he already knows my destination."

"I don't know what it means, Miss Truelove, but the fellow has a suspicious look to him, which I don't like a bit. You would do well—"

"I know exactly what he looks like. His face is sewn upon my memory, I assure you. I first encountered him on the island of

Naxos, last spring, when I traveled there—if you'll recall—to free the duke from his captors."

"Of course I remember that *disaster* of an expedition," snapped the Queen, "which brings me to my third warning—"

"It was not a disaster. We were perfectly successful in rescuing His Grace from his predicament."

"It was a disaster for *you*, Miss Truelove, for any number of reasons. One of which, I regret very much to tell you, has recently boarded this very—"

In the middle of her sentence, the door of the compartment slid open, and the cheerfully handsome face of the Marquess of Silverton inserted itself through the opening, spectacles somewhat befogged by the warmth of the atmosphere.

"Why, hullo there, Truelove," he exclaimed. "What a jolly marvel of a coincidence. Do you mind if I join you?"

The Queen disappeared, like the extinguishing of a light.

⁂

No doubt you've heard of Lord Silverton. His name, after all, figures often in those pages of the newspaper that inform a breathless public of the antics of the rich and the celebrated; they might, for form's sake, call him by the abbreviated *Lord S——*, but you must know whom they mean. After all, no other Lord S—— exists who might conceivably be confused with this one.

I regret to say that the editors of these newspapers have exaggerated neither his exploits nor his general character. If anything, he's more Silverton in person than in print. His face is dazzlingly handsome, even adorned by that pair of scholarly spectacles, and the top of his head measures nearly six and a half feet above the ground. His magnificent height and his fair hair and golden skin give you the overall impression of the sun, of Apollo, particularly during the summer: an almost stupefying effect. Sitting in that

dull compartment, taken quite by surprise, I stammered out something that must have sounded like acquiescence, for he ducked under the doorway and folded himself into the seat across—he carried
no luggage at all—and took my hands.

"My dear Truelove," he said, fixing me with a pair of familiar
blue eyes, "how very *good* it is to see you. You look remarkably
well, all things considered."

"Why, what does that mean?"

"I mean you've stuck yourself in London all summer long,
working for that damned institute of Haywood's, instead of enjoying yourself in the good, fresh air of an English summer."

"As you have, you mean?"

"Ah," he said, squeezing my hands, "just how did you know
about my summer? I hope you haven't been inquiring after me,
Truelove. Smacks of attachment, you know. Might raise my hopes."

I pulled my hands away. "Don't joke."

"You know I'm not joking. My offer still stands."

"I am not going to accept your perfectly absurd offer of marriage, Lord Silverton, even if I believed you actually meant it. Particularly after such news as I've heard of you, these past months."

"News? News?"

I turned my gaze to the handsome electric sconce on the wall
to his right. "If my information is not mistaken, sir, at least three
different women have enjoyed the favor of your company in the
months since you swore your eternal fidelity to me."

"I protest," he said, leaning back in his seat, throwing his
long arm along the row of headrests. "I did not swear any such
nonsense. My eternal fidelity to one Emmeline Truelove was
conditional upon her acceptance of my offer of marriage. In any
case, dearest girl, *that* of which you're speaking was all business.
Just ask the dowager duchess. Business, business, business."

"You must have been working *very* hard, then."

He grinned. "Very hard, indeed. And now I board the Flying Scotsman at York and discover, to my great astonishment, that my own dear Miss Truelove waits for me, prim and lovely as ever, inside a snug first-class compartment right next to the dining car. Like Christmas in August."

"I wasn't waiting for you at all, and if this meeting is a coincidence, then I'm the Queen of Morocco."

"I might possibly have had some inside knowledge."

"From the duke?"

"The thing is, I'm supposed to be up in Perth at this bloody shooting party of Thurso's, except I was unavoidably delayed—"

"No doubt."

"All in the line of duty, Truelove. Anyway, I wired Thurso yesterday to invite myself back in, and apparently Max caught wind of it and wired *me*, like the good chap he is, to let me know what a charming coincidence was headed my way." He examined his fingernails. "Perhaps I moved my plans forward a day or two."

"I'm sorry to have occasioned the trouble, since there's nothing to be gained from it."

"Nothing, Truelove? I don't know about you, but I call an hour or two of privacy in a first-class Pullman coach with the object of one's affections a very satisfactory achievement indeed. Ah, *now* you're smiling, aren't you? At last. I do like your smiles, my dear. You offer them so rarely."

"A momentary lapse. I ought to call the conductor and have you tossed out. His Grace reserved the entire compartment for my privacy."

"Wise fellow. One never knows what sort of scoundrel might gain entrance into one's compartment. Strike up a conversation and God knows what else."

"Indeed."

"And generous of him, too. Shows a proper regard for the comfort of his loyal retainers."

"I'm not his retainer at all. The duke has a new private secretary, who performs those duties admirably."

"But you're running this infernal institution of his—"

"The institute is independent of the duke's estate."

"He's paid for it all, however. And you can't deny the fact that you continue to live under Max's roof, despite having resigned your position in his household."

Somewhere in the course of this exchange, Silverton's voice lost its jocular tone. His smile disappeared, replaced by a stiff, intent arrangement of his gorgeous features, and though he kept one tweed leg crossed negligently over the other, the hanging foot gave off a series of twitches.

I wrapped one hand around the end of the leather portfolio at my side. "Are you attempting to insinuate some sort of impropriety, your lordship? I should very much like you to make yourself clear."

"Impropriety? Between you and Max? The two most upright, honorable souls across the length and breadth of jolly England? Perish." He lowered his palm to the seat beside him and leaned forward an inch or two. "But there is *talk*, Truelove."

"Talk? Talk about *me*?"

"My dear, even *you* can't possibly imagine that our little expedition last spring went without popular remark. He *is* the new Duke of Olympia, after all. Bears the unfortunate honor of being the finest matrimonial catch of the decade. The entire nation is on tenterhooks for every detail about him, and particularly the feminine company he keeps. Surely you've noticed."

I frowned. "But nobody can possibly think he means to marry *me*."

"Oh, of course not. They think you're his mistress."

"Good God."

"Absurd, isn't it?" Silverton turned his head to the country-side passing beyond the bespattered window. "All you've done is return triumphantly from the Mediterranean in his company, aboard his private yacht—"

"Confined to my cabin with seasickness."

"—resign your position as his personal secretary to take up directorship of his personal institution—"

"My capacity at the Haywood Institute is *entirely* professional."

"—and take up residence in a handsome suite in his house in Belgrave Square—"

"The suite I have occupied for the past six years, as secretary for the late duke. This is outrageous."

"Oh, bottle your outrage, my love. I'm only telling you what people are saying. Forewarned is forearmed and all that." He paused. "Is it true you're helping him find a wife?"

"He has asked my advice on the matter, and I have given it."

"No doubt, no doubt. I can just about picture the scene. Lists of suitable candidates, crackling fire, a nice pot of tea between you."

I suppose I must have blushed, because the smile returned to Silverton's face. "Well, then," he said, "any inside word for an old friend? The future of the peerage is at stake, after all. To say nothing of my standing in the wagering book at my club."

"I am not going to abet you in any sort of wagering, your lordship."

"Dash it, Truelove. You're no use at all. Well, no matter. If I had any dosh to spare, I'd place it on the head of that charming daughter of Thurso's."

"Hmhm."

"Ha! I've guessed it, haven't I? Poor Truelove. Don't feel too confounded. The whole show was blindingly obvious. For one thing, Max might be a capable shot, but he's hardly enthusiastic enough to trudge all the way to a drafty castle in the far north of Scotland without some sort of additional attraction. And she's a lovely girl, that Lady Annis. Quite exceptionally pretty. Have you met her?"

"Once, a few years ago. There was a house party at Blenheim. She came with her father."

"Ah, you see? Charming girl, eh? Beautiful as the dawn, give or take an hour or two."

"If that's the case, I wonder you didn't seek her hand yourself."

"And who's to say I didn't?"

"Because I find it difficult to believe that her ladyship would have refused a coronet so lustrous as yours."

Lord Silverton folded his arms and gazed at me. His body was so long, he sat at an angle in his seat, and his legs stretched diagonally across the compartment, careful not to crowd mine aside. Still, our knees touched from time to time as the train swayed along the line. The light sometimes reflected in the glass of his spectacles, obscuring his eyes. I had neither seen nor touched this man since April, when we parted company along a dusty path on the island of Skyros, full of grief, and yet the sight of him—the touch of him—was so familiar, he might only have popped out for an hour or two, in order to buy a ham sandwich and a newspaper. Except that my heart was beating rapidly, underneath the pressed gray wool of my jacket.

At last he turned to the window and lifted one finger to touch the folds of the curtain. "I don't know why your powers of perception should still amaze me, Truelove. I don't quite seem to have gotten used to you."

"She will make him an excellent wife, however," I said briskly. "Her kind always does. She will take to the job with enthusiasm."

"Of that, I have no doubt at all. And Max?"

"You know his heart is already lost. As long as there's liking on both sides, and loyalty, and—I suppose—a necessary degree of physical attraction, he will be content."

"Contentment. What an appalling word."

"Contentment is all most people long for."

"Do they? Poor souls. Although I suppose it all depends on what constitutes your idea of contentment."

"A clear conscience," I said. "A useful occupation."

"A useful occupation?" Silverton turned from the window. "How interesting. Do you consider *your* occupation useful, my dear? I daresay Max enjoys his little hobby immensely, but for Emmeline Truelove to make it her life's work—"

I said quietly, "You saw yourself what happened on Skyros. You know that was no little hobby. It is a power of extraordinary proportion, and I—*we*, the duke and I—are desperate to understand it."

Lord Silverton reached inside the pocket of his Norfolk jacket—the same jacket, I observed, as the one he had worn last spring—and drew out a cricket ball. "And now Max calls you urgently to his side. For what reason? I find myself asking."

"He can tell you that himself, I expect."

"He's found something, I'll bet. What is it?"

"He didn't say."

Silverton tossed the ball in the air and caught it again. "Didn't he? I suppose these rural telegraph operators aren't to be trusted. I say, I'm dashed curious to find out what it is this time. What new object has appeared in Max's universe that doesn't quite belong there. Aren't you?"

"Of course I am. I find these anachronisms fascinating. Generally speaking, there is almost always some logical explanation—"

"But not *quite* always." He tossed the ball again, a feat he managed without regarding either ball or hand, keeping his attention strictly—and rather unnervingly—upon my face. "Hence this institute of yours. The Haywood Institute for the Study of Time. And your dropping everything to gallop down the length of Great Britain to Max's assistance."

"I am always ready to help His Grace to understand the nature of this burden he bears. I—my God, what—?"

But Lord Silverton had already launched himself out the compartment door, leaving only the cricket ball to land on the carpet and roll rather painfully into my right foot.

⌀

For a moment, I sat in stupor, torn by the instinct to race after Silverton and my duty to protect the leather portfolio at my side. Then, as if electrified, I leapt from my seat, shoved the portfolio under the cushion, and threw open the compartment door.

He had already disappeared down the corridor. I cast both ways—dining car or second-class coach?—and spotted the conductor, wearing an astonished face. I dug into the pocket of my jacket and drew out a sovereign.

"Sir! The fellow who passed by, the tall one—"

He pointed to the dining car. "That way, ma'am."

I hurried toward him and pressed the sovereign into his palm. "See that nobody enters my compartment, please."

Expecting shock, or disapproval, I found instead a certain relish in the conductor's expression. "With pleasure, ma'am," he said, and I flew up the corridor toward the dining car, thanking him with a wave of my hand.

Even before I crossed the corridor between the carriages and opened the door, I knew something had occurred inside. I heard the cries of dismay, the urgent shouts. I yanked the handle and discovered a scene far different from the orderly, somnolent atmosphere I had departed an hour or two ago, brimming with hot tea and cold watercress soup. A melee of outrage, of smashed crockery and spilled potage, of white-clad waiters extracting themselves from silk-clad laps, lay between me and the opposite end of the carriage, the door of which was just now swinging shut. I dashed through it all, pushed aside inconvenient bodies, and jumped across fields of sharp white porcelain, reaching at last the end of the car just as the train made a lurch to the left and sent me sprawling into the chest of a corpulent gentleman who seemed to have been ducking beneath the shelter of his table.

"Excuse me," I said, recovering myself, and then, "Did you perhaps see a pair of men—"

"That way," he said, and pointed to the nearby door.

I thanked him and pulled the door open, continuing into the next carriage, divided between first class and third. The train began a slow curve to the left, and I swayed into the walls of the corridor, checking each compartment, until I burst through the partition to the third-class carriage, composed mostly of women and children, the children hidden behind their mothers' skirts. One woman, catching my frantic gaze, lifted her hand and pointed to the door. "Through there," she said. "God help you."

On I dashed, through the next carriage and the next—I had lost count of them by now—until I must have reached the last, because I glimpsed the pile of coal in the tender through the window glass, obscured briefly by a flash of tweed.

I ran down the rest of the corridor and wrapped my fingers around the handle of the door, just as the back of a brown tweed jacket smashed into the glass, inches from my nose, and heaved away again. Startled, I jumped back, and then tried again, this time opening the door freely and wheeling about in a cloud of coal dust.

But instead of two men before me, locked in struggle, I saw

only one: the bright golden head of Lord Silverton, bent at an angle, while his long arms braced on the railing at the side.

"What's happened?" I gasped.

His lordship turned swiftly. He had lost his cap and his spectacles, and the bone about his right eye bore an ominous red swelling. "He's jumped, the bastard. Rolled down the bank and into the woods."

I hurried to the railing and craned my neck to catch some glimpse of the path behind us, but the train was moving too fast, and the bank was already long obscured. I looked up at Silverton's frowning face. "Was it the man from Naxos?" I said. "The ginger fellow?"

"How did you know?"

"He boarded the train at King's Cross. I saw him there, watching me."

Silverton swore softly and turned his back to the blurred landscape. The coal man stood at the edge of the tender, shovel in hand, staring at us. Silverton ran a hand across his bare head and said to me, "Well, then. All's not lost. At least we can be certain of two things."

I turned my head back for one last glance. The woods had thickened alongside, and I saw only a blurred tangle of green and brown, softened by the mist. "What are those, pray?"

"One, he's bound to turn up again, wherever we're headed, since he's taken so much trouble to find us."

"And the other?"

A deep, horrified screeching had begun as the train applied its brakes, and already I could hear the footsteps of the conductors, running to the source of all this confusion. Silverton seemed not to hear them. He briefly touched the swelling at his eye and examined the pads of his fingers. Though the drizzle had lifted into a mist, his hair was already damp, and dulling rapidly into brown.

"It seems the blackguard is left-handed," he said.

∞

We stopped for nearly an hour in the middle of the countryside as the conductors investigated the incident and searched for the missing man. Of course they didn't find him. Silverton answered their questions with his usual jocular calm—*The villain picked my pocket, so naturally I gave him chase*—while I stood by silently, unnoticed by anybody except the conductor who had accepted my sovereign earlier. He gave me a single nod and kept his mouth shut.

By the time we got moving again, we were irretrievably late. We arrived at Waverley station in Edinburgh at half past seven, and Silverton, checking the station clock, checking the timetable, announced with satisfaction that we had missed the evening connection to Inverness, and would have to stay the night here in Edinburgh.

"Stay the night?" I said in horror.

"Perhaps you have another solution to our predicament? Hire a motorcar, perhaps, and drive the night?" He looked at me with earnest blue eyes, as if I might actually produce a counter-suggestion, as if I might actually agree to drive an automobile across the Scottish wilderness through the dark pitch of midnight.

"You know that's impossible," I said.

"Well, then. I suppose I'll just hop along and book us a pair of rooms in the hotel. Or one room, as you prefer."

"Two, if you please. On opposite sides of the hotel."

"Truelove. Think of the economy. To say nothing of the warmth; I'm a terribly thermal beast, I believe you'll discover."

I bent to take the handle of my valise. "It's August. I shall be perfectly warm."

"Why, don't you know, there's nothing so chilly as August in Scotland. Suit yourself, then. If you change your mind, I shall leave my door unlocked for your convenience."

"How kind of you."

Silverton reached across our two bodies and lifted my valise, before I could object. "The porters will bring mine," he said gently, and offered his sturdy tweed arm in such a way that I couldn't politely refuse, even if I had wanted to.

$$\infty$$

My father had been dead for many years—at the time of my adventures in Scotland, nearly six—but he nonetheless took the trouble to visit me from time to time. For what reason, I cannot possibly guess. When I arrived at my elegant room in the North British Hotel, in the splendid shadow of the Castle Rock, he sat in the armchair in the corner, reading from a small leather book. The air outside was still light, Edinburgh Castle outlined in charcoal against the pale sky. A steam whistle cried outside the window. I set down my valise and leaned my back against the door.

"Good evening," said my father, folding the book over his thumb. "How do you like Scotland so far?"

"I have scarcely seen it. At least the drizzle has let up."

"Has Lord Silverton been behaving himself?"

"Does he ever?" I levered myself from the door and walked to the desk in the corner, on which I placed the leather portfolio I carried under my arm. "We meet for dinner in an hour."

"Do you? I'm glad to hear it. I like the fellow."

"Yes, that's the trouble." I stared into the oval mirror above the desk. "So do I. Altogether too much."

"Can there be such a thing as too much liking?"

"When the other party is as faithless and as fickle as his lordship, yes."

"You are unfair to him, Emmeline. Haven't I always warned you not to judge a man by the mask he wears? But I think you know this already. I think you wouldn't care so much for Silverton if you didn't."

I turned from the mirror. My father sat quietly, one leg crossed over the other, fingers linked on his knee, exactly as I always remembered him. His whiskers shone in the lamplight, and his face was soft with kindness.

"I don't wish to talk about Silverton. I wish to talk about Lord Thurso and his daughter."

"You have already met them."

"Only briefly. You will recall that a secretary receives little notice from her employer's guests, except when they particularly desire something."

My father pressed his thumbs together atop the book and considered the ceiling. "He was a much younger man, when I knew him. Nor has he aged well."

"Drink?"

"Among other things. Although, when you visit the tower in which he lives, you will hardly blame him for his diversions. Even you, my upright Emmeline."

"Lady Thurso, I understand, is long dead."

"Yes, alas. In childbed. Lady Annis is the only surviving issue."

"With a nice fortune at her disposal. By special provision in the patents, the earldom may pass along the female line to the next legitimate male heir, though Lady Annis does not inherit the title in her own right."

"A considerable dowry, though it comes with little money."

"The duke does not need money. He needs an agreeable wife who will take on the duties of the Duchess of Olympia with energy and enthusiasm."

"Including the getting of heirs."

"Let us hope she proves a better breeder than her mother," I said sharply.

My father made a noise of assent. "Unfortunate, indeed, that such an old and venerable title should merely fall into the collection of the dukes of Olympia, who will hardly notice it. You know, of course, that old Thurso has a natural son, gotten of a local girl. A bright young fellow."

I sank on the corner of the bed. "Does he? Nobody mentioned it to me."

"Out of delicacy, no doubt. I am sorry to say that he was born during the period of Thurso's marriage. The mother was the daughter of an attorney in town, a not inconsiderable family. The poor girl refused to give up the child, and Thurso—by all accounts—was very much in love with her."

"How peculiar. His lordship didn't strike me as the least bit romantic. The opposite, in fact."

My father ran his finger along the spine of his book. "My dear Emmeline," he said softly, "you may one day discover that the man who feels most, shows least."

A strange, hot sensation passed across my shoulders at his words. I knit my hands together in my lap and said, "And what about the girl? Did she love him in return?"

"That, I cannot say for certain. Once the affair became known, she was ruined. Her own family renounced her. Thurso settled her in a house at some discreet distance from the castle, where the babe was born, and where she continued as his mistress. He had several other children by her, all girls, and after Lady Thurso's death everybody assumed he would marry her, once his mourning had passed."

"But he did not?"

"I understand she refused him." My father shrugged. "She lives still, raising her girls. The boy went to Oxford and has recently returned. He keeps a room in Thurso Castle and is accepted by everybody. A queer thing, but eminently civilized. I daresay Thurso's desire to see Lady Annis well settled may owe itself to his devotion to this other family."

I nodded. "So that more money can be set aside for them. I wonder how Lady Annis feels. I have always found her a proud girl."

"I have never seen any animus between sister and brother. I expect she's forgiven her parent for his frailties. As all children eventually must."

A strange note altered the timbre of his voice. I had been regarding the pattern of the carpet, too embarrassed to meet his gaze outright, but I now turned my face upward. My father was not looking at me, but at the mirror above the desk, as if he could see something in it that I could not.

"*You*, Father?" I said. "Have you some frailty to confess?"

"We are all frail," he said, and then, turning to me, "You must dress for dinner now, Emmeline."

"But—"

"And be kind to him, my dear. He has, after all, taken the trouble to discover what lies behind *your* mask. If I'm not mistaken, he has fallen violently in love with what he found there."

❦

When I arrived downstairs a half hour later, still electrified by my father's words, I found Lord Silverton resplendent in full Scottish dinner dress and a jovial mood. He kissed my hand and informed me that he had engaged a private room, so as not to start any gossip among the other guests.

"I suspect a private dinner between us will have quite the opposite effect," I said.

"Do you think so?" He looked astounded. "In that case, I

expect you'll have to marry me after all, Truelove. We can't have your reputation left in tatters."

"Unlikely, if society already believes me to be the duke's mistress."

"Well, that's another thing entirely. You can be the Duke of Olympia's mistress and still find yourself received almost everywhere. Alas, no maiden's reputation can survive the scandal of *my* bed. You're looking remarkably well, by the by. That frock becomes you extremely."

During the course of this shocking speech, he had taken my arm over his sleek black elbow and begun to lead me across the marvelous North British lobby to the hotel restaurant, and I would have been blind not to notice how many people simply stopped to follow our progress. I glanced down at my plain frock of dark blue silk—the only dinner dress I had troubled to pack—and said, "You must be joking."

"Not at all. See how everybody stares?"

"They're staring at you, O Apollo."

"Me?" He flicked his finger at the froth of Highland lace anchoring his neck. "Mere feathers. In your case, however, it's *you* who become the *dress*. There's a fascinating liveliness to your skin this evening, Truelove, which I can only hope arises from anticipation."

"Anticipation of what?"

We entered the restaurant, a grand and brilliantly lit room, where a gentleman in a starched white shirt and black jacket appeared at Silverton's elbow as if conjured.

"Your lordship," he said reverently, not daring to notice my presence, "if you will follow me."

Without missing an instant, Silverton swept me along in the man's wake, in the direction of a small door at the back of the room. I felt myself blushing, I felt every nerve coming to life beneath my clothing, and still I didn't stop him. I cannot explain why. I certainly *ought* to have stopped him.

"Anticipation of my company, of course," he said genially. "Here we are. I've taken the liberty of ordering a simple supper. I presumed you wouldn't want some kind of rich, heavy ordeal after a day of travel. God knows I don't."

The waiter was moving for the intimate table next to the fireplace, but Silverton brushed him aside and held out the chair for me himself. I sat and stared rather blankly at the delicate arrangement of silver and porcelain and crystal before me. "Simple?" I said.

"One should never sacrifice elegance for simplicity, Truelove. Indeed, the two are best encountered hand in hand."

The waiter had disappeared, leaving us alone with the table, the fire, the small and beautifully dressed room. Silverton extracted a bottle of champagne from a gleaming bucket of ice and worked at the cork while I laid my gloves on my lap and frowned at the expert movements of his fingers. In truth, I was relieved not to have to dine in the public restaurant just now; I was beginning to feel the gaze of the ginger-haired man everywhere, from every corner; I was expecting him to leap from every closet. At least here, in this room, my adversary sat in full view before me, displaying openly all his weaponry. For the onslaught of Silverton's charm, I was perfectly prepared.

The champagne, on the other hand, I eyed warily. I do not indulge frequently in wine; it has an early and alarming effect on me, which has, in the past, worked irrevocable consequences on the course of my life. I watched the bubbles rise in the coupe of delicate cut glass, poured by Silverton's generous hand, and I opened my mouth to refuse them.

"Now," said his lordship, filling his own glass, "to what shall we toast? My good friend Max, perhaps, for bringing us together this evening? Or for that ginger blackguard, who had much the same effect, if entirely unwitting?"

I frowned deeply. He urged the glass to my fingers.

"Come along, Truelove. It will settle your nerves amazingly."

"My nerves are perfectly settled."

"They are not. You're afraid I mean to seduce you, and what's more, you're afraid you're going to allow me to."

"Nonsense."

"To which suggestion? My seducing you? Or your allowing it?"

"Both."

"Well, you're certainly wrong on the first count, and I jolly well hope you're wrong on the second. Either way, however, you've earned a glass of France's finest this evening, and it's a damned shame to waste a splendid bottle like this one."

I took my lower lip between my teeth.

"Go on," he said. "I won't tell Max."

"Max has nothing to do with it," I said, and lifted the glass.

⟠

In the end, he behaved himself beautifully. Not until the coffee was set and the waiter slipped away for the last time did the conversation die away into the kind of silence that laid upon our skins, and Silverton reached one arm across the table to touch the knuckles of my left hand.

We sat without moving for a minute or two. Staring at the blurred junction of our fingers, I became aware that we had finished not just the bottle of champagne between us, but the better part of a noble Burgundy as well. Silverton had taken a gentleman's share, of course, but I had done my duty. I felt the familiar, dangerous recklessness stir in my chest, and I thought, *I must fight this, it's my enemy, it will destroy me a second time.*

And then the counter-thought: *But I don't want to fight this.*

"My dear love," Silverton said quietly, "are you quite all right?"

I looked up. He had left his spectacles upstairs, and there was nothing between my eyes and his except air, except a few feet of golden, empty space. His face was soft and earnest, his eyes exceptionally blue above the new bruise.

"I am quite all right," I said.

"Because there is a question I wish to ask you, Truelove, and I hope you'll have the goodness to give me an honest answer, for both our sakes."

The pressure of his fingers was light, a mere dance of warmth, and yet I felt it to my bones. Though the coffee was finished, a glass of water remained next to the edge of the saucer. I lifted it with my unoccupied hand and swallowed deep before answering him.

"What question is that?"

"Only this." He took my other hand and leaned forward across the table, so that I could smell the sweetness of the wine on his breath. "What the devil are you carrying in that portfolio of yours?"

I drew my hands sharply away. "I don't know what you mean."

"Ah, Truelove. You disappoint me."

"I wear your disappointment as a badge of honor."

"Where's the trust? Am I not your loyal servant?"

"You may be a loyal servant, but not mine."

"I protest. Not a hair on your head shall come to harm, if I can help it. And I *do* mean to help it, my dear. You can't shake me. Nor can you deny that our ginger friend had a particular object in mind when he approached your compartment this afternoon."

This brought me up short. "Did he?"

"Of course he did. And I suspect that object is the same one you cleverly hid beneath your seat cushion, where no reasonable thief would possibly think to look for it."

I sat back in my chair and wished for more wine. "You needn't mock me."

"I beg your pardon. But it's a damned good thing I happened along. I shudder to think what might have happened, had the fellow discovered you alone."

"The conductor—"

"Was not about to prove much use in a proper struggle, I expect."

The room was lit dimly: only the two candles aflame on the table, a pair of quiet sconces on the wall, the ebbing coals in the fireplace. Hardly enough light to understand the bland expression now laid before me, to determine how serious Silverton really was underneath the weightless tone of his words. He held my gaze carefully, neither looking away nor allowing me to do the same, and after several long seconds, he added, "If it makes any difference, it was Max who asked me to look after you, and particularly the contents of that little portfolio."

"When? How?"

"In his telegram."

There was no hesitation in his voice, not the slightest trace of guile. And I had traveled beside this man for weeks, had set my own life in the palm of his hand as we traced along the Mediterranean together, and for all his faults, he had never once betrayed that particular trust.

I rose from my chair, and he rose, too, because he was a gentleman above all things, even in this moment. I wavered tipsily, putting my hand on the table for balance, while Silverton stared at me from his great height, and I saw that his expression was not bland at all, only tender.

"If you wished to see the inside of my room, my lord," I said, "you had only to ask."

We went upstairs not by the lift but by some back staircase, with which Silverton was suspiciously familiar. He gave me his arm, and

I accepted it. Neither of us spoke until I unlocked the door and stepped inside the room, at which point Silverton slid past me and switched on the electricity. The room burst into light. He looked about, turned to me, and pulled me inside, shutting the door behind us.

"What the devil?" I said crossly.

"It is my policy, my dear, never to take the security of one's room for granted," he replied, placid as ever, "even in so respectable a hotel as the North British."

I brushed past him to the window. "If you mean the ginger fellow, he departed the train some hundred miles to the south."

"Plenty of time to reach us by now. In any case, he's not the only chap to look out for."

I turned. "Who, then?"

Silverton had already moved to the opposite side of the room, inspecting the furniture, the door to the en suite bathroom, the curtains hung at the other window. He came to me, lifted the drapery to my left, and allowed it to fall. His chest was very near mine. "About that portfolio," he said.

I pointed to the desk. "In the drawer."

"Locked?" he said.

"There is no lock."

"No, of course not." He opened the drawer and took out the portfolio. "Not that a lock would be of any particular use on a desk drawer. Any more than the flimsy mechanism on this piece of leather."

"What are you—?"

But he had already unpinned the brooch at his throat and stuck it inside the small clasp on the portfolio. It sprang open immediately. "As I thought," he said, shaking his head.

"The fellow at the shop assured me—"

"Oh, for God's sake, Truelove." He closed the clasp and stuck the portfolio back in its drawer. "You didn't go to a *shop*, did you?"

My cheeks were warm. I nodded at the desk drawer. "Aren't you going to look inside? Satisfy yourself of the contents?"

"I don't give a damn about the contents. I *do* give a damn about you."

He was facing the mirror, pinning the brooch back into the lace. Altogether he was magnificent in his Scottish attire. The black jacket fit him exquisitely, emphasizing the neat triangle formed by his shoulders and hips; the reddish plaid reached just below the knee, allowing me to glimpse an inch of thick calf before it disappeared into his stocking. The electric lights drenched his golden hair in a radiance it hardly needed. My mouth was wet, my throat dry. I asked, a little scratchy, whose plaid he wore.

"I beg your pardon?"

"Your plaid. To which clan does it belong?"

"The Elliotts," he said. "My mother's side. Lowlanders, I'm afraid, and a worse set of troublemakers you couldn't meet."

"I'm not surprised."

"No, I suppose not. It's hellish difficult to amaze you, True-love, though I shall never cease to try."

At what moment I realized he was not—as I supposed—pinning the brooch back into the lace jabot at his throat, but rather unfastening the lace altogether, I can't quite say. Sometime in the middle of this exchange, I believe, although a vital moment passed before I found the courage to address the matter. By then he had tossed the jabot on the desk and was unbuttoning his jacket.

"What on earth are you doing?" I demanded.

"What a question. As you can plainly see, my dear, I am readying myself for bed."

"But this isn't your room!"

"A tremendous inconvenience, to be sure," he said, sliding his jacket from his shoulders en route to the wardrobe, where he hung the garment carefully on a clothes hanger, "but I shall return to my little bolt-hole before the sun rises, so as not to excite comment. At least, any more comment than strictly necessary. Can I help you with your dress?"

"Certainly not!"

He closed the wardrobe door and turned to me. "Don't be silly, Truelove. I'm a dab hand with a set of hooks."

"I daresay you are, but—look here—"

Silverton had grasped my shoulders and rotated me gently to face the wall, while his long, agile fingers unfastened the hooks at my back. "You're in no condition to perform this operation yourself, my dear. Have you always been so susceptible to drink?"

"I am not," I said slowly, enunciating each syllable, "susceptible to drink."

"No, of course not. A most indelicate observation. I beg your pardon."

Several feet away, our images lay reflected in the mirror above the desk: my dark head, bowed slightly, eyes peeking up from beneath my brows; his face above mine, turned earnestly to his work; his shoulders framing my chest, his white shirt billowing from his arms. The dress loosened as he went, falling from my chest. I thought, *I must stop him, I must step away*, but I could not. The sight in the mirror transfixed me. At length, he felt my interest. He looked up without warning, and our eyes met in the flat plane of the mirror, like two animals encountering each other in a woods. I could hardly speak, but neither could I turn away. His blue eyes had grown hot—how else to describe them?—hot, yes, as if the brain behind them had gone up in flame. His cheeks were pink, his lips thin and red, his eyebrows high. He was anything but bland.

"Let me fetch you a glass of water," he said.

In the next instant, his image disappeared from the mirror, and I had to catch my dress with my hand to stop it from falling to the ground. *I really am quite drunk*, I thought, and a faint note of alarm sounded somewhere in my brain, but that was as nothing compared to the whirling in my chest, the mad note of my heartbeat, my fatal recklessness. I let the dress fall around my shoes. (*Stop*, I thought.) I stepped out of the circle of navy silk and bent to retrieve the garment. I had brought only the one evening dress; over the course of six years as the Duke of Olympia's private secretary, traveling frequently with him and his wife as they enjoyed their position at Britain's highest rank, I had learned never to expect an invitation to dinner. From behind me came the sound of running water. I straightened and walked, in so steady a line as I could, toward the wardrobe, where I hung my frock next to Silverton's black velvet jacket: so close that the sleeves touched, and the bodice of mine had communion with the shoulders of his.

"This is most unsuitable," hissed a voice at my right shoulder. "You must clothe yourself at once."

"Go away."

"I shall not go away. I shall remain exactly where I stand until you—gracious me, you are *not* unfastening your corset!"

"I can't wear it to bed, can I?"

"Intemperate girl. To be ruined once is foolishness. To be ruined twice—"

"Calm yourself, madam." I folded the corset and laid it on the shelf, before reaching for my dressing gown, already unpacked and hanging from a hook. "I don't believe it's possible to be ruined twice. Ruination is irrevocable."

She made an angry noise. "You are so like—"

"My mother?" I said tiredly, slipping the robe over my shoulders.

"Your *father.*"

I turned instantly, but no small, regal figure occupied the space by my side. Instead, Silverton stepped into view, tall and somewhat rumpled, red waistcoat unbuttoned, and offered me a glass of water.

"What the devil were you muttering?" he said.

"Nothing."

"Have you any aspirin, my dear?"

"Aspirin? Why should I want aspirin?"

"Why, indeed? Drink your water, like a good girl."

I drank the water and excused myself, making for the bathroom, and when I returned a moment later, Silverton stood at the window in stocking feet, holding the curtain slightly aside with one hand to glimpse the outline of the castle against the purpling sky. There was a glass of something in his hand; I imagined it was not water.

"You ought to leave," I said.

He laughed. "That wasn't terribly convincing, my dear."

"It's improper for you to stay."

"Oh, be honest, Truelove. You don't give a damn about propriety, not really, or you wouldn't have dined with me to begin with. You put on a fine show of correctness, but it's all a disguise. The question is what lies beneath." He turned his head over his shoulder to regard me. "What you're hiding."

I folded my arms across my chest. "It's imprudent. If you have any regard for my—for my—" I couldn't quite find the word.

"No." He turned back to the window. "I shall stay right here with you. You haven't the wits of a schoolboy at the moment. Imagine if that fellow from the train returns to finish the job."

"I can defend myself perfectly well. Besides, the door's locked, and this is the sixth floor."

"I refuse to take that sort of chance. I promised Max I'd look after you, didn't I? A most solemn vow."

"Then perhaps it's *you* who wants those papers," I said. "After all, I have only your word about the telegram from Max. What if it's *you* I should beware of? You who plied me with wine, and used your charm to intrude on my privacy."

He dropped the curtain and turned to face me. He had switched off several of the lamps, and in the darkened room, he looked decidedly rakish. His golden hair was disordered, his shirt half-tucked, his red waistcoat unbuttoned at his sides. "My God, Truelove," he said, finishing his drink, "I like the way you think."

"I have a pistol in the drawer."

"You'd miss, in your condition."

"Or I might not."

He set down the drink on the windowsill and walked toward me. I held my ground, waiting until he towered a foot or so away, looking quizzically upon my face. "Would you really, Truelove? Shoot me?"

"If I had to."

Silverton lifted his hand and laid it along the side of my face, from temple to jaw, and his face took on the heavy expression of a man whose thoughts tend to an ancient purpose. I caught his wrist. "What a shame," he whispered.

"A shame?"

"That you're so thoroughly shelved. I had *plans*, Truelove. Marvelous plans. Still, rules are rules." Without warning, he bent down and hoisted me into his arms. "To bed with you, now. I shall take the chaise and a blanket."

I craned my neck for a glimpse of the chaise in question, which might scarcely have fit the old Queen herself on its compact length. "You can't be serious."

"Why will you never take me at my word, my love? I begin to take offense at this void of trust between us." He dumped me carefully into the center of the bed and drew back the covers from one corner. "Come along, now. Sleep will cure you. Perhaps in the morning . . ."

"Certainly not."

"No," he said regretfully, tucking me under the comforter, "I expect you're right. I shall put in an early order for coffee instead. Black and strong."

"Presumptuous."

His face loomed over mine, inexpressibly kind and rinsed in gold by the lamp on the bedside table. "Ah, but it's inevitable, you know."

"What's inev—inevitable?"

"You and me, Truelove. Our souls are cut from the same strange cloth. We don't belong among the rest of them. We belong in some wilderness, with only each other for company."

I pulled my hand from beneath the covers and placed my index finger upon his lower lip.

"If you touch those papers, I'll shoot you," I whispered.

He bent and kissed my forehead.

"I'll die a happy man."

⌘

Of course I had always known that my father—the man who raised me, that is—was not the man who sired me. My parents married when I was about four years old, and my true paternity was never spoken of. Not once did I discover any hint of the gentleman's identity, and how he came to know my mother. Not once did it occur to me to ask. I needed no other father than the one I knew, who continued to love and care for me after my mother died, and whose kindness saturates all the memories of my childhood.

But I knew he existed, this other man, this genealogical father. The one who had supplied my mother with the necessary seed of my existence; the one she had known and perhaps loved in the years before she married Mr. Truelove. My mother had lain with this fellow, had known this fellow intimately; he walked the earth with one-half of Emmeline Truelove written in his blood, and yet I knew not his name, nor his face, nor his nationality, nor even whether he still lived. Whenever I entered a room, he might be in it; whenever I navigated a street or a shop or a train compartment, he might be the man who brushed my arm or found the seat across from mine, and I would not recognize him as mine, and neither would he.

Or perhaps this is not entirely true. I have one memory, or at least a thought, an image that might be a memory. I am quite young, and my parents are not yet married, or possibly even acquainted. I sit on a rug before a sizzling coal fire, playing with a toy, and a door opens, a rush of cold air. A pair of black legs appears in view, and I reach toward them, and am lifted into the air. There is a moustache and a thick brown beard, and a pair of large, warm blue eyes, which I recognize as belonging to me, as existing for my sake, as if I have some kind of dominion over those eyes.

That is all.

And I had not considered this memory in many years, had not even remembered that I own it, until the night I went to sleep in the North British Hotel in Edinburgh, while the Marquess of Silverton settled on the chaise nearby with a blanket and a pillow borrowed from my own bed. I remembered thinking about the apparition that had recently revisited me, that of the late Queen, and as I drifted into slumber I heard her say again, *You are just like your father,* and I saw again the image of those blue eyes, that moment on the rug when I was small.

I don't recall the dreams that followed, except that they were strange and intense, and I woke gasping some time later, as if drenched in water.

I flung myself upright and called out Silverton's name. The room was warm and perfectly dark, but I knew at once that I was alone, and that the leather portfolio, if I cared to look, was no longer in the desk drawer where I had left it.

One morning, when the Lady returned to shore from her morning swim, she saw that she had mistaken her distance, for the beach was not the beach from which she had embarked, and instead of the villa where she stayed with her servants and her son, she saw only a hovel made of wood and clay, and a Fisherman who sat on a wooden bench mending a net of hemp. He was tall and comely, and when he saw the Lady emerge from the sea, he fell to his knees in great wonder, for the Lady was as beautiful as she was strong, clothed in her strange suit, and her bearing was that of a goddess . . .

THE BOOK OF TIME, A. M. HAYWOOD (1921)

Two

The Duke of Olympia himself stood waiting on the platform when the train throbbed carefully into the Thurso terminus, late the following afternoon. He was dressed in tweeds and a long duster coat, and his austere face lit with welcome as I stepped from the carriage and turned down the platform to meet him.

"Why, you didn't drive the motorcar yourself!" I exclaimed.

He reached instantly for my valise. "Miss Truelove," he said kindly. "I have missed your company beyond words. I trust your journey was not too uncomfortable? The N. B. not inconvenient? I have stayed there myself."

"Extremely comfortable, certainly," I said, "but not without adventure, I'm afraid."

"Are you quite all right? You look strained. Can I offer you a cup of tea? There's a shop just inside."

"No, thank you. I've already caused you a great deal of trouble. You ought to have sent Mr. Miller for me."

"Mr. Miller has many admirable qualities, Miss Truelove, but I'm afraid I daren't trust him with the well-being of my automobile, to say nothing of *you*. But where's Silverton? I understood from his telegram last night . . . ?" He left the end of the question to dangle tactfully in the air, without the slightest change of expression upon his face.

"That, I'm afraid, is all part of the adventure."

"But where is he? Is he injured?"

"I haven't the slightest idea."

"Ah." The duke regarded me for perhaps a second or two with a solemn frown, which I returned even more grimly. He sighed and drew his watch from his pocket. "Look here, perhaps we can carry this discussion into the motorcar? We still have a chance of making dinner, I believe."

The duke's motorcar stood by the curb, a magnificent long-hooded beast from the previous duke's extensive collection. A Burke touring model, His Grace informed me, specially equipped for long journeys along rough country roads. He pointed out the excellent width of the tires, the reinforcement of the axles by vanadium steel.

"I didn't realize you were a motoring enthusiast," I said.

"I'm not. Just as a useful means of conveyance. I say, haven't you got any more luggage than this, Miss Truelove?"

"I'm afraid not."

His Grace set the valise on the rear seat and came around to open the passenger door for me. The village was sparser than I expected, the houses small and whitewashed, and when I breathed deep, I could smell the tanginess of the nearby sea. Though it was nearly five o'clock, the sun remained high and brilliant above us. I thought the weather should be damp and cloudy—this was my idea of the far north of Scotland—but instead the air was almost painfully clear, the sky a pungent blue. I glanced about, half imagining I might see the flash of a ginger head as it ducked around the corner of a building, but the streets were quiet. There had not been many passengers on the train, and I had taken note of them all.

The duke paused at the hood of the car and asked me politely to turn the ignition switch. I reached across the dashboard and pressed the lever with one gloved finger; the duke made a quick, efficient half turn of the crank, and the motor came lustily to life.

The duke was not an especially tall man—he stood just under six feet, I believe—but he was burly, made of thick, strong bones, and his size conferred a certain sense of peace as he sank silently into the seat beside me and set us off through the cobbled streets of Thurso and into the damp, clear countryside. The absence of conversation was itself a relief. I hadn't slept since waking to my empty room at three o'clock in the morning, and though I knew I must begin to explain our predicament to Olympia, my head was too tired to know where to begin.

As we gathered speed, the wind tore violently at my hat. I put one hand to the crown and closed my eyes, and the duke said, "Miss Truelove? Are you *quite* all right?"

"Yes," I whispered, and then loudly, "*Yes!* Only tired."

"But what's the matter? What's happened? Is it Silverton? He wired me last evening to say you had met up on the train—"

"Yes, we did." I opened my eyes to see that we had left the town entirely, and now hurtled along a narrow road rimmed in tough, pale grass. To the right, the North Sea threw itself upon a ragged cliff. "Do you remember the fellow we left behind in the cave on Naxos? The one with the ginger hair?"

"Yes," Olympia said softly.

"He caught up with us on the train. Before that, in fact. He followed me from London."

"By God! Did he hurt you?"

"No. He may have been after the papers. Silverton saw him lingering outside my compartment—"

"This was north of York, then?"

"Yes, after Silverton joined me. On your suggestion, I believe," I added serenely.

"It seemed convenient. I don't like your traveling alone, Miss Truelove, particularly with such a valuable cargo."

"In the end, however, I may have been better off alone. Silverton caught the fellow—actually, he threw himself from the train during the fight, and managed somehow to survive the fall—but then Silverton himself disappeared, and the papers with him."

Olympia's foot went down on the brake pedal, bringing the motorcar to a shuddering stop in the middle of the road. "*What did you say?*"

"Silverton took the papers," I said. "Last night."

"*Took* the papers? From where?"

"From my room."

I said the words defiantly. I had practiced them most of the day, inside the privacy of my compartments on the express to Inverness and then the Highland Railway branch line to Thurso, so that I wouldn't hesitate when called upon to use them. As a result, they all but exploded from my throat: *From my room!*

Underneath the Burke's long, elegant hood, the engine lost a beat, coughed, resumed. Olympia made a slight noise—*Hmm*—and coughed in sympathy with the automobile. "I see," he said.

In my rehearsals of this scene, I hadn't meant to defend myself. I had meant to state the facts of the case, without explanation, but now that Olympia sat beside me, his left arm a mere few inches from my right, his quiet breath mingling with mine, I heard myself begin, "I assure you, sir, he was only there to—"

"Please, Miss Truelove. You owe me no explanation whatever."

"We had agreed that, in light of the incident on the train, and the possible motives of the man in pursuit of me, that his lordship should join me in guarding the papers from danger."

"Miss Truelove," the duke said gravely, "before we proceed further in your account, and indeed in our relations with one another, let me first say this. I have the utmost regard for your character and judgment, and what is more, I consider you have every right to conduct your private affairs as you—and no other human being—judge proper. I hope you will do me the honor of being entirely frank with me on any subject, and I will endeavor to return the favor."

I gazed down at my hands, which were clenched in my lap, the dark leather wrinkled by the strength of my grip. "My dear sir," I said.

"Are we agreed, then?"

"Of course. As I said, Lord Silverton stayed in my room on the sixth floor of the North British Hotel last night, having stated his intention to protect me from intrusion by the ginger-haired gentleman who had pursued me from London. At about three o'clock in the morning, I woke in some confusion, having sensed something amiss. I called out for his lordship, but he was no longer in possession of the chaise to which he had retired, and indeed had departed the room entirely, together with the portfolio containing those papers you had requested me to convey."

"I say. And you heard nothing at all until then?"

"I was asleep, I confess, having drunk a little more wine than I intended during dinner. His lordship, as I remember, volunteered for this reason to keep vigil. Of course, I now suspect he urged the wine on purpose, though I have none but myself to blame for accepting it."

"Miss Truelove, there is no one I trust more thoroughly than

Silverton, except yourself. I feel certain he has a sound reason for this disappearance." Olympia paused. "He left no note? No sign at all?"

"None. I repaired immediately downstairs and made inquiry with the hotel staff, and nobody could remember seeing him, or indeed noticing anything amiss at all. No struggle, no chase, no furtive departure. No unknown characters lurking about."

"Strange." Olympia tapped the wheel.

"You will remember, of course, that Silverton serves another master than ourselves. I refer to the dowager duchess, who has inherited the work of her husband, the previous duke. You know he was Britain's great spymaster for many decades."

"But why should those particular papers hold any interest for my great-aunt, even in her new capacity? I should have thought they held no interest for anyone but us, and perhaps that damned scoundrel from Naxos, who held me captive."

I shrugged. "Once we open our minds along that avenue, any number of scenarios arise. I wired the duchess at once, of course, to inquire whether she had any news of Silverton. I hope she will answer honestly."

"You are concerned for him, of course."

"Naturally. It is distressing to find one's trust so terribly misplaced."

The duke reached out his hand and patted my own. "Have faith in him, Miss Truelove. Whatever the fellow's done, I have no doubt he's done it for the best possible reason."

"You aren't at all concerned for the integrity of those papers?"

He released the brake and set the motor into gear. The Burke surged eagerly forward, filling the clear, salt-tinged air with the scent of petrol exhaust. "Of course I'm concerned," he said. "I'm damned put out."

"I'm sorry, sir. I ought to have been more vigilant."

"Indeed you ought, Miss Truelove. In fact, if I may offer a word of advice, there is really only one way to avoid these unfortunate incidents, in future."

"Sir?"

"You must take care to keep the rascal directly by your side throughout the night. If possible, without the benefit of his nightshirt."

By the time we reached Thurso Castle an hour later, the air had turned chillier, the sky cold blue, and a stiff breeze thrust from the nearby sea against the skin of my cheeks. The towers appeared over a slight rise in the surrounding grassland, and I fell silent in the middle of a sentence. I forget the subject.

"Astonishing, isn't it?" the duke said. "I don't believe there's anything like it in England."

"Certainly not in my experience."

The ragged gray stone grew against the sky, haphazard and enormous, rising from a large, flat headland some half mile or so distant. I thought it must have been built four or five hundred years ago, at least; the walls crumbled, the battlements missed teeth, and yet the edifice stood proudly, like a terribly old man wearing the indignities of age as marks of honor. Under an overcast sky, the castle might have seemed intolerably gloomy, but the blue sky and the brilliant northern sun turned the walls nearly white. So pure and plain was its beauty, my breath stopped in my chest. I felt the duke's quick glance at my profile, his satisfaction at my awe.

"There are any number of splendid walks," he said. "I shall be happy to show you about in the morning, before the shoot."

"The shoot?"

"Thurso is an enthusiastic sportsman."

As we drew closer to the castle, I saw that the isthmus connecting the headland to the mainland was narrow and worn, reinforced by an arched stone bridge of recent construction. The sea came into view some hundred feet below, lashing against the cliffs.

"My God," I said, "it must be well-nigh impregnable."

"I believe it was, until Thurso's father had the bridge built a half century ago. You had to climb down the cliff and scale it back again, by an alarmingly narrow track that runs along the side that may, I believe, remind you of some of our adventures last spring. Makes a fine walk before breakfast, however."

"I look forward to it."

The road had narrowed into a rough track, and the duke slowed the motor to lessen the jostling as we rode along. "When you reach bottom, you'll find a scrap of beach on the more sheltered side of the neck, where Thurso's put up a sort of rudimentary dock, but it's hardly enough to land anything larger than a sporting yacht."

"A rather startling degree of seclusion, in these modern times."

"I was going to say that the entire effect is one of stepping back into the medieval age. The interior of the castle, I should add, does little to dispel this impression."

"Perhaps that's fitting, given our purpose. Will there be time to inspect this object of yours before dinner?"

He drew his watch from his pocket and glanced at the face. "I'm afraid not. These damned social obligations. Can I persuade you to join me after dinner, or would you prefer to wait until morning?"

"I have no objection at all, but I suspect Lady Annis might."

"Oh, yes. Dash it. I'd forgotten."

We were approaching the bridge. The automobile slowed further, and the duke reached for the gear lever. To the left, the sun glittered on the chimney pots hidden inside the stacks, reminding me of the domesticity that lay inside. Fires laid neatly before beautiful, moldering sofas, and ladies occupying the frayed upholstery with bare, shivering shoulders and glasses of sherry: Lady Annis, of course, prominent among them.

"Yes, I meant to ask earlier. How is your suit progressing?"

"Well enough," answered the duke. "There isn't much for me to do, really, except simply to exist there with my shiny new coronet, which conveniently does all the courting for me."

"Think of it as one of the advantages of your position, sir. Why waste your formidable energy in so frivolous an occupation as courtship?"

"Very true, Miss Truelove. I shall endeavor to look upon my situation in that spirit of optimism. Though I don't mean to sound churlish. She's a lovely girl, far lovelier than I really deserve, for my own sake. Are you afraid of heights at all, Miss Truelove?"

"Not especially."

"Excellent. Then you will, I believe, appreciate what comes next."

We were just passing the elegant gateposts of the bridge, and the landscape opened suddenly to the wide, clear gulf between headland and mainland, framed by an arc of rocky cliff to the left and the endless reach of the North Sea to the right, where the land curved away from the water. Ahead, the castle sprawled atop its flat perch, so close that I now detected the faint smudge of smoke appearing from the tops of the chimney stacks.

"You should see it in sunrise," said the duke as we passed the opposite set of gateposts to arrive safely on solid ground. "A glorious vista. Naturally, they've given me the room with the best possible view."

"Naturally. Only the finest bait will catch such a prize fish as yourself."

He laughed. "Of course, it's also the draftiest bedchamber in the entire British Isles. What I wouldn't give for my old flat in Athens. Happy, golden days, now forever lost. Here we are. Mind your head on that portcullis."

He was joking, of course, for the portcullis yawned several yards above our skulls. Still, it was a forbidding black thing, lined with fangs, and I was grateful when we emerged into the courtyard, sunlit and paved with comfortable old cobbles. The duke drew the motorcar right up the entrance and shut off the engine, but he didn't reach for the handle of the door. Instead he turned to me.

"Before you start up any nonsense about being grateful for my trouble, Miss Truelove, let me explain to you what this past hour has meant to me. The relief, I mean, of speaking frankly and rationally to someone I trust. Someone with whom I need not play the duke. No, don't say I'm too kind. Say something true."

"Sir—"

"Max."

"Max." I smiled. "Here is something true. I can think of no man more worthy of this station than you. You aren't *playing* the duke, I assure you. You *are* the duke, as naturally as any man could inhabit such an unnatural station, and I am grateful for you."

Beneath the peak of his tweed cap, the duke closed his eyes and allowed a heartfelt sigh. "Believe me, Miss Truelove. I am far more grateful for *you*."

⟢

We had arranged to meet at half past nine o'clock, in a room Olympia called the Chinese library. "It has the advantage of being private," he told me as we parted at the top of the main staircase, "since we cannot meet in either of our chambers without exciting comment."

I forbore to tell him that we had somehow already contrived to excite comment, according to Silverton. "Very well," I said simply. "The Chinese library at half past nine o'clock. Good luck this evening."

"Good luck?"

"With Lady Annis, sir."

"Oh. Right-ho." He smiled and bent me a strange, stiff little bow, right there before the amazed gaze of the housemaid who was showing me to my room.

Before the maid left, I asked her where the Chinese library might be found and memorized her directions, though her accent was so pronounced I had some trouble understanding the words. In the end, I lost myself twice, turning down one dark, empty, narrow corridor after another until I rounded a corner to a noble hallway lined with tapestries, where perhaps a half-dozen gentlemen were filing from a doorway, dressed in immaculate black and white, laughing and smoking. The duke, I saw at once, was not among them. I drew back quickly, but it was too late.

"Why, Miss Truelove!" someone exclaimed, in a familiar voice.

For perhaps three or four seconds, I stood quite still, transfixed not by any particular face but by the sovereign array of them, whiskers and collars and hair sleeked back, trailing smoke and parted lips and the thick, rich smell of cigar smoke and prosperity. I had probably met some of these fellows—if not all—during the course of my years in service of the previous duke, and yet I felt no recognition. They stared back with bright, interested eyes, the way they might observe a solitary doe that has come out unexpectedly from cover, and I became conscious of my plain dress and the shape of my body beneath it, of my hair and my mouth, my small female bones, my puny strength. The darkness of the hallway, lit by a single oil lamp burning from the wall, and the thickness of the stone walls, which cast us in utter silence, as if no other being existed for miles.

My pulse throbbed in my neck. I made a brief nod and turned, walking steadily away down the corridor, and at once the voices clamored behind me. *Who the devil was that?* asked one, and *Olympia's secretary, I believe*, said another, and yet another one began, *No, no, haven't you heard, she's his—*

By then I was out of earshot, my skin aflame, turning down a succession of corridors without any consciousness of where I was going, only that I had to get as far away as possible from those voices, from those eyes that had stared at me with such unnatural, avaricious curiosity. No English gentleman had ever quite gazed at me like that, not once while my father was alive, not once while I toiled quietly as the private secretary of the august Duke of Olympia. I had always enjoyed—had always expected— a certain status of respect in my unusual position, neither of one genus nor the other, but certainly not belonging to the species of legitimate prey.

I reached the end of a remote hallway and stopped, resting my palm against the stone, while I endeavored to catch my breath. My heartbeat smacked in my ears. My skin began to cool. A small window was cut into the stone at my right, and a cold draft poured through the cracks in the old wooden frame. I turned to gaze out the ancient glass to a smudged, distorted view of the sea, now turned gray and pink in the gathering sunset. The air smelled of brine and of sharp, wet stone.

I don't know quite how long I stood there, gathering my composure while the waves pulsed fretfully below. Perhaps a few minutes only, for I remember that my nerves were still raw enough to jump at the sound of the duke's deep voice from the end of the hallway.

"Miss Truelove! There you are! Are you quite all right?"

I turned from the window and attempted a smile. "I seem to have made a wrong turn."

"Not at all," he said kindly, offering his arm. "The Chinese library is just around the corner."

❦

The room was aptly named. Some Thurso ancestor—likely female, and perhaps a century ago—had caught the fashionable fascination for Chinoiserie, and this spacious chamber had been duly adorned in reds and golds, in geometrical furniture, in Ming porcelain and a riot of painted decoration. If the effect was not precisely authentic, it was certainly enthusiastic.

The duke seemed not to perceive this Oriental explosion around him. He ushered me inside and directed me to a table in the center of the room, on which a small, simple wooden chest rested at the edge, while he lit a pair of oil lamps with a match from his pocket. Though a series of casement windows ran the length of the room, the sky behind them was turning rapidly to a dark purple, and the seascape was nearly invisible.

"This is it?" I said. "It seems quite ordinary to me."

"It's not the chest itself. It's what's inside." Max set the chimney back atop the lamp and turned to me. "I say, are you sure you're well, Miss Truelove? Have you eaten?"

"Yes, I took a tray in my room."

"You might have come downstairs. There was an excellent venison."

"I have no doubt. But I find my presence is generally not missed at dinner. I have little in common with the ladies, and the gentlemen . . ." I turned my gaze quickly to the chest in front of me. "What is your best estimate of the age of this chest?"

"I would say quite ancient. You see the hinges—look, what do you mean, exactly? *The gentlemen.* I hope no one has dared to offer you any affront—"

"Of course not." I was sharp. "But you must understand I am welcome neither to linger among the cigars and brandy in the dining room, nor to attend the tea and cakes in the drawing room. I am a lemon placed inside a bowl of apples and pears."

"This damnable, archaic society. Even among the Moroccans—"

I moved the chest closer and bent to examine the lock. "Does the key still exist?"

"No. But keys rarely do survive the centuries."

"Then how did you open it?"

"Why, I picked the lock, of course. I have some experience in these matters, you know." He came around the corner of the table to stand next to me, facing the chest. "The mechanism gave way easily, which aroused my early suspicions."

"Because an ancient lock should have needed quite a lot of oil."

"Exactly. Go ahead and open it, Miss Truelove. You won't damage anything, I assure you."

He set one sturdy hand upon the table and leaned forward, as if anticipating me. His eagerness seeped through the formal angles of his clothes; his neck was quite pink. The scent of cigars clung to him, though he had not been among the gentlemen leaving the dining room a short while ago, and I supposed he must have excused himself early to fetch the chest. I imagined him seated at the magnificent table, leaning back in his chair, one leg perhaps crossed over the other, jiggling his hand around his brandy and pretending to care about the subject at hand. Impatient for that pause in the conversation, that turn of the tide in which he might politely rise and leave the dull company behind. I knew that impatience, that dissatisfaction; I had felt it often enough myself.

I placed my hands on the sides of the chest and opened the lid.

A scent overcame me instantly, of brine and of some other substance. I tested it inside the cavities of my nose, breathing deeply. "Rubber?" I said.

"Well done. Now reach inside and tell me what you find."

I plunged my hands into the dark interior and found a strange, cool, rather slippery material under my fingers. I grasped it by the corners and lifted it free, to uncurl in long black folds before us.

"Why, what is it?"

"It's a suit, Miss Truelove. Can't you see? You're holding it by the shoulders. Here are the arms"—he pointed—"and the legs, here."

"But it's—what's it made of? Rubber?"

"I'm not quite certain. It's rubberlike, to be sure."

I laid it carefully down on the table and straightened it out into the shape of a human being, minus head and hands and feet, almost perfectly formed, about the size of a tall adult female. The smell was strong, almost overpowering, a queer mixture of seawater and rot and rubber. Max lifted the lamp and brought it closer, so that the steady glow poured over the surface, turning it brown. I smoothed one sleeve with a kind of rapture.

"What do you think it is?" I whispered.

The duke opened his mouth to answer me, but a voice from the doorway carried over his words, young and masculine and utterly certain of its facts. The same voice, in fact, that had recently spoken my name in the corridor outside the dining room.

"Why, it's a selkie skin, of course. Isn't it obvious?"

The Lady was exhausted and bewildered, for she had swum far that morning, and though the Fisherman led her into his cottage and warmed her by the hearth, she soon fell into a dangerous fever. The Fisherman was greatly alarmed. He undressed her with his own hands and laid her upon his own couch, and for two weeks he tended her without rest and without mercy to himself, certain that each dawn would bring the Lady's death. On the morning of the fourteenth day, the Fisherman prepared himself to die, for he knew he could not bear his own agony if the Lady should expire under his hands . . .

THE BOOK OF TIME, A. M. HAYWOOD (1921)

Three

※

At the sound of the strange word *selkie*, I startled back from the table, striking the duke's shoulder with my head, and turned to the doorway of the library. A man stood there, somewhere in that fresh, exuberant age between twenty and twenty-five, clean-shaven and elegant of build. His hair, oiled back from his face, seemed to be light brown.

"Ah! There you are, Magnusson," said Max. "I have just flummoxed Miss Truelove with our mysterious find."

"So I perceive." The man walked forward, smiling, and held out his hand to me. "I understand flummoxing Miss Truelove is not an easy thing to do."

"Indeed not." I shook his hand and cast a quizzical glance to the duke.

"James Magnusson," said the stranger, before Max could speak. "Owner of said chest."

"Owner? But I thought the chest belonged to the castle."

Mr. Magnusson angled his gaze to Max. "Haven't you told her the story, sir?"

"Not yet. I'm afraid we had another matter that required our attention."

"Nothing too serious, I hope?"

Max leaned back against the edge of the table and folded his arms. He had kept on the previous duke's valet, having no man of his own, and his dress was so immaculate he nearly blinded me. To be perfectly honest, I thought he looked more himself in his worn tweeds, but the crisp black-and-white formality of dinner dress perhaps suited him better, from a purely aesthetic standpoint. He looked almost handsome, there in the golden drip of the oil lamp.

"Nothing that won't resolve itself, I believe," he said, looking at me. "It was Mr. Magnusson who brought the chest to my attention, a few days ago. He has been conducting a thorough program of refurbishment at one of the family's properties in the Orkney Islands—"

"A castle even more ancient than this one," said Mr. Magnusson, grinning widely, as if he relished the challenge, "and fallen into the most shocking disrepair."

"My goodness. Would it not be better to allow nature to take its course, and build something new?"

"Ah, well. This particular property has special significance for the family, you see, and though my father bestowed the estate on me a year ago, he wouldn't countenance my tearing it down, not for a minute. And truth to tell—"

"I beg your pardon. Your father gave you the property?"

"Yes," he said.

I looked at Max, who shrugged and said, "Lord Thurso."

"Lord Thurso! Then you're—"

"The natural son," said Mr. Magnusson. His smile grew wider

still. "Magnusson is my mother's surname. Rather too indiscreet to raise a litter of Sinclairs on the castle doorstep, you see."

"I see. And Thurso's bequeathed you a castle?"

"Indeed he has, though it's not so generous a gesture as it sounds, I'm afraid. The pile came with no money attached at all, not a brass farthing, so I've gone round to all the banks, who are lending me a frightful sum of money to fix it all up as a grand hotel, in the American style. By next summer, I hope to have flocks of tourists and holidaymakers filling the place from dungeon to rafters, enjoying all the natural beauty and health-giving advantages of the Orkney Islands."

"Which are?"

"Why, innumerable, Miss Truelove! Just imagine! Fresh air, brisk salt water, an abundant, nutritious diet, the opportunity for vigorous exercise. Combine all that with the luxurious facilities to be found in a modern hotel, and I daresay we'll be beating them from our door, come June."

"Except that the hotel has yet to be built."

"Strictly speaking," said Mr. Magnusson, "renovated."

"Which is where we come to the matter of the chest," Max interjected, faintly impatient.

"Oh, yes. The chest. Extraordinary find. I was on the island last week, supervising the work, and my foreman came to me with that." He nodded to the chest on the table, and the strange black suit laid out next to it. "Of course, I knew right away what it meant."

"I don't quite understand. What does it mean?"

"Why, haven't you heard the legend of the Thurso selkie, Miss Truelove?"

"I'm afraid I haven't. I've heard of selkies, of course, but you can't possibly think that this garment . . ." I paused and glanced at Max, who was staring intently at my face. "It's all just a myth."

"Aye, but not to the Magnussons, ye ken. It's part of our history." He spoke these words in a teasing Scottish brogue and settled himself on the edge of the table, one leg upon the floor and one leg raised, his hands gathered companionably in the middle. "Goes back to ancient times. Nobody can tell you the precise year, of course, but the family owes its fortunes to a selkie bride who came out of the waters one day and married my ancestor."

"Do you really believe that?"

Mr. Magnusson unclasped his hands to spread them out before me. "I believe *something* happened. People don't make up stories out of thin air, certainly not stories so important as that. Origin stories, you know, they're terribly important to us. I don't mean the Magnussons especially; I mean human beings in general."

"You sound as if you've given the matter considerable thought, Mr. Magnusson."

"I read the ancients at Oxford. Bloody useless, from a practical point of view, but fascinating stuff." He seemed not to notice his unsuitable language; altogether he exuded the kind of feckless, childlike attractiveness of a young dog. He was not large—his shoulders were puny next to those of the nearby duke—but he was well fashioned, neatly proportional, eager and flawless. His hair, now that I saw it closely, contained reddish tints amid the gold, or perhaps it was a trick of the light; his eyes were so colorless a blue as to be nearly gray. "Like any myth," he continued, "the selkie story must have had its beginning in something real. Something that actually happened."

"There are several theories, of course," the duke said, sounding even graver, even more deliberate than usual, next to Mr. Magnusson's rapid tenor, "which I will not trouble to enumerate at present. But the tale of the Magnusson selkie is instructive, in light of this discovery." He nodded to the rubber suit.

I looked at Mr. Magnusson. "Can you perhaps tell me more?"

"Certainly. My ancestor was a fisherman, so the story goes, plying his trade on the island of Hoy, not far from the present-day castle I'm attempting to restore to its former glory. A solitary, virtuous chap, and learned, too: taught himself to read and to decipher ancient texts and that sort of thing. One morning, he discovers a beautiful seal maiden frolicking naked on the beach, and he falls instantly in love with her. He spots her sealskin on the rocks nearby and hides it in a chest, so she can't ever swim away and leave him, and he takes her into his hut and makes her his bride. She stays by his side for seven years, bearing two children, but at the end of the seventh year she discovers the sealskin and disappears back into the sea."

"But then how—"

Mr. Magnusson held up his finger. "Before she leaves, she gives him a pearl of enormous value, and with this fortune he builds a great castle and lands, and eventually becomes laird. His daughter marries the heir to the Earl of Thurso, and unites the two estates. But all the while he longs for his selkie bride, remaining chaste throughout the rest of his life, and indeed not one of the Magnussons has ever since been happy in love and marriage, though our earthly fortunes have risen and fallen through the centuries. And it's said that when the laird's own selkie bride returns to Hoy, his heirs will find true love at last."

His eyes met mine as he pronounced this last sentence, quite warm and familiar, as if we had known each other for years. Beneath them, his smile grew bashfully.

"I—I see," I said.

The duke coughed. "An interesting story, Mr. Magnusson, but we are left to ponder how this particular object on the table ended up in this particular chest."

I roused myself. "Yes. If the laird's selkie swam away with it, into the North Sea, the suit would have been lost forever, and not locked away in a chest."

"Ah. But that's why I brought the entire matter to the duke's attention. I am hardly an expert in this field, as is His Grace, but I instantly perceived that this suit"—here he half turned and lifted one leg of the garment between his thumb and forefinger—"did not belong in a chest of such antiquity."

"May I examine it again?" I asked.

"Certainly." He moved aside.

The table was broad, and the suit lay perfectly shaped across it. The duke reached for the lamp and brought it closer. I lifted my head. "Is it possible to light another?"

"Of course."

Max vanished from my left side, and I placed my palms on the table and leaned closer, while Mr. Magnusson peered from his perch on my right. With one finger I touched the material, which was softer than I expected, almost silky in its otherworldly smoothness, and yet thick. Spongy, I thought. "It's not rubber, after all," I said. "It's something else."

Max returned with another oil lamp, burning steadily inside its glass dome. "But what, then? I'm afraid I don't recognize the substance at all."

"I've never seen anything like it. Have you, Mr. Magnusson?"

"No. The strangest thing I ever saw."

I straightened to face him. "And you found it inside that chest?"

"Yes. My foreman brought it to me, as I said. Although the suit was not inside that main cavity, when I found it."

"Where, then?"

Mr. Magnusson walked around me and grasped the sides of the chest. "When I first looked inside, I saw that the main cavity contained a quantity of old silver, which delighted me, as you can imagine. And then it struck me, once we had emptied it, that the bottom isn't quite where it should be. Do you see what I mean?" He tilted the chest. "It's a few inches higher than it looks on the outside."

"A hidden compartment."

"Exactly. Look for yourself." He stood aside, and I peered into the chest. Sure enough, as I looked inside, the bottom was too shallow. "One of those things you don't notice, until suddenly you do," said Mr. Magnusson. "And then you can't imagine not seeing it. Here, there's a little ribbon at the edge. Give it a pull."

I did, and the bottom panel lifted easily away, revealing the space beneath. I traced the true surface with my fingers. The wood was old and hard, almost calcified. "Just large enough for a suit, folded up."

"Yes."

"But when you examine the suit, there are no wrinkles at all. No sign of its having been folded."

"Another mystery," said the duke.

I looked at him. "What do you think? Can you make any guess as to its provenance?"

"None whatsoever, I'm afraid. I'm sorry to disappoint you. But those are the most interesting cases of all, I've found. The ones that confound me at first."

Max's face appeared utterly benign as he said this; as benign, at least, as his stern looks would allow. But while his expression was blank, his eyes fixed upon mine with a peculiar sharpness, which I recognized from our long hours of labor together. The fingers of his left hand played with the signet ring on the fourth finger of his right hand, in a manner most uncommon to a man so still and studied as the duke.

"Perhaps something will occur to you later," I said.

"It always does, I find. Usually about midnight, when everyone else is asleep."

"Asleep? At midnight?" Mr. Magnusson laughed. "I expect we must keep different company."

The duke straightened to his feet and looked down gravely at the younger man. I believe his mouth twitched at the corner. "I am sure we do, Mr. Magnusson, and I will keep you from it no longer. We will continue this discussion tomorrow morning after breakfast, when we have all had time to reflect on the facts of the case. Miss Truelove? Are you joining the guests in the drawing room, or do you retire?"

"Certainly I retire. My mind is now far too perturbed for intercourse. I doubt I shall sleep at all."

"Do try, Miss Truelove. Your good health is essential."

Mr. Magnusson reached for the chest and replaced the false bottom, then the lid. "Do you remember the way upstairs, Miss Truelove? I shall be glad to show you, if you need me."

"Not at all," I said. "I remember the direction perfectly. Good night, gentlemen."

As I left the room, leaving the two men side by side in front of the large table, I remember thinking how abruptly this little council had ended, and how adroitly the duke had forced its conclusion.

I also remembered wondering whether this was because Max had just seen the same curious object I saw, hidden inside the false bottom of the old wooden chest.

⁓

Now, you've likely already guessed that I was not strictly truthful when I told Mr. Magnusson that I remembered the way back to my room. Luck, however, was with me. At the end of the corridor, I turned right on instinct, and saw a wooden door hanging ajar about halfway down the hall. This proved to be a staircase, spiraling up one of the castle's lesser turrets, floor by floor, until I reached the one on which I knew my chamber lay. Sure enough, when I emerged, I recognized my surroundings, and reached my room in half a minute.

I was not, however, alone.

A woman rose from the armchair next to the fire. She was dressed in a quilted dressing gown of forest-green satin, somewhat worn, and her hair lay in a red-gold braid over her left shoulder.

"Why, Lady Annis!" I said.

"I'm awfully sorry to intrude. *Am* I intruding?"

"Not at all."

She gestured to the desk by the window. "I've brought tea. Or rather, I had someone bring tea." A small, nervous laugh. "I'm sure I should have dropped the tray if I attempted it myself."

I closed the door behind me and regarded her. Her cheeks were flushed, and her eyes almost maniacally bright. I wondered if she had perhaps had something to drink. I sniffed the air, but could detect nothing out of the ordinary, beyond the damp, musty smell of the chamber itself, on which lay a faint odor of dried flowers, in a late, ineffectual attempt to freshen the atmosphere.

"Is it still hot?" I asked.

"I believe so." Lady Annis turned and moved swiftly to the tray, as if eager to find some occupation for her restlessness. She asked my preference, and though I usually took my tea with lemon only, I said cream and just a touch of sugar, because I thought the cream might perhaps settle my nerves.

While she poured, I asked her why she had come.

"Why, I couldn't wait any longer! I was hoping to see you at dinner, but I suppose you were too fatigued from your travels?" The end of the sentence tended upward, like a question.

"In truth, I rarely dine in company."

"Whyever not?"

I hesitated. She was still turned away, fussing with the tea, and the light from the oil lamp caressed the back of her neck. I thought she was perhaps average height, or an inch above it, though she was made along such delicate lines, she appeared smaller. Her waist, cinched almost into nonexistence by the sash of her dressing gown, was immaculate. "Because I am not, by nature, a social creature."

"Oh!" Another squeak of laughter. "I'm afraid I am. Terribly. I can't bear to be alone; I feel as if the walls are moving to crush me. Here you are."

She turned at last, holding two cups in their saucers, and I stepped forward to relieve her of mine. The scent of roses caught my attention, rising from her warm, pale skin. She returned to the armchair in its favored position by the fire, taking her place thoughtlessly, by divine right, so that I was left to drag the ancient, rushed-seated chair from the desk and place it nearby, and then to add coals from the scuttle, for the fire had begun to die away. While I performed these maneuvers, she sipped her tea and gazed into the fire. Gathering, presumably, what thoughts she possessed.

I settled myself gingerly—the seat was frayed almost beyond purpose—and asked her if I might be of any use.

"How kind of you," she said. "Indeed, I was hoping . . ."

"Yes, your ladyship?"

"Oh, don't bother with that, really. You know, I've always had a tremendous admiration for you, Miss Truelove."

"Have you? I'm afraid I never noticed."

"Oh, yes. To be so independent and brave. To accomplish things, things that actually matter. Why, I can scarcely even pour a proper cup of tea!" She waved at the tray behind her. "But you. You've broken free. Everybody admires you, though they don't all dare admit it."

"Surely not."

"You caused such a flutter among us when His Grace went off to fetch you at the railway station. We were all quite jealous."

"There was no need for jealousy. The duke is only my employer; or rather, he *was* my employer until a few months ago, when I assumed the directorship of the Haywood Institute. We are now colleagues, I suppose."

"Colleagues!" She sighed and set her cup in her saucer. "Such a fascinating word. I don't think I shall ever be anyone's *colleague*."

I hardly knew what to say to this. I knew she was working her way toward something, and I had some idea what it must be. But I felt she should arrive there herself. If she had something to say to me on the subject of the Duke of Olympia, and the nature of my relationship toward him, I wasn't going to act as her midwife. I sipped my tea and cast my gaze to the old pink rug spread atop the wooden floor, and to Lady Annis's embroidered slippers that peered out in two triangles from beneath the hem of her dressing gown.

"I do hope to be somebody's *wife* one day, however," she said.

"Yes, I imagine so."

"Oh, please, Miss Truelove. Please don't be so enigmatic. You must know what he thinks of me."

"The duke, you mean?"

"Yes. Does he care for me at all?"

"Lady Annis," I said, "this is really not a question I ought to answer."

"Can you answer it, though? Has he spoken of me?"

I sipped my tea slowly. "Yes, he has."

"Oh, you must tell me. You must tell me what he said. You see—I'm going to confess to you, Miss Truelove, I'm going to place my faith in you—you see, I'm so frightfully in love with him! You can't imagine."

"In love with him?"

She set her tea on the small round table next to her elbow and rose from the armchair, wringing her hands. "Oh, I know what they say about me, how I'm nothing but a fortune hunter. And I suppose that was a little bit true. You can't blame me for that, can you? So pitifully poor as we are, I was bred to marry well, I was told from the cradle that I must find a man with a fortune at his disposal. I know you don't understand, I know you must despise me for it—"

"Of course not. I, more than anybody, understand how a young woman must make her way in the world, with whatever talents she possesses."

"Oh, God," she said. "How little you think of me. *What talents she possesses.* Yes, all I have is my beauty. I'm not fit for anything but marriage, unlike you. Which is why—oh, Miss Truelove, when I met him, when he walked into the great hall a week ago—"

"The duke?"

"Yes!" She began to pace about the room, skirting the bed, moving first to the window with the dark sea beyond, and then to the mantel. A portrait hung above it, some female ancestor or another, dressed in a rich costume of another age. Lady Annis placed her fingers on the brass plate that announced the dame's identity. "I felt it instantly," she whispered. "I could hardly speak. The strength of his gaze! It was like looking into an ocean, vast and impenetrable."

I considered pointing out to her that oceans were not, by nature, impenetrable, being composed of mere salt water. But she was gripping the edge of the mantel, as if unable to support the force of her emotion, and I withheld the observation, saying only, "He has dark eyes, to be sure."

"Such eyes!" she said. "In such a face! He has conquered me, Miss Truelove. He has rendered every other consideration insignificant."

"No doubt."

She spun around. "You think me insincere?"

"I think it is no great surprise, when a young woman falls in love with a wealthy man. You will forgive my frankness."

Lady Annis's chin tilted upward. She opened her mouth to make some imperious reply, which she bit back at the last instant, transforming the sound into a noise of anguish. "Of course you don't believe me. I don't see why you should. He's the greatest prize in the British Isles, and I am a notorious fortune hunter, aren't I? Oh, God. What he must think of me!"

"But I assure you, the duke is well-disposed toward you."

Her face lit. "Is he?"

"He is a sensible man. Naturally he realizes that his great inheritance renders his personal merit irrelevant, in the matter of matrimony. He doesn't long for a grand passion; his passions, I'm afraid, lie within the earth itself. In his work."

"In his *work*? But surely—Miss Truelove, you will pardon me—I don't know how to say this . . ." Her beautiful face turned downward, as if examining the fire, and I couldn't say whether the flush in her cheeks came from the proximity of heat or the proximity of modesty. "When he rushed away to meet you at the station, Miss Truelove, *you* of all women—"

"I hope, Lady Annis, you are not so foolish as to heed common gossip."

"Oh, Miss Truelove. Have you never been in love? Never felt the anguish of jealousy? When a woman loves as I do, loves with all her heart, without knowing whether the object of her love reciprocates it, why—why, she finds rivals everywhere, in every woman alive. You cannot possibly understand . . ."

Driven, it seemed, by the force of her feelings, Lady Annis stepped to her armchair and dropped her figure daintily into the seat, whereupon she lifted her arm and buried her face in the hollow of her elbow, and her back trembled with sobs.

I stared at her for some awkward length of time. The curve of her spine, the graceful arrangement of waist and legs, the play of light in her red-gold hair, belonged in a painting. I remember thinking how well the anguish of jealousy became her.

"No," I said, "I suppose I don't. Indeed, I find your purpose here a mystery. Do you wish me to convey these abundant sentiments of yours to the duke? Or do you merely wish to assure yourself that you have no rival for his affections?"

She looked up. "Have I? A rival?"

I chose my words carefully. "None of any threat, so far as I am aware."

"His heart is free?"

"I did not say that. But his heart is sufficiently open, I should say, for your purposes."

"How you despise me."

I rose from my chair. "I don't despise you, madam. On the contrary, I wish you nothing but success in your endeavors. I am, however, most fatigued after a long and trying day, and I beg you will allow me the peace of my own room in which to recover myself."

"Oh! How thoughtless of me!" She leapt from the chair. "Of course you're exhausted. I know I should be. Traveling fatigues me extremely. Do forgive me, Miss Truelove, for intruding on you. My passion was so strong, I forgot all courtesy. Is there anything I can do for you? Is your room comfortable?"

"Quite sufficient, thank you."

Lady Annis forced a smile. "Then I will leave you in peace, as you asked. Perhaps we shall have the opportunity to speak again, after breakfast? The gentlemen will be off shooting again."

"Perhaps," I said. "Good night, your ladyship."

"Good night, Miss Truelove."

She made for the door in her queenly way, and I remember thinking, as I watched the noble set of her shoulders, she would make an excellent Duchess of Olympia: she had the part exactly right. She reached the door and laid her hand on the latch and turned to me, wearing a smile of gleaming toothiness.

"Shall I lock the door, Miss Truelove, or do you prefer me to leave it unlatched?"

∽

Now. A word of advice, if you will allow me. When traversing a country house at night—a house in the midst of a party, that is—it's best to tread carefully and to keep your eyes cast downward, for you are likely to encounter any number of your fellow guests, intent upon some clandestine connection that will not bear the light of day.

In my years of service to the dukedom, I have had ample occasion to learn this particular lesson, and you may be sure that when I emerged from my bedroom at a quarter to midnight, I took care to open the door carefully and to examine the hallway before I proceeded. Fortunately, the housekeeper had allocated me one of the lesser chambers, as befitted my imprecise social standing; the corridor was quite empty, and so quiet I could hear the angry, rhythmic smash of the sea against the rocks below, and the faint whistle of the wind in some nearby window. I crept along the flagstones in my slippered feet, wearing a thick dressing gown against the expected chill, but I saw nobody. The staircase, spiraling down one of the turrets, contained no other nocturnal wayfarer except a plump, astonished tabby cat, who froze on the steps and suffered me to pass.

At the bottom of the staircase, a wooden door blocked my exit. I lifted the latch silently, and as I did so, a voice hissed into my ear. "You are quite mad."

The air, as I said, was cold and quite damp, smelling of the sea and of the stone itself. For a moment I thought the icy sensation on the back of my neck was a natural one, and the voice my imagination, fed by the whistle of the wind.

Still, I stopped, with my hand on the latch, and waited.

"Don't pretend you can't hear me," said the same voice, more clearly.

I turned to my left, from which direction the voice seemed to be arriving, and there she stood, bundled in a similar dressing gown to mine, in addition to a shawl of crimson cashmere. Her round, plump face was tinged in pink: whether from the chill or the slight glow of the shawl, I could not determine.

"I am not mad," I said. "I'm going to the duke's assistance."

"In the middle of the night?"

"Secrecy, I believe, is necessary to the errand. In a houseful such as this, one cannot be too discreet."

She made a deprecating noise. "It is not discreet to meet a gentleman in the middle of the night, Miss Truelove. That is the opposite of discreet, in fact."

"He is my employer, not a lover."

"That may be true, but most people aren't interested in the truth. They are interested in their own perceptions."

I reached again for the latch. "I have never allowed my actions to be guided by the opinions of others."

"Then you're a fool."

"Good night, madam." I opened the door.

"Wait!"

The hinges creaked softly. I looked up and down the hallway and, seeing nothing, stepped forward, allowing the door to close behind me. This action did not, of course, deter the Queen. In the next instant, she stepped directly in front of me, in so swift a movement that the soft fringe of her shawl rustled against her dressing gown.

"Halt at once! Halt, I say!"

"I will not. I have an appointment." I stepped around her and proceeded up the hallway, almost at a run.

"You must not! You cannot!"

"I shall!"

"It might be dangerous. There might be—"

I stopped and flung around to face her. "Oh, be quiet! For God's sake! What business is it of yours? What the devil am I to you, that you must torment me like this? Why the devil do you care?"

Her chest heaved; her fingers trembled. In her blue eyes, a bit of glitter caught the little moonlight from the nearby window cut into the stone wall. She looked as if she meant to speak, and then, just as her mouth opened, she vanished, as if she had never existed.

For a moment, I simply stood there, staring at the empty stretch of wall. I don't know why. Perhaps I wanted her to return, for some perverse reason. Perhaps I wanted to hear her answer my question. I closed my eyes and counted in my head, and when I reached a minute, feeling nothing, I opened my eyes and continued down the hallway, listening carefully for any strange sound, any sign of another being, human or otherwise. But there was nothing except the faint rustle of my own slippered footsteps, until I arrived at the Oriental library and stepped inside, shutting the door behind me, to discover the Duke of Olympia waiting for me as we had arranged.

But he was not alone. He sat in a chair next to the empty fire-place, stiff, red-faced, handkerchief in mouth, fighting the re-straint that bound his wrists together behind the chair's back.

At his side stood the man from the train, the ginger-haired man, calmly holding the end of a pistol barrel at the duke's temple.

On his knees, the Fisherman begged God for her life, and when the sun set his prayer was answered, for the Lady's fever abated and she opened her eyes, which were the color of the sea itself. 'Who are you,' she asked, in a strange accent, 'and why am I brought to this primitive house, when I am accustomed to every luxury?' The Fisherman took her hand and answered, 'Dear Lady, I am only a poor Fisherman, but my love for you is surely greater and purer than any earthly treasure, for by its power you are brought again to life . . .'

THE BOOK OF TIME, A. M. HAYWOOD (1921)

Four

"Truelove, isn't it?" the man said. "Come on in."

I was already inside the room, of course. I stayed in place, lifting my hand behind me to grasp at the doorknob.

"Oh, come on. Don't do anything stupid." He waved his other hand, the one not holding the pistol. "Come on. Step forward, where I can see you."

"You can see me right where I am," I said clearly.

He whistled. "Damn, you've got balls. Seriously, though. Chop-chop."

"For what purpose? Why are you here? Who are you?"

The duke made some sound through the material of his handkerchief, a noise of frustration.

"Oh, shut up," the man said amiably, and he gathered his fingers in the hair at the top of Max's head and jerked back violently.

I darted forward. "Stop!"

"Atta girl." The man grinned. "That's better. Now I can see your pretty face."

Max hadn't made a sound, and he didn't now, as the man released his hair. But his eyes were bright with pain, or perhaps anger, and he seemed to be communicating some fierce message as he met my gaze.

I turned to the man with contempt. "You're a fool. The house is full of people. Men with guns. They'll shoot you dead, long before the constabulary arrives, and say it was all a terrible accident."

"What, are you kidding? I know the score around here. They're all upstairs, honey. Either fast asleep or f——ing each other. They won't hear anything, trust me. Not a thing. So let's get down to business, all right?"

He spoke in a strange accent—English, I guessed, but from which county, I couldn't determine. It was neither aristocratic nor base, but a strange, slipshod mixture of the two. Back in the cave on Naxos, I had thought he was American, but now I couldn't say for certain. His language, of course, was vulgarity itself, and I ask your forgiveness for transcribing it here without omission, for I feel it illuminates certain aspects of his character, and the strangeness of the syntax in which he spoke. *Let's get down to business,* he said, looking at me with relish, and I thought, *My God, he's enjoying this.*

"Very well. Where's Silverton?" I asked.

"Silverton? You mean the blond guy? The guy in your room last night?"

"You know the man I mean."

"How should I know?"

"Because he caught you searching for my portfolio, didn't he? What have you done with him?"

Slowly, he lowered the pistol from Max's temple, until it hung at an angle near his own waist. "The f——," he said. "He's not here?"

For an instant, or perhaps not even that—a flash, a glimpse—I thought I perceived Silverton's own face inside that of the man standing before me. I thought I saw a pair of amused blue eyes, crinkled at the corners and without spectacles, and a wide, lush mouth and a glint of gold hair.

Then he was gone, vanished, and the absence of him seemed to suck my soul from my body, leaving behind nothing but blackness.

"No," I said softly. "He's not here."

The ginger-haired man whipped around and drove his closed fist against the wooden table. The table withstood the abuse; the man gave an almighty cry. "He's got the papers?" he asked.

"I believe so."

"S——. S——, s——, s——."

An angry growl vibrated Max's throat; I couldn't tell whether his captor's foul language or his mere presence had upset the duke. His eyes found mine again, and he said a short, sharp word into the thick band of the handkerchief. A command of some kind; I believe it was *Go!*

I didn't heed him. I turned instead to the ginger-haired man, because I was desperate now, my belly sick with fear. "What happened?" I demanded. "What have you done to him?"

"I didn't do s—— to him, okay? He chased me out of the room. Ran me down. Grabbed the papers and knocked me down the stairs. By the time I got my gun out, he was gone."

"Gone where?"

Until now, the man had remained bent over the table, nursing his fist, biting out his sentences in a mutter. He straightened and turned his head. His pistol lay on the table before him. I considered my distance to the table, calculated the chance of my snatching the pistol before he could react. Too slim, I thought.

And I needed him to talk. I needed to know what had happened to Silverton.

"Gone *where*?" The man made a shallow, brief laugh and nodded in the duke's direction. "Ask him. I'll bet he knows."

I startled and looked at Max, whose gaze had turned wide with shock. He looked at the intruder, and then to me.

"Are you mad?" I said.

"*Mad?* Mad, that's a good word. I like that word. But nope. Not me, not crazy at all. Come on. Don't tell me you can't guess what happened to your boy. I sure the f—— can. G——*damn* it." He slammed his fist against the table again and picked up the pistol. Turned to the duke, who stared furiously at him, fighting the cords that held him to the chair. "Dude. Duke-man. I should just shoot you now, right? J—— Ch——. If I could just reach inside your f——ing brain and grab what I need. Except it isn't there. Isn't there *yet*. Jesus. What the f—— do I do now, huh?" He let out a furious cry and aimed the pistol at me, and then at Max, and back at me, and in that moment of his frustration I leapt forward to his legs, aiming at the knees, and brought him to the ground.

As I did so, the duke roared from his seat, furious at his own helplessness, and a tremendous crash shook the floor as he broke the restraints at his legs and rose, toppling the chair. The pistol had dropped from the intruder's hand and slid across the wooden floorboards, not far, and I lurched toward it desperately, trying to grasp the handle before he could recover. But his arm found my waist, holding me back, and I saw the duke's feet pass, saw the duke kick the pistol toward my outstretched hand. I grasped it, slipped the handle into my palm, and twisted about, trying to bring the man into range.

"Feisty b——," he said, and his hand seized my wrist, while the duke spun about and delivered a kick to his ribs. He swore violently and tore the pistol from my grip and pressed it to my temple. "Touch me again and I pull this trigger!" he yelled, and instantly the duke froze.

"He's lying!" I said, and the man yanked my head back by the hair.

"I am not f—— lying," he said calmly. "Stand up. I said *stand up*."

I rose slowly, mindful of the tension on my hair, and the cold, heavy weight of the pistol's short barrel against the skin of my left temple. The man's breath came hot and damp along my cheek, along my ear, along my neck.

"That's a good girl," he crooned. "Nice and easy. Nobody does anything dumb."

I straightened myself against his body, which was flat and hard where it pressed along my spine and my head and the backs of my legs. He was not large, but his very leanness contained a tensile, ropelike strength that easily overpowered mine. Unsteady from shock and from sudden exertion, I might have toppled were it not for his arm binding my middle, like the steel cuff of a prisoner. The duke's image wobbled before my eyes. His feet were planted square on the floorboards, his dressing gown parted, the muscles of his quadriceps bulging from the material of his pajamas. The handkerchief had slipped from his mouth. Behind his back, his hands worked at their bonds: the only movement along the length and breadth of his body. His gaze was trained not on the intruder's face, but on mine.

"That's right," the man said. "That's better. Let's just figure this out, okay? We figure this out, and everybody gets what they want."

The duke's hands stilled at his back. "Very well. Lay down your pistol."

The man's hands tightened in my hair, making me gasp.

"Now, see. That's exactly what I'm not going to do. A gun gives you leverage, bro. Leverage. Means I get what I want first, you know what I'm saying? My name's Hunter, by the way. Nice to meet you both."

"Mr. Hunter—"

"Just Hunter. My first name. I ain't telling you the last."

"Hunter. I have only one request. Before we proceed at all, before we agree on a single point, you must release Miss Truelove."

"Hell, no. Next point?"

The duke merely lifted his eyebrows.

"Okay, then. You want to play it that way." Hunter yanked back my head and released the safety catch with a soft click. "See this girl here? She ain't got what you got. I can't kill you, 'cause you got the juice. Couldn't kill you on Naxos, can't kill you here. But Miss Truelove here, she's got no juice. No special sauce. Ergo, I got no problem killing her, if you don't do what I want you to do."

"And what is that, exactly?"

"So, here we go. I'm going to have to explain a few things, okay? If we're going to get anywhere tonight. Explain a few things I guess you might not know about yourself. About this thing you got."

"The juice, I believe?" Max said dryly.

"Whatever you call it. Now, let's start at the very beginning. A very good place to start." He sang the last sentence, to a tune I didn't know. "When you read, you begin with A-B-C. When you travel through time . . . ha ha. Look at your faces. Man, I kill myself. Okay. So . . . let me see. You know what you did on that island, right? When you brought that Greek brother—"

"Theseus," I said.

"Whatever. Dude fell off a cliff three thousand years ago, and you, Mr. Duke-Man, you yourself *catch him* and f——ing *haul his ass* into the twentieth century. That's some juice, right?" Hunter whistled in my ear. "Some . . . f——ing . . . juice."

"And how did you come to know that story?" Max asked.

"Because you wrote a book about it, duke-man. That story and others like it."

"I haven't written any books. Not about what happened on Naxos, anyway. I haven't told a soul."

"Let me rephrase," said Hunter. "You ain't wrote it *yet*. Not in—what year is it, again?"

"What *year* is it?"

"You heard me. 1905 or some s——?"

"1906," I said, because I was beginning to comprehend him. I was beginning to see a picture assimilate before me: a strange, wondrous, frightening, complicated picture, thick with possibility, thick with mystery.

"Fine. 1906. But this book? *The Book of Time*, it's called? You wrote it in 1921, my man. Nineteen hundred and twenty-one."

"I don't understand. Then how—if I haven't written this thing yet—how do you know I will?"

I cleared my throat. "I believe I can guess the answer to that. When were you born, Hunter?"

"Bingo!" Hunter said. "See? The lady gets it. Gold star to the lady. So listen up. You ready for this? To answer your question, Miss Truelove, I was born in good old nineteen hundred and eighty-five. 1985. How cool is that? And here I am, and the reason I'm here is because somebody sent me here, somebody with the juice, as I call it, and that somebody—"

An almighty *BANG* tore the air apart, and the instantaneous impact of a bullet into stone. Amid the shower of shrapnel, Hunter shouted something, released me, and I stumbled backward to the wall.

"Max!" I called.

Through the clearing smoke strode Mr. Magnusson, holding a cocked pistol in one hand, while Max launched himself forward to slam into Hunter's body, knocking loose the gun.

"Stay where you are!" commanded Mr. Magnusson, and Hunter swore. He turned and bolted for the window; Mr. Magnusson fired again, and the window glass exploded into tiny shards. I ducked away from the shower, and when I turned back, Hunter had vanished.

"Where is he?" I demanded, but neither man answered. Instead they rushed for the open window and gazed down, down, where the midnight sea hurled itself against the cliff some fifty feet below.

"God save him," whispered the duke.

We ran for the library door, following Mr. Magnusson, who knew the way. A succession of corridors fled past, then a long, spiraling journey down a turret staircase much like the one I had descended earlier, then more corridors, damp and dark and chill, like the catacombs of some ancient crypt. There was nothing to light our way except a curious electric torch Mr. Magnusson produced from his pocket, and this garish beam bounced along the walls at a frantic pace, bringing terrible, ragged, fleeting shadows to life, like monsters caught inside the stone. I felt them staring at me as we flew along: Magnusson first, then me, then the duke at my heels, his hands freed at last, our slippered feet thudding upon the bare floor, our breath panting in the ancient air. My lungs burned, my legs burned, but still I ran gamely in Magnusson's wake, for I knew I should never find the way back from this maze if I allowed myself to fall behind.

Quite without warning, Magnusson flung open a thick wooden door, and a gust of briny air flooded over us. So chill was the atmosphere inside, the sea wind felt almost balmy against my cheek, but as I stepped outside to the narrow stone path, a fine mist of salt water leapt from below to sting my skin. I gasped for breath. A half-moon lingered in the sky, dimly revealing our position on the cliff, upon a tiny, silver path that wound its way around the headland, up and down, following the natural contours of the tall, jagged stone, and presently about a dozen feet above the lashing of the waves.

There was no sign of the ginger-haired man.

"My God," said the duke, looking up. "I don't see how he could have survived it."

"He could not," Magnusson said emphatically. He turned and pointed upward, where Thurso Castle rose from the top of the headland, coal-dark and impenetrable, about twenty feet above our heads. "The library window is right there, you see? Halfway up the castle walls. A drop of perhaps sixty or seventy feet at least. Into that."

That was the foamy, roiling, opaque broth at our feet, slapping angrily against the sheer barrier of the cliff face. Here and there, a rock pushed up from the water, its dimensions marked by a simmer of phosphorescence. I imagined a body striking one of those rocks, a head perhaps careering against the rough, slick stone, and I shuddered. The duke's hand found my shoulder. No doubt he was thinking of his lost love, left behind on Naxos in the arms of the ancient Greek warrior to whom her heart was bound. The sea, you know. That same infinity of water that connected us to every coast in the world.

"Who the devil was he?" asked Magnusson. "He sounded absolutely mad."

"Quite mad," said Max. "How did you discover us?"

"Why, I was headed upstairs to—to find a book, and I heard some commotion. Thought it best to find my pistol and see what the devil was going on." He turned to face us, and his grinning mouth caught the silver of the moon. "Damned glad I did. Rather a tight spot, wouldn't you say? Any idea what the chap wanted?"

The duke's fingers tightened on my shoulder. "It seems he holds a grudge of some kind against me. I'm afraid I ruffled his feathers, back in the Med last spring."

"I see. Well, he's gone now, God rest his soul. I shall make a quick report to Father and inform the staff, in case the body washes ashore. Send for the constable, of course." His gaze fastened on the duke's face, eyebrows slightly ajar, as if that last sentence represented a question rather than a statement of intent.

Max said slowly, "A constable, of course. The local authorities should be informed of the incident."

"I quite agree, quite agree." Magnusson glanced at me, then back at the duke. "But . . . hmm. Not until the morning, perhaps? Nothing to be done until daylight, in any case."

"Nothing at all, alas," I said. "Besides, we should wake the entire house, even if a constable could be found at this hour."

"Well said, Miss Truelove. Very well said. That's it, then. Terrible night. I suggest the two of you pour yourselves a brandy and go to bed at once."

From Magnusson's familiar tone, and the knowing expression on his face, I could see he assumed that Max and I would do these comfortable things together. Max seemed to divine the suggestion as well. His hand slid away from my shoulder, and he stepped respectfully away. I became conscious of my dressing gown, flapping in the wind, and my nightgown that stuck to my skin, and my wet, ruined slippers. My trembling nerves. My unruly hair, which was coming undone from its braid.

Max turned to face me. "How are you faring, Miss Truelove? Shall I fetch you a glass of brandy?"

Yes, by God, my nerves screamed. I stuck my hands in the pocket of my dressing gown and said, "No, thank you."

"Are you quite sure?" said Magnusson. "A shocking episode like that. I believe I shall drink the bottle away before I retire."

"I am not fond of spirits, Mr. Magnusson."

"Ah. No. Of course not." He managed a chuckle and passed his fingers through his hair, casting a last glance toward the glittering sea. "Poor mad fellow. Happens more than you think, in these parts, though mostly in winter. Hardly ever on a fine, warm summer's day as this. Curious. Well, then. Nothing more to be done, I believe." He reached for the door and swore.

"What's the matter?" said Max.

"I'm afraid it's locked."

⟡

By the time I reached my bed, I had changed my mind about the brandy. It was too late to ring for the maid, however, and I could hardly return downstairs, so I crawled under the covers and attempted sleep, without much success. Each time I closed my eyes, I heard the bang of Magnusson's pistol, startling away what drowsiness had fallen upon me.

I stared into the canopy, counting the strikes of my pulse, and in the shadows I perceived Silverton's face, beautiful and uncharacteristically grave, gazing down upon my prone body as if to reproach me, or else to communicate some urgent message. Once I thought I heard him speak, though I couldn't make out the words, and I suppose I must have fallen asleep soon after, for I woke into a pale, chilly dawn, my heart beating violently.

A soft knock sounded on the door. It was the maid, bearing a load of coal and a telegram from the Dowager Duchess of Olympia, which informed me in staccato, capital sentences that Her Grace had not heard from the Marquess of Silverton since the day before last.

If I had any news of him, she begged me to relate it at once.

                                  *

I lay in bed for some time, digesting this message and everything else that had occurred inside this most extraordinary forty-eight hours. During that time, I had slept little, and my fatigue was now extreme, and yet my brain would not rest. An electric wakefulness sang painfully inside my skull. My eyes ached with unshed tears. My stomach, my ribs, my limbs all clenched as if locked in mortal struggle.

He is gone, I thought. *He is lost. Where do I begin to look for him?*

The maid built the fire and left the room. I waited for something to appear, the vision of my father, the vision of my Queen, anything to keep vigil with me in this lonely hour. But none appeared. The room was small and warmed quickly. I rose from the bed and went to the window, where the new-risen sun was just visible to the east, filling the sky with promise. The sea washed the rocks below me, and I murmured a prayer for the ginger-haired man, who had plunged into those waters a few hours ago. Hunter, he called himself, and he claimed it was his Christian name. A strange address. Was this the sort of method by which boys were named, eighty years hence? *Hunter?* Did they name the girls *Huntress?*

Or had the man only spun us a bizarre fiction, a madness, a fairy tale?

The room contained no clock. I consulted my own watch, a plain one made of silver, given to me by the dowager duchess at Christmas three years ago. Half past six o'clock. Nobody would be about, except the servants.

I dressed myself swiftly and went downstairs.

⁓

In the Oriental library, the old wooden chest still sat on the giant table in the center of the room, apparently untouched, though the fallen chair had been put back in its rightful place and the glass swept up. The morning breeze fluttered through the open window, cool and damp and sea-scented.

Though I had come to this room with a single purpose, I found myself stepping past the table to the window. Upon the ledge, a few minute slivers of glass remained, stuck in the gaps and the hollows of the stone, glittering by the kiss of the early sun, but there was otherwise no sign of the drama that had occurred here last night. No sign that a man had plunged to his death through this window. The morning calm of the water appeared innocent of any crime. My fingers curled into the cold edge of the stone. *This is shock*, I assured myself. *This activity in your guts, this roiling anxiety, this sickening foreboding—this is only the physical manifestation of shock.*

"My dear girl. I hope you are not considering some drastic action."

I whirled about to find my father at ease in the chair, the same one lately occupied by the Duke of Olympia. His legs were crossed, and his hands curled about the ends of the chair arms. He wore a suit I recognized, one of pale gray wool, the lightest suit he owned, when he was alive.

"Of course not," I said.

"You are greatly distressed."

"Naturally I'm distressed. You saw what occurred here last night, did you not?"

"A terrifying scene."

I leaned back against the ledge and twisted my neck to glance back down at the gray sea. "Is it really possible? Was he really born in the year 1985?"

"I'm afraid you must determine that for yourself. I have no particular insight into the matter. If he *was* born at some future date, and made his way to this age through some strange curvature in the known laws of physics, it is beyond my own knowledge. What do you think?"

"It *is* possible," I said. "I saw it happen last April with my own eyes, on the island of Skyros. You know that as well as I do. You know we have discussed the incident, over and over—"

"With the duke, you mean?"

"Yes. The duke. We discussed what had occurred, and how, and why."

"And did you conclude any of these points?"

"No. But we could not doubt the *fact* of it. We could not doubt a man named Tadeas had somehow manifested from the empty air of the Skyros cliff, at the exact spot where an ancient king was supposed to have flung a warrior known to both myth and history as Theseus to his death. And we could not doubt that this man—speaking an ancient dialect, dressed in foreign clothes—came into being at the end of the Duke of Olympia's outstretched arm."

"Quite true. We have our knowledge of science, and we have the facts as we observe them, and if one does not agree with the other, why—I suppose we must decide which one is to be trusted most."

I turned back to face my father, who sat in perfect tranquility. *Easy enough for him*, I thought bitterly. I crossed my arms and said, "But supposing Hunter's story were true, and he really did hail from another time, who had brought him into this one, if not Max himself?"

"I cannot say."

"How was it done? Why was it done? And Silverton—he has disappeared—and I am *afraid*, Father, terribly afraid that—" I felt a sob rising in my throat, and I bit off the end of the sentence rather than finish it.

My father said patiently, shaking his head, "This is for you to discover, my dear Emmeline, as human beings are called upon to investigate those things that mystify them."

I opened my mouth to reply, but he had already disappeared, like the switching of a lamp.

I swore. I covered my face with my hands and made a noise of rage.

"Ah, Miss Truelove. I'm afraid I feel much the same way."

I lifted my hands away and saw that the duke stood just inside the doorway, wearing a tweed Norfolk jacket and leather spats and an expression of deep concern. While I tried to think of a reply, he turned and closed the door behind him, locked it carefully, and walked toward me.

"I ought not to have used such a word," I said.

He came to stand before me and took my hands in his own. His dark eyes were deeply shadowed, his face drawn with long, fatigued lines. "On the contrary, I believe you summed up the situation perfectly. Did you sleep at all?"

"A few hours."

"I slept none. I expect I turned over every word he said a hundred times."

"Did you conclude anything?"

"Only a deep fear, Miss Truelove, that I myself am the unwitting cause of all our misery."

I bent my head and closed my eyes, and for some time we stood there, linked by thought and by an intensity of emotion, by our hands knit together, by an experience, an understanding we could not put into words but rather shared voicelessly.

"You're afraid for Silverton, aren't you?" he said.

"Yes."

"What pains me," he said, "what *frustrates* me, is that I believe I know where he is. Not consciously, of course. But that this knowledge exists somewhere inside my person, and I simply cannot locate it. I don't have the keys to the door that guards it." He paused. "Do you understand what I mean?"

I didn't reply. As he was speaking those words, I had become aware of something else. I felt a faint tingling enter my palms, like a tremor of very weak electricity, originating from within the duke's own body and passing into mine through the skin of his hands.

"Miss Truelove?" the duke said.

The tremor grew stronger, but in erratic, unsteady, minute surges that channeled all my thought, all my attention into that small area of flesh that connected me to Max. Behind my closed eyelids, a vision flashed and disappeared and returned, in the same tempo as the crackling in my palms: a room, a window, a fine tapestry draped upon a wall of stone. On the tapestry, a long-haired woman rising from the sea. And somewhere—not *inside* that room but near it, surrounding it—a beloved presence I could neither see nor smell nor hear, but rather felt in my bones.

"Ah," said Max, and the electricity strengthened mightily, and the vision clarified before me, and a black, cold wind seemed to gust over my head and down the strands of my hair, lifting them from my scalp, engulfing me, wrapping each nerve in agony that was also rapture; or rather rapture that was also agony.

I cried out and pulled away. The vision winked out, and I staggered back, clutching the table behind me in order to save myself from falling. The duke dropped into the chair, panting hard.

"My God," I whispered.

Max lifted his head. His expression was shocked, enervated. We stared at each other in a kind of daze. I put my hand atop my chest, atop my heart that beat like the firing of a gun.

"Are you—" he gasped.

"Yes. You?"

"A moment," he said, closing his eyes, leaning his elbows on his legs and his head into his hands. I wanted to go to him, to kneel beside him and comfort him, but I could scarcely move. My body felt as if it had been drawn through a machine. The duke still wore his peaked cap, and I could not see his face beneath its shadow. Behind him, the library shelves stood full of old books. I could smell the leather of their bindings. And yet, for an instant, I seemed to glimpse a tapestry upon that wall, in place of the shelves.

I said, with effort, "What—tell me—what were you thinking about, just now? When you—when we—"

"Silverton." He paused. "I saw a room."

"*This* room," I said.

He lifted his head. Our gazes met, and his eyes widened. "Yes."

I cannot say how long we remained like this, staring at each other inside that silent library, while the breeze pulsed gently from the broken window. We were perhaps ten or twelve feet apart, and yet this small distance was that of a gulf, unbridgeable. I made some movement toward him, and he raised his hand as if to ward me off.

"Don't." His voice was raw, as if rubbed with sand. "Don't touch me."

"It won't happen. Not unless you make it happen."

"I don't know if I can stop it. I don't know how to control it."

"Yes, you do. Max, you *do*. Don't you see? *This* is how it's done." My strength was returning to me. A swell of energy rose through my belly and down my limbs, lifting all my vital organs to a strange, sublime euphoria. I straightened from the table and stepped toward him, and at first he made some trifling movement to repulse me, but I knelt and laid my hand on his knee. "This! The force of your concentration."

"We don't know that. The danger—if I misjudge, if I have it wrong, the slightest adjustment—the consequences—"

"Don't be afraid. Don't be afraid of it. You can master it. You *must* master it, Max, you must find a way to master it, because that's the way to find him. Don't you see? This force, it's leading you to him, it's leading us to Silverton. He's *there*. I felt him."

"Ah, Miss Truelove." Max wound his hands together, away from mine. "How your faith—"

The sound of voices reached us in the same instant. The knob rattled.

"How strange," someone said, in imperious female tones, muffled by the thick wooden door. "It seems to be locked."

The Lady was much astonished, and demanded the Fisherman return her to her people, for she was proud and did not wish to live in poverty, and missed besides her young son, who was the jewel of her life. So the Fisherman took her with grieving heart upon his boat, and together they traveled the shore of the island, and all the islands around it, until at last the Lady said in despair to the Fisherman, 'It is no use, for this land is not my own, this time is not my time, and I am lost in this grim place forever . . .'

THE BOOK OF TIME, A. M. HAYWOOD (1921)

Five

For a second or two, Max and I sat frozen—he on the chair, I on my knees beside him, one hand still wrapped around the ball of his immense knee. The doorknob rattled again, and then a brisk knock sounded on the wood.

"Max!" called the woman. "Are you in there?"

"Lady Annis," I whispered.

"Damn."

"Don't, Max. Please."

He lifted my hand carefully from his knee and kissed my knuckles. "Deception only leads one further into difficulty, Miss Truelove," he said, and he summoned himself, rose with great effort, straightened his jacket, and walked to the door. I had just enough time to rise and fly to the table, to turn aside and gather my composure while Max released the lock and opened the door.

"Why, there you are!" Lady Annis exclaimed. "Why on earth—"

The sight of me interrupted her. There was the briefest moment of silence, of awkward comprehension, no more than a second. Max said, "Miss Truelove was assisting me in a scientific experiment."

"Naturally," said her ladyship. "I hope you have reached a satisfactory conclusion? The constable is here."

I looked up in time to see Lady Annis step aside, ushering a man into the room. He was elderly, diffident, wearing a rough, homespun uniform of navy blue and his cap in his hands.

He ducked his head. "Your Grace."

"His name is Mr. Eddes," Lady Annis said dryly. "I'm sure you have a great deal to discuss. I shall tell Mrs. Campbell to send in tea."

"Coffee, if you please, Lady Annis," said the duke.

"Coffee, of course," she snapped, and left the room.

"Mr. Eddes," said the duke, "may I offer you a chair?"

"If it's all the same, Your Grace, I'll just stand. I don't wish to take up your time. I understand there's a shooting party?"

The duke consulted his watch. "Not for another hour, I believe."

"This is the window, right here?"

"Yes."

Max and I exchanged glances as the fellow ambled across the room to the open window. When he reached it, he looked down and whistled. "I don't guess anyone could survive a fall like that."

"Has a body been recovered?" I asked.

"No, ma'am." The constable turned. "The fellow was known to you?"

"Only slightly," the duke said. "And not by name. He told us his Christian name, just before he leapt from the window. Hunter."

"Hunter? That's a strange name, if you don't mind my observing."

"I thought so, too. I thought perhaps it might be an alias."

Mr. Eddes reached under the brim of his cap to scratch his forelock. "And you've got no idea why he was here? That's what Mr. Magnusson said."

I cleared my throat. "He seems to have been looking for a portfolio of papers I had in my keeping."

"And where are those papers now, Miss—Miss—"

"Truelove," said the duke. "They were stolen from her room at the North British Hotel, unbeknownst to our man last night."

The constable's eyebrows rose slightly. "A fair important set of papers, then?"

"They were scientific papers, to do with an institute of which the duke is patron," I said.

"And you, Miss Truelove? What do you have to do with the institute?"

"Miss Truelove is its director," Max said.

"Director!"

"Yes. Those papers contained a number of details regarding a complex scientific experiment, one that Miss Truelove and I are presently in the process of conducting. We believe this man sought to profit from our knowledge, and has unfortunately perished for his trouble."

"I see," said the constable. He looked from the duke to me, and back again. His expression, wizened and rather stupid, seemed not to see anything at all, except perhaps something that did not exist.

"Thank goodness Mr. Magnusson happened along when he did," I said, shaking my head.

Mr. Eddes spoke to the duke. "We're fortunate, sir, most fortunate you weren't harmed. I shall ask about the village to see if anyone saw this fellow passing through. But I believe Mr. Magnusson was right, when he said we were well rid of him."

"Is that what Mr. Magnusson said?" I asked.

"Right about. If you can think of anything else, Your Grace, any other detail that might assist us to identify his remains, when they do turn up, I hope you'll remember me. I won't take any more of your time."

"But—"

Mr. Eddes turned and looked again out the window, nodded in some sort of strange satisfaction, and doffed his cap once more in farewell.

"I'll see myself out," he said, and left the room, nearly overturning the oversized tray of coffee just then borne through the doorway by an undersized maid.

⁓

"You must speak to Lady Annis before you depart with the shooting party," I told Max as we drank our coffee.

"Damn Lady Annis."

"None of this is her doing, remember." I poured another cup with a hand that, remarkably, did not shake. "Besides, if you don't, she will make my life a misery."

"Why, whatever for?" he began, and then: "Oh. I see your point."

"She paid me a visit last night, before I returned downstairs. I will not say what she told me, or the substance of our conversation. But I must warn you that her affections ought not to be trifled with."

He made a noise of dismissal. "No doubt we remain safe from *that* danger."

"My dear sir. Can you not believe the lady might possibly love you for your own fine qualities?"

"Fine qualities." He shook his head. "Miss Truelove, I'm under no illusions. I have neither beauty nor charm. What qualities

I possess are hardly the sort to recommend themselves to young ladies. I expect, if I canvass Lady Annis in my present state, I shall do my suit more harm than good."

I started to interrupt him, but he held up his hand.

"Nevertheless, there is your honor to consider, and I will not have you made the subject of malicious gossip. I will find her at once and make myself plain. *That*, at least, I am well equipped to do." He drained his cup and set it down on the tray, as if girding himself for battle.

I coughed gently. "Sir, if I may be so bold as to offer a suggestion."

"Of course, Miss Truelove. I value your opinion above all others."

"Not *too* plain, if you catch my meaning. Women like a little mystery."

The duke knit his brows and made a little groan. "I do sometimes wish we might return to days of yore, when these things were done in the proper manner."

"The proper manner?"

"By proxy. Good day, Miss Truelove. We will consult again when I return." He turned and made for the door, and just as his hand touched the knob, he stopped and patted his pockets. "Ah! I nearly forgot. See what you can make of this, while I'm gone." He struck back toward me and pulled a square of folded paper from inside his jacket.

"What's this?"

"Last night, when I couldn't sleep, I remembered what had brought me down to the library at midnight to begin with. Something I spotted inside the chest, when Mr. Magnusson was with us. I didn't mention it at the time—"

"Inside the hidden compartment," I said. "I saw it, too."

"Ah, I thought you had. In any case, there was no question of sleeping after all that damned show with Hunter, so back I went downstairs to investigate."

I took the paper. "And this is what you found?"

"Yes. Wedged in rather snugly, but I managed to pry it loose. I'm afraid I couldn't make heads or tails of it. But I expect *you*, Miss Truelove, will have no trouble at all."

~

A strange expression, *falling in love*. I have always objected to it. It implies some accident, some want of agency; it suggests a particular moment, a particular action, a particular sensation, a moment, an instant in which you travel—you *plunge*—that vast distance from indifference to adoration.

I did not fall in love with Lord Silverton, during the course of our voyage through the Mediterranean last spring. There was no sudden revelation in which I realized he inhabited my heart. I suppose you might say he crept there, inch by inch, until it seemed he had always existed inside me, even before I knew him; as if he had only given his name and his face and himself to an unknown idol I had quietly carried about in my soul.

Of all the hours I spent by his side, I remember our parting best. By then I knew each dimension of his face, each expression, the exact blue shade of his eyes in every different light, the curve of his lip, the line of his shoulders, the angle of ribs and hips and legs, every smile, every frown, the crinkle of his eyes when he laughed—which was often—the glint of his hair, the size of his ear, the rhythm of his stride, his opinion of Julius Caesar and German wines and American racehorses and Adam Smith, his taste in music (execrable) and his taste in painting (modern), his love for his father, his worship of his stepmother, his adoration for his sisters and brother, his delight in automobiles, his disgust for bicycles, his talent for cricket, his ineptitude at golf, the uncanny operation of his sensory instincts, the merriment of his wit, the melancholy of his interior, the age at which he had lost his virginity, the age of the woman who had relieved him of it, how he took his tea, how he took his women, when he took his bath, each tooth, each hair, each finger, each breath, each strike of his heart; those things he had not told me or shown me, I understood by instinct.

But as I stood in the sleepy, dusty plaza on Skyros, shaking his hand while the ferry blew its horn behind him, I realized I didn't know him at all. An hour earlier, I had made a confession to him, laying bare a secret I had never meant to reveal to anyone, and now, feeling the pressure of his palm against mine, the pressure of his gaze against mine, I had not the slightest idea what it meant to him. I had not the slightest idea what *I* still meant to him.

Next to me, the Duke of Olympia was making his own farewells. I had forgotten my hat, and the sun burned the back of my head, burned my skin through the material of my dress. The wind was strong and full of salt. Silverton's hand left mine, and his head turned in the direction of his valet, who was shouting instructions for the disposition of his lordship's many trunks. I opened my mouth to say something, to say anything, but of course I remained silent. He turned back once and waved, and I thought how large his hand was, and how competent. I remember wondering what adventures that hand would know, what women it would touch, before I saw him again.

"Well, that's that," said the duke as Silverton made his way gaily up the gangplank, and the sailor began to throw off the ropes. But neither of us made a move to return to the small villa in which we were lodged. We stood side by side, watching him go, and as the boat parted from the dock, opening a wedge of blue water between Silverton and Truelove, I was seized with panic. The blue wedge widened, and the wind blew harder, and I realized I had stopped breathing entirely. I lifted my right arm and placed it across my middle and forced my lungs to act. Max turned and asked me if I was all right.

"Yes, of course," I said, but I was lying. I was not all right. I found Silverton's blond head among the sparse crowd of tourists, all of whom turned to gaze at him as he ambled toward the stern like a negligent prince, shedding charm in his wake, and I knew he was gone. He was disappearing back into the world from which he came, a world as far removed from me as another age, a world to which I could never belong.

And when the boat had merged into the distant sea, and the duke and I returned to our lodging, I reflected that I had never really belonged to any world. I existed between them, looking inside, observing, passing through as a tourist might, and that was why I felt such sympathy for Tadeas and Desma, at the same time as I envied their belonging to each other.

Max took my elbow as we climbed the hill, and I remember thinking that casually chivalrous gesture might constitute the only human contact I experienced until morning.

❧

I thought about that parting in Skyros as I contemplated the paper the duke had given me: not because I now experienced the same panic, the same ache of separation—although I did—but because I had the feeling I was glimpsing another blue wedge, another widening gap between me and the world to which Silverton had traveled.

And this time, he might not find a way to return.

Max was wrong in his predictions; I spent the better part of an hour studying the paper, until the coffee was finished, and then I stole into the breakfast room, wrapped a sausage and a boiled egg in a napkin, and stole out again to study it anew.

I knew *what* it was, of course. I recognized the drawing immediately, even if the Duke of Olympia had not. But how had this thing come to rest inside the false bottom of an ancient Scottish chest? Who had put it there?

And the question that turned my stomach cold, turned my brain light with a peculiar mixture of fear and anticipation: *When?*

By the time I finished my breakfast, the castle was beginning to stir again. The ladies were arriving downstairs—that is, those who had not troubled to see off the gentlemen in the shooting party, as Lady Annis had—passing outside the Oriental library as they went. Fearing for my privacy, restless with a premonition both thrilling and confounding, I went upstairs for my shawl and my hat and then took myself outside for a walk.

Inevitably, the clouds had moved in. A thick, chill, overcast blanket slid over yesterday's blue sky, and the sea went dull and flat beneath it. I was glad for my shawl as I crept along the cliff path, keeping carefully to the wall, for the dampness in the air chased away whatever sunshine had penetrated the fog above. As I rounded the tip of the headland, I saw a party of ladies emerge from the castle's side entrance to embark on the path that led to the sandy cove north of the headland. I watched them descend the slope, which was much gentler on that side, and when they had safely achieved the beach, I found a small bench cut into the rock and settled myself to observe the remote seascape around me.

To my right, around the south face of the headland, lay the place where the ginger-haired man had fallen to his death last night. I glanced warily at the scene below me, but there was no sign of his remains, no bit of clothing or the body itself: only the North Sea waves, much becalmed, washing against the immovable rock. If I squinted my eyes against the horizon, I could just see the shadow of what must be the Orkney Islands, from which the wooden chest had lately arrived, under the supervision of Mr. Magnusson.

For a moment, I closed my eyes. I stretched out my mind across the gray water, as if I could actually search for him by the force of my own concentration. As if I could, like Max, penetrate these static Newtonian dimensions of time and distance and bend them to my will. Find him, wherever he was.

Him. Silverton.

But I felt nothing. Not a whisper. Only the slight breeze on my cheek.

I reached in my pocket and drew out the paper. I have something of a talent for drawing, and this sketch, inscribed by my own hand, depicted the cliffs of Naxos in pretty exact detail. Even the duke must at least have recognized the scene, for he had spent some time a prisoner in those caves, and had battled on the beach below in order to win his freedom.

There, too, a young woman who called herself Desma claimed she had crossed three thousand years of history in an instant, to escape the man who pursued her and thus emerge in our own century, though her heart remained lost behind her. Lost in the keeping of Tadeas, who did eventually rejoin her, by the Duke of Olympia's own hand.

No, Max must have recognized the scene itself, even if he didn't know the artist's identity, or where it had come from. He must have identified the subject of the drawing, even if he didn't realize that I myself—Emmeline Truelove—had carried this very paper with me from London, hidden inside my locked leather portfolio among the other documents related to our research.

That I had lost this paper during the night in Edinburgh, at the moment when the Marquess of Silverton vanished into the air.

"Why, there you are, Miss Truelove! I hope you don't mean to jump."

I startled toward the voice, which belonged to Lady Annis, standing to my right in a walking dress of Scottish plaid and a trim bonnet, though without a shawl or a jacket of any kind.

She smiled at my confusion. "We've already had our quotidian of that sort of thing, wouldn't you say? Jumping, I mean. May I sit with you?"

"Of course." I moved to my left and shoved the paper back in my pocket.

"I've been out looking for the body," she said. "Did he really just plunge through the window?"

"Yes. It was that or Mr. Magnusson's pistol."

"To think I missed it all! You independent ladies have all the jolly adventures."

"Hardly jolly, I assure you. But why haven't you gone walking with the others?" I nodded toward the cove to the north.

"Oh! Them. Silly, chattering creatures. They amuse Papa, so he invites them, along with their wretched grizzled husbands. When I have my own establishment, I shall exclude anybody over the age of forty, man or beast." She laughed. "Until my fortieth birthday, I suppose, in which case I shall offer myself a special dispensation. Now tell me what you were looking at, just now. The drawing you stuffed into your pocket. It looked fascinating."

"Merely a scene from the Mediterranean."

"Did you sketch it yourself?"

I hesitated. "Yes. Last spring."

"When you tracked down Max." She sighed. "What I wouldn't

give to visit the Greek islands. The sunlit shores of the Aegean. Instead I've got this."

"I think it's beautiful."

She laughed. "Don't be absurd. It's dull and damp and chill and remote, and that's August! Imagine it in January. No, don't. Sometimes I find myself dreaming of color. Just color. A turquoise sea and a blinding white beach and the green leaves of the olive trees and the red tiles of the roofs, everything pungent and hot and extreme. My God, how lucky you are. You will leave this place and go off on some expedition with him, and I shall—I shall—"

A small breeze found us, penetrating the soft wool of my shawl. Beside me, Lady Annis shivered and wrapped her arms around her waist. She smelled of roses and tea, of everything English, although of course she wasn't English at all. She had been born in Scotland to a Scottish father. Her mother had been English, I recalled, but that unfortunate woman had died before Lady Annis could properly know her.

I ventured quietly, "If he marries you—"

"If he marries me, it will be much the same, won't it? I shall be left behind with the houses and the servants and the endless charity committees, and the two of you will have all the fun. We Sinclairs, you know, are destined never to know happiness in marriage." She rose quickly. "I wish I had your courage," she said, and she turned back the way she had come, along the southern side of the headland, taking the path that led down to the precipice on which I had stood last night with Max and Mr. Magnusson. She moved with a splendid, nimble grace. As I watched, she unbuttoned her dress and worked herself free of sleeves and bodice and skirt, and just as I began to avert my eyes, I saw that underneath the frock she wore not the customary arrangement of corset and petticoats, but a bathing costume of dark blue serge.

She did not pause to consider her course. She kicked the dress free, stretched her long, pale arms above her head, and dove in a perfect vertical line from the precipice into the water.

✐

The shooting party did not return to the castle until past three o'clock, bearing twenty-two brace of grouse and an immense quantity of damp, muddy good spirits. I took my luncheon on a tray in the Oriental library, quite undisturbed, taking careful notes and measurements of the chest and the strange rubberlike suit inside, while the gentlemen bathed and ate and generally refreshed themselves.

By half past five, I was ready to pack up my notebooks and ruler and repair upstairs, but just as I prepared to rise from my chair, the duke appeared around the corner of the door, his hair still damp and his face full of color.

"There you are, Miss Truelove. I apologize for keeping you waiting. Mr. Miller had business for me, and I found an unexpected opportunity to speak to Lady Annis privately, which I thought I should seize."

"Of course. I hope the meeting was profitable."

The duke came to prop himself on the table nearby. "Which one?" he asked, smiling slightly, folding his arms.

"Both, I suppose."

"Yes. Quite profitable. I signed a great many papers to the estate's advantage, and when I freed myself of that duty, Lady Annis was so good as to sit with me for half an hour. She spoke frankly. I believe we shall shortly come to an understanding, thank God."

"Excellent news."

He glanced at the chest beside me. "But I hope you were not working here all along."

"No. I took a long walk in the middle of the day, although I saw no sign of our visitor's passing, nor did anyone else. His remains seem to have disappeared without trace."

"Strange. Did you find any opportunity to study the drawing I gave you?"

I glanced down at my notebooks, which lay stacked before me on the table, three of them. They were new, given to me by the housekeeper at my request, for my own notebooks—filled with numbers, sketches, diagrams, observations—had all been contained inside the leather portfolio that had disappeared in Edinburgh. "Yes," I said, and I rose from my chair and went to the door, which I closed and locked.

"What's the matter?" asked Max. His heavy cheekbones were stained raspberry, his mood transformed since the morning's malaise, giving me leave to wonder just how frank Lady Annis had proved after her bracing dip in the sea.

I stood with my back to the door, still holding the knob with my right hand. "You'll think me mad."

He laughed. "I have long since lost the right to think anyone else mad, Miss Truelove."

"You know, of course, what the drawing depicts."

"The caves of Naxos."

"Yes." I walked back to the table and drew the scrap of paper from within the first notebook. "Did you know that I drew it?"

"I presumed you must have. It's extraordinarily well done. But that was what troubled me, you see. How *this* particular drawing made its way inside a hidden compartment in *that* particular object." He was sobering already, his skin regaining its customary pallor. He nodded toward the chest itself. "Did you bring it with you from London?"

"Yes. It was inside my portfolio. The one that disappeared with Lord Silverton."

He uncrossed his arms and rested one hand on the edge of the table. "My God."

"Yes. But there's something else. This figure, here by the mouth of the cave."

"The woman?"

"I didn't draw her."

Max took the paper from me and frowned. "Are you quite sure?"

"Yes. She's a striking figure—look at her face, so carefully done—but she isn't—well, she isn't—"

He handed back the paper. His face was now quite pale. "She isn't Desma."

"No."

"Then who is she? And how did she come to be sketched into your drawing?"

"I don't know," I said, "but I spent the day considering various scenarios by which it may have come to pass—all of it—the paper, and the chest, and the strange suit. Silverton's disappearance, and what that fellow Hunter told us last night—"

"Presuming he spoke the truth."

"I believe him," I said. "Perhaps I ought not to believe him, but I do. Because it is the only explanation that makes any sense, when we consider your particular powers, and the strange events of the past several months."

The duke detached himself from the table and walked swiftly to the window. He crossed his hands behind his back and said, "Tell me what you think. Tell me what you think is the most likely scenario."

I hesitated. "This is the mad part."

"Just tell me."

"Very well. I believe that what we are seeing now, these events that have come to pass since the autumn of last year, are occurring by the actions of your future self. A man, we must presume, in full control of the powers that God has granted him, and employing those powers according to some method we do not, at present, fully understand."

He did not reply. He seemed to be staring at some distant point across the sea, wholly absorbed by the vista before him, paying not the slightest heed to what I said. The slight breeze moved his hair. From this angle, I could not quite see his expression: only his clenched jaw, and the taut tendons of his neck.

"I know this explanation makes no rational sense—" I began, and his laugh interrupted me.

"No rational sense," he repeated. "My dear Miss Truelove. When did any of this make any rational sense? From the moment she appeared at Knossos . . ."

She. He meant Desma, of course: Desma, who had traveled three thousand years in an instant, escaping a villain's trap on Naxos to find herself marooned in the twentieth century, without friends or family, without language or knowledge, without the man whose heart and whose child she carried inside her. Desperate, abandoned, she took ship to the island that had once been her home, and there she had encountered one Maximilian Haywood, who eventually restored her beloved Tadeas to her side. We had left them together in a daze of bliss in Skyros; in June, Desma had presented Tadeas with a bonny daughter, a child conceived three millennia before her own birth.

But one mystery remained. How had Desma come to this century to begin with? What force had transported her from an ancient Naxos beach to a modern one, at the exact instant when she might otherwise have perished?

"According to our own philosophy, it makes no rational sense," I said. "Which means we must endeavor to learn a new one. We must endeavor to understand the rules of this new logic. And I believe—I am certain, sir, *certain* this logic exists. This morning, when you held my hands, I felt it inside you, communicating itself to me. If we had continued . . ."

"Yes, Miss Truelove?"

"If we had continued," I whispered, "we would have found him."

"Silverton?"

"Yes. He was there. Somewhere inside that connection, somewhere inside that place to which you were propelling me." I drew in a deep breath. Max was looking down now, staring at his hands, which he spread before him, palms upward. "He was there because you sent him there."

"Sent him where?"

"To wherever—*whenever*—you required him. Just as you sent Desma from ancient Naxos to the exact moment you required her to appear in your life, in order to begin the course of events of last winter and spring."

"No." He turned to face me, and his expression was bleak. "I haven't sent her yet."

"But you will. One day. Do you remember what Hunter said in the cave, last March? *It's not what you've done, it's what you will do.*"

He was quiet for some time before replying. "Yes, it's possible."

I rose from my chair and held up the paper. "And what I thought to myself—as I studied this thing, wondering what it was—I realized it might be a clue. A clue you have sent to yourself, so you would know how to act in this moment."

"A clue sent by my future self, you mean."

"Yes! You *see*, don't you? It's all—it's not in a straight line anymore. We have this scientific idea of time, based on our own observation, that it occurs in sequence, from past into present into future, but what I've been thinking—" I set down the paper and rummaged into my notebook. "Here. It's like this. I've been trying to sketch it. It's all laid out, your life, my life, all our lives, all at once, all at the same time. These circles I've drawn. Here is Silverton, at the hotel in Edinburgh, gone in an instant. But he isn't gone. He's *here*." I pointed to another circle. "And he's hidden this paper in this chest, knowing we would find it, knowing we—the two of us, here in Thurso in August of 1906—would recognize that he left it there, because *that* already exists, you see. Your future self exists in this moment, over here, placing pieces on the chessboard, saving Silverton, saving Desma, putting them somewhere else—some*time* else—where they will act as you, sir, as *your future self* knows they will act. How they *must* act, in order for all of these events to occur. For this paper to arrive to us in this chest. For Desma to arrive in Knossos in November of last year, when you happened to be there."

I stopped, breathless. The duke had come to stand by me, to stare without speaking at the strange sketch in my notebook. I couldn't tell if he understood me at all, let alone believed me; I could scarcely understand myself. There were no words in the English language, no words in the great scientific tradition of the past two thousand years to describe what I meant.

"Are you telling me," he said slowly, "that we have no free will at all? This is our fate, laid out in a map, and we cannot escape it?"

"Not exactly. We can choose not to act. But we won't."

"Why not?"

"Because Silverton's life depends on it. Because Desma's life depends on it."

"Ah," he said as if someone had stabbed him.

"Because you love her so well, you will save her life in order that she can live that life with another man. You will do this thing, one day, even though you know the pain it will bring you."

He reached across me and spread his large hand over my circles and arrows and notes, passing each one under his fingertip. "And you," he said, turning to face me. "Do you love my friend Silverton so well as that?"

I looked away. "It's not a question of love. It is simply humanity."

"Humanity." Max settled himself back against the table and crossed his arms. "But what do you propose we do? This future self of mine might be in full control of his powers, but my present self hasn't more than the most rudimentary knowledge of what I'm capable of, and how to control it. We have discussed over and over the circumstances by which I caught Tadeas from the brink of the cliff, but the truth is I don't *know* how it happened. I simply felt this compulsion possess me, when we came to that point on the cliff."

"Then perhaps you must be standing in the right spot."

He frowned. "But I didn't feel this sensation in the morning, when you and I stood here. Nothing overcame me. It was something else. I was thinking about Silverton, and where he had likely gone, and you—"

"I was thinking the same thing. And I could feel—this thought connected us somehow, and we held hands, and that's when I felt the power rising, and so did you. And I could feel him there, somewhere, as if he was beckoning us. Guiding us." Gently I took the duke's hands. "Try it. Try it again."

"No." He pulled his hands away. "Don't you understand? If I'm holding you, touching you, then it's *you* who will be sent to *him*, not the other way around. That's what was happening this morning, Emmeline. That's why I stopped it. You were rushing away from me."

"Was I?"

"Couldn't you feel it?"

"I don't—I can't remember—I saw a room—"

"*This* room, but different. I saw it, too. I saw you hurtling toward it, and I stopped, because I could not—"

"Couldn't what?"

The duke made a sound of frustration and walked past me to the giant, empty fireplace. He laid one elbow on the mantel and ran the other hand through his black hair. He seemed to be staring into the face of the clock resting in the exact center of the chimneypiece, an ormolu affair of gilt cherubs and scrollwork, in which the time itself seemed an afterthought. He said quietly, "I could not—I cannot—bear the thought of causing you any harm, Miss Truelove. I should never forgive myself. You have seen enough peril, because of me."

"The *danger*? The danger is nothing, sir, nothing at all compared to the marvel. My God. To be so close to such a sublime mystery, a miracle, a thing I never imagined possible—"

He pounded his fist on the mantel. "A curse."

"It is not a curse! It's a gift from God. An immense, extraordinary power to do good, such as no man has ever before known."

"That's the curse of it. I wasn't made for this." He turned to me, and his face was bleak and hollow, each thick bone casting a deep shadow upon the skin beneath. "I am a scholar, Emmeline. A plain scholar. I have not an ambition in the world, except to study the past. Now God has seen fit to make me a duke, and at the same time to endow me with an immeasurable power over my fellow creatures that I neither want nor deserve."

My chest seemed to hollow out and fill with pity. I made my way across the floor to where he stood, and so great was the agony in his expression, I lifted my hands and placed the palms along the sides of his face. "He has given you nothing you cannot bear, my dear sir. Nothing you are not good and worthy to do. We have no choice in the burdens that are laid upon us, but we can choose to accept them. To bear them with grace."

The duke closed his eyes and bowed his head. He made no move to touch me, nor did he move away from my touch. For some time we stood there in contemplation, while the clock ticked softly nearby, and the breeze spun from the window. At the tips of my fingers, I felt his pulse, measured and heavy, like the beat of a great drum.

"He has given me something else," the duke said at last, lifting his head a little. "He has given me *you*, Emmeline. Your quick mind and your immense fortitude and your good sense."

"They are all at your service, sir."

He smiled. "Max."

"Max." I slid my hands from his face to take his hands. "I am determined to help you."

"And yet, you need *my* help, don't you? You need me to find our missing marquess for you."

"Only because it is our duty to find him."

"Since I have apparently mislaid the poor fellow." He walked past me, back to the table, and picked up the notebook I had shown him. "And how do you propose we attempt it, hmm? We have this morning inadvertently discovered how this power of mine might be persuaded to send a person to another age, but I hardly summoned Tadeas into ours by my own will. At the time,

I never even imagined I could do such a thing, not in my wildest supposition. I only happened to be at the right place at the right moment—" He checked himself.

"What is it?"

"Of course. My God." He set down the notebook and bounded to the open window, gripping the edge with both hands as he peered northward. "The chest. Magnusson brought the chest here from the castle on Hoy, didn't he?"

"Yes. But why should that matter?"

Max turned from the window, and I can only guess what he saw out there to sea, for his face was now transformed, lit with excitement. "Because Silverton must have been there. According to Magnusson, the chest has lain in that castle since its earliest days. Don't you see? It's a clue. If I did send Silverton back in time, he would have done this deliberately, to give us some sign where to find him. If we go to Hoy, to the castle, where Silverton lived at some point during his adventure, if we map the place thoroughly—"

"You'll find him."

"I *might* find him. If this thing works again, the way it did on Skyros. If I can somehow find the exact place—the moment— find a way to replicate—"

As he spoke, our gazes met, and I noticed that the sun, out of sight to the west, must have emerged once more from behind the clouds, for the space around the window had filled with a molten afternoon light that touched the duke's head with gilt. The sight made me think of Lord Silverton, and for an instant the two men seemed to merge into one, and I could not say which stood before me. I could not say whether his hair was black or gold, whether his eyes were dark or blue, whether he was built like a Thoroughbred or a destrier. I couldn't breathe; I couldn't blink.

Then the light shifted, and Max reassembled before me, plain and solid, his gaze still fixed upon mine.

"A tower of ifs," he said. "*If* I sent Silverton to some ancient age. *If* he left this drawing in a chest in order to communicate with us. *If* the chest really lay in that castle undisturbed, during all those years lying between us. *If* it's possible for me to find him at all."

"It's the smallest chance in the world," I said, "and yet it's not. If the first thing occurred, then the rest follows."

"How do you figure that?"

"Because you knew," I said. "You wouldn't have sent him back if you didn't already know we would save him."

The duke stared at me, incredulous, and walked back to the table in the center of the room. The suit he wore was an old one, fitting comfortably over his broad, thick shoulders, and I stared at the point between the shoulder blades, the ordinary cloth covering an extraordinary mystery. I wondered where it originated, this power of his. Did he generate it inside his own body, or was he merely a convenient channel for a force beyond our human senses?

He reached forward and lifted the notebook. The pages wavered not a millimeter as he held the book open in his hand, frowning at the map I had drawn there.

"Well, then, Miss Truelove," he said, without turning, "it seems you must steel yourself."

"Steel myself?"

Max looked over his shoulder at me, and his face wore a devilish grin.

"We travel to Hoy in the morning. And if I'm not mistaken, the journey requires a spell on the water."

So the Fisherman brought the Lady back to his hovel and allowed her to mourn, and every day he went out in his boat and brought back fish for her to eat and to sell in the market, while the Lady tended the cottage and learned to cook and to mend, to grow vegetables in the garden and to repair the nets and to dive for pearls by the shore, though her heart still ached for the son she had lost. One evening, when the Fisherman returned from his work, the Lady looked up from her mending and saw not his poor clothes nor his rough hands, but his great strength and noble face, and she put down her mending and said to him, 'Fisherman, there is something caught on the hook of my dress, perhaps you can help me to unfasten it . . .'

THE BOOK OF TIME, A. M. HAYWOOD (1921)

Six

Among her many virtues, Lady Annis Sinclair was apparently not subject to seasickness. I took note of this fact as I hung by the rail of the ferry, attempting to hook my gaze on any object other than the tilting horizon, while her ladyship laughed merrily at some quip from her friends near the shelter of the deckhouse.

Once the Duke of Olympia had made known his intention to visit and inspect this fascinating project of young Magnusson's, the entire house party decided it would be a jolly lark to join us. I suppose there was no polite way to dissuade them. Magnusson himself made all the arrangements, from picnic baskets to ferry tickets to transportation to and from the relevant docks, presumably in order to heighten interest in his grand new resort. Now he stood in the center of his party, almost on his tiptoes, holding forth on the laziness of workmen and the healthful benefits of the seaside climate, in reckless disregard of the energetic pitch of the deck beneath his feet.

"Why, I glory in storms!" he said. "I like nothing better than to watch a good blow come across the harbor. The howling winds, the churning surf. Washes away everything old and stale, scrubs the air clean. I find it invigorating!"

His voice carried across the deck; he nearly jumped from his shoes from sheer enthusiasm. My breakfast sloshed helplessly in my belly. I turned and hurried to the larboard stern, out of sight, just in time to pitch my all into the deep.

When I raised my head, a handkerchief hovered respectfully near my hand. "Terrible, isn't it?" said a woman's sympathetic voice. "Would you like to sit down? There's a bench right here."

I was too weak to protest. I took the handkerchief, which smelled of lavender, and allowed the woman's arms to propel me to a seat. The bench was hard and narrow, exactly the kind of implacable furniture one expected to find on a ferry plying the water between the northern shore of Scotland and a weather-beaten island in the Orkneys.

The woman sat down beside me and asked if I was always subject to seasickness.

"I'm afraid so," I replied. "It comes on almost immediately, and I am never fully well, even on a long voyage."

"What an awful shame. Isn't there anything you can take for it?"

There was something in her voice that made me raise my head. She sat about a foot away, a respectful distance, wearing a plain dress of navy blue and a gray woolen cardigan so similar to my own, we might have acquired them together. Her hands, covered by a pair of dark kidskin gloves, lay in a snug knot upon her lap. But it was her face that astonished me. She was exquisite. Her face was a perfect oval; her eyes huge, a lustrous gray-green, fringed by the thickest, longest black lashes I had ever seen. I thought she was perhaps twenty-five or thirty, but an instant later I changed my mind: the size of her eyes and the luminosity of her skin made her seem younger than she really was. There was a look of knowingness about her, a faint network of lines about her eyes and mouth. She was one of those rare women more beautiful at forty than at twenty.

She must have seen my confusion, because she smiled and patted my arm in a way that was almost motherly. "Don't worry, it's only another hour," she said. "Pregnancy's worse, believe me."

A second tremor passed along my nerves. In my bemusement at her unexpected beauty, I had forgotten that uncanny something in her voice that had caught my notice to begin with. It was not her accent precisely. She spoke like a well-bred girl from somewhere in the Home Counties; the unmistakable cloth of an expensive finishing school burnished her vowels and her consonants. But she delivered those words with a certain ease, a casual syntax that I cannot quite describe; she uttered the bald word *pregnancy* without a hint of shame.

"I'm afraid I wouldn't know," I said.

"Well, I've had three children, and I was miserable for weeks with all of them. Except this one." She laid her right hand over her belly, which I now saw was not plump but gravid. "He went easy on me. I suppose it's the least he could do."

Her intimacy amazed me. I have never had much connection with other women; having been raised and educated by an elderly father, having been employed by an elderly duke, I had no opportunity to form the usual female friendships. Such girls as I encountered in my childhood were either the daughters of servants or of aristocrats, and neither were encouraged to play with me. By the time I reached adulthood, I had no notion of what interested other girls, what they discussed, what they dreamt of. All I knew was that I had not marriage in my future, but employment. That alone set me apart. In time, I suppose I developed a kind of aversion to other women, and they of me. We might have been two separate races, eyeing each other suspiciously. I have never been the sort of person to reveal my inner soul to anyone, but if I did, I should open myself to a man: solid, honest, practical, and unsentimental.

But this woman. I wanted to pull away, and yet I found I could not. Her firm hand on my arm held me fast; her frank expression mesmerized me. "I beg your pardon," I said. "Have we met?"

She lowered her face, but her eyes continued to hold mine. "My name is Helen," she said.

"My name is Truelove."

"Yes, I know." She squeezed my arm and rose. "I shall tell the duke to fetch you a cup of water."

"No, don't—" I began, but she was already walking away, around the corner of the deckhouse, and I was so miserable I couldn't find the strength to follow her. I sat on the hard bench and gazed at the shrinking Scottish shore, clutching at something in my hand. When I looked down, I realized it was the lady's handkerchief, smelling of lavender.

An hour later, exact almost to the minute, the ferry began to slow and change course, the engines to thud and grind. I lifted my head from the bench and forced myself to sit up. I had been left mercifully to myself for the remainder of the voyage, and there was nobody nearby, though I could hear a multitude of merry voices from the other side of the deckhouse. Perhaps the woman Helen had failed to find Max in the crowd; perhaps he had been too engaged with the other members of the party. The boat lurched, finding its bearings in the confluence of current and tide at the harbor's mouth. I gripped the edge of the bench, rose unsteadily to my feet, and staggered to the rail. We were coming into Hoy at an angle, and I could see the land to my left: soft, round, grassy hills, ending abruptly in a sheer gray cliff, and a stone village nestled by the shore, in the crook of two green slopes.

"Why, there you are, Miss Truelove," said the duke. "I thought you must be in the deckhouse, in this drizzle."

I looked at my woolen sleeve, on which the dew had laid a thick sheen. The air sang with mist. "It's nothing," I said.

He offered me his arm. "Are you well enough to walk?"

"Of course."

"I have been thinking," he said as we walked around the corner of the deckhouse, toward the buzz of voices, "how we shall effect this investigation of ours, without undue notice."

"As have I," I said. "I can easily plead sickness to avoid the picnic. You shall have to find some other excuse."

"A false telegram, perhaps?"

"Perhaps. I suspect an opportunity will present itself. Did you speak to Helen?"

"Helen? Who the devil's Helen?"

We were now joining the tail of the throng of passengers, waiting to disembark. The duke lowered his voice, and so did I.

"The woman who assisted me, when I was sick. A beautiful woman. She was going to find you." I paused. "I thought you knew each other."

He looked astounded. "Nobody approached me. I don't even know a woman named Helen. Are you quite sure?"

I cast my gaze over the small crowd spread before us, already streaming down the gangplank to the dock. Lady Annis's pale, wide-brimmed hat hovered joyfully near the front, while Magnusson, in his peaked cap of gray tweed, swiveled back and forth somewhere in the middle.

Nowhere did I spy Helen's plain, modest straw hat, rimmed only by a grosgrain ribbon the color of strawberries.

"Quite sure," I whispered.

Nobody doubted me when I staggered down from one of the wagons Magnusson had hired to transport us to the castle and said I should prefer to rest indoors.

"My poor Miss Truelove," said Lady Annis, looking deeply concerned, "I understand you suffer from *le mal de mer*. How dreadful that must be for you."

"It is an inconvenience to me," I said, "but I hope it won't deter you from your picnic."

"Not at all, I assure you. Can I offer you a ham sandwich? A deviled egg, perhaps? I believe Cook packed along her pâté de saumon fumé, such a treat."

The blood drained from my head. "No, thank you," I said, rather more wanly than I intended.

"Dear me. How pale you look. Magnusson!"

Her brother ranged up magically by her side. "Yes, my dear?"

"Miss Truelove looks decidedly pale. She won't be joining us for the picnic, I'm afraid. Have you got a cot of some kind, inside that pile of yours? I'm sure she doesn't require much. Do you, Miss Truelove?"

"Not much at all," I gasped.

We stood in the castle's courtyard, surrounded by stones and dust and pounding workmen. The clouds had parted briefly, and in the glimpse of watery sunshine, the castle looked magnificent despite its spider's web of wooden scaffolding. Like Thurso Castle, it was perched on a cliff by the sea, and as Magnusson took my arm and led me up the steps and into what had once been the keep, I remarked on the similarity between the two buildings.

"Oh, they aren't just similar, Miss Truelove," he said, "they're identical."

"Identical!"

"Almost to the stone, at least in original design. Naturally the lords of Thurso have made alterations to suit the convenience of modern inhabitants, but—oops, watch that chisel—the plan, the footprint, as they say, varies hardly an inch." He spoke loudly, above the clang of tools around us, and while I had not directed much attention to my surroundings during our approach to the castle—my attention being focused rather more inwardly—I now cast about and saw that the room we now crossed contained the same vast dimensions as the great hall of Thurso Castle. There loomed the main staircase, there and there stretched the hallways toward the formal chambers. Though the walls were bare and the space filled with workmen and materials, the proportions aligned exactly with my memory of Thurso.

The sickness fell away, replaced by the buzz of discovery. "How extraordinary!" I exclaimed. "Were they not built centuries apart?"

"It's a bit of a mystery, really. There aren't any records."

"Not at either castle?"

"No. It's as if they both rose up by themselves. As near as we can figure, they were built sometime before Norway relinquished the islands to Scotland. Naturally this one seems older, as it's ruined. But ruins—like people, I suppose—have a way of looking old before their time. Mind the stairs, now."

He kept a firm hold on my elbow as we climbed the massive staircase, which had evidently undergone recent restoration—the stone was sharp-edged, the wood raw and unpolished, the air suffused with the scent of fresh timber. "We had to replace all the banisters, all the steps," Magnusson was saying. "The wood had rotted, of course, and the stone was crumbling. We used the staircase at Thurso as a model. Dashed fine work, don't you think?"

"How fortunate that the two castles are so alike."

"Isn't it, though? Of course, we aren't trying to re-create Thurso—it's meant to be a hotel, not a medieval fortification—but it does add a fine dash of authenticity, don't you think? And then there's all the rubbish that turns up as we go. The dungeons, for example."

"Dungeons!"

"Oh, yes. Fearsome stuff. But so convenient for stashing away unwanted items, so to speak. That's where we discovered our mysterious chest, you know."

"I didn't realize that. What was it doing in the dungeons?"

"God knows. Perhaps it had misbehaved. There's no way of telling when it was put there, of course. Or perhaps it lay in the dungeon all along, who knows? Here we are. My office, such as it is. There's a sofa in the corner that should do very well. I nap in it myself, from time to time." He winked broadly. "Do you need a blanket or some such thing? Water, perhaps?"

I stared around the room, which was large and bare, the walls unfinished, the floor uncovered, containing a desk and chair, a pair of threadbare armchairs, and the sofa in question: a masculine, deep-seated Chesterfield of brown leather, missing a number of its buttons. A pair of casement windows looked toward the sea.

"Nothing at all except privacy, thank you," I said.

⚭

I waited some minutes after he left before I rose from the sofa, which smelled of leather and damp. Though the fickle sun now shone through the window glass, the room was chilly and suffered from a draught—from what source, I couldn't tell. The windows were shut tight.

According to our plans, the duke would find his excuse to leave the picnic in about an hour. I knew I ought to rest, but I was seized by restlessness, by a compulsion to discover something. Around me, the castle seemed to be lying in wait for me, seemed to beckon, desiring to be explored. I tightened the belt of my cardigan and slipped through the doorway into the hall.

Though the building crawled with workmen, this particular corridor was empty and silent, nothing but bare stone walls and bare stone floors and thick wooden doors at irregular intervals. I tried to remember the hallway to which it corresponded at Thurso and could not—the morning room and sitting room? the state bedrooms?—and yet I had the strangest sensation that I knew my surroundings. I set off down the narrow space, away from the main staircase, and I thought I had walked here many times. The height of the ceiling above me, the exact width, the shadows; the rectangular shapes of the doorways, rounded slightly at the tops—all of it, all of it settled familiarly on my eyes. Not just my eyes. Something inside me, in the region of memory. My steps quickened. I turned right at the end of the hall, then left, stretching out my fingers to pass across the smooth, dark stone as I went, until they encountered a small door cut into the wall. I opened it. Up wound a narrow staircase, following the curve of a turret.

For a moment, I leaned against the doorframe, gathering my breath. The perfect arc of the stairs mesmerized me. Like the rest of the castle, it was empty and unadorned, and the steps were worn in their centers, as if Magnusson's program of refurbishment had not encompassed this column of the castle. I thought, *I ought to be exploring the dungeon, where the chest was found,* but instead I found myself yearning upward. I placed my right foot into the soft groove of the first one. Through the walls came the sound of hammering, of hard male voices, of the clatter and clang of tools. A faint whistling floated somewhere above me. I felt like a thief as I climbed upward, floor by floor, until I reached the top and looked briefly through the small, arched window. It was speckled with mist, affording a blurry view of the harbor.

I turned away, opened the door to the hallway, and gasped.

Not only had Magnusson's workmen failed to set about returning this portion of the castle to its former glory, they seemed not to have visited it at all. The space was a ruin, open and without partition, the stone crumbling. The wind sang through the gaps in the outer walls—a noise I recognized as the whistling I had heard on the stairs. A roof existed above me, at least, held in place by thick, sturdy beams, or else I might as well have been outdoors in a loggia.

"Miss Truelove?"

I spun around. The duke filled the doorway from the staircase, one hand on the frame and the other at his side. His head bent slightly under the lintel. I put my hand on my heart. "I wasn't expecting you yet."

He stepped forward into the room. "I claimed indigestion."

"It's too convenient. They'll suspect us."

"I don't particularly give a damn what anybody *suspects*, Miss Truelove. You looked genuinely ill outside. Are you certain you're recovered?"

I turned away to survey the attic before me. "I should not have climbed those stairs if I weren't. How did you find me?"

"A lucky guess, I suppose. One of the workmen directed me to Magnusson's office, and when I saw you weren't there, I wandered along until I spotted that open door to the staircase. Have you discovered anything?"

"No. Mr. Magnusson informed me that the chest had been found in the dungeons, but he allowed that it might have been moved there at a later date."

"The dungeons!"

"They seem to have incarcerated more merchandise than criminals there."

"Ah. Have you gone down there yet?"

"No." I paused to kneel beside a pile of cut stones. "The stairs only went up, and besides . . ."

He put down a knee next to me. "Besides what?"

"I wanted to go up. How long have these stones been here, do you think? There isn't any dust on them."

He picked one up with his gloved hand and turned it about. "A great many years ago. Look at the marks."

I looked, but my eye was not as expert as his. "How many years?"

"Over a century. Why did you want to go up?"

"I don't know. I was curious."

"Because I felt the same curiosity," he said softly. "A sort of compulsion."

I turned to face him. He wore his usual implacable expression, shadowed by the brim of his tweed cap. The weather had brought out a flush of red along the broad blades of his cheeks. He stared down at me, and though his eyes revealed no more opinion than usual, I had the idea that he was troubled, and that he looked to me for relief.

I dropped my gaze to his hands, encased in black leather, still holding the ancient stone, and then back to his face.

"A compulsion," I repeated. "The same kind of compulsion as on the cliffs of Skyros?"

"Yes. No. I'm not quite sure. Not as powerful, I think. Here I am, after all, talking sensibly to you, instead of being out of my mind." He looked at the stone again. "But there's *some*thing here. Like a field of energy."

"Describe it."

"My methodical Miss Truelove. Very well. If I must describe

it, I suppose the sensation originates somewhere in the stem of my brain."

"The seat of instinct!"

"I believe so. It seems to guide my actions, in place of conscious resolve. At this point, however, I can resist it. If I had wanted to, I could have remained at the bottom of those stairs, just now. On Skyros, I could no more have remained where I stood than I could have commanded my heart to stop beating."

I took the stone from his hand and laid it back on the pile. "Shall we walk about the room? See if the feeling grows stronger in any particular place?"

"You might," said a voice from the stairway, "but I'm afraid it won't do any good."

⤲

Even before I turned, I knew who stood there. She smiled and advanced toward us, and in the diminished natural light of indoors, she looked even more beautiful than she had upon the deck of the steamship. I thought there was something familiar about the shape of her eyes, about the angle of her jaw, but I could not quite understand how. As she walked, she turned her gaze to the duke and said, "Max, it's good to see you."

He started. "I beg your pardon."

"Don't you know me? It's Helen." She came to a stop before us and removed her hat. Her hair was blond and thick, parted neatly down the middle and wound in a simple Psyche knot at her nape.

"I—I am at a loss," he said. "Have we met?"

"I guess not. Well, then. How to begin." She spoke in that same accent as before, distinctly English and yet impossible to pin down. "I do have instructions, but they're not—"

"But who *are* you?" I interrupted. "Helen whom?"

"It doesn't matter. I can't tell you, anyway, not in any way you'd understand. I don't really understand it myself. I wouldn't believe it, if I weren't standing here. If I hadn't spent the last seven years somewhere else, and before that—well." She replaced her hat snugly. "I know what you're trying to do, anyway. You're trying to bring somebody through, aren't you?"

"Through what?" the duke asked warily.

"Through time. But it won't work, not like that. You have to be standing in the right place, and you have to be carrying something."

Max and I turned toward each other, eyes wide, and then back to Helen.

"Carrying what?" he asked.

"Something. It doesn't matter what, apparently, so long as it's something that belongs to the person you're trying to summon. Some physical artifact that connects a person in one time to a person in another." She shrugged. "So I'm told, anyway."

The duke and I stood there silently, shocked, teeming with questions, afraid to ask them. I wanted to take him aside and confer, but this was not a court of law. This was the attic of a half-ruined Scottish castle, and we had to decide, right now, separately and simultaneously, whether this woman might be trusted. Who she was. How she had come here, and how she knew all this.

And why.

Max spoke first. "Told by whom?"

"By you, of course. You told me."

Max swore so softly, I almost didn't hear him. I felt the change in him, however. There was a winding of tension, a sense of electricity so strong, I thought I heard it crackling. I wanted to lay my hand on his arm, on his shoulder, to offer him some kind of comfort, but of course that was impossible, too.

Helen continued, watching Max's face as she spoke. "You said you would know what I meant by that."

"Yes, I believe I understand," he said. "What else did I tell you?"

"Just that, really. There wasn't much time."

She shifted her gaze to me as she said this, and I knew she was lying.

"Tell me," I said, speaking with as much authority as I could muster, "are we to understand that the duke has met you in another time? That you have traveled here from some other age?"

"Yes."

"When? Where?"

A small hesitation. "I can't say."

"Why not?"

"I shouldn't even have come to you, except that I need—" She looked again at the duke, and again I experienced that jar of familiarity, that sense of having seen this movement before.

"You need my help," he said.

Helen drew in a deep breath, and as she did so, she placed her hand on the stout rise of her belly. I saw that her skin was so pale, it matched almost exactly—in color, if not in texture—the creamy wool of her cardigan.

"I need you to send me back," she said.

⌁

"She might be lying," I said. "She might be trying to trick you."

The duke spoke solemnly from the window. "That may be true, of course, but not wholly so. How else would she know as much as she did? Why, she knows more than we do."

"So did Hunter."

I sat rigid upon the sofa in Magnusson's office; Max stood, as

I said, by the window nearest me. In order to obtain this privacy for us, I had claimed a sudden return of illness, and Max played his part as if born to intrigue: solicitous, insisting upon my immediate removal to a place of resting, brushing off Helen's offers of assistance. Miss Truelove needs utmost quiet, he had told her imperiously. He would rejoin her upstairs when he was satisfied with Miss Truelove's health and comfort.

At this moment, my health and comfort seemed the furthest objects from his mind. He stood with one hand braced on his hip, the other on the window ledge, motionless. His brow was keen. The light through the glass was strangely white, turning his skin pale. I wondered what he was staring at. What he was thinking.

"Yes," he said absently. "Poor Hunter."

"*Poor* Hunter?"

"After all, he's dead. What do you think of this proposition of hers? Of Helen's, I mean. This idea that I must possess some sort of object upon my person, some link to the person I'm trying to summon."

"I suppose there's a certain logic. If an object existed in a previous time, does it not then contain some link to that moment?"

"But when we were on Skyros, I had no object upon me that belonged to Tadeas."

"Yes, you did. The medallion. The one I found in Desma's bedroom at Knossos. Didn't it once belong to him?"

He started. "By God."

In some corner of the castle, not far away, a workman began to hammer in slow, steady strokes, like the beat of a drum. I thought it sounded like chiseling, like the battering of metal upon stone. The smell of sawdust seemed to hang in the air, and beneath it something more foul, like manure. Above it, another smell entirely, one I knew intimately but could not name. I opened my mouth to ask Max whether he smelled it, too, whether he recognized the particular scent, but he spoke first.

"You would think—wouldn't you, Miss Truelove?—that with all this power of mine, this apparent ability and even *inclination* to move events like the gods on Olympus, I might have troubled to send myself some damned *CLUE*"—he brought his fist down on the stone, suddenly and mightily—"how to proceed."

"But you did not," I said. "You did not plant some clue. Which means that whatever it is you decide, whatever it is you do, it will be right."

He turned to me with deliberate slowness. His eyes were bright and incredulous. At first, I thought he had seen something out the window, some extraordinary object, but then I realized this extraordinary object was me. That I was the source of his amazement.

"Why, you're right," he said. "I must act, that's all."

I rose from the sofa. "Yes. Simply act. Do something."

"Act *what*? Do *what*?"

He spoke intently, one hand still gripping the edge of the window, and as I stared at him, helpless, the strange illusion came upon me again: the duke, before an identical window, blurring and transforming into Silverton. The sunlight in his hair became the gold of Silverton's crown. I shut my eyes and opened them again, but the illusion remained, the blurring, and within me grew an unstoppable urgency, a craving that seemed to travel within the channels of my blood.

"We are in the library!" I gasped.

"What's that?"

"The library! This room—Magnusson's office—it's the library! The Oriental library."

I could not see the duke's face—it merged into that of Silverton, so that the expression hid itself from me—but the head moved, allowing the gaze to travel around the room.

"By God," he said, in Silverton's voice, "you're right."

Now the craving strengthened, electrifying my nerves. I stepped forward, and as I did, I recognized the faint scent, carrying above the almost barnyard odor that had filled the room.

The smell belonged to Silverton. His soap, or his skin, or whatever its source. I had smelled it last in the hotel room in Edinburgh, as he bent over my body in the bed.

I staggered forward and seized the duke's hands, driven by a compulsion I could not name. "Send me back!" I gasped.

"Send you back?"

"Yes. Now. That's what you must do. That's how you must act. Send me back to him."

"To Silverton? Here? Now?"

"Yes! That's the easiest way, don't you see? We might spend weeks combing this place, and never find the right spot. Send me back, and I'll bring him there."

"Where?"

"Anywhere! Here. Right here. In this room."

"What if it's not built yet?"

I turned to the window. The hammering was growing louder. We were speaking in short, quick sentences, as if time were of the essence, as if some devil stung our heels. My heart was hammering, too, so hard and so fast I felt dizzy. "What were you looking at, out there?"

"Nothing. That point, I suppose. That crest of rock."

"There, then. I'll take him there."

"You can't. Miss Truelove, you can't. It's far too dangerous."

"Don't say that."

"My God, anything might happen! I don't know what the devil I'm doing! You must consider—you might be lost to me forever—"

I shut my eyes and gripped his hands with all my strength, while my pulse shattered my ears and my brain turned to flame. "Don't say that. Don't make me consider. Just do it. Send me. You must. Right now. This is what you must do."

"How do you know that?"

"I can't explain—"

"Miss Truelove—"

The smell of sawdust and manure and Silverton grew inside my nose and occupied my head. I thought I heard voices, footsteps.

"Someone's coming," I said. "Quick."

"Nobody's coming."

"Please!"

He hauled me down on the sofa, and the first sparks tantalized the nerves of my palms.

"Keep going!" I gasped.

Something sang in my ears. My palms turned hotter, began to burn. The rush of separation began, of otherworldliness, of hurtling toward some distant destination, surrounded by electricity.

"Wait!" cried the duke. "Wait! The object! I need an object, something of yours."

I opened my eyes. Away from the window, away from the sunlight, he had regained his own face, Max's face, and he was gazing upon me like a man in torment. His black hair seemed to have gained twice its volume, as if a force had taken hold of each strand. So red was the skin of his cheeks and his nose, it might have been burnt with a hot iron. I thought, *I have nothing, nothing except my clothing.*

But that was not quite true.

You must understand how desperate I was. You must understand the compulsion I felt, the extraordinary necessity, as if I were galloping to catch a train that, if it left the station without me, would surely crash and be destroyed.

Without thought, without the slightest sense of regret or loss, I untied the belt of my cardigan and found the chain of my father's plain silver pocket watch, pinned to the pocket of my skirt.

I unpinned the watch and thrust it into Max's hand.

"Here," I said. "If that can't summon me back to you, then I am forever lost."

"It won't work," he said. "It can't work."

"Try. Try!"

He took my hands again, and the force of contact struck me like an engine. In the space of an instant, I was hurtling backward, or forward, or upward, propelled toward some magnetic pole. I heard a voice calling my name from the end of a long tunnel: a voice that began in Max's dark baritone, and ended in something else.

The Fisherman did as the Lady asked and unhooked her dress, and he said to her, 'Lady, if you do not mean to lie with me, you must tell me this instant, for the sight of your beauty is too much to bear.' And the Lady replied, 'Then my beauty is yours, as poor as it is, for by your dear love you have purchased mine, and yours it shall remain unto eternity.' So the Fisherman took her to bed and loved her mightily, and in the morning they went to the village and were married, and the Fisherman and the Lady gave thanks to God for their happiness.

But that night, while the Lady lay asleep in the deep thrall of nuptial pleasure, the Fisherman stole from their couch and hid her strange suit in the false bottom of an old chest, for he took no chance that his bride should disappear back into the sea that had brought her to him . . .

THE BOOK OF TIME, A. M. HAYWOOD (1921)

Seven

I smelled the smoke first. Though I couldn't realize it then, a long time would pass before the scent of a peat fire did not constitute some part of my awareness.

I cannot say whether I was conscious yet. My head was heavy and dark, and I could not move my limbs. I remember thinking I was dreaming, that I was caught in some dream from which I could not wake, and that my surroundings, my person, my own name were a mystery. I realized I was cold, but that even the relief of shivering was beyond my power.

I stirred slightly, trying to lift my head, but some warm, constraining force held me in place. In the instant before I slipped back into the void, I understood that this force was an animate one: the arms of a human being.

And I heard a voice, hushing me gently. Telling me to rest a while longer.

$\mathcal{\infty}$

The next time I woke, the break was sharp. I jolted upward, and now the unknown human arms released me. Though I was still weak, I could turn—indeed, you could not have stopped me from turning—and saw a bearded face before me.

Its lips moved. "Feeling better?"

I kissed him. That was our first kiss: an act of reflex. Because he was Silverton, who never refused a kiss in his life, he embraced me back. I wish I could recall how it felt, how long it lasted, whether our lips parted, how he tasted, but the memory is too confused. I only remember how glad I was, how relieved, though I could not quite determine *why* I should be so glad and so relieved. And the scratch of his beard on my skin, that is indelible. I can feel it still.

At length our mouths parted, and he set me against his chest. I believe he was laughing, or at least chuckling. My head moved in rhythm, and the vibration filled me. "Don't try to move anymore, my dear," he said, and his voice sounded different somehow, not in timbre but in accent. "You're quite safe, at least for now."

"Safe?" I whispered.

"In my little hut. Nobody bothers me here."

I had so many questions, but no strength or wit or sense to put them into thoughts. Only the single word: "Where?"

"*Where?* Oh, my darling girl," he said, laughing again, though it was not a joyful laugh. "I'm afraid that's the wrong question."

$\mathcal{\infty}$

I suppose it was several hours later before we talked again. He left me to heat some broth in the iron pot on the hearth, and as I lay back upon the pallet and watched him, I realized I was covered by several lengths of fur. The room was not large, perhaps twelve feet by twelve, containing only a pair of chairs and a small table, a large chest, the primitive fireplace, the pallet on which I lay. A rough, earthen substance formed the walls around us. On the wall to my right, a window seemed to have been cut, but it was covered by a cloth of some kind.

What lay beyond, I was terrified to discover.

My little hut, he had said. He crouched before me now, his tall frame cramped by the small room, his limbs even leaner than before. Instead of his usual impeccable suit, he wore a tunic of homespun wool, belted in leather, and dark hose of the kind an actor might wear, and I thought, for the first time, shivering not with cold but with fear—

My God, my God. What have we wrought?

Silverton seemed not to notice my awakening. When he returned, he bore the broth in a cup made of pewter, and he spooned it to my lips himself, as if I were an infant. He was not without reason. I had no more strength than an infant, and I continued to shiver, despite the fur. He remained patient and told me the coldness would ease soon. That was why he had kept me close, these past hours, piled with fur, the peat fire blazing extravagantly, though it was August.

"Still August?" I said, rather hoarsely. "Then how have you grown such a beard?"

"What do you mean?"

"It's only been a few days since—since—since I saw you last."

He set the spoon in the cup and stared at me. "Truelove. My dear, dear Truelove. I've been wandering these blasted lands for three years now. Are you not aware?"

"Three years!" I started a little, and realized, as I did so, that I wore only my chemise beneath the fur. Neither dress nor stays nor petticoats belonged to me. I hardly cared, however. My attention was fixed on the face before me, its lower half covered by stiff golden whiskers, a shade or two darker than the hair on his head, which was quite long and bound in a queue at the back of his neck. The truth of his words now stunned me.

"Yes," he said, more gently. He set down the cup on the stone floor beside him. "Are you saying you've passed only a few days, in that time?"

I nodded.

"Well, I'm dashed. I suppose I must look a beast to you." He ran a hand through his hair, loosening it, and then smoothed his beard. "By God, it's good to speak English, however. You're confused, of course."

"Oh, how can you be so cheerful?" I said, and burst into tears.

For a moment, he only stared at me in astonishment. Well he might. I have never been the sort of woman to weep; I have learned, over the course of a life spent chiefly in the company of men, that tears must be kept strictly on the inside. I don't know what broke me then. The idea, perhaps, that Silverton had lived three long years alone in this place, while I had lived only three days. In my state of physical and mental enervation, I couldn't bear it.

At length he conquered his amazement and reached for me. I sobbed against his homespun shoulder and found that while the odor of his expensive soap had disappeared, the familiar scent of his skin had not. Silverton. His voice came like a miracle into my ears.

"Because I'm used to it, my dear. That's how I can be cheerful. And I'm so damned glad to see you again, I might sing." His hand stroked my hair. "I never imagined I should have this chance again."

"No faith at all?"

"Faith? Faith in what? Luck? Though I suppose my luck is

your misfortune. How the devil did it happen to you? I still can't quite work out how I ended up in this mess. One moment I was chasing a villain into the street, and the next—hmm. Something to do with Max, of course, the damned beast. Perhaps you can enlighten me?"

We had never touched so intimately—I in such shocking undress, he clothed scarcely more decently—and yet I felt no embarrassment. No constraint, no sense of doing wrong. The strict code in which I had been bred seemed to have lifted from my shoulders and flown away. I lifted my head and met his soft, curious gaze, and I told him the truth.

"I came back to find you, of course. I made Max do it. It seems he has the power, you see, not just to summon but to send, almost at will."

"I see."

"At first, we tried to bring you back, but we couldn't find where, or how. So there was no other way. I had him send me to find you."

The room was quiet. Through a crack in the curtain covering the window, I perceived that it was daylight, but what hour? Morning or afternoon or evening, I couldn't say. With my eyes, I traced the fine new lines etched upon Silverton's face, the expression of grim wonderment. His lips were cracked and full, his beard glinting faintly in the glow from the hearth.

"My dear, brave Truelove," he said. "As game as they come. And now we're both in the soup."

I seized his sleeve. "No, we're not. How can you possibly think me so heedless? We made a plan, the duke and I—"

A series of loud, rapid thumps shook the wood of the door. Silverton swore.

"Who is it?" I exclaimed, in a whisper.

He sighed and detached himself from me. "It's your welcome

committee, of course. I'm afraid I was expecting this. Tuck yourself back under those blankets, my dear, and attempt to look as if you're sleeping off a night of carnal debauchment."

"*What?*"

Silverton kissed my forehead and rose to his feet, and so small were the hut's dimensions that his dear, golden head bent at the neck, in order to avoid brushing the ceiling. He said, with a note of apology, "I'm afraid I told them you were my concubine."

❦

I obeyed him instantly, at least in the first directive. Whether I actually contrived to look like a prostitute—that tip of my head showing from the edge of the furs, that is—I know not, for I kept my eyes shut tight, and the voices I heard, masculine and rough, almost guttural, spoke no language I recognized.

Silverton answered them in the same tongue, however, and at one point the sound of laughter drifted from the doorway. My cheeks turned hot, chasing away the last of the chill.

Then footsteps, heavy ones, and a sharp word from Silverton.

I lay perfectly still. I believe the side of my face showed above the covering, but that was all. A rank smell found my nostrils, and a wave of disgust and terror passed through my belly. How close was he? I couldn't tell. I didn't dare open my eyes. Silverton was saying something, and somebody answered him, and there was another round of male laughter, of the kind I recognized from my own age. Certain things were eternal, it seemed. I began to perspire, in my cocoon of animal hides, and just as I thought I couldn't bear the tension, the loathing, for another instant, something took hold of the furs and yanked them away from my body.

I gasped and sat up, and Silverton let out the kind of roar I had never before heard from his throat. Before I could even comprehend the appearance of the man who stood next to the pallet—closer, far closer than I had imagined—Silverton was between us. I snatched up the furs. From the doorway, men laughed. Silverton had whipped out a blade of some kind, a knife or a dagger, and held it now against the other man's throat. I saw black hose and thick leather gaiters and a tunic much like Silverton's, and also a sword, raised slightly, which I now realized was the object that had pulled back my covering. The metal glinted in the light from the open door. I remember thinking how battered it looked, how scarred. Silverton was speaking, or rather he snarled words I could not understand. From the doorway, the other men roared happily.

Then a curious silence fell upon the small, smoky room. The two men stood a few feet away from me, Silverton and the intruder, poised against each other. From my perspective on the pallet, I could see nothing of their expressions, but I knew better than to intercede, or even to move. Or perhaps I was too stunned to do either. Some strange, primitive drama was unfolding before me, some ritual. Silverton's back moved as he breathed, and I found myself counting the long, slow beats of his respiration. The fresh air moved inside the hut, summer-mild, laced with the familiar scent of the sea. The sword moved slightly; Silverton hissed some quick word, and the other man drew back, laughing. Silverton laughed, too, but I knew him too well. I knew he didn't mean it.

All at once, the tension dissolved. The man tucked his sword into his belt, and as he moved to the door, I caught a glimpse of his face, his dark beard and his pale face, and the scar that creased the skin above his left eyebrow. I remember thinking it was not a face you could easily forget.

∽

When the door closed at last, I rose to my feet.

"Have you any clothes for me?" I asked.

He faced away from me, one hand still braced against the door, his head bent as if in prayer. "Not as such," he replied, rather dryly.

"I suppose I might borrow one of your tunics, then."

"Why?"

"I must—there are certain—I require a moment of privacy."

Silverton straightened and turned. His face began to crinkle. The laughter built slowly, as that of a man not quite sane, and proceeded into helpless whoops. "Oh, Truelove," he said, wiping his eyes. "My dear Truelove. You are so damned—so damned— my God. You're just the same. Perfectly, beautifully unchanged, the truest Truelove there ever was. God forever bless you."

"Sir—"

"Sir." He sagged back against the door. "A band of ruffians turns up at your door. The breadth of a mere hair stands between you and a most brutal rape. And you—"

"Rape!"

"Yes, Truelove. Did you not divine their purpose?"

I shook my head. My throat had closed in shock, making words impossible.

"Dear chaps. They'd decided I'd had time enough with you, you see. Fair's fair. They wanted their turns."

He said it lightly, but his face was grim and exhausted. I thought, for some reason, of our earlier kiss, and how heartfelt it was, and how curiously innocent. How tenderly our lips had moved each other. How I had then rested myself against his chest and thought myself safe, as safe as I had ever felt in my life.

I made myself speak. "What did you tell them?"

"That you were mine."

I must have frowned, because he pushed himself away from the door and said, "I realize that sort of thing goes against your noble principles, of course, but I felt I had no other choice. Possession is the creed here. Possession, enforced by strength."

"I see."

"No. I don't believe you do. You are to go nowhere without me, is that clear? Not one step outside this hut."

"This is nonsense."

"I'm afraid not. It's deadly serious. You've got no idea—" He shook his head and moved to pick up the cup and the spoon that sat next to the pallet. "It's damned lucky I came upon you first. I don't know what sort of all-powerful Providence was keeping watch over you, Truelove, but you should offer up your orisons forthwith. Still hungry?"

I shook my head.

He set the utensils on the table and went to the wooden chest under the window. "In the meantime, if you'll be so good as to pop this tunic over your fair form and follow me, we shall proceed to the privy."

"*We?*"

"You still stand, I presume, in need of relief?"

"Yes, but—"

"Come along, then." He handed me the tunic and winked. "I won't watch, I promise."

⁓

Outside, it was drizzling, and my need was urgent. I wasted little time inspecting my surroundings, which were gray and shrouded, but hurried the few yards to the tiny shed that served us, while Silverton's hand gripped mine. He stood outside, stalwart, until I emerged, and invited me to rinse my hands afterward in the bucket beneath the eaves, which caught the rain from a wooden spout. Some small distance away, I heard the soft crash of the sea against the rocks, but I could see nothing through the mist.

The expedition exhausted me. Inside, I sank back on the pallet while Silverton heated more broth. All this we did in silence, and when we had both drunk our fill, he sat comfortably next to me on the pallet, a few inches away, as if we were housemates of long standing. I had neither strength nor will to banish him. I asked him what time it was.

"Time?" he said. "No such thing, my dear. Not of the clock, in any case."

"Is it morning or evening, then?"

"Coming on to evening. I'll cut a bit of bread and cheese for supper. Ale to wash it down. Humble rations, I'm afraid. Nothing like the champagne and whatnot we enjoyed during our last evening together. I hope it agrees with you. If not, I suppose I can—"

He was nervous. I inched closer and laid my head on his shoulder. "Don't trouble yourself. I'm not hungry."

"You'll need your strength, believe me. You won't feel properly yourself for a week at least, and even then . . ." The sentence faded ominously.

"It doesn't matter. We're going home tomorrow."

"Home?"

"Yes, home. Max is waiting for us, he's ready. I'll show you where." I yawned. "It's all arranged."

"Ah. Of course it's all arranged. Each detail absolutely failproof. I would expect no less of you."

His arm was around my shoulders. We leaned back against the wall and stared at the dull orange glow of the fire. Silverton had removed his leather shoes, but his stockings remained, loose and woolen, bound by leather gaiters. I found myself wondering what his feet looked like.

"And here I am, before the fire, Emmeline Truelove tucked under my arm," he said softly. "Who would have thought it possible? By God, I would have traded my soul for this, two days ago."

"I imagine any woman would have sufficed."

"Perhaps for the purpose of an evening's cuddle," he said, "but I shouldn't trade my soul for her. Tattered and unworthy an object though it is."

"Well, here I am, and your soul remains your own. No cost to you whatsoever."

"Except three years of my life, of course, but that hardly signifies."

"Three years. Have you really been here three years?"

"It passes belief, doesn't it? There are times I felt as if I'd lived here forever. As if I'd been born again into a new world. Three years." He shook his head. "Three lifetimes. You can't imagine."

"Tell me. Tell me everything you've done."

He laughed. "I'd be rattling on for weeks if I did."

"Tell me something, then. What happened when you first arrived?"

"Well, I woke up much as you did, inside the hut of some kindly bystander, except—I imagine—a great deal more confused. For some time, I thought I had died altogether, and this was purgatory. Eventually I pieced together what had happened. The essentials, I mean. That I had passed through some portal of time in the manner of our good friend Tadeas on Skyros, and that Max must somehow be behind it all. The *why* of it remains a mystery, however. Perhaps you can enlighten me, when you're up to it."

"Not now." I yawned. "When we're home again. With Max. We'll talk about it then."

"Oh, I shall demand a proper reckoning from Max, I assure you."

I wanted to say more, to tell him that Max had little more notion than I did how all this had come to pass, but fatigue made my tongue and my wits too slow. Instead, I asked him how he had survived.

"Training, I suppose," he said simply. "You'll recall I've spent the last decade of my life dropping into various corners of the globe, living by my wits and my good right arm. And I have a certain aptitude for language, God knows how. Once I picked up the lingua franca, I began to get along well enough."

"Thank God for that."

"Mind you, it was a lonely existence. Not a friend, not a soul to whom I could unburden myself. The odd moment of black despair."

He spoke in perfect tranquility. I slid my hand beneath the blankets and laid it upon his chest.

"But surely you must have met somebody sympathetic. Some friend you might trust."

"The first rule of survival, Truelove, is that you trust nobody. I haven't sat like this with another human being since—well, since our last dinner in Edinburgh. And I would have bartered anything for a kiss such as the one you gave me this morning."

So great was my surprise, I found the strength to lift my head. "Are you telling me—why, you cannot have been chaste all this time."

"I have."

"But you—you're Silverton! And there are women—there must be women—"

"Of course there are *women*, Truelove. But I am not the same man. I hardly even remember him. Life, you see, has shrunk to its essentials. During the day, I occupy myself with remaining in one piece. During the night, I sleep. When I long for a woman, when I long for a companion of an evening, when I long for anything at all, Truelove . . ."

His gaze was steady, looking not at me but at the fire. So blue were his eyes, I could still discern their color, even in this faded light, although the fire turned the shade closer to green. I lifted my hand and touched his beard, and I remembered how he used to shave twice a day, and that his cheeks were once smooth and bare. The arm, the shoulder that supported me, was hard with muscle and bone. There was not a spare ounce to him, not a breath of softness. And he was Silverton. The same man I had known a moment ago, except he had changed form, changed voice, changed dress, changed everything.

I waited for him to finish his sentence, but he did not.

"There was a more practical reason, too," he said. "Because there were times when I had no hope, I'll admit. No hope of you or anything else, these past three years. But in these unenlightened times, I had no means of preventing the consequences of union."

"Has it ever stopped you before?"

"Why, Truelove. What an awful beast you think me. Of course it has. I don't get women with child, my dear. My father laid down a thunderous lecture on the matter when I came of age, and I never forgot it."

"I am—I am astonished," I whispered.

"You wound me. Well, there it is." He paused. "A good man, my father. A good man, a faithful husband. I always hoped . . ."

"Hoped what?"

"Nothing." He kissed the top of my head. "Go back to sleep. In the morning, God willing, we shall see what fate has planned for us."

⌘

In the middle of the night, I woke suddenly, as if someone had prodded me. Except for the remains of the fire in the hearth, glowing like a soft beacon on the opposite wall, the room was utterly dark, and for an instant I lay in terror, thinking myself alone in a void.

A noise came to me, the rush of a man's heavy breath, not far away.

Silverton, I thought, and I remembered the thought that had woken me. The question I had not asked, and the answer he had not offered.

My earlier mood of drowsy languor was gone, replaced by a fine-tuned alertness. I listened to my companion for a minute or two, the steady sounds of his slumber, until I could just pick out his shape on the floor nearby, wrapped in a blanket like some sort of long, gold-tipped sausage. A strangely virtuous sausage. I remembered the gentle way he had removed me from his embrace, just as my eyes began to close, and how he had murmured something to me as he tucked the blankets around me, though I could not recall the words. In my unguarded mood, I had wanted him to stay, and I think I may have told him so.

Evidently he had found the strength to resist me.

Outside my little cocoon, the air was not cold, only close and damp. The air smelled of old, stale smoke and human flesh. My mind teemed. I thought about the territory outside these walls, hidden by mist; the same island I had left a day ago, the same rocks and earth and water, and yet belonging to a different people, a foreign world. The enormity was beyond my comprehension. And yet Silverton slept nearby. He was proof. He was indisputable. I could not be dreaming him; his shoulder had been too firm, his words too clear. And now, his sleeping form, too solid.

I lifted the furs slowly from my body. I still wore Silverton's borrowed tunic, covering my chemise and my skin, though it reached only just past my knees, like a child's nightshirt. I slid from the pallet without a sound, not the slightest rustle of linen and straw, and for a moment I crouched there in the darkness, trying to detect any change in the rhythm of Silverton's breath, trying to orient myself to the room around me. The dim orange glow of the fire's end, straight ahead. The window, then, lay to my right.

Below the window, Silverton's wooden chest.

The floor was made of stone and beaten earth, covered by rushes. With each step, they made a slight noise, like a whisper. I kept my gaze on the fire, because that was the only thing I could see in this thick, wild darkness; my right hand I stretched out in front of me, searching for the wall and the window.

As I said, the hut was not large. Three, four, five steps—five soft whispers of my feet on the rush-covered floor—and my fingertips brushed the rough surface of the wall. I felt along until I discovered the corner of the window, and then I bent to place my palms on the lid of the chest below.

How smooth it was, almost slippery. In the absence of light, I couldn't tell whether this was the same chest that had made its way to our modern age, only that they were about the same size, and also the same simple shape, rectangular, unadorned. The lid curved slightly, like the side of a barrel. I slid my hands down the sides to the corners and lifted it open.

Last spring, when Silverton and I embarked suddenly together on a voyage to the Mediterranean Sea—upon a vessel no less august than the Duke of Olympia's private yacht—he had traveled with no fewer than a dozen handsome steamer trunks, the exquisite, well-tailored contents of which were tended by an exacting—if rather fearsome—valet. Now, it seemed, his entire wardrobe existed within this small wooden box. My searching hands found a few layers of rough wool, folded neatly, and a coil of leather. More folded wool, narrower and thinner in texture, which I imagined must be hose. A large, shapeless garment, possibly a cloak. Something else made of leather. Underneath these few items of clothing, I found the bottom of the chest, and I was just trying to judge whether its location hinted at a cavity hidden underneath when a hand came to rest on my shoulder.

"Just what the devil do you think you're doing?" asked his lordship.

✎

My father and I hardly ever spoke of my mother, who died when I was not yet six, but I know she was given to deceit. Once, I asked her about my real father, the man who sired me, and she told me he was a great prince, handsome and rich and charming; she used to spin other tales when she settled me in bed at night. I don't remember them all, but I can still hear the persuasive lilt of her voice as she built me castles, stone by stone, and whispered promises she had no means of keeping.

All mothers say these things, I am told, and I suppose she meant to comfort me. But as time went on, and I learned the truth of her past, of my own conception, I resented her falsehoods bitterly. Better to tell me the truth, that I was begotten of a brief, lustful encounter with some carnal-minded gentleman; a transaction, no more, a commercial exchange. I sometimes wondered how much he had paid for the privilege of starting me in her womb, and whether he ever knew the result of his few minutes' recreation.

A short time before she died, when her belly was just beginning to round out with a true, honest babe, conceived in matrimony with Mr. Truelove, she told me the greatest lie of all. She took my small, frightened hand and told me that she would be well again soon, should shortly rise from her sickbed and join me for tea in the nursery, and she said this thing with such conviction—I can almost see the sincere slant to her beautiful eyebrows, even now, though I never can recall the shape or the color of her eyes themselves—that my fears dissolved at once.

Only later did I realize how skillfully she had misled me, and I have hated a lie ever since, even those small, harmless ones in which most people trade daily.

You can imagine, therefore, the sickness in my heart when Silverton laid his hand on my shoulder, in the black, damp netherworld of his hut on the island of Hoy, my own palms deep inside the contents of his private chest, and asked me what the devil I was doing.

The lie came easily to my lips, as it had to my mother's.

"I was cold. I thought you might have another tunic. A blanket, a cloak."

He reached around me and closed the lid of the chest. "My dearest love. You should have woken me."

"I have already troubled you enough."

An instant's silence settled upon us both. In this strange, primeval world, not a single noise disturbed the stillness, not the slightest sign that another human being existed on the earth. Not the sea, not the wind outside. Even my breath seemed to have stopped in my chest, and so did his. Only the warmth of Silverton's flesh reached me through the darkness, spreading softly along my back and my arms. My hands dropped away from the chest.

"Come to bed, then, Truelove," he said at last. "We'll make you warm enough."

He took my elbow, and I followed him obediently to the pallet and climbed under the furs. My heart smacked, my breath turned shallow at the thought of my deception. I nearly blurted out the truth, I nearly demanded the truth from him, and to this day I don't know why I didn't. Perhaps I was too frightened to hear the answer. Instead I lay on my back, staring up at that shadow that must have been his head, expecting his lips to find mine, his long limbs to slide down the furs and warm me with the compressed, violent heat of his own body.

But he only drew another length of fur over my body and tucked them all snug, the way a mother might do to an infant, hardly touching me at all. He asked me if that was warm enough, and I said it was.

"Good," he said. "We'll find our way home in the morning, never fear."

For seven years the Lady and the Fisherman lived in peace in the cottage by the sea, where she bore him a girl and a boy, and their passion for each other grew with the setting of each sun. By day the Fisherman plied his trade on the water while the Lady taught her children to dive for pearls by the shore, and by night they lay in the Fisherman's bed and discovered every carnal pleasure, until the Lady's heart was whole once more, and a new babe quickened in her womb, and she knew she had nothing left on earth to desire.

Then one morning, at the beginning of the eighth year, their daughter rose from the sea with a pearl of such size and beauty, it might make their fortunes forever . . .

THE BOOK OF TIME, A. M. HAYWOOD (1921)

Eight

⁂

In the morning, the mist had lifted, though the sky remained gray. When Silverton led me outside to the privy, I gasped at the sight around me.

We stood in a field that sloped to meet the wet, pebbled shore, about a hundred yards away; above us, perhaps a mile or two distant, a castle rose from the cliffs and merged with the clouds. Further down the line of the shore, where the land became flat, lay a cluster of modest houses—two dozen, no more—from which the steeple of a church emerged like an arrow pointing to heaven.

"Why, it's the village!" I exclaimed. "There's the harbor. There's where we landed on the ferry."

Silverton followed my outstretched arm. "Is it? I'm afraid I wouldn't know. Never having visited the place in its modern setting."

"And the castle. Except it's—it's—I don't know, it's different. The same size and shape . . ." I couldn't finish the sentence, because I could not put a name to the change. A pennant snapped breezily from the middle tower; perhaps that was it. The building seemed alive somehow, fulfilling some higher purpose. At work, instead of inert.

"All right?" Silverton said quietly, touching my arm, and I realized I had been staring, without sound or movement, for some time.

"Yes. Quite all right." I resumed my progress to the privy, and once inside, cramped, covered by darkness and the reek of human waste, I stared at a long crack of daylight between two wooden boards and wept.

✑

When I emerged, Silverton stood respectfully away, staring down the slope of grass toward the lapping shore. I had forgotten how tall he was, and the unfamiliar, homespun tunic made him somehow larger. I touched his shoulder and he turned to me. He made no comment on the lapse of time, or the redness that no doubt marked my eyes and skin.

"What brought you here?" I asked.

"Here? This island?"

"This village, this castle. How did you know?"

"I don't understand. Know what?"

"Know to come here and wait for us. That this was the place we'd find you."

His face was puzzled. "I didn't know anything. Wait for you? I hadn't the faintest idea. I thought I was stuck here forever, that I had no hope of seeing my own world again."

"Then why—" But I stopped. There were new lines in his face, spreading from his eyes and his mouth. I reached up and smoothed his forehead with my finger. The skin flattened away under my touch, and I thought, *It was the other way around, wasn't it? We were led to you.*

"That face," he said. "Those eyes of yours, frowning at me. I never imagined I should see them again."

"I'm not frowning. Only thinking."

"What are you thinking?"

I allowed my hand to fall away and turned to the sea. "So you traveled here from Edinburgh, did you?"

"Yes. Well, Edinburgh as it exists, which is rather different than we knew it, Truelove. I only recognized it by the Castle Rock. I suppose that's how I deduced what had happened, because there was the Castle Rock, except without the castle, without anything else familiar. I spent some time there, until the local folk became suspicious of me, and then I left." He began to tug at my hair, which lay loose and tangled around my shoulders, and I realized he was combing it with his hand. "I met a fellow at a tavern, an earnest Christian chap who had traveled to Edinburgh on trading business, and helped him out of a tight spot. In return, he offered to take me home with him, to his village in the north."

"And you've lived here ever since?"

He hesitated. "Yes."

A note of melancholy had entered his voice, so new and so entirely unlike the Silverton I had known that I turned back toward him. His hand, which had been combing my hair, slid to the center of my back. I put my arms about his waist and laid my head against his chest, and I spoke fiercely into the rough wool of his tunic.

"You're going home now. I'm taking you home."

He said nothing, but his arms wound around me and held my body snug against his. I listened to the slow beat of his heart, the tide of his blood. The clouds were thinning, and over the ridge of his shoulder I saw the battlements of the castle, and the pennant that snapped in the freshening wind. The damp, tangy air of this strange world filled my lungs. I knew I should move. I should step away from his arms and lead him to the jagged point of rock that the duke and I had designated as our rendezvous. But I didn't move, and neither did Silverton. We stood locked together, as perfectly fit as a pair of spoons, unable to part.

"Are you ready?" I whispered.

"The question is not whether *I'm* ready, Truelove, but whether *you* are."

I pulled back. "Of course I am. The sooner we leave this place, the better."

"But you've only just recovered from the journey here. Are you sure you wish to attempt the return passage so soon? Rest awhile longer?" He assumed a solemn, innocent expression, reminding me of the old Silverton. "Naturally, I'd take the most splendid care of you. Bring you back up to fighting strength."

"I'm strong enough already, I believe. And I don't wish to spend another minute here in this uncivilized world, among your barbarian friends."

"They're not such bad chaps, once you get to know them."

"You'll forgive me if I'd rather not take that chance."

"Now, Truelove." One of his hands still remained at my waist, and he raised it now, grasping my fingers. "You know I'd never let anyone harm you. Not while I've breath in my body."

I pulled my hand away. "That's precisely what worries me. Come along. Let's make ourselves ready."

He sighed and followed me back into the hut, where we smothered the fire and washed and put away the cook pot and utensils. The atmosphere took on a strange quality, as if we were preparing for an afternoon's picnic instead of a journey some several hundred years into the future. I asked Silverton where he had put my modern clothes, and he pointed to the chest beneath the window.

"But why do you want them?" he asked.

"Because I ought to be suitably dressed, upon our return."

"My God. Suitably dressed? How does one dress for this?"

"I don't know. I don't wish to excite comment on our return, that's all."

"Truelove, I don't mean to alarm you, but I expect that's inevitable. Our clothing's the least of it."

I could hardly answer his logic, so I made a stubborn noise and turned to the chest. Before I could lift the lid, however, his lordship darted in front of me and took hold of it himself.

"Here," he said. "I'll find them for you."

"It's no trouble."

"Nothing's ever any trouble for you, Truelove, but I shall continue to hammer away at your confounded self-sufficiency until my dying day. Ah, here we are." He turned abruptly and handed me a small stack of folded clothes. "I would have had them laundered, except there's no laundry, as such. I hope you'll forgive me."

I couldn't see around his shoulders, and in any case he had already lowered the lid of the chest with his other hand. I took the clothes instead. "If you'll excuse me," I said.

"Excuse you? Excuse you where?"

"I require a moment of privacy."

He threw back his head and laughed. "My dear girl. Who do you think removed those clothes from you in the first place?"

"I've endeavored not to think about it at all."

"Well, not to belabor the obvious, but I was your lady's maid, Truelove. Good old Frederick, at your service. Every last button and hook and lace, so that nobody would call you a foreigner or a witch or worse, as they did me. I took the most conscientious care not to uncover any more than was necessary, of course, but I'm afraid your modesty is forever compromised. Do you mind awfully?"

I moved to the wall and turned my back. "At least have the goodness to look away, if you can't bring yourself to leave the room."

I heard his footsteps, and then his voice, more distant, somewhat muffled, as if he were speaking into the opposite wall. "I see I've offended you."

"Of course not. I know you meant me no ill."

For a moment, he didn't answer. The rustle of my garments made the only sounds in the room. I knew he was turned away, so that we stood back to back, separated by twelve feet of empty, charged space.

He cleared his throat. "You see, Truelove—don't laugh—I imagined myself a sort of bridegroom. I imagined you had arrived here to stay. With me. If that makes any difference."

I had just removed the woolen tunic, and stood there in the corner of the hut in nothing but my chemise, holding one petticoat in my hand, shivering a little. I remember the smell of peat smoke, and the faint, briny whiff of the sea.

"A foolish presumption, I soon learned. But what I saw—what I *did*—I did in reverence," he continued, in the same quiet tone.

I turned my head and saw his broad, homespun back, his bowed head, the glint of his long hair. He stood in the farthest corner of the hut from me, like a boy being punished, except a boy so overgrown you couldn't see the corner for the body that occupied it.

If he turns, I thought. *If he turns.*

I didn't finish the sentence. I didn't dare.

The air was quite cool on my skin, but I had stopped shivering. I was flushed and warm. I said lightly, "At least now you have better prospects. Instead of sharing your exile, I've come to lead you back to freedom."

"Freedom. How jolly."

"Aren't you happy? Don't you want to return? Your family, your friends. Think of your poor father. Your sisters and brother, your dear stepmother. Surely you miss them."

"Of course I miss them. Every day, it's a hole in my chest. I've already told you how lonely it's been."

"You're a lord, Silverton, you're the heir to a dukedom. You have everything."

He raised his head and turned, but his eyes didn't widen or wander at the sight of me in my chemise, in a state of near undress. His gaze rested on my face alone, as if that was the only thing that mattered.

"Yes," he said. "I have everything. Now for God's sake, let me help you with those damned petticoats, or we'll never get there before nightfall."

⁂

Silverton held my hand as we climbed the mile or so of hilly terrain toward the plain on which the castle stood, and the promontory beyond it. I was grateful for his support. My limbs lacked strength; my head was light with fatigue. Though the clouds were breaking apart, and the sun sometimes warmed our shoulders, I still felt chilled, as if the exercise and the sunshine weren't enough to chase away the strange, cold sense of dread that overcame me as we approached the fortress. A soldier of some kind came into view, atop one of the towers, and I tightened my grip on Silverton's hand.

"Why, what's the matter?" he asked.

"Nothing." I nodded toward the castle. "There's nothing to fear, is there?"

"From the chaps on the battlements, do you mean? No. They wouldn't waste their time on us. In any case . . ."

"Yes?"

A shout drifted downward from the tower. I squinted up to see the guard's arm raised, his attention fixed in our direction. Silverton raised his own hand—the one not holding mine—and answered with a hail of his own.

"In any case," he said, "I happen to know a few of them."

"Of course you do."

"Walk on. And keep that cloak close about you."

The cloak was far too long—it belonged to Silverton, who had at least ten inches on my height—but that was the point, wasn't it? To disguise my extraordinary clothes. The wool swished around my heels and toes, scarcely clearing the earth, and I began to think that Silverton had been right. I should have kept my strange tunic. I felt the eyes of that guard on my figure as I walked along the narrow path, hand in hand with Silverton, bundled in an oversized cloak despite the August sunshine. Not warm, perhaps, by the standards of a twentieth-century London, but no doubt positively tropical in medieval Orkney.

I turned to Silverton. "What year is it?"

"What year? Don't you know that?"

"I never asked."

He looked amused. "It's the year of grace 1316, at least so near as I can determine."

"Aren't you certain?"

"Record keeping is less precise than you'd imagine, dear one. Care to rest a moment?"

He spoke casually, but I knew he was concerned for me. My stride was dragging, my breath coming far too fast. We had nearly finished the hill—the castle was now a hundred yards away, to the right—and I said, "No, thank you. I'd rather not stop."

"You're quite safe, I assure you. Nobody will trouble you, as long as I'm here."

"Just as nobody troubled us in the privacy of your own home?"

"That was different," he said, and I waited for him to explain this distinction in circumstance, but his attention had turned to the sea that washed the cliffs to our left. I followed his gaze and saw a cluster of small ships—boats, really—plying the water of the channel between this island and the next.

"Not warships, are they?" I said.

"Warships? Wherever do you get your ideas, Truelove? That's the fishing fleet. Humble fisherfolk, drawing a living from the water. Just because they speak a different language doesn't make them fearsome, you know. They're just like us. As strange as that sounds. Underneath it all, we are mere human beings, the lot of us, fourteenth century or twentieth, plying the same water. Men and women, seeking only to exist and to procreate, to leave some little mark on the world before we vanish from it. Careful!" He caught me as my foot found a rock. "You're awfully winded, Truelove. We must stop."

"No. We're nearly there."

"As game as they come," he said, sighing, but he didn't try to stop me. We reached the plain, and the path became easier. The castle passed to our right, without any disturbance, and my breath returned to me, though not my strength. Ahead, I saw not one promontory but two: two long, jagged teeth biting into the sea. I paused, and Silverton asked me what was the matter.

"Nothing," I said. "It looks different, that's all."

"I daresay it does. Time and tide. Do you see anything familiar?"

"I'm sure I will, when we draw closer."

He went along willingly, as if we were choosing a spot for our picnic. He'd insisted we bring a bit of bread and cheese, some ale in a flask, in case our mission took longer than we supposed. He'd said this in a careless voice—*In case things take a trifle longer than planned, my love*—as if it didn't matter, as if the success of our mission had little consequence. But he was always like that, wasn't he? Even in the Mediterranean, he had treated everything like a lark. Only the strength of his grip around my fingers betrayed any conviction.

On we walked, and the shape of the cliffs became clearer now. I raised my hand to shade myself from the sun, which had reappeared with sudden, blinding intensity, and tried to remember exactly how the promontory had appeared from the window of Mr. Magnusson's office, overlooking the sea. I knew there was just one, covered in tufted grass that had thinned into bare rock as it approached the brink, but only because I hadn't noticed a second outcropping. Had the other crumbled away in the centuries since? Which one, then?

"Come," Silverton said. "Let's walk to the edge. Something might trigger your memory."

We angled away from the path, toward the cliffs. A breeze whistled in from the sea, laded with all the smells of the ocean: salt and fish and that sort of indefinable green-tinged marine tanginess. The sun vanished again, as suddenly as it had appeared, and now I felt the wind's chill on my bare cheek.

"You're shivering," observed Silverton.

"Only nerves."

"Well, I'm damned glad to hear it. I thought I was the only one dreading the ordeal to come."

"Don't you want to go home?"

There was the slightest pause. "Of course. It's the getting there that's the trouble. Are you quite sure Max knows what he's doing? Not going to lose us in the void somewhere?"

"There are no guarantees, of course."

"As I thought. At least we're together this time. That should be a comfort. You must hold me tightly, Truelove, so I'm not afraid."

"Don't joke."

"I'm not joking, believe me." We had reached the ledge, and he stopped a few feet away. "Here we are. I don't know about you, but this rather reminds me of a certain extraordinary cliff on Skyros."

"Much smaller," I said.

"Same notion, however." He still held my hand. His palm was warm and dry, a great comfort. He looked upward to the mottled sky, and then down. "Anything nudging your memory, Truelove? We can walk about a bit."

I followed his gaze tentatively downward—I am not afraid of heights, but the edge *was* rather close—and saw to my surprise that the cliff was not a sheer one. The rock tumbled downward at a comfortable angle to a shingled beach, quite deep, and on this beach rested a hut of some kind, larger than Silverton's, although fallen into disrepair.

"Why, what's that?" I pointed to the beach.

"That? Oh, some old fisherman's dwelling, I suppose. Decent, sheltered position, though rather inconveniently far from town. See anything you recognize?"

For some reason, the hut held me transfixed, and only with the greatest effort did I turn my gaze to the side, and the shape of the outcroppings nearby, none of which matched the picture in my head from Magnusson's window. I made a noise of frustration. "Perhaps we should simply walk along the edge," I said.

"And what? Wait for Max to find us?"

"It's about being in the exact right spot, you see. Some particular location that connects us."

"Ah. And what if that location doesn't exist, from one century to the next?"

"Then I'm sure . . . I'm sure . . ."

"Yes?"

"I'm sure we'll find a way. Max will find a way."

"No doubt. Magnificent, all-powerful Max. He is, after all, the Duke of Olympia. I say, can we stop for a bite of bread? I'm awfully famished."

I tugged his hand. "We're almost there. I'm sure of it."

"You're sure? How? Feeling some sort of tingling?"

I wasn't. I felt nothing at all, in fact, none of that familiar electricity that had charged me in Max's presence. Only the chill of wind on my cheek, and the heat of Silverton's hand in mine. And a slight swirl of unease in my belly, one that was not supernatural but merely human doubt. I thought about the chest in the library, about the sketch in my own hand on the paper that lay inside it. The paper that had once lain inside the leather portfolio I had brought from London—where was it now?

"Not tingling, exactly," I said. "Look! That rock ahead. I think—yes, I'm quite sure. That's certainly it."

"Excellent. Good show. Off we go, then."

I kept my gaze fixed on the rock, about a hundred yards ahead, which did indeed strike a chord of memory. That shape— not quite the same, but similar. My skin began to prickle underneath my clothing, like a buzz of static. Excitement, or Max's power, gathering me toward him? The formation was quite large and dark, so deeply charcoal it might have been wet. Not a blade of grass or moss grew upon it. The distance closed. My heart was beating hard, my breath short. About twenty yards away, I stopped and turned to Silverton.

"Yes? Something wrong?" he asked. "Is this it, or not?"

"You don't believe me, do you?"

"Of course I believe you. You're here, aren't you? We're both here. Something sent us here."

"Max. It was Max."

He lifted his hand and rubbed his beard. His gaze shifted out to sea. "I was there on Skyros. I saw what happened. If Max can yank a damned mythological Theseus off a cliff three thousand years in the past, without even stopping to think, I imagine this ought to be child's play."

"And us? You're not afraid?"

"Afraid of what?" He turned back to me, and his eyes were terribly blue in the pale midday light. The curling hairs of his beard glinted softly. I couldn't resist reaching up to touch his jaw, to feel the strange texture of his whiskers under my fingers.

"Afraid of the journey," I said.

"A little. But I can't very well leave you to face it alone."

I tried to smile. "Just think of everything waiting for you on the other side. Your cricket ball and your pipe. Women at your feet."

"Just one woman is quite enough for me, these days."

"Oh, don't—"

"It's true. Now, don't look away. Look back up at me, the way you were doing just now. As if you were thinking about kissing me."

"I wasn't thinking about kissing you."

"Because this is important, Truelove. This is vital. I won't take another step until we make something clear. If we do this thing, this mad scheme of yours, if by some miracle we actually make this terrifying journey and survive it—"

"Survive it!"

"—I want you to promise me you won't abandon me on the other side."

He had taken both my hands and held them close to his belly. His cheeks were pink beneath his beard. Only a week ago, he had stood before me in much the same way, in a bedroom of the North British Hotel in the middle of Edinburgh, trimmed and sleek and beautifully dressed. I thought how different he looked now, how that long golden hair and that scruffy face, that lined skin and rough tunic had transformed him, how only the color of his eyes remained the same as before.

Only that wasn't quite right, was it? It wasn't his appearance that had transformed him. It was the other way around.

"What nonsense," I said, "when it's you who will return to your splendid old life. Gallivant about on the dowager duchess's behalf. Doing whatever it is you do, whatever it is you're so marvelously good at doing."

"The *duchess*? Good Lord. You don't think—my God, Truelove. Those days are long over."

"By my count, those days were only a week ago."

"By mine, it's a trifle longer. It's another age. You can't imagine what I've seen, what I've done, the length of days between us. You can't—I don't—my God, that old cricket ball." He made a small, sad chuckle. "My dear Truelove. I don't even know that man anymore. As far as I can remember him, he had only one good idea."

"What's that?" I asked.

He leaned down and kissed me. "This one."

His kiss was brief and gentle, his lips warm, and when he raised his head, I couldn't speak. If he had kissed me fiercely, I might have resisted him, but this tenderness left me without the breath for words.

"I'll follow you anywhere, Truelove, even if it kills me. God knows this life of mine isn't worth saving. But I'll be damned if it was *duty* that sent you here to rescue me. Not even you could pretend that."

"Of course it was duty. And—"

"And?"

"And—we share a certain—I have always—since our time together last spring—"

He stepped close and bent to speak in my ear. His beard tickled my jaw. "Admit it. Before we touch that damned rock. Before we go back to that old world, Truelove. Admit it."

With great effort, I put my hands on his chest and pushed him away. It was like tearing a strip from my own skin. We stared at each other, panting a little. His figure began to blur in my vision. I turned and stepped toward the monstrous outcropping of rock.

"Are you coming?" I asked, over my shoulder.

He let out an almighty roar. I started forward, walking quickly, and an instant later I heard, or rather felt, his footsteps on the soft turf behind me. Another instant, and he took my hand, then my arm, and the world slanted as he swooped me up in his arms and carried me across the final yards. The action so startled me that I couldn't tell whether the splintering of my nerves came from shock, or from the supernatural power gathering around us. The air roared in my ears, or perhaps it was Silverton's angry breath. Together we crashed into the rock, although Silverton took all the impact upon his own shoulder. He leaned back and stared at the sky, still cradling me against his chest, and he whispered something I couldn't make out. I thought it was a prayer. I closed my eyes and listened to the pounding of his heart, the rasp of his breath, and I waited for the hair to lift on my skin, the otherworldly energy to rush over us both. For the world to blacken and empty, and our entangled bodies to lighten and dissolve into the void.

But there was nothing. Only Silverton's arms, holding me close, and the gentle scratch of his tunic. The salty scent of his skin, the heat of his bones. The muffled thud of his pulse.

A bird sang out. I opened my eyes and saw the straight gray lines of the castle's westernmost turret, the one overlooking the sea, and the blue pennant snapping in the breeze.

Silverton had stopped whispering. The seconds passed, tick-ing off some invisible clock, and because I was listening so care-fully to the world around me, I caught the faint chime of bells, ringing from the village below. Bells, because that was how you kept time in this world. Your life was ruled not by clocks, but by bells, rung from the steeple of a stone church in the middle of a village. By the movement of the sun across the sky.

Not by a clock.

"Truelove," Silverton said at last, "I don't mean to doubt you, but are you quite sure this is the rock in question?"

"I believe so."

"And Max? He couldn't mistake it, all the way over in the twentieth century, could he?"

"I—I—don't think so."

"But it's possible?"

"Of course, anything is *possible*," I said reluctantly.

The arms loosened around me. I slid to my feet on the solid ground and stared at Silverton's tunic.

"Perhaps we might walk around a bit," I said, "just to be thor-ough."

❧

Hand in hand, we trod the landscape, drawing long, even lines along the turf, the way a gardener might mow a lawn of grass. Silverton walked patiently by my side, offering only the occasional mild observation, until the rumbling of his stomach betrayed him. I said that we might pause for a moment and eat, if he liked.

We sat facing the sea, upon a small stand of rocks. Silverton insisted I rest between his knees, so that we remained in physical contact in case Max found us while we ate. Rather, while Silver-ton ate, because I wasn't hungry.

"You must have something," he said. "You need your strength."

"I can't eat."

I was leaning against his lean, bony knee. What excitement had animated me earlier had now dissolved, leaving me weaker than before, and yet—as I truthfully told him—too listless to contemplate eating. Silverton's hand began to stroke at my loose hair. The waves stirred below us. I closed my eyes.

"When I was first starting out in the game," Silverton said, "I used to get most damnably nervous. Couldn't eat, couldn't sleep. Took me weeks to recover afterward, from some silly show of a few days' work. Eventually I learned to set my terror aside."

"Terror? You?"

"God, yes. And then one night, lying there in some cheap hotel in Budapest, waiting anxiously for midnight, I thought, *What does it matter, if you die? Father's got another heir now. Nobody depends on you. You've had a good run, an immensely rich life. Why not end with a bang?* I sat up and ordered myself a good dinner, and from then on . . ."

"Are you saying I should stop caring?"

"No, Truelove. I don't recommend that at all." He reached down and held a piece of bread before me. "But I do recommend that you eat something. If not for your sake, then for mine."

I took the bread and put it in my mouth and began to chew. It was different from the bread I was used to: dense and unleavened, heavy on my teeth, nutty in flavor. I swallowed and said, "Did you bake this yourself?"

"Of course not. Where do you get these ideas? There's a baker in the village. Pleasant chap. His five children do most of the work, while he chats with his customers."

"What about his wife?"

"She died in childbed a year ago."

I accepted a piece of cheese and ate that, and I thought I had never tasted cheese so delicious.

"It's sheep's milk, actually," Silverton told me. "Sheep being in far greater supply than kine. Feeling better?"

"It's not working," I said. "I don't know why it's not working."

"Have some more, then. I brought plenty."

"I don't mean the cheese. I mean Max. We agreed—he was supposed to—"

Silverton brushed the crumbs from his tunic and took my hand. "It's all right, my love. We'll find him. Come along, up we go. We'll keep on bloody walking until—"

"No. It won't work." I pitched forward from the rock and knelt in the grass, staring across the channel to the island that lay faintly in the distance. "I don't feel anything. Before I left, with Max, when it was working"—I drove my fist into the turf—"I *knew*. I could feel it in my nerves, my skin. There was this energy. And here, now, there's nothing. He's not here at all."

"If we keep walking—"

I turned and grasped the neck of his tunic with both hands. "He's not here! Don't you see? I'd know if he were here. I'd know."

"We could try again tomorrow."

"It won't make any difference. It doesn't matter. Today or tomorrow or a year from now. Either he's here, or he's not. If he's not here now, he never will be."

Now I was leaning into Silverton's chest, and his arms came around me. My knees scraped on the rough, hard rock. My throat stung.

"I see," Silverton said slowly.

"He promised me. We agreed how to do it."

"Perhaps he can't. Perhaps he tried and failed."

"It's my fault. I was so certain. It was an impulse, I had to find you, I didn't stop to work it all out—"

"Truelove, don't—"

"And Max said we should wait, but I wouldn't wait, I couldn't wait—"

"Because you love me."

"—compulsion—"

"It's all right. We'll find a way."

I looked up. "There *is* no other way. There's nothing. I've trapped us both with my stupidity, my headstrong—"

"Headstrong? You?"

"Oh, stop. Don't you see? Don't you care? There's no chance of going home. No hope at all."

His face was soft and kind. He touched my cheek and said, "My dear, dear girl. I never had any hope. Not until three days ago."

"Well, now it's gone."

"Not true. Not true at all. I'm filled with hope, in fact."

"You're wrong. It's a chance in a million he'll find us by accident."

"I wasn't talking about Max."

I stared at him in amazement. The wind lifted the ends of his hair, and the tip of his nose had turned as pink as a raspberry. His thumb found my cheek again, brushing along the underside of the bone, and I opened my mouth to say something, I forget what.

And I don't suppose I shall ever know what I intended to say to him at that moment, because a shout broke apart the fragile air between us, and Silverton leapt and spun in the same motion, drew a weapon from the folds of his tunic, leaving me sprawled behind him at the edge of the cliff.

The Lady said to the Fisherman, 'Let us throw this pearl back in the sea, for I need no riches except your heart, and our children I have borne you, and our babe that quickens in my womb.' But the Fisherman knew that his wife had forsaken luxury for his hand, and he replied, 'No, I will take this jewel across the channel to sell in the city, and I will return to you with rich clothes to adorn your beauty, and furniture for the great house we will build together.' The Lady's heart misgave her. She pleaded with the Fisherman to stay, and in bed that night she worked upon him all her wiles to change his mind, yet still in the morning the Fisherman embraced her tenderly and kissed their children good-bye, and sailed his boat across the channel to the city on the mainland . . .

THE BOOK OF TIME, A. M. HAYWOOD (1921)

Nine

I thought you said you knew these people," I muttered as we marched across the grass toward the castle's grim walls.

"I don't know *all* of them." Silverton kept my hand firmly inside his grip. "But never fear. I do know the right ones. We shall straighten the whole mess out directly, once I speak to Magnus."

"Who's Magnus?"

"Just a chap I know," he said serenely. "How are you holding up?"

"Oh, beautifully."

"Ah, the same dear Truelove. I can't tell you how delighted I am to hear you haven't lost your essential vinegar. Just let me do the talking, is that clear?"

"My dear Silverton, I'm afraid we have no choice."

There was the briefest pause. "You magnificent woman," he said. "I want very badly to kiss you right now. If they kill me, will you promise to press my lips in a final embrace?"

"*Kill* you?"

"There is the smallest possibility. But don't worry, you'll be safe enough. They've got a shortage of women on the island, at the moment."

"How fortunate for me."

He didn't reply, and as the three men around us exchanged words, I realized he was listening to them. His hand remained steady and warm, and I'm afraid I clung to it shamelessly, as an anchor. We were approaching the main entrance, which had seemed so harmless on that August day in 1906, almost inviting, and was now harsh and forbidding. The sharp teeth of the portcullis hovered close. I glanced at the man nearest, a few feet to my right, whose thick, dark beard and white face sickened me. He was saying something, laughing as he talked, and he must have felt my gaze because he turned in my direction, grinning— an expression that deepened the scar above his left eye.

But I had no time to wallow in fear. We passed beneath the thick black iron of the portcullis, and for an instant I recalled how I drove beneath the portcullis at Thurso in Max's splendid, shining motorcar—was it only a week ago?—and the memory was so thorough, so acute, I thought I could smell the sultry petrol exhaust, I could hear the sublime roar of the Burke's massive engine. I remembered the strange shimmer of terror I had experienced then, until the peaceful, lichen-crusted courtyard had opened around me. Thurso's footmen in plaid. Crumbling, damp, relaxed gentility.

No lichen now. The reek of manure assailed me, of unwashed flesh, of smoke, and though it struck some familiar chord, I couldn't say what it was. There was an air of purpose. Perhaps half a dozen men milled about, dressed in tunics and hose of homespun wool, shaggy-haired; two of them attended to the unloading of a cart stocked with large woven baskets, pulled by a stocky pony, while others hung from ramshackle scaffolding and repaired the stonework. I heard their strange words drifting down, incomprehensible, and I turned to Silverton.

"What language is this? Gaelic?"

"Gaelic? No, no. It's a form of Norse. Orkney's subject to Norway, didn't you know that? The Scots aren't due to arrive in force for some years yet, as I remember, although the present Earl of Orkney is a Scotsman. All very complicated." He made some friendly gesture at the guard who stood near the steps to the keep, and the guard nodded slightly. "It all started with the Vikings, as these things so often do."

I glanced back at the man with the scar, who was starting up the steps to the keep. "They're Vikings?"

"Descendants, at any rate. I expect they found these islands an excellent place from which to base raids, until they became too troublesome and the King of Norway stepped in, four or five hundred years ago. Then it was all Norsemen coming in. Luckily I had some Norwegian already. One of my few talents, language."

"Lucky indeed," I whispered, and then I fell silent, because the men were casting us suspicious looks. We climbed the steps into the keep, and again I experienced that frisson of familiarity as the walls took shape around me, the same dimensions as before, except the floor was covered with rushes and the walls hung with tapestries, and in the middle of the hall stood a giant rectangular table lined with rough benches. At one end of this table, three men sat eating from a platter of meat, using their knives and the fingers of their right hands. The fellow at the head, somewhat broader than the others, turned to us in mild surprise.

"That's Magnus," whispered Silverton in my ear, just before he strode boldly forward past our phalanx of grim escorts—still holding my hand—and dropped to one knee. I followed suit. I felt I had no choice.

Magnus nodded, releasing us to our feet, and addressed some question that ended in a gesture, indicating the whole lot of us. Silverton and the scarred man began to answer him at the same time. Magnus held up his hand—silence—and repeated the same words, gazing at Silverton.

I felt an angry, restless silence gather behind us as Silverton spoke in the unfamiliar Norse tongue. His words rang about the stones, filling the vast, chilly hall. Magnus glanced at me, but it was not a lascivious gaze, merely curious. He was a plain man, and though he still sat on his chair—the men on either side of him occupied the benches—I perceived he was quite large. His shoulders were wide, his neck thick; his tunic covered a bulk of muscle on his chest and arms, as if he were accustomed to rigorous physical labor. I liked his face, which was not handsome but thick-boned and honest, covered by a bristling ginger beard. He turned his gaze back at Silverton, and this time it remained there, steady and penetrating and intelligent. I thought his eyes were gray, but it was difficult to tell in the muted light of the hall, and they were overhung by a pair of large ginger-thatched brows that disguised them further. And yet I felt I could trust this man. Some primeval instinct, perhaps, or else some clue in Silverton's manner, for of course I couldn't understand what Magnus actually said. I wasn't even certain of his position here. A lord of some kind, but hadn't Silverton said the islands were ruled by a Scottish earl? Surely not *this* man, then. In any case, an earl would have kept his seat on the main island, not Hoy.

Silverton stopped speaking and raised my hand to his lips, turning his body a few inches toward mine, and just as he kissed my knuckles, the scarred man jumped forward and began to jabber angrily. Magnus looked at him and frowned, the way a schoolmaster might regard a troublesome student. He lifted his hand and drank from a pewter tumbler, and I saw how enormous his fingers were, the last one encircled by a plain gold ring.

A real man, I thought. Not some flattened figure in a history book. A real man, wearing a real ring, made of battered gold. Fully alive in his own present.

The future—*my* present—did not exist. Only this world. These people. Living and breathing, eating and drinking, talking and fighting and loving, with no possible knowledge of the world that lay a hundred years, five hundred years in the distance.

Their present. *Their* bodies, arms and eyes and hair and fingers, as real as mine.

So transfixed was I by this thought, by the sight of this hand and the ring upon it—so incomprehensible were the words bursting from the scarred man's mouth—I hardly noticed when the speech became heated, when Silverton's hand tightened on mine.

When, without warning, the scarred man turned around and tore Silverton's long cloak from my shoulders.

A dozen gasps drew the air from the room. Magnus bolted to his feet. I remember the sound the chair made as it scraped along the stone floor, and for the first time I noticed the tall gray dog who rested there, and who now rose on his paws and growled.

But only for an instant. Silverton made a noise of fury and yanked me behind him, and the world became a jumble of movement, a flash of light on a short silver blade. Somebody grabbed at my waist. I threw him off with a strength that must have surprised him, for I had time to spin around and snatch one of the knives from the table before he lunged at me again. I slashed at his face, then at his grasping hand—two quick strokes, a spurt of blood, and he fell back howling. To my left, Magnus roared. Footsteps pounded on the floor. A company of guards formed a half circle around us. Silverton straightened away from the scarred man's throat and let his blade fall to his side. He made an apologetic swoop of his head in Magnus's direction, to which Magnus scowled ferociously from the middle of his magnificent auburn beard.

He spoke in a low, rumbling, ominous voice. I could not strip my eyes away from him. Both Silverton and the scarred man stood before him, arms lowered, and because I saw nothing else, I didn't notice that every other man in the hall—every man, for there were no women—was staring at me.

Me, in my plain dress of navy blue, fastened at the back with horn buttons, pleated at the waist, shaped by the undergarments of another age. I was no slave to fashion. My corset did not bend my figure into the elongated S then in mode; I disdained the explosion of ruffles and tucks, the excess of decoration, the gargantuan hats worn by Lady Annis and her set. I dressed with a view to practicality and comfort rather than style, but the materials, the details, the needlework, the shape of my dress did not belong to this world, any more than Max's motorcar would.

And because we humans are still animals, after all, and retain certain animal instincts, I realized sometime in the middle of Magnus's thunderous lecture that these gazes lay upon me. That all the men in the hall now stared at me, at my unnatural dress, so violently exposed by the scarred man when he tore away Silverton's long cloak. My skin flushed, my pulse sped. I moved not a muscle, but I felt the weight of all those staring eyes, pressing against my flesh, until at last Magnus himself turned to regard me.

I met his gaze without flinching, though I knew I should not. The lot of women in my own time is not without its injustices, but we may safely look a man in the eye when the occasion demands it. Here, I knew, I enjoyed no such privilege. The very absence of women in this hall spoke to my precarious standing. More. I felt the antipathy, the affront of nearly every man in that hall, the way your skin feels the sting of a slap long after it's delivered. Somewhere to my right, a man stood bleeding from the wounds I had just delivered him. I, a woman! The shame of it! His hatred was a palpable thing, pulsing, close to strangling me.

But still I returned Magnus's gaze squarely. I could not do otherwise; I could not cast my eyes downward and still be Emmeline Truelove.

Magnus came to the end of his sentence, and it sounded like a question, delivered to me. I raised my eyebrows and spread my hands. Silverton spoke up, in measured words. Magnus turned and asked him a short question. Silverton answered. Magnus turned back to me.

To my amazement, his face was kind, if grave. He stepped toward me and held out his hand. A draft blew across my skin from some unknown quarter, making me shiver, but I went forward regardless and placed my hand in that rough, enormous palm. The contact electrified me. This man, this hand created and born in the thirteenth century, now clasped mine. The fear I had held at bay now engulfed my belly and my brain, and it was all I could do to remain standing.

Magnus turned to Silverton, still holding my hand, and gestured to his lordship. Silverton went readily forward and made a movement of obeisance, which Magnus waved away. Instead he drew my hand forward, placing it in Silverton's palm, and then he wrapped his own fingers around our bound fists and said a short, reverent sentence.

A burst of astonished conversation broke out around us, which Magnus quelled with a single word. I heard the frustrated rustle of feet behind me, though I didn't dare look. Magnus was speaking again, almost in a chant, and then he released our hands, looked above our heads—we were both kneeling—and addressed the men assembled there.

"What on earth is going on?" I whispered to Silverton.

"It's the devil of a thing," he replied, in the same low voice. "It seems he's just married us."

✑

"I was only trying to protect you," Silverton explained, across the table. Around us, a banquet was taking shape. Perhaps two dozen men had gathered along the wooden benches, and serving maids were now emerging from some hallway to the right, bearing platters of bread and meat and fruit. Several rounds of ale had already filled the tumblers laid out before us, and the men had emptied them just as rapidly. Under the effects of this bounty, the atmosphere had turned buoyant. Even the man I had bloodied now rose to his feet and began a ballad, in a voice not quite precise. His companions joined him, and under cover of this noise, I replied to Silverton.

"Protect me? But what did you say to him?"

"That I had fallen in love with you." He drank from his tumbler, without breaking his gaze from mine. "That we were betrothed."

"I see."

"I had no choice. Thorvar—"

"Thorvar?"

Silverton gestured to his right eye. "Chap with the scar, the one who broke into the hut the other day. He was accusing you of sorcery, just now. Your confounded dress, our strange behavior on the ledge outside. He said you were a magical creature, not human, and that therefore—well."

"Therefore what?"

"You must understand, my dear, it's a different age. A brutal age. A less abundant age. They haven't the luxury of broadmindedness. That's the sort of rubbish that can get you killed."

"So they want to kill me first, before I can infect them with my strangeness."

"Or banishment," Silverton said cheerfully. "We may still have to leave the island, if Magnus's little maneuver here isn't enough."

I turned to look at Magnus, who sat at the head of the table, directly to my left. He was watching the ballad singer thoughtfully. One hand gripped his tumbler, the other lay gently fisted on the table. His nose was large, and looked as if it had been broken at least once. A serving woman reached between us to lay a platter of meat on the table, and I turned back to Silverton.

"But by what authority has he married us?"

"Why, he's the Earl of Orkney's vassal here in Hoy. He can pretty much do as he pleases."

"What about a priest?"

Silverton shrugged. "There is no Marriage Act, Truelove. No regularization of these matters. Remember divine rights and all that. Your ruler is nearer to God than thee."

"But we can't be *actually* married." I leaned forward over my empty plate. "My God. This is absurd. I never consented. I don't *feel* married."

Silverton's gaze had wandered down the table toward the man singing the ballad, who seemed to be reaching a chorus of some kind. He now returned his attention to me. "I imagine—" he began.

But Magnus rose to his feet, bringing all conversation and ballad singing to an abrupt end. I would have said he was frowning, but that wasn't quite right. His expression was heavy, thoughtful, and those thoughts—so I imagined—were not joyful ones. He raised his tumbler and said something in his massive, rumbling voice, and the other men answered him in a roar.

Then he set down his tumbler and stretched his hand to me.

"Stand up," whispered Silverton.

I stood and placed my hand in Magnus's palm.

Magnus turned to Silverton, who also rose and made fist with his leader. And Magnus spoke again, and the men answered once more in unison, making the stone walls ring with their full-throated, masculine voices, and Silverton's words returned to me: *If Magnus's little maneuver here isn't enough.*

But it is enough, I thought, looking back to Magnus's rough profile, his grave, ageless expression. In one gesture, in one spontaneous wedding banquet, arranged with a snap of his fingers and a few words, he had united us.

‽

Though the meat was unfamiliar to me—tough, stringy, greasy— I ate as much as I could bear. I had little else to do. Magnus, unable to speak to me, engaged Silverton instead, so I swallowed my notions of hygiene and stuck my fingers into the pile of viands that Magnus himself had carved for me, by the slice of his own knife. I had thanked him, and he had nodded. There are certain words that may be understood across all human civilizations. The meat was mutton, I thought. I sopped it up with the same coarse, brown bread I had eaten with Silverton.

But then the servers arrived bearing more platters, and these were loaded with something else: fish. Great filets of cod, dressed with herbs and fruit; whole trout, baked in its skin; herring, saithe, other varieties I didn't recognize.

"Ah, there we are," Silverton said.

"I never knew you admired fish so much."

"You might say it's grown on me."

It was strange, speaking like this, knowing that we couldn't be understood, the way some people spoke in French in front of the servants. Without asking—of course, he couldn't ask— Magnus filled my plate and then Silverton's, and lastly his own. There was nothing to wipe my fingers on, no way of cleansing myself, so I simply dipped my fingers bravely into the cod and ate, and the freshness of the flesh astounded me.

"This is quite good," I said to Silverton.

"Of course it is. Plucked from the seas within the past few hours, I'll bet."

He turned to the man on his left, exchanging some joke, and I took another piece of cod and thought, *This is my wedding banquet.*

A serving maid passed by, wearing a loose homespun robe bound at the waist. A pair of long dark braids wound about her head, and as I examined her, I realized she was casting me the same curious gaze. Our eyes met, and she looked away swiftly, but not before I felt her hostility penetrate the layers of my modern clothing to strike my bones.

I ate another bite.

Before me, Silverton's head still turned to the side, and though the beard disguised his face, it could not disguise his handsomeness, his glamour, the peculiar ease with which he met every strange turn in his life. I stared at the tendons of his neck, flexing with speech, and I thought, *This is my husband.*

Except he wasn't. Of course he wasn't. I hadn't said any vows, and neither had he. I hadn't said, *I will take thee, Frederick, as my husband.*

I drank from my tumbler, which somebody had refilled without my noticing. It wasn't quite the same ale I knew, but it was fermented, only more sweet and spicy. At my feet, something stroked my ankles—something wet—and I looked down to see the large gray dog earnestly licking my stockings.

I bent and rubbed his ears with my left hand—not my right, greasy with mutton and fish—and he gave off licking and looked at me lovingly.

"What a wicked fellow you are," I murmured, "a very wicked

fellow," and when I straightened once more, I discovered Magnus's face studying mine, no more than a foot and a half away.

I confess, I startled slightly. His expression was so fierce, his eyes a terrible blue, and everything so *large*: his nose, his brows, his mouth, his bones. My breath froze somewhere in my ribs, a strangled noise rather like a hiccup. But I did not look away.

"I'm not afraid of you," I said aloud, not for his benefit but for my own.

His face changed. His thick eyebrows lifted; his eyes crinkled at the corners. His mouth stretched into a wide, toothy smile, like that of a playful wolfhound, and he nodded—just once, deeply, a bow of acknowledgment.

Then he spoke.

"No, you are not," he said, and he turned to signal the serving maid for more ale.

"You're quite sure he spoke in English?" Silverton said. "There are certain Norse words that—"

"Quite sure. His accent was deep, of course, but I didn't mistake him." I paused to frown at the wall next to Silverton's neck. "Even if I did, he understood me. That was clear."

"Hmm," Silverton said.

"*Hmm?* Is that all? You don't find it extraordinary that a medieval Orcadian both understands and speaks modern English?"

Silverton crossed his arms and tilted his head upward, as if discovering some flaw in the ceiling. "I might have taught him a few words, that's all."

"*You* taught him? *Why?*"

We stood in a snug corridor off the main hall, which led presumably to the jakes. This was the excuse I'd given Silverton for our departure from the table, that I required the privy. In fact, I did, but I had no intention of subjecting myself to the sanitary whims of a medieval public convenience, particularly in a building so thoroughly masculine as this one. The hallway was dim and cramped, smelling of damp, and the shadows lay at strange angles across Silverton's face. We stood close, whispering, and I felt the heat from his body seep into mine, felt his ale-saturated breath touch my forehead. My head was a little dizzy from the spiced ale, or whatever it was, and the seconds seemed to stretch into infinity as Silverton considered his reply.

"Well?" I demanded.

"It's rather a long story."

"Then you had better speak quickly, hadn't you? Why did you teach him English?"

He lifted his hand and rubbed his forehead with his thumb. "Because he was the fellow who brought me here from Edinburgh. The one who rescued me from imminent disaster at the hands of a pack of fearsome chaps who—as I believe I already explained—had taken a violent dislike to my unusual bearing."

I stared at his shadowed, unblinking face in shock. "That was Magnus? Why didn't you tell me?"

"Didn't I?"

"Don't look angelic. You know very well you didn't."

"Ah, you're cross with me." He hung his head.

"Of course I'm cross! You're supposed to trust me."

"I do trust you. I wasn't trying to *hide* anything, Truelove. Only I saw no reason to burden you with any unnecessary information. After all, weren't we supposed to be back in the good old twentieth century by now, the two of us, six hundred years away from all this?"

"But I don't understand. What was he doing so far south? Visiting the Scottish court?"

"Well, no. Not exactly. He wasn't lord then, you see. Just an ordinary man, transacting a bit of business. But he's a fair man, Magnus, the truest fellow you'll ever meet. Rather like you, in some respects, now that I think on it. In any case, he saw an injustice being done, and he set about mending it. Luckily he's got a measure of might to those shoulders. Afterward, he offered to bring me home with him, and it seemed to me like a gift from God. So I took it."

"And you taught him English along the way?"

"Something like that. It's a long journey, you understand, without the assistance of the Highland Railway, or even a friendly horse. In return, he taught me his own language."

"How friendly."

Silverton shifted his long limbs, uncrossing his arms and looming over me, so that I stepped back and pressed my spine against the wall. He placed his palm on the cold stone next to my ear.

"I owe Magnus my life, Truelove. Not just the physical miracle of my existence, but whatever scrap of faith has driven me out of bed and into the light, each morning of the past three years. There's no amount of loyalty on earth to equal what I owe him. Nothing at all I wouldn't offer him in return—my life, my blood, my fortune—except one thing."

"What's that?"

"You, of course." He touched the side of my face. "And now I owe him that debt as well. So let's—"

An enormous hand landed on his shoulder. We startled around to find Magnus himself, as if summoned by our conversation, blocking whatever meager light found its way down the hallway with his two massive shoulders. He nodded politely to me and addressed Silverton tersely in Norse, and Silverton answered with a sound of affirmation.

"What's the matter?" I asked.

Silverton gathered up my hand and inclined his head toward Magnus's jaw.

"It seems our presence is required at the banquet, Lady Silverton." He kissed my knuckles, and even in that dusky light, his blue eyes gleamed with the old charm. "As you'll recall, we *are* the guests of honor."

~

I had drunk too much ale, I thought, or perhaps it was all the shocks, delivered one after the other, making me so numb and yet so reckless, the way you might act in a dream when you expect to wake up at any second.

Except there was no waking up. I knew that.

I stared at the scene around me, and in the way of dreams, nothing seemed strange. The homespun clothing was perfectly ordinary; the furniture, the walls, the rushes spread upon the flagstones had become familiar. Across the table, Silverton shared some joke with his companion, and while I couldn't understand the words, the sounds of the vowels and consonants fell easily on my ears. He must have known I observed him, for he turned to me and tilted his head.

"Everything all right?" he asked loudly, for the room was growing hot and raucous.

"No, it is not all right," I shouted back, but I was lying. Or rather, it was not all right because it was. It was strange because it wasn't strange, because my senses had so quickly adjusted to this new world around me, because my human nature was adapting with such frightening ease to these circumstances that ought to level me.

Silverton's eyes narrowed in concern. He started to rise, but Magnus placed a hand on his shoulder to stop him and climbed to his own feet. Instantly the hall went quiet, but still Magnus waited. He looked down one side of the table, fastening on each man, and then down the other side, and his inspection was so thorough I had time to sit there and wonder how he had man-

aged this impromptu feast, how he had accomplished this afternoon's work without the slightest sign of strain. His big fingers
rested on the edge of the table; his eyes shone keenly beneath his
thick brow. When he spoke, he said the words slowly, as if to
make himself plain to the meanest understanding, and I gazed at
his extraordinary face in something like rapture, the way certain
objects fascinate when your senses are confused by drink. The
smell of fish and grease and ale was beginning to make me
queasy, but I didn't care. I heard Silverton's voice in my head.

The truest fellow you'll ever meet.

I owe Magnus my life.

As I stared, I noticed for the first time that he wore a simple
gold chain about his neck, more like a symbol of office than decoration, and that the center link in this chain was larger than the
others. It bore a design of some kind, and I angled my head to
see it better. The men around me were echoing back some kind
of assent. Magnus turned his head a few degrees, addressing
someone, and I lost sight of the link entirely, forgot its existence,
because something else intruded on my attention. Some animal
instinct, I believe, for when I snapped toward this thing, I found
a man staring at me fiercely, from a seat halfway down the opposite side of the table.

The man with the scar. Thorvar.

He didn't look away, as one usually does when caught staring
at someone else. He kept his gaze upon me, challenging me to
break first, and though I was softened by drink, I wouldn't yield.
He looked sloppy and angry, as if he'd been drinking a fair quantity himself, and his dark beard bore the crumbs of his dinner.
Hostility crackled between us. In my belly, I felt the coldness of
fear, but also anger. I moved my hand to my pewter cup of ale,
half-full, and I never knew whether I meant to finish the drink
or to hurl it at him, because someone's hand closed around my

elbow and urged me upward, and it was not Magnus but Silverton. Silverton, who had come around the table and now clasped my hand with both of his, looked upon me with adoring eyes, and around us both the men roared a kind of approval that crosses all bounds of time and language.

"What's happening?" I asked. But I knew. I felt it in the heat of the men along the table, in the nature of the sounds they made. I felt it in my crashing heart, my shaking fingers.

Silverton said, "Our wedding night, apparently."

Then he bent his head and kissed me, right there in front of everybody, right there beneath the gaze of his lord.

∽

The room to which he led me was a large, familiar rectangle, hung with tapestries. A brazier stood in one corner, and several rugs covered the stone floor. I went to one of the windows, set deep in the wall, and I knew before gazing through that it overlooked the sea cliffs. "Whose room is this?" I asked.

"Mine."

"Yours?" I turned in amazement. He was stretching his long arms to the ceiling, and beyond him I saw a pair of chairs and a carved wooden bed, overhung by a canopy and clothed in rich blankets. "But this is a nobleman's room!"

"How do you know that?"

"Because I've seen it before. It's one of the principal rooms of the castle."

He shrugged. "I happen to be a terribly important man, Truelove, at least as far as Magnus is concerned. Mind you, I don't sleep here very often. I don't like the life at court, such as it is. I prefer my hovel near the sea, where nobody finds me odd, and there aren't quite so many barbs pointed in my direction. Still, it's nice to have a bolt-hole handy, when one's up late with the minstrels and doesn't wish to walk home through the wind and rain in the dark of night."

"Minstrels."

"Do you disapprove of minstrels, too?"

My head spun with questions, but I was too tired and had drunk too much ale. I set my hand on the window ledge and remembered how Max had stood right here, had placed his own palm exactly where mine now rested. For an instant, I closed my eyes and tried to find him. But there was nothing. No tingle of electricity in the bones of my fingers. No faint pulse reaching me across the abyss of time.

I opened my eyes. "You found me here, didn't you? In this room."

"Not quite. Magnus found you first."

"What?"

"You lay asleep on my bed. He sent for me straightaway."

I stared at the bed, and then at Silverton. "I see," I whispered.

"So I carried you back to my hut, in the dead of night, so as not to attract any unwelcome attention. The trouble is, one can't really keep a secret so delectable as yourself, Truelove, in a small village like this."

I shook my head. All at once, the room seemed large and cold and alien. I suppose I must have wavered or some such sign of weakness, because Silverton stepped forward and caught me by the shoulders.

"Look at you," he said. "I ought to have stopped that nonsense downstairs hours ago."

I shook my head again.

"Time to rest, Truelove. Come to bed."

"It's not bedtime."

"Yes, it is. Come along, now."

"But I need—I require—"

"There's a pot under the bed. I shall give you a moment's privacy, if you like."

I stood for a moment or two after he left, not because I was loath to make use of such a primitive device—those of you who regularly visit English country palaces, as I must, will surely know what still awaits you—but because I could not bring my thoughts into order. I felt myself balancing on the verge of madness, as if one step might send me falling from the brink. The evening breeze tumbled through the window, full of the endless light of a northern summer, and for a flash of an instant I imagined how it would feel to force myself through the opening and spring free, free.

Don't be a fool, snapped a voice nearby.

I whirled around, but no other creature inhabited the room with me. No small, queenly image. I pressed one hand to my forehead. A gust of wind flew through my hair, so sharp and cold it might have been November.

Don't be a fool, the voice said again, more kindly.

I closed the wooden shutters over the window and stumbled to the bed.

✍

When I was finished, I covered the pot with a cloth and closed the remaining shutters. The brazier was unlit, and my eyes took some time to adjust to the darkness. Silverton had been gone for some time. I reached without thinking for my father's silver watch, but my grasping fingers found only the cloth of my dress and nothing more. No watch. Not even time itself.

"Oh, God," I whispered. The distant sounds of merriment drifted through the walls. I sat on one of the chairs next to the cold brazier and gazed around the dusky room, and for the first time I noticed the shape of a small wooden chest resting against the wall, opposite the foot of the bed, nearly lost in the shadow of the tapestry that hung above it.

A rush of blood filled my veins.

It's only a chest, I told myself, just an ordinary chest. *There must be dozens of them inside these walls.*

Still, I found myself rising from the chair. The dark, cool air moved against my skin. I grasped the bedpost for support—my limbs were so weak, my head so muddled—and stepped carefully around the corner of the bed to kneel before this object, this thing, this wooden capsule. I ran my hands over the top and down the sides—was it the right size? I couldn't positively say— to grasp the edges of the lid.

It was locked.

What did you expect? demanded an imperious voice, from the opposite corner of the room.

I jumped and turned, and again I saw nothing there.

"Where are you?" I called out.

Here.

A faint blue light seemed to shimmer by the window. An instant later, it was gone.

"Why can't I see you?"

Why do you think? I had trouble enough finding you as it is. Foolish, foolish girl. Did I not warn you—?

A knock sounded on the door. "Truelove! It's me."

"It's Silverton," I whispered.

Well, answer him! He's your husband, after all.

"He's not—"

The door swung open. Silverton's face appeared in the crack of light, all bent with concern. "Truelove? Can I come in?"

"Of course."

He sidled through the doorway and shut the portal firmly

behind him. "Why didn't you answer me? And what the devil are you—"

"This is locked."

"Of course it's locked."

"Do you have a key?"

"Perhaps," he said suspiciously. "Why do you need one?"

I held out my hand. "To open it, obviously."

"Well, I don't have it with me."

"Why not?"

"Because I wasn't expecting to spend the night here! I say, you're acting rather queer. What the devil's so important about that chest?"

I hit the lid with my open palm. "Because it might be the chest I'm looking for. The one that lay in the dungeon all those years, the one with the suit inside."

"Suit? What suit?"

"The selkie suit!"

He blinked—twice, slowly, as if waking up from a long nap. "I'm afraid I haven't the slightest clue what you're talking about. A selkie suit? There's nothing inside that chest but a few clothes of mine. Ceremonial stuff. Are you saying you found it? On the other side, I mean?"

I sat back on my heels. "I don't know. It might be this one, or another one. The point is, it exists somewhere, and I think—I wonder—maybe in order to go home, in order for Max to find us—"

Silverton strode across the room, fell to his knees in front of me, seized my shoulders. "Go *home*? For God's sake, Truelove. We're not *going* home. Don't you realize? *This* is home."

"This is *not* home!"

"Maybe not, but it's all you've got, Truelove. There is no hope of anything else. Nobody's going to save you, nobody's going to send you back where you came from. There's no hope."

"That's not true. I won't give up."

"It's no use. Don't you see? This is all there is."

"That's not true. That's not true."

He slid his arms around my back and gathered me to his chest. "I know. I know what you're thinking. How you feel. Believe me. My God, how I railed. How I raged. But it's no use. That world, it's gone, it's lost."

"It is *not* lost. It is *not* gone."

"Not forever, maybe. But we'll be gone by then. This is our world now, Truelove, and believe me, it's infinitely better now that there's two of us in it. At least as far as I'm concerned. I only wish—"

"Wish what?"

He sighed into my hair. "Of course I would have done anything to spare you this. But since you're here—since it's done—"

My arms had crept around his waist. I was not quite sobbing, but I was close. *Gone. Lost.* The finality of those words, the desolation. I thought of Max, of the great mansion in Belgrave Square, of my comfortable bedchamber and my dear, dirty, bustling, striving London. Of railway carriages and hot tea and the familiar, sensible sound of the English language.

"It's not done," I said. "There's always hope."

He sighed again, more deeply, and we knelt there on the flagstones while the salt wind whistled through the cracks in the shutters. Beneath my head, Silverton's heart thumped steadily, the same heart as ever. The heat of his body seeped into mine.

He is your husband now, said the Queen, in a tone of either satisfaction or resignation: I couldn't quite tell.

I lifted my head.

"What's the matter?" asked Silverton.

"We aren't really married, are we?"

He paused delicately. Lifted one eyebrow. Looked terribly

handsome, even underneath all that golden beard. "Why do you ask?" he said.

"Because it matters!"

"Does it?"

"Of course it does. We can't possibly be married."

"Magnus says otherwise."

"Damn Magnus."

"Now that's ungrateful. He saved our hides, didn't he? Anyway, we've got to be married. It won't work otherwise."

"What won't work?"

He frowned. My hands fell away from his waist. After a moment, his arms dropped, too. He rose to his feet and helped me up, one aching knee after another, and turned me around to unbutton the bodice of my dress.

"This damned dress," he said. "The cause of today's mischief. If you will insist on wearing unusual clothing—"

"It's not unusual. Where we were going, where we were *supposed* to go, it's not unusual."

"Truelove. We're not going back. Strike that idea from your mind. It will only bring you misery."

The dress fell away from my chest. I stepped out of it. My shoes were already off, lying side by side next to the chair I had occupied earlier. I didn't remember taking them off. Silverton found the laces of my corset and loosened them.

"Will you please consider it?" he said softly.

"Consider what?"

"Me."

I moved away and removed my corset with my own hands. I stood in my petticoats without embarrassment. Perhaps I ought to have felt embarrassment, but I didn't. The drink, maybe, or my own fatigue, or shock, or the sense of intimacy that had grown between us. And yet my fingers were trembling. My skin was warm, despite the chill Orkney draft. I crept to the bed and pulled down the bedclothes.

Silverton followed me. "I don't understand. Is it such a terrible thing, to be my wife? You can't possibly have the same objections as before. I've got no awkward bloody title in this world, no dukedom in my future. No clandestine career, chasing treason across the globe. Nothing to do but devote myself to a quiet, faithful life with you." He touched my hair. "And you care for me."

I paused with my hand on the linen. A bed, I thought. A real bed.

"Yes," I said. "We're equals here. But what happens when we return?"

"Damn it all, Truelove! We're not going to return. Will you listen to yourself? What happens if some mystical wand waves over our heads and sends us six hundred years into the future?"

"Max sent us here to begin with. He will not rest until he's found us again."

"But he won't succeed. Think. If he had, he'd have done it by now."

The bed was quite high. I lifted my foot and braced my toe on the bedframe, and then I heaved myself onto the feather mattress and brought the bedclothes up to my chin. Silverton stood nearby, glowering and shadowed. I saw the outline of his long hair, the tiny glint of his beard.

"You're welcome to share the bed, of course," I said generously, "since there's nowhere else for you to sleep."

The Fisherman was gone for seven nights, while the Lady grew more wretched each hour, for he was dearer to her than her own flesh, and his absence was like the absence of her own breath. On the morning of the eighth day, she went to the shore to look for the return of her husband, yet instead of the Fisherman's humble boat she saw a strange craft sailing toward her with all the might of the wind. The Lady turned to her children and said, 'Go, my darlings, hide in our cottage, and if some evil befalls me, run for the village as fast as you can and ring the bell of the church three times, for then I will know you are safe . . .'

THE BOOK OF TIME, A. M. HAYWOOD (1921)

Ten

I woke on my stomach, to the gentle prodding of somebody's hand on my shoulder. For a moment, I thought I was a child, and the hand was my father's.

"Come along, Truelove. Rise and shine."

Silverton's voice, abundantly cheerful. I bolted upright and felt a wash of cold air upon my skin. I looked down in terror. To my relief, my chemise remained in view, crumpled and far, far too thin. I crossed my arms over my chest and looked over my shoulder at Silverton, who was fully dressed and presently opening the wooden shutters wide to the early sunlight.

"Are you mad? Close those at once!"

"It's morning, my love." He braced himself on the ledge and breathed in deep. "Good, clean sea air. Take in a lungful. Clears the head wonderfully."

I wrapped the bedclothes around me and glanced at the hollow by my side. "Did you—?"

"Sleep with you? Of course I did. As you so astutely pointed out, I had no choice, except to creep downstairs and find a pallet in the kitchen, which would certainly excite comment in a new bridegroom." He grinned. "You cuddled me."

"I did not!"

"I'm afraid you did. Took me rather aback, at first. And then I understood you might be cold, so I did what was proper."

"And what was that?"

"Cuddled you right back, of course. Do you mean to say you don't remember?"

"Not a thing."

"Dash it all." He tossed a woolen garment on the bed. "In any case, while you were wallowing in luxury, I made my way down-stairs and found you some suitable clothing. Don't thank me. It's no more than any devoted husband would do, to ensure his wife's properly dressed. Why, what's the matter?"

I snatched the dress and made a tent with the bedclothes. "You're far too cheerful. It's oppressive."

"I'm afraid I'm always cheerful in the morning, Truelove. Another of my many sins. Don't you remember, when we were in the Mediterranean together, hunting after Max?"

"I always assumed it was because of—*well*."

"Not at all. You'll recall, that charming interlude with Mrs. Poulakis took place but once. You and I shared a great many more mornings together that had nothing to do with—*well*. More's the pity."

I emerged from the bedclothes, fully dressed. Silverton stepped back to inspect me, and his eyes grew soft. "Here," he said, and he drew a thick silver chain from the leather pouch at his waist.

"What's this?"

"A belt. You link it around your waist, like so." He reached around me and fastened the chain in place. "A wedding gift."

"From Magnus?"

"No. From me." He gave the end a little tug, as if to make sure it was properly fastened, and then he stepped back again. Though the sunlight doused his face, I couldn't read his expression. He neither smiled nor frowned, only studied my midsection as you might study a portrait on a wall. "The married women generally wear them here."

"But we're not married."

"Maybe not," he said, "but the point is that everybody *thinks* we're married. Wouldn't you agree?"

He held out his hand. After the slightest hesitation, I placed my palm against his, and he drew me gently to stand before him on the floor.

"The stone's cold," I whispered.

"I'll get your shoes."

By the time we reached the gatehouse and ducked outside, the clouds had rushed in to cover the sun, and a fine drizzle came down on our heads. Silverton didn't seem to notice. I drew up the hood of my cloak and glanced sideways.

"Aren't you going to get wet?" I asked.

"Why, yes. I suppose I am." He took my hand and hurried me across the courtyard, whistling.

"Don't you mind?"

"Of course not. When it rains, the fish come to the surface."

"The fish? What fish?"

"The fish I catch, Truelove. Didn't I tell you? I'm a fisherman by trade."

We hardly spoke as we walked down the wet lane to the village, and to Silverton's hut beyond. I wasn't sure what to say. He must have been joking, of course; he was a man of some standing at Magnus's court, despite his preference for simple living, and I simply couldn't imagine the charming, gregarious Marquess of Silverton engaged in so humble and so solitary an occupation as fishing. So I didn't ask him any questions, for fear he would mock me for believing him. I hunkered deep into my cloak instead, as the drizzle turned into a shower, and tried to make sense of everything. How I might make some kind of contact with Max, how I might help him to help us.

"Who's J——?" Silverton asked suddenly, just as the hut came into view.

I stumbled on the path, and his hand tightened around mine, saving me from the fall. "J——? I don't understand."

"Last night. When you cuddled into my chest. You called me J——. Is that the chap, then?"

There was no point in lying. "Yes," I said.

"Ah." His hand stayed snug around mine, the rhythm of his stride remained steady. "Your life is your own, of course. I only wish to know whether he hurt you. And whether, I suppose, you still have some regard for him."

"I have no regard left for him at all," I said. "I can't imagine why I said his name."

"Habit, perhaps?"

"The habit was of very short duration. But I suppose it's possible." I hesitated. "I'm sorry if I caused you any pain. I assure you—"

He lifted my hand and kissed it. We had nearly reached the hut, and I saw something I hadn't noticed before: a length of netting, hung neatly upon a row of hooks along the back wall of the hut.

"Think nothing of it, my dear. I was only curious. Here we are. Shall I carry you over the threshold?"

"Certainly not."

But he scooped me up anyway and heaved me through the doorway, groaning so loudly as he went that I couldn't help laughing. He set me down in the middle of the floor and said he'd be back directly, he was just going to fill the bucket from the well.

"I can do that," I said.

"Do you know how?"

"I can learn."

So we filled the bucket together and brought it inside, and Silverton laid a fire and showed me where to find yesterday's bread and the cheese and the apples, if I was hungry.

"But what about you?" I asked.

"Me? I'm going fishing. It's late, of course, but not too late to catch something for supper, if I'm lucky. Tomorrow, on the other hand—why, what's the matter?"

"I thought you were joking!"

"Joking? Why should I joke about a thing like that?"

"But I don't understand. Why on earth?"

"To make a living, Truelove. Everybody has to make a living."

"But you're—you're—"

He smiled. "Not anymore, am I? And I couldn't simply live off Magnus's largesse. For one thing, the other men were jealous enough of my influence. It doesn't take much to get a man accused of sorcery and magic and all manner of dangerous habits. Or a woman, as you've learned. Magnus was the one who suggested the fishing trade. Gave me the boat and the nets."

"But what am I to do while you're gone?"

"My dear. I suppose you'll have to discover that for yourself. You're a clever, resourceful woman. The island is your oyster, I believe. I'd ask you to join me, but I well remember your unfortunate aversion to seaborne adventure." He was gathering apples and bread and putting them in the leather pouch at his waist. "Don't worry, you'll be all right. They daren't touch you now.

And you've got your silver belt for good measure, just in case anyone's minded to forget whom you belong to."

"I belong only to myself," I began, but he was already pulling a blade from the basket near the hearth and testing its edge with his finger and didn't seem to notice.

"Of course," he said, holding it out to me, "it never hurts to have an insurance policy, of sorts. You can stash that in your pocket. Just don't fall on it."

I snatched it from his hand and started to make some indignant reply. He leaned in and kissed my open mouth.

"Ah, that's better," he said. "A tender kiss good-bye from my bride, before I stride out the door for the day's labor. I suppose it's too much to hope that you'll have my pipe and slippers waiting for me on my return? Newspaper folded and dinner hot on the table? Cherubs scrubbed and cheerful on the rug before the hearth?"

With that, he fled for the door while I searched for something to throw.

ℐ

Not until later did I realize what he was about that morning, with his good cheer and his kiss and his swift absorption into the routine of daily labor. I only remember staring at the door and listening to the sound of his whistle in the cool, damp air, rising above the noise of the drizzle on the roof, and feeling nothing but a profound, almost admiring astonishment.

And then, as the whistling died away to leave only the miserable rain, the creep of uneasiness.

I stood for some time in the center of the room, considering the unexpected turn of the day's events. It was still early, and the hours stretched ahead, as interminable as the rain. First I went to the window, trying to catch some glimpse of him, and then I put on my cloak and went outside, down to the pebbled edge of the shore, and at last I saw him, scrambling about what must have been the harbor, untying a long wooden boat from its mooring against a crude dock. The wind was picking up, but he didn't seem to notice, any more than he minded the rain. He climbed into the boat and found an oar, which he used to maneuver the boat into open water, at which point he unfurled a sail from the single mast. His movements were sure and graceful, and I remember thinking to myself, *Why, he's happy. He's enjoying himself.*

The sail filled with wind, and Silverton settled down to the tiller in the stern. The boat swept past the shore, and as he came alongside that piece of rock—you couldn't really call it a beach— on which I stood, he looked toward me and raised his hand, as if he'd known I was there all along. I couldn't see his face, but I knew he was smiling.

✒

When Silverton's boat had shrunk to a mere speck on the rough, rippling sea, I turned and went back into the hut. I was cold and wet, and I warmed myself by the peat fire, which had gained strength in my absence. I added more fuel and longed for tea. Just one cup. Even coffee would do. Something civilized. I stared at my pink, chilled fingers and said aloud, "It's up to you, Truelove. You're a clever, resourceful woman. The island's your oyster."

I half expected an answer from some corner of the room. A queenly voice admonishing me for my folly, offering imperious advice I had no intention of taking. But there was nothing. No Queen, or my father, either. I was alone.

I rose from the fire and went to the chest under the window.

It wasn't my chest, of course. It was too big, and there was no secret compartment. No, this was an ordinary chest, containing only Silverton's ordinary things, but I opened it anyway. The hinges squeaked faintly. The scent of damp wool and leather rose from within, and I lifted a few layers of clothing, neatly folded, until I came to the object at the bottom: the object for which I had searched the other night, before Silverton himself interrupted me.

I drew it out from beneath the clothes, the various items, and carried it to the pallet by the wall. The leather was smooth and unmarred, almost exactly as it had looked in the shop where I had purchased it; almost identical to its appearance in the railway carriage en route to Edinburgh; practically the same as I had last seen it, in my bedroom at the North British Hotel. Perhaps the buckle was a little tarnished, and no wonder, in this climate. It was not locked, however, so I sprung open the fastening without hindrance and stuck my hand inside.

If Silverton were speaking the truth—and I had no reason to doubt him—the papers in my fist had lain inside this portfolio for three years, even though by my own clock, I had placed them there only a week earlier. The paradox was nearly impossible to comprehend, and as I stared at the first page, and the neat, familiar lines of my own handwriting, it seemed I had laid that ink in another age. Well, I had. But another age in my own lifetime, more like the years that had passed in Silverton's reckoning. How quaint, how earnest, how utterly naïve were those words I had written in my study in Belgrave Square, the one Max had kindly fitted up for me in the ducal town house until my office at the Haywood Institute for the Study of Time should be ready for occupancy. The words blurred before me, and I wiped at the corners of my eyes.

I don't know what you expect to find.

I looked up.

Over here. By the fire.

I turned my gaze to the hearth, and I thought I saw a faint shimmer in the air, distorting the black curve of the cook pot, the iron tongs resting against the stones of the fireplace.

"I don't know, either," I said, "but at least it's something, isn't it?"

No answer.

"Why did you take the trouble to find me here, if you haven't got anything useful to say?"

Because I must, I suppose. One does one's duty.

"And how am I your duty?"

My dear girl. Haven't you discovered the reason for that yet? I sometimes believe you aren't nearly as clever as your mother. Certainly not in the essential ways.

"I haven't the slightest idea what you mean. How do you know my mother?"

Did. How did *I know your mother.*

"Isn't she there with you?" I asked, with a certain degree of irony.

There was a faint sniff. *No.*

"I don't know why you should haunt me like this, when my own mother doesn't. You're the last person I need about me. I don't even know you."

But I know you, and that's all that's necessary. Your father—

I sat forward. "Yes? My father? Is he there?"

Not at present. This sort of journey requires a great deal of effort, you understand. I don't know why you must insist on getting yourself into these terrible fixes. And even now—

"I only did what I thought was right."

Yes. (A sigh.) *That's the trouble, isn't it? These things always begin with someone meaning to do right. Well, you've done it now, and I can't say I'm as disappointed as I ought to be. You have that scoundrel Silverton to keep watch over you, and given the available alternatives, I suppose you've done well enough. He has his faults, but he shall take great care to ensure that your days of unseemly adventure are quite over. I must admit, as I watched the ceremony yesterday, I felt a certain—*

"You were deceived. I am not married to Lord Silverton."

I beg your pardon. I saw a marriage ceremony.

"Nonsense. It was a farce, a convenience. I never gave my consent."

Phisht. You're married in the eyes of the law. The eyes of the world. In my eyes, which are the only eyes that matter.

"And when we return to the twentieth century? Our own world, our old habits. He will regret matrimony soon enough, and as for me . . ."

She waited, shimmering, for me to finish my sentence. She seemed to have moved closer, near the chest, where the grim light from the window distorted her shade into tiny ripples of air.

As for you? (Gently.)

"I will be miserable at his misery."

Either she was thinking this over, or she was fading entirely. She seemed to make some movement, and I had the idea she was sitting on the chest. As I turned my attention back to the papers in my lap, she spoke at last.

And if you never return, my dear? You are prepared to forgo all the pleasures of marriage, all the comforts of a family to sustain you in this wilderness?

"I shall never give up trying to return. I shall never give up hope."

You haven't answered the question, my dear.

I stared keenly at her, or rather the disturbance of light and atmosphere that marked her presence. "Why do you ask me these things? *Will* we return? Can you tell me that, at least?"

No, she said simply, and before I could ask her what she meant—whether she was forbidden to tell me, or whether she really possessed no knowledge of my future—the air next to the window went still.

I rose from the pallet with a cry. The papers slid to the floor.

I stepped over them, toward the window, and fished the empty space frantically with my two hands, calling her name, but my palms remained empty, my cries went unanswered. A few drops of rain reached through the deep window recess and wet the side of my cheek. I let out a long, wild scream of frustration and dropped to my knees, hitting the chest over and over with my fists, until all my remaining spirit was gone and I rested my head and my arms on the smooth wooden lid and lay there, staring at the wall, gasping for breath.

At what time I realized I was not alone, I cannot say. I felt the stir of wind first, the chill, damp breeze cutting through the warmth of the peat fire. I thought this was only a gust making its way through the window, for I had not closed the shutters, and then I felt his presence: hot, large, steaming with rain and patience.

I lifted my head and turned. My right hand reached for the dagger in my pocket.

The room was dark, and he stood silhouetted against the gray sky outside, filling the doorway, smelling of smoke and wool and perspiration. It was not until he stepped forward into the room that I saw who he was.

Magnus.

❦

I am accustomed to large men. They seem to recur in my life with extraordinary persistence. My father was of average height, but His Grace, the Duke of Olympia—not Max, but his august great-uncle and predecessor, that great lion of the previous century—was a giant. He reached nearly six and a half feet, topped by a head of hair so silver as to be white, and the loose-limbed breadth of him, even as he reached his ninth decade, made him seem as if he contained all England inside his skin. Sometimes I believed he did.

But for all his great size and formal bearing, the duke was only a man. He ate and drank, he laughed and occasionally swore, he suffered deeply and he triumphed mightily, he fell in love late in life and never stopped until his last breath. When my father died, the duke informed me that he should be grateful if I did him the honor of stepping into Mr. Truelove's position as private secretary, and he said this in so kind and so delicate a manner, so changed from his usual air of immense authority, that I accepted at once. Thus the fateful trajectory of my present life began.

I remember one day in particular, the first day of my employment. I arrived early in his study in Belgrave Square, dressed in mourning, eyes and fingers sharp with nervousness. I remember staring at his hands in awe, at his brow, at the size of his jaw. His coffee cup was empty. In my anxiety, I asked if I could bring him more. He stared at me in amazement and rang for the maid instead, and I sat there in my chair before his desk, crushed and inadequate, until the duchess blew into the room. (She is an American, you know, and will insist on blowing into rooms.) She looked at me and she looked at him, and she asked her husband what the devil he'd said to dear Miss Truelove.

How bemused he looked! I can see that expression even now, bewilderment mingled with adoration for the woman before him. He said he'd no idea. Something about coffee.

The duchess sighed and went to the tray of liquors on the elegant Chinese chest along the wall. She uncorked a crystal decanter of what I later learned was an aged Scotch whiskey and filled his coffee cup. "There," she said. "That should tide you over."

Then she turned to me. "Darling, he may be twice your size, but I daresay he's nervous as a rabbit to have a pretty young thing like you in his study, taking down his every word. Do try to be kind to the poor fellow. He's only a man, after all."

She left the room, and I fully expected His Grace to bluster and storm, but instead he reached for his coffee cup, sat back in his chair, and drank the whole measure without pause. "She's right, of course," he said, sighing. "She always is."

As the days and weeks went on, a succession of terribly important men went in and out of the Duke of Olympia's study, many of them large in physical dimensions as well as grandeur, but I never forgot the duchess's advice. However grand, however tall, however strong, they were only men, nervous as rabbits in the presence of a woman.

For the most part, I tried to be kind.

ℐ

So I held my ground before the advancing Magnus—I had not much room to maneuver, in any case—and kept my right hand in my pocket, wrapped around my dagger.

He is not so tall as old Olympia, I thought. Nor so broad as that fellow who visited once, the pugilist with the broken nose, who looked so fearsome until he broke the duchess's favorite Ming vase and cried with remorse.

I met Magnus's bright, keen gaze. *The truest fellow you'll ever meet*, Silverton had said. *Rather like you, in some respects.*

He married me to Silverton with his own hands, I thought. His own words.

He stopped in the middle of the room, a few feet away. Opened his mouth and frowned, as if groping for words.

I stood expectantly, trying to remember if there was any tradition of droit du seigneur among the Norsemen. (Or, God forbid, the Vikings.)

"Hello," he said at last.

"Hello," I replied, and then added, "my lord."

He shook his head, whether to dismiss the honorific or to express his own frustration with the English language.

Try to be kind, I thought.

I cleared my throat and spoke carefully, pronouncing each sound. "What brings you here, my lord? Silverton is out fishing."

He frowned. "Sil-ver-ton?"

"My new husband."

"Oh! I forget this. His name is Fingal here. This means *fair-haired stranger*."

Magnus's accent was thick, unpolished, as if he didn't have much practice speaking English. Well, of course he didn't. And yet he was trying hard; I could almost feel his concentration on each word, his determination to get it right. To please me.

I released the knife and drew my hand from my pocket. My palm was damp. I wriggled the fingers, which had grown stiff with tension. "Thank you for helping us yesterday," I said.

"You're welcome." He hesitated. "I want to question—I want to ask to you—"

I gestured to the stools next to the wooden table. "Maybe we can sit down?"

He smiled. "Yes, please."

We sat. Magnus overflowed his stool, each sturdy leg planted like a tree on the floor, bent at each massive knee. In my own world, I would have rung for tea. Would have poured him a cup and asked if he took cream or sugar. Offered him biscuits. Here, I had nothing to offer. I felt he wouldn't take it, anyway. He had something to say to me. Something, as he said, to ask me: something important, something vital to him. He rested his forearms on his thighs and linked his fingers as a bridge between his two legs, twiddling the thumbs as he stared fiercely toward the window.

"This is like my hut," he said.

"Your hut?"

"I was a fisherman. Fingal, he has my boat now. My nets."

"I know he's grateful for them. He wants to make his own living. I think he likes the peace. Before, he lived a life of great—"

"I had a wife." Magnus turned his gaze back to me, and I was startled by the ferocious longing in his expression. "She is gone now."

"I'm so sorry. How long ago?"

"Three years."

"How terrible for you." I moved to touch him, and held back at the last instant. He was not at peace, not wanting to be touched; he was scintillating, burning with something. His knuckles were white, his thumbs pressed together like a pair of steel plates. I ventured, "Was it—was she—"

He struck suddenly, grabbing my hand with his own and holding it so tightly, I could scarcely breathe. I gasped and tried to rise, but he held me down and leaned toward me, so I could see the streaks of his irises, even in this dim, gloomy light.

"She came from the sea," he said. "She came from a different land. Like you."

"Oh!"

His hand relaxed around mine. "We have two children."

"Then at least—I'm so sorry—when she died—"

Magnus's hand tightened again, more fiercely than before. "Fingal. He loves you. He says—said—many times of you. Now you are here."

"Yes. Now I'm here."

He turned toward me and took my other hand, holding them both within his. His expression lost a little of its ferocity, but remained earnest. Still containing some tension I could not comprehend. Grief, I supposed. The grief of a good, faithful man who had loved his wife.

"You will love my friend Fingal," he said. "You will be his good wife. You will stay in his house and have joy."

"I don't—I can't—"

"He will protect you."

"Yes. He will protect me."

"And you will stay with him."

"Of course."

Magnus nodded and released my hands. "I will protect you, too. I hope—Fingal and you, sometimes you come to visit me. I like to speak the English. To keep—to speak—"

"To practice speaking?"

"Yes! To practice. Maybe you practice the English with my children."

"If you like," I said warily.

He gazed at me without speaking. The bones of his face were so thick and heavy, so plain as to be almost beautiful. His skin covered them like a thin, finely worked leather, and I thought of Silverton's skin, taking on the same texture, and knew it was the North Sea, the Orkney weather, a fisherman's skin. That was it. Silverton was not Silverton anymore. He was not a marquess or a spy or a dashing chap about town. He was a fisherman named Fingal, living quietly in his hut in a remote, windblown village by the sea, six hundred years ago.

And maybe Magnus was thinking about my skin, the bones of my own face, because he lifted one of his huge hands and cupped my cheek gently, testing the texture with his thumb.

"Stay," he said. "Stay with Fingal. He loves you so."

⁂

By afternoon, the drizzle had eased. I ate some bread and cheese and went outside for a walk; in the village, I found the bakery and the blacksmith and the alemonger. In the harbor, the fishing boats began to return, selling the day's catch to the fish merchant, but Silverton was not among them. Though the men and women cast me curious gazes, nobody approached me. It was as if I carried some kind of disease. No matter. I walked because I needed to think, that was all. Certainly not because I desired intercourse with my fellow human beings.

The hour grew late, and still there was no sign of Silverton. I returned to the hut and studied the notes and drawings I had made—these notebooks of research on the nature of travel through time, which had then traveled through time itself. None of it was much use. Max and I had learned so much more in the few days of our stay in Scotland. But I didn't really consult those papers for the information they contained.

One page only interested me: the drawing on the cliffs of Naxos.

Still inside its notebook, one page among many. The lines of ink so familiar to me, I could see each one when I closed my eyes.

And the figure of the woman—the one I had noticed on the drawing inside the secret compartment of the chest Magnusson had shown us—was not there.

I wiped my finger delicately across the empty space where she ought to be, as if I might rub her into existence, but the paper remained exactly as I had first created it. The woman did not exist. She had not yet been drawn.

↼⟆

I had no way of knowing what time it was when the door opened at last and Silverton arrived home, looking as if he had been run through a steam engine, and smelling rather strongly of fish.

"Why, what's the matter?" I asked.

"Oh, a spot of bother with the winds, that's all. Then some net to be repaired." He tossed a package on the table and followed it with a pair of coins. "There's our supper. I was late getting in, after everybody else had sold his catch, so I wasn't able to get much for my trouble. If you don't mind, I'm just going to wash. Can you cook a fish, do you think?"

"I'm—I suppose I can."

"Just chuck it in that iron dish and bake it in the fire. I'll be back in a quarter hour."

He turned and left before I could reply. I stared at the lump on the table, wrapped in cloth, and went to the hearth to find the iron dish, which turned out to be a shallow pot. I unwrapped the fish and, having never cooked such a thing in my life—having never really cooked much at all—followed Silverton's brief instructions exactly. It was a large fish, silver-scaled, still whole, eyes round and shocked at this unexpected turn of events. I stuck it in the pot and stuck the pot in the fire, directly on the glowing peat, and rinsed my hands in the bucket by the hearth.

Silverton returned a few minutes later. His hair was wet, his skin was pink. He set a bottle on the table and went to warm his hands at the fire.

"What's this?" I asked.

"Wine. I keep it in the storehouse for special occasions."

"You look exhausted."

"I'm afraid I am." He stared at his hands. "It's not an easy life, I suppose. What did you do all day?"

"I walked. I thought. Magnus came to visit."

Silverton turned. "Did he?"

"You don't seem surprised."

"Maybe I'm not. What did he have to say?"

I considered Silverton's weary face for a moment and went to inspect the fish in its primitive oven. "Just to wish us well, really."

We ate and drank in a strange silence. The fish was delicious, white and flaky and mild. The wine was mere sack, too sweet, but not unpalatable. Outside the window, the sky was deepening in color, and the air grew dim and thick and smoky. Silverton's charm had deserted him. He looked at his food, at the walls. When a gust of wind came through the window, he rose and closed the wooden shutters, and then went to light the crude oil lamp in the middle of the table.

"So, my dear," he said, sitting down again, "what have you been thinking about, all this time?"

"I've been thinking about how we are to return home."

"Of course you have. Did you conclude anything useful?"

"Yes. I've realized how I went about it all wrong. When I had Max send me here, my only object was to rescue you. To bring you back safely. I forgot there's a greater purpose in all this, and my task wasn't—*is* not—to serve my own selfish desires, but to discover that purpose."

Silverton drank his wine, set down the tumbler, and stared at the rim. The lamp's small flame wavered in his eyes. "I don't quite follow you. Am I to understand that *I'm* the object of your selfish desires? You came here only for my sake?"

"I mean I thought my only task was to find you. In my eagerness—in my *determination*—"

"Don't mistake me, Truelove. I have no quarrel with your selfish desires."

"Perhaps not." I finished the wine and cleared our empty plates from the table. "But they shorten our vision, don't they? They make us impatient."

He rose to help me, but I motioned him back. I thought he was weary enough already. He crossed his arms and watched me as I rinsed the plates in the bucket and dried them with the cloth and put them away on the shelf.

"Tell me something, Truelove," he said. "How did you know I was here? How did you know where to find me, I mean. And why the devil did Max send me here in the first place, three years ago?"

"To the first question, because you showed us where to find you. You left us clues."

"Did I? I don't remember doing any such thing."

"Because you haven't, yet. That's in the future, your future. Our future, whatever it is."

"*Our* future," he said slowly.

"And to the second question, I don't know. But I'm beginning to understand, I think, that *this* is why we failed to connect with Max yesterday. We haven't earned it. We haven't yet achieved what we're meant to achieve. And it's not possible for us to return home until we've done it."

"Done what?"

"I don't know! I think—I believe it has something to do with a woman."

"Ah, yes. It always does."

"A particular woman, lost in time as we are. I can only imagine it will become clear, somehow. We'll know what it is when we discover it."

There was a long pause. "I see."

I turned from the shelf and hung the cloth on the hook in the wall. With my hands, I smoothed the folds of my woolen dress.

"And I realized, too, that while Max and I discovered the signs of your having lived here, of having done something vital here, we can only guess whether you then returned—*will* return—to your own world. Our own world. So perhaps—"

"Perhaps what?"

"Perhaps you were right. Perhaps there *is* no returning at all. Perhaps this is all there is. Just to give ourselves up to fate."

He nodded. In the small, flickering light from the lamp, his skin had lost its weary cast, though his face was still too thin and too hard. His hair, loose from its leather tie, fell along the sides of his face in unruly pieces. I went to the chest and opened it, looking for the comb I had seen there earlier. It was made of bone, and the teeth were wide. I closed the chest again and went around the back of Silverton's stool and began to comb his hair.

"So yes, I have been thinking," I said, "and what I think is this. I should set aside any plans for our immediate escape, and instead try to discover why Max sent us here in the first place. What we're meant to do."

"Didn't he remember to tell you that, when he sent you?"

"I don't mean Max as he is now. I mean some future Max, some wiser, more experienced Max, who knows how it all turns out. Who's sticking us about time and place like chess pieces."

"My dear love," Silverton said slowly, almost dreamily, as if his eyes were closed and he was already half-asleep. "You're not making the slightest amount of sense."

"No, I suppose I'm not. Never mind." I laid the comb on the table and ran my fingers through his damp, smooth hair. I felt his fatigue, his longing. He reached up and wrapped his hand loosely around my wrist.

"What are we to do, Truelove?" he asked. "Tell me."

I had no answer. Inside, I was trembling, I was roiling with fear and anticipation and confusion. I felt myself balancing, I felt myself back on that tenuous brink, not quite brave enough to step off and entrust my fate to another. I pulled my wrist free from his grasp and returned the comb to the chest. His gaze followed me; I felt it caress my back. I turned to face him. He rose from the chair. I thought how plain he looked, how noble. I put my hand to the back of my neck.

"I can't reach the fastening," I said. "Could you help me, please?"

He stepped forward. I turned around and lifted my hair as his hands undid the simple ties. He helped me pull the garment over my head, so that I stood in my linens. When he spoke, his voice was hoarse.

"If you don't mean to lie with me, Truelove, tell me now. For God's sake, I can't bear it."

He smelled of the sea, of salt and fish and life. I felt his warmth along the length of my back, his hands around the balls of my shoulders. I took his fingers and led them forward, across my chest, over the curve of my breasts to my stomach. The floor seemed to drop away beneath us, and I was falling irretrievably into light.

The Lady waited bravely by the shore for the arrival of the strange ship, while the wind howled in her ears and the waves rolled at her feet, for she was certain it must bear evil news of her husband, and her grief would know no end. At last the craft made land, and a young man jumped upon the pebbles, wearing a suit such as that in which the Lady herself had arrived in this land. She cried out in fear, but he clasped her hands and said to her, 'Lady, do not be afraid, for I am your son now grown, who has sought you these many years, and I will carry you back to your own country, and the luxury you once knew in my father's house . . .'

THE BOOK OF TIME, A. M. HAYWOOD (1921)

Eleven

❦

Seven months later

The nights had been growing shorter for many weeks, but the air was still dark when I awoke. The force of habit, I suppose. I lay quietly, listening to the soft whistle of the wind against the wooden shutters. Last October, when the weather turned bitter, Silverton started hanging a length of sheepskin over the shutters before we retired to bed, but no amount of insulation could banish the noise of an Orkney gale.

"You can't go out today," I whispered. "It's too fierce."

"Nonsense. A mere zephyr."

"Stay home," I said. "Please."

He didn't answer. His heartbeat struck gently at my back; his breath warmed my hair. Of course he was awake. He always woke before I did, long before the sun found the horizon. The earlier we woke, the longer we could lie like this, not moving, snug in our chrysalis of bedclothes, while the wind blew and the morning gathered, cold and damp, around our noses. I had long since stopped thinking in hours and minutes; time had lost its boundaries, its neat compartments, and we lived by the sun. During the darkest days of winter, we must have spent half our lives in slumber.

In bed, at least. Not always slumber.

When we did sleep, it was the deepest sleep I had ever known, dreamless, so rich and velvet that waking felt like emerging from the bottom of the ocean. I became aware of myself in slow stages, detail by familiar detail, my face and arms and legs, my heavy stomach, the weight of Silverton's arm along my ribs, empty of any desire to be anywhere else except right here, in this particular hollow of this particular bed, enclosed by these particular arms.

By the slight stirring of his body, I knew Silverton would rise soon. I turned in his embrace and tucked my nose into the hollow at the base of his throat.

"Now, Truelove," he said softly. "You know I've got to make a living."

I loved the taste of his skin, the smell of him, the texture. He washed every afternoon when he came home from the harbor, but still the scent of fish clung faintly to his pores, and I loved it, I loved it. How strange that a smell I had once considered disagreeable was now my favorite smell in the world. I touched his collarbone with the tip of my tongue and he let out a long, slow breath. His hand moved down my back to cup my buttocks. I couldn't keep him out of his boat today, I knew, but I could at least keep him in bed with me a little longer before he left.

We took our time, because we had so much of it to spare, handfuls of time that had no meaning and no measurement. Dawn crept around the cracks of the window when at last he finished, gasping, and fell to the sheets beside me. We both wore nightshirts because of the cold, and mine was rucked up almost to my shoulders. He pulled it back down and drew up the blankets to cover me. "Stay here," he said, kissing my lips. "I'll start the fire."

I rolled on my side and watched him drowsily as he threw on his tunic and bent before the hearth. He seemed too lean to me, his muscles too tough and too flat, battered by winter and the hard labor of harvesting the sea. We had plenty to eat, but the food was simple and plain, lacking any richness, and since my courses had ceased in the third month of our union, he made me eat his share of cheese as well as my own. The baby worried him, I knew. When I first told him my suspicions, his face had filled not with joy and pride, as I expected, but with remorse. And though I went on to experience hardly a moment of sickness, though I remained strong and healthy and disgracefully sound, that misgiving had never quite left his eyes. He worried about my confinement, he worried about the crisis of birth. He worried about providing for us both.

"Really," I said once, exasperated, "did the possibility not *once* occur to you, when you were committing yourself to me three times daily?"

"Of course it did. But there's a great deal of difference between the theoretical and the actual. A theoretical infant, sometime in the distant future, is a marvelous thought. An *actual* infant increasing within my wife's womb is positively terrifying."

"This from a man who has cheated death a hundred times."

"But that was only *my* death, Truelove. I can face that possibility with perfect tranquility. *You*, on the other hand—"

I never let him complete that sentence, and to his credit, he was easily distracted from morbid thoughts. He was too naturally ebullient, too naturally amorous to regret the act of love. Instead, he fussed, as he did now. While the fire caught, he poured me a cup of ale and made me sit up and drink every drop—it's good for your lactation, he informed me, having had a long and unembarrassed conversation the other day with the village midwife, who had been scandalized by his interest.

"Lactation? But the babe won't be born until summer," I said.

"It can't hurt, can it? Now, drink up, there's a good girl, while I make your breakfast."

"I can make my own breakfast."

"That doesn't mean you should. Look here—"

But I was already swinging my legs out of bed, already reaching for my woolen dress. "Your health is just as important as mine. Think what it would do to me, if something were to happen to you."

"Nothing's going to happen to me. I'm as strong as an ox, and besides, I've got luck on my side. Tremendously important, luck."

I sliced the bread and laid it on the plates. "Luck? You've been transported without consent from a world of wealth and privilege and railways to a world of primitive barbarism and unsatisfactory wine."

He turned, caught me around the waist, and pulled me against him for a long, deep kiss. "As it happens, Truelove, I consider that the luckiest thing that ever happened to me."

"Then you're mad."

"Consider, my dear. Would you ever have agreed to marry me, if you weren't so utterly devoid of alternatives as you are here?"

"I never *did* agree to marry you, if you'll recall. I only resigned myself to the necessity, after the fact of our *soi-disant* wedding. In any case," I said, pulling away, "I expect you'd have plied me with wine and seduced me eventually, with the same result."

"Ah, you're happy, Truelove. Admit it."

"I admit nothing."

"I make you happy. You're splendidly happy, the happiest, most adored, most well-loved woman in the British Isles—"

"These aren't yet the British Isles. And even if they were—"

He dropped the apple he was slicing, gathered me up, and carried me to the bed. "Admit it," he said, stabbing my neck with kisses, "admit it."

"Stop! Oh, God, your beard—it tickles—"

"Admit it!"

"Yes!"

"*Yes, dear husband, I'm deliriously happy here in this crude hovel with you.* Say it, Truelove."

"Yes—dear husband—oh, stop! I'm happy, yes!"

"*In this crude hovel—*"

"This awful, dirty, cramped, fish-smelling hovel—"

"*Because I love you.*"

"Because I love you," I said softly, and he stopped kissing me, stopped tickling me, and we sat together, limbs tangled, watching the fire gain strength in the hearth, while the March drizzle began to crackle against the roof.

෴

The bed had been given to us by Magnus, as a wedding present. If it was not exactly magnificent—that would have been ridiculous, in a cottage like ours—it was sturdy and comfortable, furnished with a feather mattress, and I made it up neatly after Silverton left, whistling, into the rain. The dishes were already washed, our few possessions put away. I drank another cup of ale—Silverton's orders—and went outside to gather up net for mending.

Among the skills I had learned since falling into Silverton's bed that August night: how to mend a fishing net, how to scale and bone a fish, how to skin rabbits and pluck fowl, how to bake bread in a peat fire, how to make cheese from sheep's milk, how to seal a boat with resin, how to gather and dry peat for the fire, how to draw water from the well, how to keep a house clean with only water and sand, how to darn stockings, how to mend clothing, how to speak Norse, or at least the rudiments. Once spring was under way, I had plans to start a vegetable garden, for I understood the soil here was exceedingly fertile. I learned and did all these things not because I expected to end my days as a fisherman's wife on this dreary, dark, chill, windblown island off the northern coast of Scotland, but because I should otherwise have gone out of my mind with boredom when Silverton left each morning in his boat to make a living.

And because it was needful. Because my husband—for so I came to think of him, whether or not we were truly married—returned home exhausted with a fish and a few coins each afternoon, and I loved him too much to do nothing for him in return.

But there were only two of us, and by noon my work was finished. I fastened the silver chain about my waist, took my cloak from the hook and my notebook from the chest, and I headed out into the chilly March day.

⁊

It may surprise you to learn that I had my own boat, a sort of crude dinghy I used to row across the harbor, or else to the little inlet on the other side of the shore, away from the village. Silverton taught me to use the oars, and I discovered that I experienced no sickness at all when operating the boat myself. I liked the independence of rowing, the exercise and the exposure to the rough, wild elements of the Orkney climate. I liked to test myself, even in my new condition, and most of all I liked to explore.

By the time I emerged into the early afternoon, the rain had cleared, although the wind blew cold against my cheek and the clouds lay low and thick. I turned to look at the castle on its hill, gray-walled and toothy, and for an instant I remembered it as I first saw it, half-ruined, crawling with builders and scaffolding and bathed in a mild picnic sun. My heart ached. Poor Max, he was likely frantic with worry for us, searching desperately for a way to bring us back.

Max. How I missed him, and the calm, easy, almost intuitive nature of our friendship. I missed his steadfast manner, and the long hours we had spent together, engaged not in battles of wit but in deep conversation, untangling long threads of logic, charting out plans. When I thought of him, I remembered all we had left undone, the mysteries left unsolved, and the memories shattered my hard-won peace.

Helen, I thought. Maybe Helen was trying to help him. Helen, who had some strange connection to the castle, who came from some other time of her own. Who carried some babe of her own.

I put one hand to the new, gentle curve of my belly and closed my eyes. *Show me, Max. Show me what I'm supposed to do.*

The wind howled around the corner of the cottage. A gull called nearby, and another. My eyes opened, and the castle stood imperviously above me, whole and solid, pennants snapping angrily. I slid my woolen mittens onto my hands, picked up the oars from against the side of the hut, and started down the path to the harbor, where my little craft bobbed at its mooring.

I saw nobody in the harbor. Perhaps half the fishing fleet was out; the other fishermen stayed sensibly indoors. That was why Silverton went out when the weather was bad—or rather, worse than usual—because he could get a better price for his catch. I swallowed back my anxiety and stepped into the boat. Shipped the oars and untied the knot. A faint queasiness overtook me as the boat rocked beneath my weight, but only until I dipped the oars into the water and began to row. Then the rhythm took hold, the exhilaration of physical exercise. I maneuvered around the other boats and slipped around the little headland protecting the harbor, staying close to shore to avoid the current that ran along the channel between this island and the next.

Many times before, I had made this journey. I knew the outline of the shore, the way the pebbled beach gave way to the rise of the cliffs, and then the abrupt bite of the first inlet. Silverton rowed with me the first time, and we brought the boat to shore there and ate a little picnic. That was at the end of August, when the sun still offered a little heat; in fact, the day had been unusually warm, and we had basked on the rocks and contemplated swimming.

"We can't," Silverton had said sadly. "For one thing, it's jolly cold. For another thing, the castle overlooks this little inlet, and we can't have anyone see us."

"Why not? Surely they can't see us properly from so far away."

"Maybe not, but they'd know it was us. None of the locals swim. The fishermen consider it bad luck, and the rest of them just think it's a sign of witchcraft."

"And they already think I'm some sort of witch, don't they?"

"Well, they can plainly see the spell you've cast over me," he said, touching my hair, and we didn't speak any more about swimming, or anything else, for some time.

Now, as I rowed past the mouth of the inlet, the tranquility of that summer afternoon seemed terribly distant. The wind blew in stiff, cold gusts, and the sky hung drearily above my head. The waves slapped against the hull of the boat, sending a salt spray across my cloak and my face, and still I rowed, bending my strength into the oars, thrilling to the pulse of my own effort. The terrain began to rise again, the inlet slipped from view. Now the cliffs, jagged and without mercy. The waves sloshed around the base, carving delicate features into the bare rock, and I kept well clear, though the wind blew from the northeast and I was not in any particular danger. Silverton had lectured me about the perils of a lee shore, to be watched carefully under oar and avoided at all costs while under sail.

As I drew in another great gust of air, I thought I smelled a faint hint of roses.

Is this sort of expedition really wise, in your condition?

The right oar skipped painfully on the surface of the water. I swore—in Norse, I hasten to add, which lends such exclamations a certain panache. "What the devil are you doing here?"

Sitting in the stern. I suppose you can't see me in this light.

I resumed my rhythm, pulling hard to right myself. "I'm perfectly capable of rowing a boat, madam."

I don't mean the exercise itself, although I should prefer you to undertake it with a degree less vigor. I mean rowing out so far, by yourself, in such weather. Should you meet with an accident, you would have little recourse.

"I don't intend to meet with any accidents."

Nobody ever does. But think of your poor husband. Think of the child.

"I assure you, I think of them constantly. You, on the other hand. You haven't intruded yourself on my company in months. Have you something particular to tell me? Some choice piece of advice that can't wait for a more opportune moment?"

(A sniff.) *I was only trying to give you a little privacy, during your honeymoon.*

"Honeymoon, indeed—"

You seem to have enjoyed it well enough.

"I did, thank you."

With the expected result, of course. That rascal Silverton. Naturally he took no care for your own convenience.

"I need hardly point out that your own husband is guilty of the same offense."

Procreation was our duty, my dear. Still, a most inconvenient condition. If the cause were not so supremely enjoyable, I should never have endured it once, even for the sake of Great Britain, let alone nine times. And then, at the end of a miserable nine months, the further misery of bringing forth. Thank God for chloroform.

I pressed my lips together and studied the wooden slats at the stern of the boat. If I narrowed my eyes, I could just detect a blurring at the point where the boards came together, and a faint impression of the color blue.

The Queen went on blithely, as if the lack of blessed chloroform in medieval Orkney had not occurred to her.

However, the deed is done, and I urge you most firmly to turn this—this little craft of yours about and return to shore, for the sake of the life within you, if for no other consideration. Your husband—

"Silverton is hardly overjoyed at the prospect of fatherhood."

Nonsense. Of course he is. He's only daunted by the responsibility, as he should be. Whatever is he thinking, to support a wife and child as a fisherman? I had hoped better for you. Still, he's a fine, strapping fellow, and will get healthy enough infants on you, I dare guess. If one must endure the indignity of childbearing—

"Really, madam. This is not a matter I wish to discuss with you."

If not with me, then with whom? A girl ought to have somebody with whom to discuss these matters, at such an interesting time of life.

"Certainly. But why you?"

There was a small, defiant harrumph from the stern, and then silence. I thought perhaps she had gone, and yet instead of feeling relief, I experienced a pang of longing. Or perhaps it was only indigestion. In any case, I went on rowing, while the cliffs fell back into another inlet, and I realized I had never roamed this far. I had always turned back, made uneasy by the sheer, cruel height of those cliffs.

Put to shore here, the Queen said sharply.

"What? Why? I thought you wanted me to turn back."

Put to shore, I say.

"I am not in the habit—"

There was a flash of light, and I knew she was gone, re-absorbed by whatever force had concentrated her spirit before me. I paused mid-stroke, while the waves buffeted the boat, and began to turn.

But I did not turn all the way around. As the inlet slid past my gaze, I saw the shallow, pebbled shore, and the grass-topped landscape that led toward it, and something attracted me, I don't know what. Some tug of memory, or magnetism, or perhaps only the breathtaking fairness of the scene, the tender slope of grass softening the horizon, the elegant crumble of cliffs into shore. The calm surface of the sheltered little cove.

I brought the boat in along the south bank, beaching it carefully among the pebbles before I stepped out and dragged the craft above the faint line of the high tide. The quiet surrounded me, empty of any hint of human habitation. I might have been standing there at any moment since the earth's creation. Beneath my feet, a few shells crunched among the pebbles. I laid down the oars and started to walk.

Even now, I can't say what guided me to this particular beach. It was not the Queen's order to make land, though she would likely insist otherwise. I walked along the rim of the shore, just along the tidal line, all the way to the tip of the opposite headland, and then back again. Not far from the boat, I found a rock and sat. The wind had calmed, and the clouds were breaking apart—a rare sight, and one I drank in gratefully, trying to calculate whether the sun might find one of those promising blue patches of sky. Then it did. A fragile warmth bathed my face. I closed my eyes and slid my hand beneath my cloak to caress the small, solid bump that was my child. My *child*. The word seemed so strange, so impossible and yet so natural, all at once. My child, Silverton's child. Of course, it was no surprise we had conceived a babe. It would perhaps be stranger if we had not, so frequently and so passionately had we united as summer wound into autumn; as the connection, as the *fascination* between us grew and strengthened by our constant physical communion. I thought of his face, his shoulders, his laughter, so inexpressibly dear. The deep, splendid shudder of his body inside mine, time and again. No surprise at all that we had conceived life. *This* life, stirring now beneath my hand, like the pulse of a butterfly's wings. *This* child, created from Silverton's essence and mine, brought miraculously together on this strange, remote shore.

And it was exactly at that moment, exactly when the stirring of life engaged in me a feeling of profound wonderment, that I opened my eyes and allowed my gaze to fall upon an object, half-hidden among the shells and the shingles of that uncanny Orkney beach.

A small, shapely, conical metal bullet, as from the barrel of a modern gun.

Anachronisms. As I said before, the present Duke of Olympia made his name in the field of archeology, and particularly by his expertise in analyzing those objects unearthed in strata at a time and place in which they could not, logically, have existed. In the vast majority of those cases, Max was able to find an explanation for their paradoxical presence—accident, or mistake, or outright fraud.

But not always. Locked inside those storerooms that temporarily housed the collections of the Haywood Institute for the Study of Time—as of the summer of 1906, that is, while the institute itself was under construction—there existed several boxes that contained certain objects, along with their accompanying notes, which the best efforts of Max's brilliant mind could not interpret.

Now, I am not and have never been an expert on firearms, still less on the ammunition that feeds them. I could not have told you what sort of gun that bullet belonged to; I couldn't guess what caliber or material or particular qualities it possessed. I knew it was a bullet, that's all, and I knew that even the earliest guns were unknown to northern Europe in this year of grace 1317.

Moreover, this bullet was surely no round, primitive musket ball.

I stared at it for some time before I dared to touch it. During that moment, the sun slid behind a cloud and emerged again, glinting dully on the bullet's side. It was about an inch long— perhaps a little less—and the rounded tip of its cone was shrouded in copper. It had sunk comfortably into the space between two pebbles, as if it had rested there for some time and meant to stay, if it could. I reached down at last and pried it loose. Brushed off a bit of sand. A trace of rust discolored the groove at the bottom, or perhaps that was something else, some product of the sea. The bullet seemed to be vibrating in my hands, until I realized it wasn't the bullet at all—it was my fingers that shook, my heart that hammered in shock, the hairs of my neck that prickled with the sensation of being watched by a pair of hidden eyes.

I spun around and scanned the beach, the cliffs to the side, the long roll of hills gathering inland. I saw nothing, nobody. No hint of animal life amid the still, green landscape.

I slipped off the rock and stood, looking out to sea, shading my eyes with my hand, but there was nothing there, no sail or slim, dark boat disturbing the water. Only the gentle ripple of the little bay, and the chop of the water beyond. The sun slipped behind a cloud, a large one, and I dropped my hand and opened my palm, staring at the small metal object there.

A pair of gulls called overhead, making me jump. I ought to be getting back home, I knew, but instead I turned to the cliffs to my left, along the southern rim of the inlet, which tumbled down to shore from a height of perhaps a hundred feet.

I looked again at the bullet. Was that really rust? How long had it lain there, nestled among the stones and shells? Certainly long enough that whoever had dropped it, or fired it, had forgotten its existence. Had left and gone . . . where?

Perhaps more important: Who?

In the absence of sunshine, the chill crept back under my cloak, but I hardly noticed. My mind began to spin with possibility. If this person had left one object, he must have left more. Some clue as to who he was, and how he had gotten here, and what he was doing. I shoved the bullet in my leather pouch and cast about the surrounding ground, the rocks, the shingles. The beach was narrow, perhaps twenty feet from the line of high tide to the edge of the turf. Along the southern rim, the driftwood had collected, carried there by the prevailing wind. I set off in that direction, walking slowly, inspecting the terrain as I went. My nerves sang, my mind raced. I felt as I had in Magnusson's office all those months ago, as if something lingered nearby, something important, and if I cast out the net of my senses, if I absorbed every surrounding vibration, I might discover an extraordinary truth.

Within a few yards, the driftwood began to collect in tangles, some of it quite old and smooth, bleached by sun, and some of it so new it was still wet. There was one enormous log, hollow in the middle, and as I clambered over it, I lost my balance and spilled to the ground on the other side. For a moment, I lay there, stunned out of my fervor. My elbow hurt. When I raised it, I saw a small patch of blood darkening the wool of my tunic. I half expected to hear a queenly voice admonishing me for my impetuousness—my clumsiness, at least—but there was only the gentle wash of the waves on the beach, and the screech of the seagulls passing overhead. I rolled on my side and sat up, facing the cliff, and in doing so caught sight of something I had missed earlier: a shadow that was not a shadow, but a recess in the rock.

I braced myself on the log and stood. My right ankle wobbled and held. I limped carefully in the direction of the recess, holding my right elbow with my left hand. The space deepened as I approached it, almost a cave, surrounded by curious piles of driftwood that were all roughly the same size—too similar for mere chance, as if someone had gathered them there for a particular purpose, and the wind and weather had since undone it. A few long, flat branches stood propped against the entrance to the recess, and when I reached it I peered inside, behind the wood. The air was dim and chill, for the cave faced north, cast in shadow by the cliffs above. I couldn't see much. I ducked past the branches and stepped fully into the shelter.

At once the sensation of power enveloped me, so electric, it was as if Max himself had laid his hands upon my skin. I flung out one hand to find the wall, to anchor myself while my eyes adjusted to the darkness. The rock was cold and damp, the daylight faint by the time it found its way between the gaps in the driftwood at the entrance, but I could see that the space stretched farther into the rock than I had imagined. So far, in fact, that I wondered if nature could have created it on her own. I felt the buzz of human habitation, the flavor of it on my tongue. I stepped forward, tracing my fingers along the wall for guidance, and went about eight or ten feet before I found the opposite wall. My nerves burned, my hair lifted. I cast about—the ground, the ceiling of rock above me, the walls—and saw nothing, nothing, but I felt everything. The bullet was like an anvil in my leather pouch, so heavy I imagined its gravitational field tugging my awareness downward, until I actually set one knee on the ground and found not rock or rough shingle, but something soft, like cloth.

I leaned down and groped about with my fingers. Slid my knee away and lifted this thing, this cloth that was not actually cloth.

It was a suit of some rubberlike substance, made to fit the human body.

I made a noise of wonder, an exclamation, and a voice answered me. Silverton's voice, calling my name.

✑

Since the night last August when we had first lain together as lovers, as husband and wife, Silverton and I had not discussed the possibility of returning to the twentieth century. I remember waking up the next morning, immersed in warmth, immersed in the sensation of Silverton's body curled around mine, and thinking I never wanted to leave. To leave this pallet was to return to our old habits, our old constraints, and to stay was the purest joy. So I lay there without moving, breathing in the scent of his skin, and eventually I realized he was awake, too. Equally still, and for the same reason. We were thinking the same thought, praying the same prayer.

Eventually I spoke. One of us had to. I asked him if he was happy.

"My dear Truelove," he said, pronouncing my name slowly, as two separate words, *true love*. "I am the happiest man alive, just now."

Then he turned the question around. Was I happy?

No, that's not quite right. Here is what he actually asked me: *And you? Have I made you happy at last?*

I wanted to say that this was the happiest moment of my life, that I had never felt such joy as I felt during the night just past, that my every sorrow had dissolved in the draught of his love.

But I couldn't say those words. I wasn't the sort of woman who spoke like that. I only whispered, *Yes,* and I believe he must have understood the rest of it. He turned me in his arms and kissed my forehead and my nose and lips. "That's all that matters to me, then," he said. "You're all there is."

"You're everything," I whispered back, and I meant it. I had given myself up to him, I had given myself up to the possibility that I might never return home, and sometime in the night Silverton had built me a home here, in this hut, on this humble pallet, and I didn't need another. I didn't want another. I didn't want to leave.

And I knew that he didn't want to leave, either.

⁖

So when I heard his dear, familiar voice calling my name, echoing from the walls of the strange cave hidden along the cliff wall, I dropped the suit back into the shadows and called back, "I'm here!"

He appeared an instant later, blocking what little light made its way into the cold, dark space. I saw only his hair, like a nimbus.

"Thank God," he said.

I started forward and met him halfway in a crushing embrace. "Why, what's wrong?" I asked.

"What's wrong? I came home to find you gone, your boat gone from its mooring."

"I only went for a row!"

"In this blustery weather. Haven't you any sense?"

His left hand stroked my hair; his right arm lay tight across my back. He was breathing hard, almost panting, and underneath the damp heat of his body I could feel the agitated smack of his heart.

"I'm all right," I said. "I only went for a row. You didn't need to come after me."

"Well, I couldn't sit around and wait, either. The baker said he'd seen you head up the western side, so I went out after you, had to put down the sail and row because the wind was coming from the wrong quarter. And then your boat here, empty, no sign of you."

"I was just exploring."

He pulled back at last, and I felt him examining my face, though he couldn't have really seen my expression in the darkness. At least, I hoped he couldn't. His arms fell away, and he took my hand. I cried out at the pain in my elbow.

"What's the matter?" he asked.

"My elbow. It's all right. I scraped it up a bit, going over that fallen log."

"You did *what*?"

"I was only exploring," I said again.

He swore and lifted me in his arms, carried me outside into the daylight. The sun still hid behind its enormous bank of cloud. He set me down on the log and knelt before me to examine my elbow.

"It's nothing," I said.

He looked up at me reproachfully. His hair was tousled and salty, tied back in its leather thong, and his beard needed trimming. How changed he was from the old days of valets and impeccable grooming. In the dull light, his eyes had lost their extraordinary blue, but none of their old magnetism. I stared back helplessly, praying he wouldn't see what lay in mine.

"Truelove," he said, "my own Truelove. You know how I admire your pluck. Never in life would I seek to clip those marvelous wings of yours. But I ask you—I beg you—just think a little. Think what you mean to me. If I should lose you—the both of you—"

I put my hands on his bloodless cheeks. "Never. Never."

"This past hour—no sign of you—"

"Never." I kissed him. "Never."

He allowed my kiss, but didn't return it. He was too shocked, I suppose, too relieved to feel anything. I slid down the log to kneel next to him on the pebbles.

"I feel the same way, each morning, when you set out in your boat," I said. "I watch you make sail. I watch you until you're out of sight, and I wonder if I shall ever see you again. Especially when the weather's like this."

"I came home early. That's why I came home early. I thought you might worry."

"Well, I do. Every time. I have to keep busy, to keep occupied so I won't think of you out there."

"Why haven't you told me?"

"Because I know how much you love to go. I know you need your solitude, your peace, I know you need the sea, and since I can't go out with you—"

"Oh, Truelove." He gathered me against him and buried his face in my hair. "Damn the bloody sea. I can do without *fishing*, for God's sake. Particularly in the middle of winter. What I *can't* do without is you."

He was leaning against the log. His tunic was soft against my cheek; he wasn't wearing a cloak. He never seemed to mind the cold. I lifted my head and rose to straddle him. Slid my hands along the roughness of his beard until I cradled his jaw.

I wanted to tell him that I couldn't do without him, either, that I worshiped him, that I had just been sitting in the sun and reflecting on the nature of this life he had made in me, how I loved the little butterfly in my belly because it was a small piece of his own essence, a living amulet I carried within me.

But I said none of that. Of course I didn't. I only kissed him, and this time he kissed me back while the sun slid out at last and warmed our heads, our shoulders. His hands disappeared underneath my dress and my linens, and to this day I remember the awkward, hurried, desperate way we came together on that beach, his hands underneath my clothes, his flesh sliding into mine, the crash of pleasure at the end, so unimaginably intense I lay reeling against his chest while the world blurred around us. Cold and damp and uncomfortable and it didn't matter, nothing else mattered, only his body and mine and the small, budding life between us.

♒

"There's another reason I came home early," Silverton said, "other than the weather, and I couldn't find any damned fish."

We sat together against the log, facing the water, cushioned from the rough texture of the beach by my cloak underneath us. My head lay comfortably in the hollow of his shoulder, and everything smelled of the sea.

"Hmm," I said drowsily.

"Are you listening to me, Truelove? I sometimes imagine I'm speaking into a void, at a moment like this. You lying there in a trance and all that, overcome by the sorcery of my lovemaking."

"I'm listening."

"Excellent, because this is important. I've been thinking about giving up the fishing trade altogether."

I lifted my head. "What's that?"

"Giving up fishing. A chap with a wife and a baby on the way, he can't afford to take chances like those afforded by the North Sea in January. To say nothing of the laughable compensation in exchange for such risks."

"But you love fishing."

"I *did* love fishing, when I had only a chill, empty hut waiting for me on my return, and no hope for the future. Now I begin to see its disadvantages. Particularly when one would rather stay tucked up luxuriously in bed with one's wife, instead of rising before the sun."

"I see."

"You don't agree?"

"Of course I agree. It's just—and I don't mean to argue against my own interests—but what else could we possibly do? Acquire a farm? I'm afraid I don't—"

He shuddered. "Perish the thought. If you don't like me smelling of fish, my dear, only imagine the sorts of perfumes I'd bring home from a barnyard. No, no. That's too hard a life for you, anyway. A farmer's wife, that's real work."

"I don't mind working."

"I mind it for you. No, I had in mind something a little more prestigious."

I peered into his face, which was angelic, bathed in light from the mild afternoon sun, the lines smoothed away by content-ment. He had one arm back behind his head, cushioning him from the wood, and I supposed he looked like what he was: a man who had just experienced a satisfying out-of-doors tryst with his wife.

"What, exactly?" I asked.

"Well, the other day, as I was haggling with that old villain Christof for a price for my fish, I happened to run into our good friend Magnus."

"What a tremendous coincidence."

"Yes, it was, wasn't it? Only it wasn't, really, because he had gone down to the village to find me."

"Why didn't he come to the house, then?"

"Because we had things to discuss, Truelove. Manly things. Chests were beaten, jests were exchanged. Do you know," he said, patting his tunic, "at times like this, tucked up cozily together after a good bout between the sheets—"

"Sheets?" I said dryly.

"—I really do long for my old pipe. I suppose tobacco's a long way off yet, isn't it?"

"A very long way. Don't change the subject. What did you and Magnus speak about?"

Silverton sighed. "He was offering me a job, in fact. I believe the same thought had occurred to him, once the news began to spread—"

"News?"

"That you're breeding, my dear. I'm afraid that midwife isn't the sort of woman who holds her tongue, and babies are about the only news there is in a village like this. In any case, he thinks fishing's a bad show for me, in my present situation, *your* present situation, and he wants us to move to the castle, where I can advise him in a political capacity. Be a sort of grand vizier. How does that sound?"

I spoke slowly. "It sounds like exactly the sort of thing you didn't want. What did you say? All the barbs pointed in your direction."

"Oh, I don't mind, not really. I've regained a bit of my old spirit in recent months, after all. I can't imagine why. In any case, it would relieve my mind of a great deal of worry. Plenty of dosh, plenty of food and clothing and shelter for you and the child." He lifted his arm from behind his head and laid his hand over mine, atop his chest. "I never meant to be a fisherman forever, after all. I relished the danger when I had nothing to live for, but now . . ."

"Only if you want to," I said. "Don't make yourself miserable because of me."

"Miserable? I have a life now, because of you," he said. "A future. An entire lifetime, here with you. It's high time I set about making something of it. There might be more children, after all. All those long winters ahead of us, and you so damned insatiable in bed. There are consequences to that kind of wantonness, Truelove. Terrible consequences."

I thought about the rubber suit, back in the cave. The small metal object hidden in my leather pouch. The electricity that had crackled along my nerves, the sense of returning purpose, the presence of a power I knew in my bones.

Now here I sat, tucked into the curve of Silverton's chest. His arm lay about my waist; his hand covered the ball of my belly, as if to protect the infant within.

Silverton squeezed my hand. "Well, Madam Grand Vizier? What do you think?"

"I don't know what to think. I suppose I wouldn't mind living in a castle," I said. "Back in your old chamber, I suppose?"

"Not just my old chamber, but an entire apartment, all to ourselves. Sitting room and bedroom and nursery. They're fitting it all up now."

"What, already?"

"The sooner, the better, don't you think? You'll have a waiting woman, too, all to yourself. I made sure of that." He pulled me on his lap, kissed me heartily, and hauled us both to our feet.

"Magnus will be over the moon. I don't know if I should tell you this, but I believe he's taken rather a fancy to you."

My head was spinning, trying to fasten itself on all of these new facts. "Has he? He's hardly spoken a word to me, since that day he visited me in the hut. The day after our wedding."

"Well, he will tomorrow, won't he?"

"Tomorrow?"

"Yes, tomorrow. Didn't I mention it?" Silverton took my hand and led me carefully over the driftwood to where my little boat sat on the shore, ten yards away from the sailboat bobbing at its mooring. "Magnus's father and stepmother have just arrived from the mainland. The feast begins at the usual hour. I shouldn't be surprised if it goes on until sunset. What's the matter?"

"I've just—I've left my cloak behind."

"I'll get it."

"No, that's all right. I'll fetch it while you ready the boat."

I turned and hurried back past the driftwood, where my cloak lay rumpled on the shingles. I picked it up and shook out the dirt and sand. Behind me, Silverton was still busy with the boat.

Quick as a minnow, I darted into the cave, snatched the rubber suit from the corner, and wadded it into the folds of my cloak.

✎

I woke in a jolt, sometime in the middle of the night. Another gale had started up, and the wind howled miserably around the cracks and corners of the cottage. Beside me, Silverton stirred and lifted his head.

"What's the matter?"

"Nothing," I whispered, and settled myself back in the bed-clothes.

But I did not return to sleep. I had been dreaming that I was back in my old life, before the old duke died, inhabiting my elegant room in Belgrave Square, devoting myself to some tedious, shallow task that, for some reason, I couldn't complete. And when I woke, I didn't recognize myself. This cold, dark cottage; this warm bed, inhabited by this vital man; this marriage, this pregnancy, this primitive, passionate life—surely *this* was the dream, *this* could not belong to me. This couldn't be *me*, Emmeline Truelove. I was not given to wanton adventure. How had I woken up inside this woman's body? Inside this strange world?

The man beside me made a sleepy noise and gathered me snug against his chest, spoon-fashion, as we were in the habit of sleeping. The warm marine smell of him filled my head. His flesh lay solid against mine. I laid my hand along his forearm and said to myself, *This is why you're here. This is what you came for.*

But the thought gave me no comfort. Something else lingered outside the comfort of Silverton's body, outside the stone walls of our cottage, biding its time for me, and it was this that had jolted me awake in the middle of my dream.

And as the hours of the night bled into dawn, I did not rest, but instead lay hovering between sleep and wakefulness, neither of one world nor the other.

The Lady fell to her knees and begged her son to let her stay upon this shore, for she had fallen into love with a Fisherman here, and pledged herself to him by sacred vow, and his babe even now quickened in her womb. But her son grew angry and dragged her to the cottage, where he opened the false bottom of the Fisherman's chest and showed her the suit that lay hidden there. 'See how your lover has deceived you,' he said, 'for he has kept the means of your escape from your hands, so that you would remain here in poverty to keep his house and serve his vile lust, and to bear his bastard children . . .'

THE BOOK OF TIME, A. M. HAYWOOD (1921)

Twelve

✦

In the end, I must have slept a little that last night in the cottage, because I woke to Silverton's kisses—not on my lips, but my belly, where his beard both tickled and aroused me. I cried out and grabbed his hair. Thus encouraged, he moved lower.

He took his time dispatching me, and made his own pleasure last as well, rocking gently inside me as if he meant to go on all day. Why not? He had no fish to catch this morning, no dawn launch from the harbor. He meant to enjoy himself in his favorite occupation, and he meant me to enjoy it, too, and such was his happy dedication to marital duty, his infectious delight in the act of love, I gave myself up and joined him in that netherworld of carnal copulation. We sprawled on the bed afterward, too depleted to move, until the growl of Silverton's stomach could no longer politely be ignored. He turned his head and grinned at me.

"Do you know what it is with you, Truelove? You're game."

"Game? Game for what?"

"For this. For anything. I knew it the moment I spotted you

at Olympia's funeral, wearing your prim black dress and clutching your little glass of punch. I said to myself, Silverton, old boy, that woman is game. From that instant, I wanted you."

"How flattering. I remember thinking you were an idiot and a reprobate, and I wanted nothing to do with you."

He climbed on his elbows and crawled to me, pressing kisses into my neck and bosom. "Now look where you are, rosy-cheeked in my bed, great with my child. Life has a bloody marvelous way of working out, doesn't it?"

"I don't know how you do it, really."

"Do what?"

"Get everything you want."

"Oh, that. It's a matter of perseverance, that's all. Single-mindedness. I decided you were the only woman in the world for me, and once I did that—narrowed my efforts, I mean—you stood no chance at all, Truelove. Why are you laughing?"

"It just seems a Pyrrhic victory, that's all. You've got me trapped in your bed, right enough, but at what cost?"

Silverton lifted his head from my breast and considered me with his blue eyes. He stood on his hands, one on either side of me, like a cat with its prey, long and lean and wonderfully scruffy. "I don't count the cost, Truelove," he said quietly.

"Why not?"

He rolled to his side and propped up his head with his elbow. "I've told you about my mother, haven't I?"

"Your stepmother? Or the bolter?"

"The bolter. My real mother. Or rather, the woman who gave birth to me. Immensely beautiful, I'm told. She and my father, they were madly in love, and then my father went off to war and got himself wounded, terribly disfigured—have you ever met him?"

I thought of the Duke of Ashland and his missing arm, his

mangled jaw in an otherwise perfect face, visiting Olympia in his study one afternoon. "Yes," I said.

"Well, you can imagine my mother's reaction when *that* monstrosity returned home to her, calling itself her husband. She jumped straight into another man's bed, and then she bolted with him, and I never saw her again."

We lay facing each other in a tangle of bedclothes, in a fog of human musk. I laid my hand on his cheek, wound my fingers inside his short, rough beard, and the old Emmeline Truelove receded, receded, until I could not recall her at all. Who was that woman in her prim black dress, clutching her wine, terrified of the high animal spirits scintillating the man standing next to her? Disguising her terror with disapproval.

I touched the corner of his mouth with my thumb. "You're wrong. I can't imagine her reaction at all."

"I hope not," he whispered. "I don't think I could survive it."

⟨✦⟩

I tell you all this not to arouse or titillate, but to explain the intimacy of our mood as we made our way along the lane to the castle, followed by a cart that contained our few belongings. Magnus had sent the cart—the driver arrived at our door a few short minutes after the conversation I related above, causing us to scramble for our clothes and our dignity—and I watched as Silverton helped the man load the bed, the table and stools, the dishes, the wooden chest underneath the window. We left the door unlocked. Silverton took my hand as we started up the road, and it seemed to me, as the castle grew to a monstrous size before us, buzzing with activity in anticipation of the feast to come, that we were walking into a vast, unknown future, with only each other to cling to.

The bustle of the great hall astonished me. I had thought our wedding banquet, as impromptu as it was, had been a lavish event, but that was nothing compared to this hurly-burly of servants and furniture and decoration. There were new, fresh rushes on the floor and banners hung from the walls and railings. Men stood about, already half-drunk, and Silverton hurried me past them to the staircase. As we climbed the steps, I felt the seriousness of his mood.

"What's wrong?" I asked, in a low voice.

"The whole damned village, that's all."

"What's wrong with that? I daresay they'll appreciate a bit of merriment, after the dark winter months."

"Just stay close to me, that's all."

We reached the landing and went down the hall to the chamber we had shared on our wedding night. I paused in the doorway, but Silverton urged me through and shut the door firmly behind us. The wooden shutters were closed tight over the windows. I walked to the middle one and opened it, and a gust of wet, fresh wind struck my face. I leaned out regardless, craning my neck to see around the edge of the recess.

"Why, there it is!" I said in surprise.

"What?"

"The inlet from yesterday. You can't see the beach, but there's the tip of the headland, and the gap between them." I pulled back so Silverton could look, but he paid little notice. He was walking restlessly about the room, inspecting the furnishings. "Is something wrong?" I asked again.

Before he could answer, a thunderous knock struck the door, and without any further preamble the driver entered, followed by a train of men, carrying our things from the hut. I stood aside while Silverton argued and instructed, and the table and chairs went out again, along with the dishes and cookware. They were dickering over the chest when I spoke up.

"That stays here, please," I said in Norse, and the man must have understood me, because he shrugged his shoulders and set the chest against the wall, next to the one already in place. They were similar in size, but the one belonging to the castle was built along more elegant proportions. I stared at them both, side by side, and a shimmer seemed to pass over my skin.

The last man left and closed the door. I looked for Silverton, who had stopped beside the bed. A pair of garments had been laid out on the covering, considerably richer than those we were wearing. "What the devil are you playing at, old boy?" Silverton muttered, crossing his arms.

"I don't understand."

He looked up. "He's making a show of strength, that's all. The feast, the garments. Me, hurriedly installed as grand vizier. You, as some sort of hostess."

"Is that what I am?"

He held up the dress, which was made of rich blue velvet, nearly purple, and trimmed with fur. "You're no lady-in-waiting, that's certain."

"I hope I'm not too large to fit inside it."

"I expect your belly will be part of the show, my dear. Nothing so extravagant as a woman increasing." He walked to me and held the gown to my shoulders. "A good fit. I wonder how he guessed so well."

"He's a man, that's all."

"Exactly. Come along, then. Let's get you into it. I'll be your lady's maid. There's no point trying to find servants; I expect it's all hands downstairs at the moment."

He helped me lift my old woolen surcoat over my shoulders,

and then eased the velvet garment over my kirtle. The fit was snug; I stared down in dismay at the bulge of my abdomen. "Don't worry," he said. "You look ravishing."

"But I don't want to look ravishing."

"Well, my good friend Magnus apparently wants you to look ravishing, so I expect we had better not disappoint him." He reached for the silver girdle and wound it around my waist, just above the curve of my womb. "You might as well accustom yourself, in any case. This is nothing to how you'll look in a couple of months. Why, when my stepmother was carrying my brother—"

"Oh, stop."

"—like she had swallowed a cannonball, or else a cook pot, that's it, a very large cook pot—"

"For God's sake, it's your own fault, you devil!"

His smile faded. "Yes," he said softly. "My fault."

"I didn't mean—"

Silverton knelt before me, put his hands to the small of my back, and kissed the center of my belly. "You are to behave yourself in there, is that clear? Not to injure your mother in any respect. Maintain a modest size, turn about smartly, enter the world headfirst and double-quick when summoned."

"If he's anything like his father, he'll do none of those things. Especially now that he's been told."

"Then he had damned well better turn out like his mother."

"Or *she*," I said softly. "Just imagine you rearing a daughter."

"Ah," he said, expelling his breath, and for a moment we didn't move, not a flicker, except my hands caressing his hair, except the butterfly stir of the baby against his cheek. At last he rose and held me against him. "That's why we're here. For your sake, for the child's sake. You can't raise a child in a hovel."

"And you? What about your sake?"

"My dear," he said, "they are one and the same."

The wind blew through the window, striking the side of my cheek. The faint noise of revelry rang in the air, muffled by stone and wood, laughter and voices and musical instruments playing snatches of music. I said, "It sounds the same, doesn't it? That's the strangest thing of all. The words are different, but the voices haven't changed. Men are still men. Rain is wet. It's the same sun, the same clouds. Flowers, birds, fish. Life goes on."

"Except these men will be long dead by the time we're born. Bones rotting in the ground, forgotten utterly. Not even a tombstone left to mark them. Nobody will know exactly how all this was. Scholars will wonder. Archeologists like Max will dig and dig, and they'll never know the truth of it. The essence."

I listened to the beat of his heart, the whoosh of his blood, and my arms moved to encircle his waist. I closed my eyes and for a moment, for an instant, I forgot where we stood. The cold wind blew on my neck. My scalp began to tingle in a familiar way, my bones to lighten. I felt as if we were hovering between the two worlds, and the sounds beneath us were the sounds of builders and picnickers, and Max . . . and Max . . .

My eyes flew open.

"What's the matter?" Silverton asked.

I looked up to meet his gaze, which was narrow and quizzical. His thick gold beard, his long, unkempt hair, the lines about his eyes and mouth. I tried to remember what he had looked like before, clean-shaven and immaculate, the polished, dazzling heir to a dukedom, and I couldn't.

I said hoarsely, "You had better change your tunic."

❧

While he changed and washed in the basin, I folded my plain dress and put away my things. From our chest I retrieved a comb, which I used to smooth and plait my hair. I had no mirror, no glass of any kind. My trembling fingers kept slipping on the long strands. Still, the rhythm of the work soothed me. Returned to me some sense of the ordinary to anchor me back to the world.

Before we left for the feast downstairs, I opened my leather pouch and searched for the bullet inside. It had nestled into the corner at the bottom, like a small, oval pebble. Except it wasn't. I ran my finger around its base to be sure. The metal had the cold, perfect touch of something machine-born, something deadly modern. A bit of sand came loose from the tiny groove.

"Missing something?" asked Silverton, by the door. He had trimmed his beard and combed his hair, and in his new tunic of velvet, in a shade of blue almost matching mine, he took the breath from my lungs. He couldn't be mine. In our own world, he never would. I might have him for an instant, for a week or a month, but not like this. Not seven months as we had just lived them.

"No," I said. "Nothing's missing."

He held out his hand to me.

I set down the pouch and fastened the tie at the top. Tucked it into the wooden chest along the wall, the one we had brought from our little cottage by the sea.

I placed my hand in Silverton's, and he brought it to his lips.

"Why, you're as cold as ice," he said. "Is everything all right?"

"Yes."

"I didn't disturb you with all my morbid talk, did I?"

I shook my head.

"Truelove." He took my other hand. "Something's bothering you. Is it this damned show downstairs? Are you nervous?"

What could I say to him? Confess what I had discovered on the beach? Describe the instincts clamoring inside me, the proximity of the supernatural in this room? The premonition of something hovering outside the perimeter of our contentment, preparing to rupture us? After seven months of perfect peace, in which the twentieth century had become the dream, and the stones and sea of Orkney had fixed themselves into permanence.

"A little," I said. "So many strangers, and I can't speak more than a few words. And everybody will be staring at me and my fat belly."

He must have believed me, because his expression softened. He released my fingers and wrapped his hands around the sides of my face, so I couldn't help but meet the warmth of his eyes. "Here's the honest truth, Truelove," he said. "You've never looked more beautiful. Do you know what I was thinking just now? *I can't believe she's mine. Can't imagine what I've done to deserve her.* Ah, don't cry."

"I am not crying."

He wiped the corners of my eyes with his thumbs and lowered his forehead to mine. "And I was wishing—I was wishing—"

"Oh, don't—"

"—that my father could see you. See I've done something sensible at last. My God, how he'd love you. His face—"

I was gripping his waist now, digging my fingers into the muscles along his sides. I whispered, "Let's not go. Let's stay here."

"A very tempting thought."

"Then stay with me. They don't really need us. They won't miss us. Please."

He laughed. "I'm afraid they will. Magnus will, at any rate."

"Damn Magnus."

"No, no." He drew back and took my shoulders. "Buck up, Truelove. Time to tap that extraordinary courage of yours. We shall march straight down those stairs with our heads high—I shall, at any rate, I'll be proud as a bloody peacock with you on my arm—and we shall damned well enjoy ourselves."

"I won't understand one word in five."

"I shall translate for you. I won't leave your side for an instant, I promise. Then we'll leave early and come upstairs and frolic all night, if you like."

His eyes were very bright. I realized he actually *wanted* to go downstairs and share in the revelry. Of course he did; he had always loved a good party, loved to lose himself in communion with his fellow man. Then, afterward, to lose himself in communion with a woman. He craved all this. He was emerging from his solitude and becoming himself again. A wiser and more somber Silverton, perhaps, but drawn inevitably to the old joys.

"Will we really?" I whispered.

He kissed my forehead. "I'm at your service."

My heart was so full, it hurt. I rose on my toes and kissed him back, except on the lips, and I felt by the movement of his mouth that I had surprised him. I don't know why. I had kissed him often enough before. Maybe it was the force of the kiss, the ardor of it. When I drew away, he was smiling.

"As game as they come," he said, and he took me by the arm and ushered me through the door.

❧

The night after his funeral, my father appeared in my room for the first time. I had dressed for bed, but I couldn't bring myself to rest. His presence ought to have shocked me, but it didn't; I think I was beyond shock, beyond sense, having endured both the grief of his passing and then the burden of planning his funeral within the space of five sleepless days. It was autumn, in the last year of the century, and I felt as if the entire world were passing into eternity.

I became aware of his presence as I sat in my armchair before a meager, dying fire. I lifted my head and there he was, wearing a dressing gown of dark green paisley over a pair of blue pajamas, one leg crossed over the other. I suppose I thought he was a hallucination. My mind was so exhausted, you see, even if my body refused to settle into sleep. He spoke first. He told me how sorry he was to have left me by myself, without family, but he trusted to the goodness of the duke and duchess to stand in his place, as guardians of my interest.

"But what am I to do?" I asked him. "Where do I belong?"

"My dear Emmeline. I'm afraid you must choose that for yourself. You have the wit and the strength to make your way along any path, wide or narrow."

"A lonely path," I said.

He had uncrossed his legs and leaned a little forward, and his dear face was soft with kindness. "You're wrong," he said. "You have friends you know nothing of, and I have no doubt they will one day make themselves known."

"I don't need friends. I need my father."

"My dear," he said, "remember you are fortunate to have two fathers. One of them still remains to you."

"That man is nothing to me. No more than I am to him."

My father sat back again and smiled faintly. "Perhaps," he said, and his edges blurred, and in the next instant he was gone, and I blinked, staring at the void he had just occupied, feeling as if I had just woken from a dream.

In the ensuing years, he appeared to me regularly, if not often, but he never again referred to the unknown man who had fathered me on my mother. I suppose I forgot the substance of that first conversation entirely. But I never quite got over the habit, which I had formed as a child, of looking, half consciously, for my mother's lover. On the streets of London, the drawing rooms of my employer, the opera house, the department store, the railway carriage—he might be any man, any fellow of a certain age, and sometimes, as one of them perhaps felt the weight of my speculation, he turned to look at me. Turned to look, and my heart lost itself, my breath died, until he turned away again.

He always did.

Except here, in this strange, primitive century. Without thinking about it, I had stopped looking for my sire. I hadn't thought about him at all. My real father—Mr. Truelove, I mean—no longer appeared to me in this place, and in his absence, in the absence of all familiar things, I almost forgot I had any parents at all. I had only my life with Silverton, and his proximity was enough. So great was his devotion, it banished that loneliness I had felt since childhood.

It was only when Silverton mentioned his own father that the idea of fathers rushed back to me. That, and Silverton's tender embrace, his cheek absorbing the movement of his child inside me. As we walked down the staircase to the noisy hall below, I caught the scent of smoke and charred meat and perspiration, caught sight of all the men milling happily, of Magnus's large frame towering above them, and I stopped and turned to Silverton.

"My father!" I said.

"What's that?"

"My father! I wish you could have known him. I wish you could see him."

He gave me a strange look. "But I *have* met him, on several occasions. In Belgrave Square, when I had business with Olympia. Capital fellow, your father."

"I mean that you could have known him *as* my father. That he could see how good you are. How happy you've made me."

We still stood on the stairs, about a third of the way down the final, wide stretch. There was no rug, and the soles of our shoes rested on bare stone. Below us, the noise of revelry blurred into a single boisterous roar, like a sea in which you might drown.

"Have I made you so happy?" Silverton asked.

"Yes." I gripped his arm. "I want you to know how happy I've been. My father would be so grateful."

"*Grateful?* I'm your husband. It's my duty to make you happy."

"You have. You have. You've been wonderful."

"Truelove, what's wrong? You're shaking."

"Nothing's wrong. It's only nerves."

"My dear—"

"Fingal!"

We turned so quickly, I lost my balance, falling against Magnus's sturdy shoulder before Silverton could catch me. He took the blow without flinching, simply wrapped an arm around me to steady me, and then restored me to the step.

"My God," Silverton said, "don't do that to a fellow."

Magnus shrugged. "The baby. Makes it hard to—" He jiggled back and forth.

"Balance," I said. "I know."

Silverton drew my arm back through his elbow and secured it with his other hand. "You've got a big feast down there," he said in Norse. (I translate roughly, you understand, for my Norse was not fluent.)

"The Earl of Thurso visits us. We must make a good feast."

I looked at Silverton. "I'm sorry. Did he say the Earl of *Thurso*?"

"Yes," Magnus said, this time in English. "My father."

❧

"He's a bastard, of course," Silverton said, when Magnus had escorted us to the bottom of the stairs and then vanished with a peculiar agility. "His mother was a girl in the village. But the earl did right by him. Took him in when he was breeched—or whatever it is they call it these days—and had him properly educated."

"You said he was a fisherman."

"Well, that came after. I believe he had some sort of falling-out with the old man, and moved himself to the Orkneys, to this island, as a fisherman."

"Then how did he come to be lord of Hoy?"

"Damn it all, Truelove. Can't the questions wait until after the party?"

"No, they can't. And why didn't you tell me about all this before?"

"It never came up. But I'd be happy to—oh, look here."

I followed his gaze and saw Magnus advancing back toward us, except this time he was accompanied by two children—a boy of about ten who held his hand, and a girl of about five who sat like a doll in the crook of his massive elbow.

"Well, well," Silverton said, in undertone. "This is unexpected."

I had no time to ask him why. The three of them stopped before us, and Magnus allowed the little girl to slip carefully to the floor to stand shyly by his side. "My little ones," he said, in English, "this is the lady Fingal, who is wife to our friend Fingal."

I cleared my throat. "Hello."

"Lady Fingal. I give to you my son Henry and my daughter Olivia."

I bent and took each of their hands. "What lovely names," I said slowly. When I straightened, I saw the color in Magnus's cheeks, the extreme focus of his gaze upon me.

"I hope you will be friends," he said.

"Of course. As you know, we shall have a child of our own this summer."

"Yes, I know."

His gaze continued to penetrate mine, as if he meant to look within and observe the memory of the babe's conception. Beside me, Silverton cleared his throat and bent from his great, lanky height to address the children.

"And *I* am the lady's lucky husband. Delighted to meet you, Master Henry." He shook the boy's hand. "And the fair Mistress Olivia." He held out his first two fingers to the girl, and I'll be damned if the little minx didn't smile and cast down her pretty blue eyes and touch Silverton's outstretched fingers as if they were made of porcelain. I suppose I couldn't blame her; I knew the effect of Silverton's charm all too well. No doubt his eyes were twinkling, or some such nonsense.

"Do you mean to say you've never met?" I asked.

"I'm afraid not. Magnus keeps them under snug supervision, don't you, old boy?"

"Then how do they understand modern English?"

Magnus frowned in confusion, and Silverton said something in Norse I couldn't pick out. I returned my attention to the children: first the sturdy, dark-haired boy, who stood solemnly at his father's side. His skin was pale and his eyes were round and startlingly blue, and he was possibly younger than I first realized; he had inherited his father's robust proportions, which gave him the look of an older boy. The girl was a little fairer, her hair a lighter brown, her eyes a lighter blue, and she hid behind the edge of her father's tunic and regarded us intelligently.

Magnus and Silverton were still talking. I knelt before the girl and asked her if she had a doll, and she said yes. The doll's name was Margaret and she was upstairs. Daddy had made her a cradle of her very own.

"Daddy must be very clever with his hands, then," I said, and Olivia nodded yes. I turned to Henry and asked him if he knew his letters.

"Yes, madam," he said, very correctly, "and my numbers and sums, too."

"Does your father take you outside with him?"

"Yes!" Olivia said. "We ride our punnies."

"*Po*nies," said Henry witheringly, sounding very much like a big brother.

"Ponies." I straightened. "Very good."

The men had stopped talking and stood facing each other, arms folded. A fine tension hummed between them. I put my hand on Silverton's arm and felt its tautness. Along the line of Magnus's throat, a tendon flexed.

"What's the matter?" I asked.

"My dear," said Silverton carefully, "Magnus proposes you accompany him and the children upstairs to their rooms, while he settles them with the nurse. Is that agreeable to you?"

"But what about you?"

"I shall remain below and make merry." The words *make merry* were uttered dryly. He turned his head to look at me, and his expression was stiff. "I believe he has something to say to you."

"Say to me?" I looked between them. "What? Why can't he say it here?'

"It has to do with the children, I believe, and such conversations are better done in private."

I turned to Magnus. "But—"

Silverton took my elbow and maneuvered us a step or two away. "Just go with him, Truelove. It won't take long." He paused to adjust the long plait of hair over my shoulder. "He's about the only fellow in the world I'd trust with you, except perhaps Max himself. And for the same reason."

"What's that?"

"Because he's desperately in love with someone else."

The children occupied a suite of rooms on the highest floor of the castle, which we reached by means of a staircase curving around the walls of a turret. I led the way, Magnus at the rear, the children between us. As I climbed, I marveled at the newness of the steps, the crisp, fresh-cut stone in its familiar spiral. The height made me dizzy, or maybe it was my own anticipation. Before I left, I had kissed Silverton good-bye. I don't think he understood why, and I couldn't tell him.

I did my best to ignore the tremors around me. I shoved them aside as mere imagination. Behind me, the children chattered away in Norse, and Magnus sometimes replied in the patient, measured way of fathers with small children. The air grew fresher. The noise of the feast faded and died away below us. I counted the steps to steady my nerves, and by the time we reached the landing at the very top, by the time I reached for the latch on the door, I felt a great calm settle over me. My hand, as it pushed the door free, was marvelously steady.

The scene that opened before me was not what I expected. The vast, open space of the attic was now partitioned into rooms, and dry rushes covered the stone floor. The outer walls were sound and strong, holding the Orkney gales at bay. Somewhere within, the peculiar smoke of a peat fire made the air snug.

As I stood, transfixed, the children ran past me down the hall, toward a door near the end that stood ajar. Magnus came up beside me and said, "Thank you."

"For what?"

"Come here."

I thought it was a command, but he didn't move, and so maybe he meant *for coming here*. He was thanking me for making this little journey with him. I turned to look at his face, which followed the progress of his children down the hall and around the corner of the door. When they disappeared into the room, he ducked his head to look at me.

"But why?" I said. "Why am I here?"

He picked up my left hand and examined it: first the back, my knuckles, the bones of my fingers, and then the lines of my palm.

"Come," he said, and this time the command was clear.

So I followed him down the hall, tracing the same path that the children had just blazed, and entered the room at the end of the hall. The chamber was smaller than I expected, empty of furniture except for a few stools and a brazier that burned in the middle, attended by an elderly woman in a plain woolen dress much like the one I had doffed an hour earlier in Silverton's bedchamber. In the corner, Henry and Olivia were playing with some sort of spinning top. The wooden shutters were closed firmly over the window, keeping out the cold, and the room had the dim, opaque quality of an overcast sky.

Magnus took a step inside the doorway and stopped to cross his arms and observe the children. The woman at the brazier made a curtsey and kept her eyes cast down. I stood at Magnus's elbow, slightly behind him, and from this vantage his size seemed insurmountable, almost grotesque. For an instant, quite without intending to, I thought of his poor wife, trapped beneath all that bulk while he used her in bed. Silverton might have been tall, but he was also lean, agile, supremely considerate—I would almost say *inventive*—in the employment of his own weight.

"My wife," said Magnus.

I startled and stepped back. Magnus caught my elbow and turned me to face him. I knew I was flushing; I felt the surge of blood in my cheeks. I couldn't quite meet his gaze. I addressed the tip of his nose instead.

"What about your wife?"

"She is like you."

"My hair, you mean? My face?"

He took my other elbow. His grip was strong but not ungentle. I forced myself to look upward, to find his eyes, which regarded me with such ferocity I lost my breath.

"No. She is beautiful—"

"Thank you terribly."

"—I mean, like you, she is beautiful. But not this." He gestured to his own face. "Words. The same words. Like Fingal."

I glanced at the children, who had stopped playing with the top and were staring at us, Olivia with curiosity and Henry with suspicion. "English, you mean?"

"Your English."

"I see."

He made an impatient noise and looked at his children, at the nurse, who swiftly turned away. "Come," he said, and dragged me from the room to stand in the hall. I felt the hot frustration raging from his skin, his inability to make himself understood. My own heart smacked and smacked against the bones of my chest. The walls were made of wood, unplastered, unfinished, and I thought of the pile of stones that lay in the attic of Magnusson's castle. *This* castle, six hundred years in the future, *this* attic, in which Max and I had held our brief conference.

And the woman. The woman, five or six months gone with child, who had walked inside and interrupted us.

Magnus's hand still held my elbow. I laid my hand on his sternum, and the thunder of his heart startled me.

"Like you," he said again. "From different place. Different time."

"Oh, God. Oh, God."

"You know?"

My hand fell away from his chest. I pulled back and stood against the wall, laying my palms on the rough stone, and stared hopelessly at his face. The electricity buzzed in the air, numbing my cheeks, raising the hair on my head and my arms.

He opened his mouth, and I knew what he would say. I could have said the words for him. But I didn't.

"Her name is Helen," he whispered.

The Lady was afraid that her son might discover her children by the Fisherman and destroy them in his rage, so she returned with him to the edge of the shore, though her heart nearly stopped under the weight of her grief. When they reached the small boat that was to carry them to the ship at anchor in the bay, her son set her before the eyes of the sailors and said, 'Now, strip away your clothes and stand before us in your shame, for you have dishonored my father and lain in lust with a poor Fisherman, and your womb even now quickens with the bastard babe gotten of his seed . . .'

THE BOOK OF TIME, A. M. HAYWOOD (1921)

Thirteen

Silverton was deep in conversation with a flushed, small-boned woman wearing a gown of embroidered amber velvet. I took him by the arm and spun him around, mid-sentence.

"You knew!" I said.

"Knew what?"

I leaned forward. "Magnus's wife."

"Ah."

"Don't say *Ah*. Tell me the truth!"

Silverton looked back over his shoulder, as if just remembering the woman he was speaking to, but she had already cast me a look of deadly hostility and turned away. He sighed and rubbed his beard at the end of his chin. "I *have* told you the truth."

"*All* the truth."

"Of course. Whatever you want to know. Where has Magnus gone?"

"I don't know. I didn't stop to see if he was following me."

"Well, it seems he has. Followed you, I mean." Silverton nodded over my shoulder.

I didn't turn. "I don't want to speak to *him*. I want to speak to *you*. I want the truth from you, the entire truth, the whole story. And I'd very much like to know why you haven't told me any of this before."

"Not because—oh, damn." He slipped his arm free and took my hand firmly in his own. "Step back."

"Why—"

But my words were drowned by the noise of trumpets from the gallery above. The din of gathered humanity settled into quiet. A pair of men had stepped in front of us, so I couldn't quite see what was going on, but I didn't need to, did I? I heard the final flourish, heard Magnus's voice boom out in Norse, something about welcome and drink and the bounty of God. I thought he sounded urgent somehow, as if he were straining to get to the end of each rote sentence. Before me, one of the men shifted position, opening up a narrow vantage, and inside that gap stood Magnus, looking mighty in a pool of sunshine from some window above, next to another man in a rich tunic and robe. Older, gray-haired, nearly but not quite so large as Magnus himself.

"Is that the earl?" I whispered to Silverton.

"I expect so. Never met the chap."

A hurrah swept the crowd. Laughter, high spirits. I looked around the room and saw a few faces I recognized, but mostly strangers. They could not all have belonged to the village. They must have come from throughout the islands, the other towns and hamlets scattered about these fertile rocks, and probably the Earl of Thurso's own retinue as well.

"Why is he here?" I asked. "What's going on?"

"I'm not quite sure. I gather he's making a sort of state visit. He's never been here before, not even unofficially."

The trumpets began again, and everyone moved to the long trestle tables laid out in a rectangle in the middle of the hall. To my surprise, Silverton led me toward the head table, raised on a dais above the others, where Magnus and the earl were taking their seats, next to a richly dressed woman who wore a fillet of gold across her forehead and an expression of pained disapproval, close to mutiny. The Countess of Thurso, no doubt, who was perhaps not pleased to attend this celebration in the home of her husband's bastard offspring.

The table itself was scarcely visible under the candlesticks and dishes and bowls of fruit. Silverton led me directly to Magnus's right side, and Magnus turned and took my hand and pressed it with his lips, while the guests below us stood by their stools at the long tables arranged below. I was too stunned to make any reply. I felt the eyes of the crowd upon us, and I felt the weight of my rich clothes, the slight but unmistakable curve of my belly beneath the snug velvet gown and the silver chain, the shadow of Silverton's body hovering at my shoulder. Magnus straightened and, still holding my hand, introduced me to the notice of the Earl of Thurso, his father.

I would like to say that I saw some resemblance between this earl and my host, six hundred years later, but this man—if he was indeed a direct ancestor of the Thurso I knew—would have contributed only one line on the family tree among thousands. Thus the multiplication of generations. He was large, as I said, and beginning to run to stoutness. His silver hair grew long and loose, and his beard covered half his face. From the middle of it, he curved his narrow lips and greeted me in Norse, though his native language surely must have been Gaelic.

I wished him well in the same language, and Magnus pulled out my chair and urged me to sit. I turned to Silverton at my right. "What in heaven's name is going on? Why has Magnus seated us with him?"

"Because of our new status, I suppose. Or perhaps he wants everyone to know that you—that *we*—are here under his direct protection."

We spoke in undertone, while the hum of gaiety went on around us. Next to me, Magnus had not yet taken his seat, nor had his father to the left. They stood quietly, facing the assembled company. I felt tiny as they towered by my side, and yet terribly exposed. How often had I attended grand occasions, in my service to the duke and duchess? I couldn't count them all, the parties and dinners and ceremonies and performances. But always hovering in the background, always tucked in some obscure corner. Never like this, within the exact center of the room's gravity. The blood rose in my cheeks. Magnus's hand rested on the edge of the table, not far from my own, large and gnarled from years of casting his nets into the North Sea. The fingers curled with tension. For the first time, I noticed the priest who had come to stand in front of the table, just to my left, facing the guests.

I glanced at Silverton, whose brow was heavy with speculation as he gazed up at Magnus's profile.

"Something's going to happen, isn't it?" I whispered.

"Hmm. Yes. But what?"

"Don't you know? Hasn't he told you?"

"Not a thing."

Gradually the assembled guests became aware of the two men standing at the head of the room. The air filled with an expectant silence. Someone suppressed a cough nearby. The servers backed away and stood at the perimeter.

But it was not Magnus who spoke into that fragrant hush of people. It was his father.

The Gaelic words rang out in measured phrases, translated into Norse at intervals by the priest who stood before me. I was too rapt, too astonished to concentrate on the words. The expression of the guests transformed from curiosity to amazement. A gasp swept along the tables. I looked desperately at Silverton, whose own face had hardened in that way he had when something important was taking place, too important for emotion.

The earl finished, and Magnus's voice boomed out in Norse, a single sentence, and the guests answered him with a cheer.

"My God," I said to Silverton, "what's happened?"

Next to me, Magnus and his father took their seats, and evidently this was a signal of some kind, because the rest of the company sat, too, and the musicians struck up from the gallery above our heads.

"A rather extraordinary thing, I believe," said Silverton. "The earl's just made Magnus his heir."

"Can he do that? His natural son?"

"In this age? Yes, I believe he can. The nobles are more autonomous. Like little kings."

The serving maids and men began to circulate with jugs of wine and platters of meat and stewed fruit, which they first laid before their lord. Magnus helped himself and his father, who served the countess. We could not eat until he had taken the first bite. Not that I had any desire to eat. The sight of the food was making me ill. I felt overturned, disorientated by all the revelations that had just uncovered themselves before me, one after another. Silverton reached with his knife and speared a slice of meat—duck or partridge or some sort of bird—and laid it on my plate, and I put my hand on his wrist.

"I'm not hungry. You must speak. You've got to tell me about Magnus's wife."

"Not here, Truelove. In front of everybody. After the feast."

"Now. Don't you see, it's vital, it can't wait. You *must* tell me about Helen."

Silverton went still beneath my palm. "How do you know her name?"

"Because I've *met* her, you fool. Don't you understand? She was here, in the castle, the day Max and I came here. *She was here.*"

I had always thought it was impossible to shock Silverton. You might startle or surprise him, perhaps, in an entirely superficial way, but after a decade spent undertaking the most dangerous, clandestine errands imaginable on behalf of his country, he had long ago conditioned himself to expect the unexpected. That was how he had survived in the twentieth century, and that was how he had survived in this one—the extraordinary strength of his nerves.

But now. *She was here*, I said, and his hand froze, his body froze. He seemed to be staring at my fingers, where they encircled his wrist, and I felt the quick stutter of his pulse through his skin.

I tightened my grip. "Do you hear me? She isn't dead. She's with Max, here, in this castle. She went through time. She's still alive."

"I heard you." He withdrew his hand, and I released him. "Does Magnus know?"

"Of course not. How could I explain to him? We can scarcely exchange the simplest ideas. I only realized the connection because I remembered what Helen said, before I—before I came here. And because the children speak English as we do, without any instruction from you."

Silverton glanced across me to Magnus, who was speaking to his father. "Then why did he want to speak to you?"

"I don't know. I think he realizes there must be some connection, or else why should all three of us find our way into his life? But I didn't wait to find out. As soon as I realized, I ran downstairs to find you."

"Of course you did."

Everybody was eating now; the feast had begun. Silverton reached to the platter and filled his own plate, but instead of eating he picked up his cup and drank his wine. His hand seemed steady enough. I envied him. I could not keep my nerves in place; the rest of the world seemed to exist at the end of a tunnel.

"You have to tell me what you know," I said. "There's something—something's going on, I can't explain it, but I need to know everything, straightaway. Everything you know about Helen and how she disappeared."

"I don't know anything. Neither of us knows anything. I've never even met her. She had already disappeared by the time I arrived."

"Oh, for God's sake, start from the beginning!"

Magnus turned to us. "What is it? Something happens?"

"No, old boy," said Silverton. "I'm afraid she's not feeling well."

"What?"

Silverton spoke in Norse—I caught the word *sick*—and Magnus put his hand on my chin and turned my face toward his. He looked worried, almost thunderous, and said something to Silverton.

"I'm not sick," I said clearly. "For God's sake. I just need to know. Will somebody please tell me what the devil happened here three years ago!"

Magnus gestured to Silverton. "You tell her. Go. Now."

"Are you sure?" said Silverton.

The two of them shared a heavy look. Above us, the minstrels played some light, cheerful tune with pipes and strings; the men and women around us were drinking wine, were eating rich food; somebody burst out into laughter and was joined by his fellows. The hall had been transformed into color and light and sound, was saturated with the smell of human sweat and an-

imal food, and yet for an instant I glimpsed its bare, gray, half-
ruined shell, scaled by scaffolding, ringing with the lonely beat
of hammers and chisels, so clear and sharp I couldn't breathe. I
put my hands on my temples and closed my eyes. The vision
passed, but I felt its absence inside me like a poison.

"Take her," Magnus said urgently. "Take her now."

But Silverton was already pushing himself from his chair,
wrapping his arm around my waist, lifting me to my feet. "Come
along, Truelove. That's it. Let's find somewhere private, hmm?"

He led me along the row of stools, stepped me down from the
dais, called out for a cup of wine for his wife. His voice sounded
like an echo of itself. I felt his hand at my waist, his arm across
my back. The great hall slid past, a blur of colors, and something
appeared before me, a cup. We paused. Silverton said, *My thanks
to you*, in Norse. Took the cup and continued on, brushing past
the servant who had brought it, a man wearing a plain gray tunic, smelling of something I couldn't quite place. My head came
up. I turned and looked over my shoulder at the man, but he had
already turned away, and I couldn't see his face, even if my eyes
could properly focus.

We reached the end of the hall and turned down a narrow,
quiet passage, and in the diminishing of sight and sound my
mind seemed to find anchor again. The whirring slowed, the
objects around me took shape. Silverton led me to a small window recess and sat me on the bench. The wind sang through the
shutters, but I was not chilled—the opposite. A strange friction
heated my skin.

"Here," said Silverton, offering the cup to my lips, watching
me closely. While I drank, he said, "I met Magnus as I told you,
in Edinburgh. What I didn't say was this: he had rescued me
from those chaps at the tavern because he'd heard me swearing
in English, the same native language as his wife."

"Helen," I whispered.

"Yes. He told me the story as we made our way northward. His English isn't fluent, as you know, so I had to piece it all together. He said that she had come from the sea, half-dead, wearing clothes like the skin of a seal and speaking a strange language, and he had taken her into his hut by the sea and nursed her to health. Had fallen deeply in love with her. Eventually she loved him back, and bore him two children."

I set the empty cup on the bench beside me. "Did he actually believe that? That she was a selkie?"

"He never said the word *selkie*. But he seemed to think her a magical creature of some sort. Until they learned a little of each other's language, he didn't know what else to think. And I don't believe she trusted him for some time—trusted him to believe her, I mean, because the truth, as you know, is too fantastic for belief, unless you've seen it happen for yourself. Even now, I think he sees you and I and Helen as coming from another world, a sort of realm of the gods, like Valhalla. I don't think he can properly get his head around the notion of traveling through time. God knows I don't blame him."

He took my hand as he spoke, and I stared down at our linked fingers, resting atop my own lap. I had thought the wind created all that noise coming through the shutters, but now I perceived the rush and crash of the sea as it beat the cliffs below. I smelled the brine, the hint of ozone. "What happened to her?" I asked.

"Well. We were making our way up from Edinburgh, as I said—"

"What was he doing in Edinburgh?"

"One of the children had found a treasure of some kind, a stash of pearls, and he had gone to sell them. So we were carrying a fortune with us, though I didn't know it at the time, which he meant to bring home and shower his Helen with. He meant to buy land and build a manor, to become a lord in his own right, because he hated seeing her labor as a fisherman's wife when he knew she hadn't been brought up to it."

"Then he might have made up with his father and found some occupation in the castle," I said, "instead of a harebrained scheme like that."

"Ah, well. A chap likes to make his own way. In any case, they were much at odds in those days, and I daresay he didn't want to put Helen in that position, living in the castle while the countess made her life miserable. You women can be devilish territorial. In any case, where should I be if he didn't go down to Edinburgh on his harebrained scheme? Dead on the floor of a tavern, without much skull left to speak of."

I gripped his hand. "Oh, don't."

"In any case, as we got near to Thurso, Magnus became more and more animated. He'd been away longer than he expected, and he missed her terribly. Couldn't wait to see her again, to see the children, to show her what he'd brought, to introduce her to me. I was rather charmed by his ardor, though it made me ache for you, Truelove. But when we arrived at last, she was gone."

"You mean—"

"No, not gone like that. At least, not until later. The hut was empty, and he was frantic, went into the village for news and found the children in the church, as he had told them to do if some danger threatened. And the children told him that a boatful of men had landed on the shore near their cottage, had made Helen put on the suit in which she had arrived there seven years ago, which Magnus had stashed away in an old trunk, and she had swum away with them."

"My God. It's just like Magnusson's story."

"Magnusson? Who's Magnusson?"

"Thurso's son, the modern Thurso," I said, and then, more slowly, "His natural son. He's the one repairing this castle. He's turning it into a hotel of some kind. And he discovered the chest that— And he told us the legend of the castle—but it doesn't make sense."

"My dear, none of this makes any sense."

"I mean that the story he told us—the family's selkie legend—took place here in Hoy. It's associated with *this* castle, not Thurso."

Silverton leaned back against the wall. "There are dozens of selkie legends in these parts, Truelove, and it's been hundreds of years. Things get muddled and merged together. Interpreted according to one's own superstitions. Isn't that what we talked about, back in Greece? How myths are made."

"Yes, but—" I looked down at our clasped hands. A delicate movement stirred inside me, the baby quickening, and for an instant I forgot all of it, the tangled history, the banquet taking place nearby, Magnus and the Thursos and even Silverton, while an ocean of ferocious love drenched me. I put my other hand on the underside of my abdomen and closed my eyes. Next to me, Silverton moved.

"Something wrong?"

"No."

He made a little sound and laid his hand over mine. I opened my eyes and found he had turned toward me and watched me anxiously. I tried to smile.

"You're certain?"

"Yes. How did everybody end up here in Hoy?"

"We followed her. One of the fishing fleet had seen them, heading in that direction, toward the Orkneys, so Magnus swallowed his pride and went to old Thurso for help. That was my idea, by the way. Old bury-the-hatchet Silverton. And I'll be damned if the old man didn't come bang up to scratch. Gave him men and boats and everything he needed."

"And you reached Hoy . . ."

"And we reached Hoy and traced them north, along the coast, until we reached—well, as it happens—"

"The same inlet where you and I met yesterday?"

"Why, how did you know?"

"Because I found her suit. Helen's sealskin."

"By God! Where?"

"In the cave where you found me."

His hand released mine. He straightened and stared at me. "Why the devil didn't you say anything?"

"Because I didn't want to alarm you. Because I didn't know you knew anything about Helen. Because I simply couldn't explain what I felt in that cave, without terrifying you."

Silverton took me by the shoulders. "What? What did you feel in that cave?"

"Max," I said.

"You can *feel* Max?"

"I can feel his power. It was there in that cave, and it's upstairs in the attic, and it's in your bedchamber and God knows where else. In the great hall, I think, though it's more diffuse there."

He gazed at me steadily, his expression fixed in such stern lines, I couldn't tell what he thought of this revelation. Whether he was angry with me for keeping it secret, or mystified, or even believed me altogether.

"He's reaching for us," I said.

Silverton swore. Released me and leapt to his feet. "I'll swear we searched every inch of that beach. She was gone. No sign of her."

"The cave is very dark."

"It wasn't until we found our old friend Hunter and his men—"

"Hunter?"

"Oh, yes. You'll remember him. The ginger chap who caused all the trouble in the first place, first on Skyros and then on the damned train into Edinburgh, and then at the North British while you lay in your drunken stupor."

I whispered, "He was here?"

"Him and a half-dozen men. They raided our camp during the night, while we were entrenched near the inlet, searching for Helen. It was a damned close thing. He had a pistol with him."

"Oh, God. The bullet!"

"What bullet?"

"The bullet I found on the beach."

He was staring out the window, which overlooked the sea, and now turned his head over his shoulder and frowned downward at me. "Did you, now? Was this before or after you seduced me on that particular beach?"

"Before, of course. I kept it in my pouch."

"And the sealskin?"

"I brought it back with me, wrapped in my cloak. But Hunter! What happened to him? Did you kill him?"

"No," he said slowly, "I didn't. Why do you ask?"

"Because he paid us a visit at Thurso, two days after you disappeared. He surprised us in the library."

"You and Max?"

"Yes," I said. "Max and I were examining the contents of the chest, you see, the one Magnusson had discovered here. The reason Max summoned me up to Thurso to begin with."

"Yes, I remember. So that was what Hunter was after? This chest?"

"No. He was after Max, actually. I think he wanted Max to send him somewhere, but Max didn't know how, hardly even knew what he was talking about, and wouldn't have done it in any case.

We managed to take back his pistol and he leapt out the window and into the sea. He must have killed himself; I can't imagine anyone surviving that leap, let alone swimming to safety afterward."

Silverton folded his arms. "Then how did he turn up in Hoy?"

"I don't know. I presume he accomplished all this before we met him in Greece. He must have first come to Hoy and found Helen, and then managed—God knows how—to get himself sent to the twentieth century—maybe Max accidentally—"

"But that's impossible."

"Not quite. You see, we think of time as a sort of line, when it seems to me—"

Silverton sat down on the bench opposite and leaned his forearms on his knees, so we were face-to-face, almost touching. "No, darling," he said quietly. "I mean it's impossible because he's still *here*. He's locked up right here in the dungeon of this castle, where Magnus imprisoned him three years ago."

℗℗

There is a ring on the fourth finger of my left hand, made of gold. Silverton placed it there himself, the morning after we consummated our marriage, or whatever it was that Magnus had made between us in the great hall of the castle of Hoy.

He knew, of course, that I didn't consider us properly married. He said as much, as we lay facing each other on the pallet at dawn, the blankets wound shamefully around our nakedness. *You're everything*, I had told him. His arm stretched over my head, and the other hand caressed my cheek, and for some time we contemplated each other. Contemplated this new, intimate kingdom we had entered during the night.

"And of course you think we've sinned just now, don't you?" he said at last.

"Yes."

"You do realize the modern Marriage Act is centuries away. You and I could marry each other right now, in this bed, just by saying a few vows and then copulating afterward, if Magnus hadn't already done it. Married us, I mean."

"I didn't say any vows, and neither did you."

"Then I'll say them. I, Frederick, take you, Emmeline—"

I put my fingers on his lips. "Don't blaspheme."

"I wasn't. We don't need a church, Truelove. Not even a priest. Not in this age. God Himself is the only necessary witness."

"It doesn't matter. I don't give a damn if we're married or not. What does it matter, after all this?"

"It matters to *me*. It matters to *me* whether you think I'm your husband or not." He sat up. "Let's get dressed."

"Oh, God. Must we?"

"Yes, my dear. We must."

He had risen and dressed while I watched him dreamily, and then he had persuaded me to rise and to dress. Out in the cool, foggy morning, he had led me down the path to the village and the small stone church at its center. I stopped at the sight of it.

"What about banns?" I said.

"Merely customary."

I looked again to the wooden doors of the church. It was a Thursday, I believe, and they were shut.

"Must we?" I said again.

"Well, no. Of course not. But I should very much like you to believe in this marriage as I do. I should very much like to hear the word *husband* from your lips, and have you believe it."

I looked up at his dear face, the blue eyes I loved, the familiar shape of his jaw and the color of his damp hair, and I thought, *He means it.*

So I went into the church with him, and he roused the sleepy priest and said his vows to me before the humble altar. I repeated them back. The priest proclaimed us man and wife and Silverton drew the gold signet ring from the fifth finger of his left hand and placed it on the fourth finger of my left hand. It was too big, of course. We later went to the blacksmith and had it properly fitted, in exchange for a large, handsome cod.

The point is this. I stood before Silverton on that misty August morning and watched him slide his own gold signet ring over my knuckle, lifted up my face to be kissed as his bride, and I—foolish creature—thought we were therefore united. I thought the ring I wore signified the infinite trust between us, the union of our bodies and minds and secrets. The circle we had drawn between ourselves and the rest of the world, inside which there was only the two of us, our true selves, nothing else.

And I suppose, since I then went on to keep certain truths from him, I shouldn't have felt betrayed or even surprised to learn that he had kept certain truths from me.

But I was.

⚬

"My God," I said. "My God. Right here in the castle, right here below our feet. Why didn't you tell me?"

"For the same reason, I expect, you didn't tell me about the bullet or the sealskin. I didn't wish to alarm you. And there was no need."

I stared across the small space between us, so short a distance that I could see the tiny streaks of brown leaking from his pupils into his blue irises, I could see each line around his eyes and his mouth, I could count each eyelash. I thought of the past seven months, sharing our little hut, sharing our bed, each daily joy, each daily bread. I looked at his lips and remembered how they felt on my breast; I looked at his golden, thatchy beard and remembered how it felt between my legs.

My mouth was so dry, it was difficult to speak. "All that time. All this time, he was a mile away, a short walk, and you *knew*."

"He's locked in the dungeon, Truelove. There's no danger at all."

"If he had escaped?"

"He can't escape. The guards—"

A faint shriek floated down the corridor. Somebody's laughter.

"For what reason?" I asked. "What reason does Magnus keep him there? Why didn't he just kill him?"

"He couldn't do that. He couldn't bring himself."

"Why not? My God, why not?"

Silverton opened his mouth to speak, but the sound of footsteps came down the hall at a frantic pace. A man bolted past, and another.

"What the devil?" Silverton said, rising from the seat.

I rose, too, and looked around the corner of the window recess, into the corridor. The music had stopped, the gaiety had stopped. Somebody screamed. The sound carried like a banshee's wail, and abruptly cut off.

Silverton turned to me. "Stay here," he said, and pushed me back into the recess.

"But—"

"This *one* time, Truelove, for God's sake! Do as I say and stay there!"

Before I could answer, he bolted down the passageway toward the great hall.

❦

Of course I didn't obey him. I sat stunned for a second or two, trying to comprehend the turn of events, and then I rose from the seat and followed my husband at a stealthy, safe distance.

I couldn't let him see me. If he saw me, he would bend his

attention in my direction. He would try to save me instead of himself. I kept back, concealing myself in the corridor's many shadows. My dagger, my leather pouch were both upstairs in the bedchamber, out of reach. Ahead of me, Silverton slipped around a corner and disappeared. The walls now echoed with an ominous silence, except for a single voice, a male voice, issuing commands I could not hear.

Surely this was all part of the feast, I thought. Surely this was some kind of entertainment being practiced on the guests. Two hundred men guarded the castle, and the Earl of Thurso had brought fifty men of his own in their ships across from Scotland.

A scuffle of voices broke through the silence, and another shriek. I stopped and flattened myself against the wall, listening.

Think, Truelove. You can't just walk right into the hall.

Footsteps. Heavy, loud, quick, numerous.

I dashed for the nearest corner and whipped myself around it just in time. Three men ran past toward the hall, bearing arms, wearing leather armor, and I couldn't say if they were guards or attackers, hunters or prey. I flattened myself against the wall and prayed they wouldn't see me in the darkness. Prayed Silverton would find the same luck, wherever he was.

When the noise of their passing faded, I nudged myself out into the corridor and hurried in the same direction Silverton had taken, ducking around the same corner, which led not to the great hall itself but to a narrow, plain staircase. A faint light glowed at the top. Behind me, the sound of footfalls smacked against the stone. I dashed up the steps, breathless, to find myself in the gallery above, which bordered three sides of the great hall at a height of perhaps fifteen or eighteen feet.

I stopped and stared at the opposite side, where the minstrels had played, but there was no sign of them. They were either ducking beneath their seats, or had abandoned their instruments altogether. I looked to my right, the long side of the hall, and a hint of gold flashed from the darkness. Silverton?

I stood with my back to the wall, and I couldn't quite see over the edge and into the space below. I was expecting the noise of a melee to rise into my ears, but instead it was strangely calm, just a single voice calling out commands, and the rustling sound of footsteps on rushes. If I crept to the edge, would I expose myself? Carefully I edged along the wall, out of sight, in Silverton's direction. The gold flash had disappeared back into the shadows, but I knew he was there. My head ached; my eyes were starting to blur. I kept myself upright by sheer force of will, inch by inch, until I reached the end of the wall, facing the open space of the long side of the gallery, and stifled a scream.

Three men lay motionless on the ground. Silverton bent over one of them, working his hands at something on the man's body, over his lifeless shoulder. I wanted to call out, but my throat was too stiff. I moved forward to the pillar at the corner of the gallery, thinking I could grip it and brace myself, and as I approached the gallery's edge the scene in the hall itself became visible. I gathered the details in an instant—tables overturned, guests in a huddle, presided over by a very few men, something going on at the head table, where was Magnus?—when a movement caught my eye from the gallery. Silverton. He held a simple crossbow in his hands, into which he had already loaded an arrow. As I watched, wavering, he coolly brought it up to his chest, aimed, and fired. A shout came up from the hall below. Silverton was already reloading. I peered over the edge and saw a blur of movement, an arrow flying back in Silverton's direction, a ginger head attached to an enraged, familiar face.

And in the way of memory, I now recalled the hooded servant

who had passed me the wine, on my way out of the great hall. The swift duck of his head. I had time and strength to shout something across the gallery to Silverton before my legs failed, but I don't remember the words, or whether they made any sense at all.

The Lady cared not for the shame of her nakedness, for her heart was given over to grief. She stripped away her clothes, and when she stood bare and shivering in the cold wind, she said to her son, 'I see your soul is as empty as that of your father, and I have nothing left to me except the joy of those hours with my Fisherman, and his babe that yet lives in my womb.' But her words only fueled the rage of her son, who sent away the sailors in the boat, and said to her, 'Then you shall swim to my father by your own power, and by the time you have reached him, this sin-begotten infant shall have withered in your lustful belly . . .'

THE BOOK OF TIME, A. M. HAYWOOD (1921)

Fourteen

⁂

When I came to my senses, it was twilight. I knew this because my eyes opened to a window, and the slivers of sky visible between the slats of the shutters had the indigo quality of a day on the point of death.

That was my first thought. My second thought was that my head was split open.

"Handsomely, now," said a voice I knew I ought to recognize. "Don't try to move."

I wanted to say that I *couldn't* move, but that wasn't quite true. My hand went to my belly, even before I remembered the child within, and I discovered that my wrists were bound together. I found the firm roundness with my fingers and groaned with relief.

"Don't worry," the voice said, more gently. "Little lad seems all right."

Silverton, I thought. *What's Silverton doing here?*

I lifted my head, and a sensation of pure agony sliced right through my skull. A hand fell on my shoulder, urging me back, but not before I perceived I was lying on a bed, in a room that was somehow familiar, the walls hung with tapestries. And my feet were bound as well, around the ankles.

"Max?" I murmured.

There was a slight hesitation. "No, my love. Only me. Max remains quite some distance away. Six hundred years, to be precise."

"Oh!" I struggled again and managed to sit up at last.

The room took shape, the world took shape. The man propped up next to me on the bed, wearing only a linen shirt and hose; a bruised, bearded face etched with dried blood. "Silverton," I whispered. "What's happened?"

"We have been taken prisoner, Truelove." He held up his hands, which were tied together with a length of rope, like mine. "Our captor has been so kind as to allow us to remain in our bedchamber. I expect that's due to your interesting condition. I have the idea he wants you to remain in one piece, at least for the time being, and has extended that privilege to me, as your husband."

The word *husband* jolted me back into the world. The history of the past seven months, Hoy, the castle, the village, the hut by the sea, Magnus, Silverton.

For some reason, I had forgotten it all. I had expected a prim, comfortable, modern English bedroom. A coal fire simmering in the grate. I had some vague idea I was going to the opera tonight. *Parsifal.* I looked down at my hands, gathered in my lap, and saw the gold signet ring.

The feast. The children, the attic. Oh, God. The gallery.

"Our captor?" I asked.

"You'll never guess."

"It's Hunter, isn't it? I think—he was down there—"

"Yes, my dear. You've hit the nail bang on the head. It seems our ginger-haired friend has escaped his prison cell, exactly as you predicted."

"How?" I whispered.

"Apparently Magnus's guards aren't so loyal as one might have hoped."

The pain in my head overcame me. I lay down again, staring at the ceiling. "You should have told me. Why didn't you tell me?"

"You're quite right. I should have told you. But I didn't, and you kept a few things from me, and it's nobody's fault, Truelove. I don't think we could have stopped any of this." He paused. "It was Thorvar. Thorvar's among the guardsmen. He wasn't pleased with the events of seven months ago, and so Hunter found a ready ear for his plot. They put some kind of drug in the wine and gave it to the loyal soldiers, so there was nobody to defend the hall when the rebels attacked."

"A coup."

"So it seems." Silverton shifted position, wincing, as if the bruises on his face were only the start of his troubles. His feet were likewise bound at the ankles, and the tips of the stockings hung almost comically from the ends of his toes. "And the earl's visit was a plum dropped in their laps. Making Magnus his heir. Gathering everyone together in one place, and then drowning them in their cups—"

"Magnus! Is he—"

"Still alive. They threw him in the dungeon, along with the countess and a few of the other chaps from Thurso. At least, that was the last I saw, before they took us up here. How are you feeling?"

"My head's pounding. My wrists hurt. I don't believe I'm injured, however."

"It was the wine that brought you down. I was afraid you'd hit your head when you fell, but there aren't any marks. Tried to beat them off when they came for us, but it was no use. And then Hunter came up, like the cat—oh, God, whatever it is. Cream or canary, I can't bloody remember—you're laughing?"

"It's just—you said something like that when we were on Olympia's yacht, just after we met. And I thought you were a terrible idiot. And now—and now—"

"Ah, sweetheart, no tears. We'll find our way out of this, never fear."

"You and your ridiculous optimism. And I'm not crying. I just wish to God . . ."

We lay there on our backs, a foot or two apart, hearts beating into the dusk. The wind blew through the open window and chilled the air.

"At least you're awake now," he said. "That's something. Although you're a fascinating subject, while drugged and asleep. It was not a peaceful slumber. You kept going on about Parsifal."

"I spoke? What else did I say?"

"Nothing of any import," he told me, like the gentleman he was.

I turned carefully on my side. My brains sloshed a half beat behind. "What do we do?" I asked.

"Do? Now?"

"You *have* got a plan of some sort, don't you?"

"Why on earth should I have a plan? Do I have to do all the thinking between us?"

"So you *do* have a plan."

He sighed. "Just rest, Truelove. We can't accomplish anything until your strength is back."

"And then?"

"And then we'll see. By the by, if your wrists pain you overmuch, you'll find that the rope gives way if you give that loose end a bit of a tug."

I held up my wrists. "What? But why would they make a knot that comes apart so easily?"

"*They* didn't, Truelove. *I* did." He maneuvered the fingers of his left hand to the loose end on his own binding, pulled gently, and the rope fell away. "I am a trained professional, after all."

❧

An hour later, the door opened, and Hunter entered the room, bearing a torch that he set in the sconce on the wall.

As we had agreed, I rolled on my side and closed my eyes, as if still under the effects of the drug. Silverton whipped the rope back around his wrists and sat cross-legged on the bed. I had wanted to clean his face and examine the cuts left by the guardsmen, but he shooed me away. *The weaker I look, the better,* he said. Always encourage your enemy to underestimate your powers.

"Damn, it's cold in here," Hunter said. The sudden intrusion of his voice made me shiver: that cadence, that accent unlike anyone else, as familiar as if I had last heard it yesterday. "What, isn't she up yet? Everyone else is up."

"Afraid not, old chap. She's been out like a light. Snoring like a soldier."

"Bulls——," Hunter said.

He marched up behind me and jerked my shoulder toward him, so I rolled on my back. I let out a small, surprised cry—I couldn't help it—but kept my muscles slack, my eyes closed, while he stared down at me. He reeked of wine. *Good,* I thought. Next to me, Silverton made a noise of outrage. I felt him coil up.

"Look here!" he exclaimed. "That's my wife!"

"Your wife? Are you serious? I thought she was banging the duke." He laughed. "They sure the f—— *looked* like they were banging each other, back in Thurso. Come on, b——. Wakey, wakey."

He took my shoulder and shook me, hard, and there was no point in feigning sleep any longer, not while Silverton wound himself into a ball of dangerous fury beside me. I opened my eyes blearily and made noises of confusion, to which Hunter only laughed.

"Oh, b——. You were awake all the time, weren't you? Why don't you sit up and we can have a nice little chat. Come on. Now. Down on the floor." He motioned with his hand, which contained a pistol much the same as the one he had threatened us with in Thurso. God only knew how he had obtained it here.

"The floor?"

"You heard me." He stuck the pistol in his belt, looped his arms under my shoulders, and dragged me off the edge of the bed. My feet hit the floor with a painful thump.

"By God!" exclaimed Silverton.

"Silverton, no! Just wait. I'm all right."

"Chill out, bro. Listen to the lady." Hunter dragged me across the floor with an ease that astonished me, propping my torso roughly against the hard stone wall opposite the door. He straightened, flexed his arms, and grinned down at me. "Pilates, right? You know they invented that s—— in prison? No lie."

"If a single hair on her head—" Silverton roared from the bed.

"Just shut up, all right, bro? *You* I don't trust. So I want you to swing your legs out, nice and easy, and get down on your back."

"On my *back*? Are you mad?"

Hunter swung the pistol toward my head. "Do it," he said calmly, "or I pop her. What do you think of that?"

I knew he was bluffing. He wanted me alive—needed me alive, I expected—or he would have killed us both by now. But I couldn't say that aloud, and in any case, Silverton had undoubtedly made that calculation already. He was tilting his head, gazing speculatively at the pistol in Hunter's hand. The light from the torch lit his beard into shimmering gold.

Make his move now, or bide a little longer?

For God's sake, bide, I thought.

"All right, then," Silverton said at last. "As you like."

He swung his feet off the bed and sank gracefully to the floor. Like an earthworm, he inched on his back along the flagstones, over the rug, past the cold, unlit brazier in the middle of the room. The torch illuminated his bruised face, clenched with pain. My vision blurred as I watched his suffering, and yet I couldn't turn away. His head reached my feet and paused, as if to rest. I gazed at his hair, mottled with blood, where it touched the hard, round knobs of my ankles, and my fingers hurt with longing to take that head in my lap, to stroke the blood and the dirt from that hair.

"Hurry up, all right? And move away from her. No touching." Hunter laughed suddenly. "Unless I say so. Man, *that* would be a good show."

Silverton edged a few inches away and continued, until his head found the wall and he turned on his side and levered himself up in a sitting position to stare defiantly at Hunter. He said not a word. I stared at his battered profile and felt the coldness of his regard. I still wonder that Hunter didn't freeze by the force of it.

But Hunter only grinned and looked back and forth between us, until his gaze came to rest on me. He lowered the pistol. "Damn, it's good to see you. I don't know how the f—— you ended up here, but welcome to Hoy." He flung out his arm. "Glad you stopped by."

"May I make a small suggestion, if you don't mind?" said Silverton, under perfect control. "Kindly cease referring to my wife in vulgar terms. She is not a dog, nor has she engaged in any manner of carnal conduct with our good friend the duke. Moreover, in consequence of our marriage last summer, she presently finds herself in a certain delicate condition for which even a blackguard like you owes her a modicum of deference."

"A delicate condition. Yeah, I can see that. Wasn't going to say anything in case she's just been eating too much haggis or something. I don't know. Is haggis a thing around here? The cr—— they fed me in the dungeon, I couldn't put a name on it."

"Not in its modern form, I believe."

"Well, anyway. So Miss Prim and Proper got herself a little old bun in the oven. Did you put that sh—— up there all by yourself, bro? Nice work, my man. Respect."

"I don't believe you properly understand the meaning of the term, sir, or else I should actually have killed you for that." Silverton delivered this sentence so carelessly, he might have been referring to the weather. "As it is, I feel compelled to begin your education in the matter."

"Yeah? With what gun, bro?" Hunter held up his hand and waggled the pistol. "Because the only heat I see in this room—"

"Oh, stop!" I said. "Stop it, the two of you. For heaven's sake. Mr. Hunter—"

"Just Hunter."

"Hunter. Am I to understand that you traveled here to Hoy, six centuries in the past, *after* you paid your visit to His Grace in Thurso?"

Hunter looked back to me and sat down on the edge of the bed with the gun in his lap. His hair had grown long and greasy, hanging to his shoulders without any kind of binding, and his eyes were quite blue, a detail I hadn't noticed before. The mattress bent beneath his weight.

"You understand correct," he said.

"Correct*ly*," said Silverton. "Grammar makes the man."

"For heaven's sake, Silverton, be quiet." I narrowed my eyes at Hunter. "Do you mean you survived that plunge into the sea? We thought you were killed."

"Nope. I just dove, that's all. Dove and swam to shore."

"Dove? Swam? But—my God, it must have been forty or fifty feet!"

"Something like that. Don't worry, I can handle it. My mum taught me to swim when I was about six months old. She dove in the Olympics, you know that? Won bronze in the platform."

"In the Olympic Games?" asked Silverton. "A *woman*?"

"Man, you are some Neanderthal. Sexist a——hole. This was the '84 Olympics. Los Angeles? She met my dad there. Long story. Anyway, diving's in my blood. I'm like a f——ing porpoise. That ledge in the castle? Not much higher than a ten-meter platform. Like a knife through butter, you know?" He made a slicing motion with his hand, the one with the gun.

"And then somehow you found your way here," I said. "Three years ago, just as Silverton did. Or was it more?"

"I guess it was about three years. But I didn't know *he* was going to turn up in the same spot. That kind of threw me at first. But then the sh—— made sense. I mean, he sent *that* dude there"—he pointed to Silverton—"because he knew that's where *I* was going to be. Kind of like chess."

"I assume we're talking about Max?" Silverton asked.

"Yes, bro. Yes, we are. I got to give that dude some credit. He is one bad motherf——er. Every time you think you got him cornered, he comes right back at you. I mean, I thought I was a goner. I thought the jig was up, man. Sitting there in that damn dungeon. No way out. Biding my time, learning the local lingo. Ticktock. And then, boom! The duke makes a mistake at last."

"What's that?" I asked.

"You. He sent *you* here. What a dumbass move that was. I mean, in chess, you keep an eye on your queen, right, bro? You keep her safe?"

"In fact, the king's the chap you want to protect. The queen's the most powerful piece on the board," said Silverton. *"Bro."*

"Whatever. King, queen. Only a dumbass takes them out of the game."

"Actually, it was my idea."

"Well, you're a f——ing idiot, pardon me. You were *in* there with the duke. I mean, I saw it, b——. He was all over you. He was right up in your attic. And then, boom! You're stuck here in this sh——show, married to this loser."

"I say," began Silverton.

"Sorry, man. The truth hurts. Never mind, though. It's all good. Miss Prim and Proper starts the whole ball rolling. Turns up one day and gets the menfolk hot and bothered, the natives get restless, that's where I come in. Easy peasy, like Mum would say."

"Well done," I said. "So what do you intend to do with us? Now that you've got what you wanted."

"Got what I wanted?"

"Yes. You've overthrown Magnus. You've turned the tables, you've got your revenge. You're lord of the castle, aren't you? By right of arms."

"Lord of the castle? Hell, no. You think I want to be lord of some castle in the middle of nowhere? Like some f——ing Viking?"

"They're not Vikings. They're Norse."

"Whatever. This? *This* is not the plan. This is the means to the end."

"Then what the devil is the end?" asked Silverton. "What do you really want?"

"Wait, wait, wait," Hunter said. "Hold on a sec. You really don't know? You don't have a clue? All this time?"

"My dear fellow, of course not. There's no point trying to understand a madman."

Hunter clutched his heart. "That hurts. Not really."

"Look," I said, "do you mean to illuminate this vast mystery or not? Because I'm afraid I shall shortly require a moment of privacy. As is natural to my condition."

His gaze slid downward to my abdomen. "Oh, snap. Didn't think of that. You know what, bro? She's all yours. Pregnant ladies are not my cuppa." He stretched and rose to his feet. "See you two jailbirds in the morning, okay? Sweet, sexy dreams."

"Wait—you can't just—"

Hunter walked to the door, lifted the torch from the sconce on the wall, and knocked three times. The portal swung open, revealing a guard in armor, whose grim, heavy face I recognized as among those who had attended the wedding feast, seven months earlier.

"Eric!" shouted Silverton.

"Don't waste your time, fool. He's mine. Aren't you, buddy?" Hunter struck the butt of his pistol against the guard's leather shoulder. "Yeah, doesn't talk much, but he can guard a damn door, all right."

"Wait! You can't just leave us here!" I said.

Hunter turned in the doorway. I couldn't see his face, but his voice carried cheerfully into the room, as if borne by the light from his torch. "I know, right? Sucks to sit there in a room, dark as s——, nowhere to go, nothing to do, no f——ing clue when they're going to let you out. If ever. Anyway. See you later, alligator."

"What about food?" Silverton demanded. "My wife's got to eat something!"

"In a while, crocodile."

The door slammed shut, leaving us in darkness.

∽

For some infinite time, which was likely only a minute or two, we sat quietly. Adjusting, I suppose, to the absence of light.

"Was this part of your plan?" I asked at last.

"I suppose that all depends on what you mean by the word *plan*. One's always prepared to improvise, should circumstances take an unexpected turn. But I believe we're back on track now. Everything in hand."

I bent my head and tucked it into the soft hollow of Silverton's shoulder.

"All right," he said. "All right. Shall I untie you?"

"I don't think it matters. I don't even feel them anymore. Hands or feet."

"Well, you should. Come along."

He plucked at the loose end of the rope. My hands fell free, and he repeated the process with my feet.

"What if he comes back?" I gasped.

"I don't give a damn if he *does* come back, at this point." Silverton loosened his own bonds and rubbed the newly freed skin. "Anyway, he won't. Not right away. He's left us to stew in our juices. A classic technique." He turned to me and began rubbing my ankles, my wrists. Asked if they felt any better.

"Yes, a little," I lied.

"Come along, then. Up we go. You've got to move those legs and arms, my love."

He stood and helped me up, supporting me carefully as I rose and wavered on my feet. The room shimmered around me. I closed my eyes and concentrated on Silverton's hands at my waist, his breath at my hair. The air still smelled of Hunter, of wine and blood. Or perhaps the blood was Silverton's. I turned in his arms and rested there, thinking how we had stood like this only this morning, just before he took my hand and led me down to the feast below.

"How is Magnus?" I whispered.

"He took a few blows, I'm afraid. Still alive, so far as I know."

"If only he'd killed Hunter outright, three years ago. Why didn't he kill him?"

"Damned if I know for certain. I presumed he took pity on him. Or perhaps he recognized that the fellow came from another world, like his wife. Like me. Thought the fellow might somehow be the key to getting her back."

"As we are." I looked up. "That's why he took such care of us, isn't it? Because we're linked to her. To Helen."

"When a chap loves a woman like that, Truelove, the mother of his children, he's liable to do any number of foolish, reckless acts to get her back." His arms dropped away. He took my hand and tugged gently. "Come along. You need to move a bit. Loosen those stiff joints of yours."

We walked to the bed, but he wouldn't let me sit. Instead we walked back and forth, back and forth, holding hands in the cold, velvet darkness.

"I don't suppose you happen to feel any of Max's vibrations, at the moment," Silverton said.

"Not at present. Why?"

"Because he couldn't choose a more opportune time to flex those extraordinary muscles of his, don't you think? Would solve our difficulties in an instant. Imagine Hunter walking back in to discover you gone."

I stopped and turned. "What about you?"

"My dear," he said softly, "I can't possibly leave my friend Magnus in such straits as these."

"I'm not leaving without you!"

"I don't believe you have a choice. If Max gets hold of you, I mean."

"Neither would you."

"Can he do that, however? Two people at once?"

I opened my mouth, and the words died in my throat. A gust of wind rattled the shutters and whistled through the cracks to strike my back. The faint sound of shouting seemed to carry along the air. Silverton gripped my hand.

"It's always seemed like a tremendous feat, to me," he said. "One's amazing enough. But two at once? How would he manage it?"

I whispered, "All this time. Have you thought this all along?"

"I didn't want to dampen your enthusiasm."

I bent my forehead into his chest. "You knew we had no chance. You knew from the beginning."

"My dear, that depends on how you define the word *chance*. I thought *I* had a chance of heaven on earth, living here with you. I only regretted that my good fortune came at the cost of your own happiness."

"But I *am* happy. I have been happy."

"Your face said otherwise, when we stood on that damned windswept headland seven months ago, having lost any hope that Max would turn up and do his bit."

"That was before. That was only because I didn't *know* yet."

"Know what?"

I shook my head mutely. He sighed and took my face in his hands and kissed me.

"Never mind, Truelove," he said. "I understand what you mean."

I put my hands on his chest and stared at my fingers. "Besides, what if *you're* the one he brings back, and I'm left behind?"

He laughed. "I doubt that extremely. Max and I may be good chums and all that, but I can't imagine he'd go to all that trouble to haul *my* amiable carcass back inside his century, instead of yours."

"It's not necessarily his choice, is it? He didn't choose to bring Tadeas through. He didn't even know he could, or that Tadeas was there to begin with. The power—whatever it was—

guided him to that spot, to that cliff. Max was only the instrument."

Silverton went still. His lips rested against my forehead, his hands still clasped the back of my head. He smelled of wool, of dirt and perspiration. I could hear his heartbeat, I could feel the whir of his blood as we stood there near the window on our aching feet, surrounded by night. The absence of light heightens all the other senses.

"What are you thinking?" I asked.

"Rules, Truelove. I was thinking about rules."

"Like a schoolroom?"

"Like the universe. Everything's guided by rules, isn't it? Even the things we don't understand. Our whole lives are spent trying to determine what the rules are. Whether to follow them, how to break them. Whether they can be broken at all."

"That's a fascinating observation," I said, into the hollow of his throat, "but apropos of what?"

He stepped back. "Could we possibly manage to get this brazier lit, do you think?"

✑

My notebooks were still in the chest we had brought from the hut. Silverton drew out the topmost one and thumbed through the pages. "To think all our troubles were caused by this damned little book," he said. "If Hunter weren't so seduced by its possible contents as to enter your hotel chamber in the middle of the night—God, the good old North British—"

"I don't know why. We knew so little when I composed these notes."

"What's this here?" He pointed to a page.

I peered closely. We were sitting on the rug by the brazier, trying to read from its feeble light. "It's a sort of diagram," I said.

"I was trying to come up with a possible chronology. To find a pattern. But I was looking at it the wrong way. This notebook is useless, really."

"Are you certain?"

"Yes. It was Hunter who gave me the necessary insight."

"That's decent of him."

"He didn't mean to, of course. But when he spoke to us in Thurso, he told us he was born in 1985, and suddenly it all came—"

"I beg your pardon. Did you say he was born in 1985? Seven decades from when we first met him?"

"Didn't you know that? You didn't blink when he mentioned the Olympics."

"I wasn't thinking. I suppose I thought he meant 1884. Although that wouldn't make sense, either, since they've only held the Games since—what was it—'96? I just never imagined . . . How extraordinary . . . Are you quite certain?"

"Quite certain. He meant the 1984 Olympics, not 1884, which means he was born a year later. And that's what he meant, back on Skyros, when he told Max that it wasn't what he'd *done*, it's what he *would* do, some day in the future. You see, Max is apparently going to write a book about all this, and Hunter's going to read it—"

"But wait a moment. Won't we all be dead by then? By 1985?"

"Yes, I suppose so."

Silverton sat back on his heels and frowned at the notebook. "Well, it doesn't make sense. If Hunter's come from the future, when we're all dead, then who did the hocus-pocus? Who sent him to us?"

"I—I don't know. I suppose I thought—somehow Max—"

"Sent himself into the future, just to send Hunter back to plague us?"

"Well, but Hunter's necessary, in his way. None of this would have happened if Hunter hadn't arrived in our time, starting things in motion. Tadeas would have died, falling off his cliff. So Hunter's a neccssary evil."

"Only if everything works out, however. But assuming that's true, how does Max get to the future in the first place? Is it even possible?"

I took the notebook from him and flipped through the pages, until I came to the drawing of the cliffs of Skyros. I touched my finger to the empty space that contained no sketch of a female figure. No embellishment, like the page we had discovered inside the chest from Hoy. "I've come to believe that anything's possible," I said.

"Possible, then," said Silverton. "But I'm afraid we're going to have to consider another explanation entirely, and one that throws a wrench into all our philosophizing."

"What's that?"

Silverton stared into the meager fire inside the brazier and rubbed his bearded chin. "The possibility of another actor. Somebody else who shares Max's power, at some point in the future. Somebody, it seems, who doesn't wish us well."

The hours fled without measurement, with no sign of food or company. The immediate crisis past, I became aware of a deep, almost painful hunger, and realized I hadn't properly eaten since breakfast. My stomach growled angrily. I asked Silverton whether we should attempt to escape. Surprise the guard outside our room, overcome him, and flee before anyone could find us.

"It's too risky," he said. "If we're caught, God knows what he'll do to us."

"We don't know what he plans to do to us, in any case."

"Bide awhile, Truelove. You can't rush these things. You have to strike when the moment's right, when your chance opens."

"What if this *is* our chance? Our only chance?"

"Then it's a rotten one and not worth the trouble. Go to sleep. I'll keep watch."

I wanted to say that I couldn't sleep, not famished like this. But Silverton hadn't eaten, either, had he, and he didn't complain. There was a little water left in the pitcher. I swallowed a mouthful and we returned to the wall, where Silverton carefully retied our bindings and settled me into his lap.

"I'm damned hungry, Truelove," he said, stroking my hair. "Are you hungry?"

"A little."

"A little. Well, I'd make love to you to help you forget your miseries, but I'm too damned bruised, and we'd only end up hungrier than before. Besides, I've already trussed us up again. Mind you, there are some who prefer it that way."

I laughed softly into his velvet tunic.

"I shall get you out of this, Truelove," he said. "I promise."

"We'll get out of this together." I said it with conviction, a little too loud, as if I were trying to convince us both. And maybe I did convince myself that we would escape this prison together, for I fell deeply asleep, there on his lap while his hand stroked my hair.

I know this because when I woke sometime afterward, a faint dawn had just begun to creep through the shutters, illuminating the figure of a woman who must certainly have belonged to my dreams.

I raised my head. "Helen?"

She crouched down next to me, and her face was more ghost than dream: pale, drawn, lined, unbeautiful.

"Come with me, quickly," she said. "I need your help."

The Lady begged her son for mercy, but his soul was cold and empty, and her pleas fell upon indifferent ears. Her son handed her the suit she had once worn and said, 'Take this and cover your nakedness, so that my father will not see your shame, and the body you have defiled in the squalor of an adulterous bed . . .'

THE BOOK OF TIME, A. M. HAYWOOD (1921)

Fifteen

At the sound of Helen's voice, Silverton startled awake, knocking his knee into my ear. "My God!" he exclaimed. "Who the devil are you?"

"You must be Lord Silverton," she said. "My name is Helen. Magnus's wife."

"But what—the guard—"

She held up a knife.

"You killed him?" I gasped.

"He may live," she said, shrugging, "and if he doesn't, it's no more than he deserves. There's a reason the punishment for sleeping on sentry duty is death."

I tried to rise, but the cords around my wrists and ankles hampered me. Helen leaned forward with her knife, but I waved her away and pulled the loose end, as Silverton had shown me. I still felt I was in a dream. My mind was slow and clumsy, and so were my hands. The brazier had gone out, the room was cold.

My fingers were so frozen, I could scarcely feel them. "How did you get here? Max?"

"Yes. I wish I could explain, but we haven't any time."

Silverton had already slipped free from his bindings and helped me with mine. "You're mad," he said. "Have you got any idea what's going on? A damned foolish—"

"Yes, I know. Why do you think I'm here? I need your help."

"Our help? I thought you were helping us!" I said.

"To do what?" asked Silverton darkly.

Helen was rubbing my ankles—not out of sympathy, I suspected, but to get me on my feet as quickly as possible. "To free him," she said. "To free Magnus."

"You realize he's languishing in the dungeon right now, don't you? Guarded by a dozen men, at least."

"Of course I do." She straightened. "Why do you think I came to fetch you first? Now hurry, before someone walks by and discovers what I've done to that chap outside the door."

༄

Dawn lay chill and quiet about the walls of the castle as we stole down the corridor to the rear staircase. Silverton led the way, because he was the one who knew where to find it—a small, narrow set of steps that led down to the storerooms, through which the dungeons might be accessed.

Though the eerie stillness allowed us to creep undetected, it fed my anxiety. "Where is everybody?" I whispered to Silverton as we paused to turn a corner.

"I expect they're asleep," he whispered. "Magnus's men in the dungeon, Hunter's chaps either drunk or exhausted, or both."

"They're drunk," said Helen, in disgust. "Every last man."

I wanted to ask more, but Silverton gave the all clear and we scurried painfully down the hall to the next corner. When we

reached the relative privacy of the staircase, I whispered to
Helen again.

"What about Hunter?"

"I haven't seen him. I hope to God I don't. I couldn't bear it."

She spoke so coldly, I stifled any further questions, and in any
case we had just reached the bottom of the staircase and entered
the dark, dank space in the castle's netherworld. Silverton paused
at the corner and stretched out his neck. With one hand he motioned us forward, and we followed him down a narrow walk-
way, until he ducked to the right, into a small, windowless room
filled with baskets, smelling powerfully of fish. Helen put her
hand to her mouth.

"I apologize." Silverton drew the door in behind him, allowing a few inches of light. "It seems they use this space for storing
the dried cod in winter."

I turned to the baskets and lifted the lid, and Silverton was
right—it was half-filled with filets of white, dry fish. "Thank
God," I said, and put one to my mouth. It was like chewing
leather, only it tasted of fish, but I was too hungry to care.

Silverton watched me. "Do you know, I've been flung together with any number of unusual colleagues in my years of
service, some of them more striking in their habits and persons
than others. But I've never had the pleasure of undertaking a
mission with two gravid women."

I handed him a filet. "Here. You'll be glad for it later."

He frowned and took it, and after a certain mature consideration, Helen accepted another. I propped myself against one of the
baskets, and for a moment we stood there, recovering our breath
and our wits, while the air made clouds of our breath. I had slipped
on a woolen overdress, and Silverton had done likewise. Helen's
costume was similar but too short, as if she had taken it from
someone else's wardrobe. Well, presumably she had.

Silverton swallowed and said, "We haven't much time. Hunter's chaps will be awakening soon, and even if they're not quite in fighting form, we're only three, and largely unarmed."

"Not quite," said Helen. She reached into the folds of her cloak and pulled out a gun: not the sleek machine Hunter had brought with him, but the more rounded, familiar shape of a modern revolver. She handed it to Silverton. "I presume you're the best shot. I have only a dozen bullets, so you must use it carefully. The chambers are fully loaded, at present."

He took the gun reverently and turned it about in his hands. "Max's?"

"Yes."

"Good man. If you see him again—"

"I don't mean to see him again. My life is here. I've already taken the children and their nurse to a place of safety—"

"When was this?"

"During the night. Hunter seems to have forgotten their existence, or perhaps he didn't know where they were being kept."

Silverton nodded. "Magnus only allowed a few people ever to see them. How did *you* know where they were?"

"It's too much to explain." She finished the fish and brushed her hands on her skirt. "They're waiting for us in the cove, with a ship. There's not a moment to lose."

"Yes, let's get to it," Silverton said. "Before Hunter decides to kill him."

"Oh, he won't kill him, not yet," Helen said. "He needs Magnus."

"For what?"

"For me, of course. All of this, everything he's done, it's to get me back. But I won't go."

"To get *you* back?" said Silverton. "I always thought he took you for ransom, when he came for you three years ago. That it was something to do with Magnus's new fortune. Do you mean he wants you personally?"

"Yes. He wants to take me back with him. Back to our own time, our old life."

"I don't quite—I beg your pardon—were you lovers? Man and wife?"

She recoiled. "Oh, my God, no! I mean, I had a husband, of course. Hunter's father."

"His father!" I exclaimed, forgetting to be quiet.

"Yes." Helen looked at me, and though the light was dim, I could see the agony in her face. "Hunter was my little boy once. My wee treasure. And when I disappeared into this world, his father raised him instead. His father raised him to be just like himself. And now he wants me back."

"Who wants you back?" Silverton asked. "Hunter, or his father?"

She put her face in her hands. "Both."

❧

The plan was a simple one. Those were the ones that worked best, Silverton explained, for the obvious reason that fewer things went wrong. He was to go ahead and find the cell where Magnus was being kept, while Helen and I kept watch at either end of the long corridor encompassing the dungeon. I took Helen's knife, while she took the gun back from Silverton. Max had shown her how to use the thing, whereas I knew nearly nothing about revolvers.

But as we crept down the dark, silent hallway from the store-rooms to the dungeon, I wondered if perhaps we would have done better to wait. To go into the village and find help and weapons, to construct some robust plot to take back the castle by force. Except, by then, the alarm would be raised. Hunter would have discovered our absence, and we would have lost the element of surprise.

Better to act now, I told myself, keeping my gaze on the faint shadow of Helen's back as we moved along the flagstones, clutching our weapons. My ears strained for noise, for any clue that the castle had awakened. There was nothing. Only the rustle of our own passage. Only the smell of our own bodies, and the damp sourness of the dungeon itself. As if the walls themselves were lying in wait for us.

For an instant, my mind flew back to that stealthy journey through the bowels of Thurso Castle, following Magnusson to the ledge by the sea to find the place where Hunter had plunged. *Well, he's gone now, God rest his soul*, Magnusson had said confidently— my God, I could almost hear the philosophical cadence of his voice—and where were we now? Creeping along a different corridor, in a different castle, behind a different man, but it was all the same. Damp, chilly, dark, the stone walls pressing upon you, no end in sight. My body ached, my feet and my wrists hurt. I wiped my damp right hand on my dress and clutched the knife more firmly into my palm.

Just ahead, Helen stopped and made a motion with her arm. I paused obediently behind her. I saw that her hand was shaking, that her profile—scarcely visible in the charcoal light—seemed sharp and keen, almost beatific in her longing for the man imprisoned in one of the cells nearby. Imprisoned by her own son. The hair tingled on the back of my neck. I put my left hand to my abdomen and looked over Helen's shoulder at the gray smudge that was Silverton, moving cautiously ahead to check for guards, his blond head finding what little light worked its way through the darkness. In that moment, every ounce of love I had ever felt for him, every atom, seemed to rise up in my chest and

choke the air from my lungs. I flung my arm out to brace myself
on the wall, and Helen half turned to see what was wrong.

Ahead of us, Silverton turned and motioned. That was the
signal. I remained in place, turning to keep watch on the corridor we had just crept down, while Helen went ahead with Silverton to the other corner. In the middle, according to Silverton, a
hallway split off to the cell blocks, like the stem of a T. Helen
and I should wait on our corners, watching for the approach of
any additional guards, until Silverton emerged again. With
Magnus, God willing.

I watched them go, over my shoulder, until the darkness
swallowed them. Two gravid women, Silverton had said. *I've
never had the pleasure of undertaking a mission with two gravid
women.* He'd said the words cheerfully, as if this were an im-
provement over his usual circumstances, but as I stood there in
the hallway, nearly blind, stiff with cold, I saw the hopelessness
of it. One man, two women in the family way. What chance did
we have against a dozen guards, even drunk?

I kept my gaze—such as it was—on my assigned corner, but
my ears strained to hear the sounds from the territory behind
me. If I went absolutely still, if I tuned my entire body into a
mere conductor of atmospheric vibration, I could just detect the
stirring of human bodies. Not the sound, exactly, but the sense
of them, respiring and moving and existing. The smell of human
perspiration. Human excrement. Foul human breath.

Footsteps.

I straightened and peered into the gloom.

Yes, footsteps. Quiet, muffled, distant. A single, quick pair of
feet. A woman? I adjusted my grip on the knife, touched my
thumb to the razor edge of the blade. My heart flew, my blood
warmed. My God, could I do it? The beat of feet grew sharper,
and then a light appeared, soft and golden, bouncing in the same

rhythm as the footsteps. It grew in a lurid halo along the stone wall, while my muscles tensed, my mind keened to absolute attention. Larger and larger the light grew, until the shape of a human body appeared suddenly around the corner, approached, saw me, froze.

My God, I knew her. The serving maid who had poured my wine at the wedding feast. A comely girl of perhaps sixteen, round-cheeked, dark-haired. She carried a candle in a plain pewter holder, which she shielded with one hand. The rank smell of tallow crept into my nostrils. We stared at each other. Her eyes widened with recognition. I put one finger to my lips, and she nodded, turned, and flew back the way she had come.

As I sagged in relief against the wall, a faint shout sounded from behind, and cut off abruptly.

Silverton, I thought.

I wanted to run, I wanted to find the source of that noise, I wanted to know what was happening, but I could not. I was chained to this damned corner. I was no soldier, but I knew this was my post, and I should hold it at all costs. How many of Hunter's men were guarding those cells? Were they all awake? Were they armed? I flattened myself against the wall and tried to watch both sides, back and forth, the corner of approach and the hallway where Silverton had disappeared.

There was no clock in this vast space, no way to count the seconds and the minutes that passed after that first faint shout. I counted them anyway. I felt the beat of time in my bones.

I have to go, I thought. *I can't wait here any longer.*

Just as I pushed myself from the wall, another sound reached my ears, echoing from the stone: the sharp, surprised cry of a woman, calling my name.

I bolted off down the corridor, toward the corner assigned to Helen, passing the hallway to the dungeon cells, running so quickly, so heedlessly that I ran into her almost before I saw her. She was not alone. Holding her right arm wrenched behind her, pressing a pistol to the back of her head, was Hunter. Was her son.

When I first showed signs of being with child, I confess, I avoided them. I knew the possibility existed, even the likelihood; as the summer passed into autumn, Silverton had spent himself so often inside me, we might have conceived an army. But I had never thought of myself as a mother. I had so little knowledge of maternity; my own mother died when I was five, and my father had never remarried. I had never expected to marry; I had certainly never expected to have children.

But when couples meet in bed, without any modern means of keeping the essence of life at bay, children are the likely result. I entered willingly into the pleasures of Silverton's bed, knowing these facts, yet still I waited patiently for my courses to make their regular appearance; and as the days passed, the weeks passed, I felt a little betrayed that they did not. Until my body began to swell and grow tender, and my appetite grew fussy, and one fine, frosty morning in late autumn, I looked down at my breasts and I looked at Silverton, pulling his tunic over his head, and I heard myself say, "I believe I may be with child."

I believe. That's what I said, and yet a small part of me did not believe it. Did not translate this idea of pregnancy into a real, living child, until the day when at last the babe grew large enough to flutter against the sides of my womb and make himself known to me. I remember I was lying in bed in the moments before sleep, my husband stretched soundlessly along my side, the still, black night pressing around us, and there came a tickle. The delicate beat of a butterfly's wings.

And I felt that flutter in wonder, and put my hand on my belly for the first time, and for the first time I said the word *mother* to myself. I tasted it on my tongue. I saw a baby before me, I saw a pair of round infant eyes, I felt the quickening of a brand-new passion inside me. I remember thinking how strange a bond this was, host and parasite, the advantage all to one side, and yet I knew I would pour all my life's blood into that growing creature, if I could. If I had to.

I would die for him.

⁓

Now this bond stood before me in adult form. Mother and son, the advantage all to one side, the child poised to kill the parent. There was not enough light to see their faces properly, but still I found the terror in Helen's eyes, the fury in Hunter's. He was a few inches taller than she, and her temple banged on his chin. In the flat, dim light, his ginger hair was the same color as hers, so that you could not quite tell them apart.

"Don't do it," I whispered. "You can't do it. Your own mother."

"B——, you don't know. She *left*," he said. "She f——ing left us to live with *him*. She had his f——ing babies."

"She couldn't help it. She didn't know *how* to return to you."

"She f——ed him. She was married to Dad, and she f——ed *him*. Giant ugly-a—— cretin."

"She thought she would never see your father again. Isn't that right, Helen? She fell in love again. It's nobody's fault, least of all hers. Don't you want her to be happy?"

As I spoke, I slipped the knife into the fold of my dress, out of sight. Helen's face was frozen in terror. Where was her revolver? Had she dropped it?

"Actually, I don't give a s—— if she's happy or not. We've just got some unfinished business back in the good old twenty-first century, that's all. Nothing personal. Granddad's inheritance. Unless she turns up, it all goes to the f——ing RSPCA. Sooo . . ." He shrugged as he stretched out the word.

I thought of Silverton. I heard his voice, echoing back: *She jumped straight into another man's bed, and then she bolted with him, and I never saw her again.*

"You're lying." I shifted the knife lightly in my palm. "It is personal. You wouldn't have done all this if it weren't. You've been obsessed with this all your life, haven't you? Your mother leaving you."

"You know what? Pretty sure you're not a qualified therapist, Prim and Proper. So you just b——er off, all right? Go back to f——ing your cretin. Pretend you never saw anything. I'm done here. Got what I wanted."

Behind me, the shouting had started, and my mind seemed to divide into two—one side listening painfully to each noise, each thump, each clang, each exclamation, and the other side focused upon the man in front of me, holding a pistol to Helen's petrified head.

"No, you haven't," I said. "You may have won back your mother's body, but you've destroyed her soul. You can't have back what you lost. But you're an adult now, you can give her back what *she's* lost. You can give her back the man she loves. The life she loves, the children who need her. Your brother and sister."

"Oh, f—— off. I told you, I don't give a s——. I'm in it for the money."

"And I say you're not. You wouldn't still be standing here—"

But my words were swallowed up in the tide that engulfed us. Hunter looked up in amazement to the hallway behind me, and I lunged without thought, knocking the pistol from his hand. It struck the ground and went off, and somebody screamed. Helen staggered backward against the wall of the corridor.

I turned and raised my knife against the oncoming scramble of shouting, bearded men, but somebody grabbed my elbow and my wrist, forcing the blade free. I swung my head and bit his hand, and he dropped the knife. I watched it fall, threw myself downward to grab it, and Helen screamed, "No! God! Don't hurt him!"

Hunter turned to her, as if he'd forgotten she was there, and reached for her arm.

A roar filled our ears. In the next instant, a massive bulk blurred between Hunter and me. Magnus, streaked with blood, both old and fresh. He took hold of Helen's shoulders and lifted her away from her son as easily as you might lift a baby from a cradle, and she cried something out in a voice that sounded as if it were dragging across shoals.

But Magnus did not stop to answer her. He turned in fury to Hunter, raising his enormous fist. Hunter dove for the floor, and I thought he was only avoiding the blow, but when he stumbled back to his feet he held the pistol in his left hand.

"Watch out!" I screamed. I tried to kick it from his hand, but I was too far away and lost my balance, crashing against the wall. Hunter switched the pistol to his right hand and rose to his feet. Magnus whirled around to insert himself between Helen and the pistol. Lifted his elbow to dislodge the gun from Hunter's hand. The gun went off, a shower of chipped stone came down from the ceiling, and a pair of men flew past Magnus and Helen to tackle Hunter to the ground.

One of them was Silverton.

"No!" Helen screamed, darting around Magnus, reaching for Silverton's arm. In confusion, he loosened his grip, and Hunter writhed free.

"Get him!" I called. I levered myself from the wall and started forward, but I was already too late. Hunter bolted down the corridor and melted into the darkness.

Silverton scrambled to his feet, turned to me, and took my elbows.

"Are you all right?" he demanded. Bright, new blood flowed from a cut above his left eyebrow.

"Yes! Your face—"

He released me and whipped down the corridor, where Hunter had vanished.

I started off after him, but a hand gripped my arm and kept me back. I turned my head and saw it belonged to Magnus, who held Helen against his chest with the other arm. His face was haggard and thunderous. "Stay," he commanded me.

"But the men—"

"Are mine. Fingal opened the dungeon. The castle is ours."

⸎

We made our way, dazed and shivering, into the great hall. The morning sun dazzled the air through the open windows, illuminating the shambles of the day before. The tables were overturned, the food and wine spilled across the rushes. A pair of dogs moved about, stomachs bulging, picking at the destruction.

It's all right, I thought. It's over. Thorvar and his band of traitors now inhabited the dungeon, in place of Magnus's men, and I hardly dared to think of their fate in this brutal, pitiless world. It would be swift and final. Danger sliced off at the neck. Peace restored, the castle cleaned and returned to order.

But the knot of worry remained in my chest.

I turned to Magnus, who stood aside with Helen near the enormous, empty fireplace. Her face was turned into his chest, and he was stroking her hair. He had sent two men after Silverton and Hunter, and none of them had yet returned.

I opened my mouth to demand news, but I had no chance to speak. A small, keening cry rose behind me, and a figure in blue darted past to throw herself on the body of a man who lay near the dais at the end of the hall. Her bare head shone silver in the sunshine, and I recognized the Countess of Thurso.

Helen raised her head and made a noise of sympathy. She detached herself from her husband and followed the countess, and I observed Magnus's face as he watched her go. Adoration so intense, it was almost agony.

I moved to his side. "What is it?"

"My father," he said tonelessly. He lifted his hand, stained with blood, and made a motion to his neck.

"My God! Why?"

"Why?" He looked at me in amazement. His eyes were wet. He gestured with his giant arm to the scene around him. "Why this? Why man is cruel? God alone is good."

I burst out bitterly, "How can you say that? How can you look upon all this, your own dead father, slaughtered before you, and say God is good?"

Magnus sighed and wiped his cheek with his thumb. He looked back at his wife, who knelt on the stones, holding a sobbing countess in her arms.

"God is good," he said. "Man is cruel."

As I put my hand on his thick arm, I heard my name called out behind me, in an exhausted voice. I turned my head toward the sound. Silverton staggered into the hall, followed by two of Magnus's guards, and perhaps it was only chance that the morning sun passed through a certain window along the eastern wall and struck his head at such an angle, he was drenched in gold. Or perhaps the light would have found him anyway, would have disobeyed the puny laws of physics and bent in his direction. I stared at his tall, graceful figure, his shoulders bent by weariness, his dirty, bloody clothes, and my misery slid away.

I ran toward him and flung myself into his outstretched arms.

"Did you find him?" I gasped.

"No. Wretched bastard." He held me tight against his chest, kissing my hair, kissing my temple, smelling rank and unwashed and beautiful, and then he set me back and looked over my shoulder at the scene around us. "My God. The poor woman."

Helen looked up and saw us. She detached the countess carefully and hurried to intercept Silverton. "Hunter!" she said, grabbing his arm. "What's happened?"

"I don't know. We tried to follow him, but he seemed to know the place better than we did. Lost him."

"Lost him where?" asked Helen. "Where did you lose him? Where was he going?"

"Near the granary," he said.

Helen turned to Magnus. Her face had lost all color.

"The children!" she said, and I shall never forget the tone of her voice. I shall never forget the terror of it.

✑

She had left them inside the granary, in the care of the nurse, because it was quiet and unlikely to be disturbed at such a time, and because it was located near the path to the village, where she had a fishing smack fully rigged and waiting to sail.

She explained all this to me, panting, as we ran from the great hall to the stairs leading down to the working part of the castle, not far from the storeroom where we had made a breakfast of dried cod an hour before. I didn't need the explanation—all that mattered was that they were safe, that Hunter hadn't found them, that Hunter hadn't already known where to find them—but she needed to give it.

Because if she had left Olivia and Henry untouched in the attic, they would be in no danger.

Neither of us could move swiftly, weighed down as we were

by pregnancy and exhaustion and injury. We lost sight of Magnus and Silverton at the bottom of the stairs. The underground engulfed us, and as I felt the cold, damp air on my skin, the familiar smell of damp and human confinement, I had to force back a surge of panic. Helen clasped my hand and pulled me down the corridor, turned a corner and then another, past the narrow staircase we had taken earlier, until I felt a cold wind rush against my cheeks. The light grew. We turned a final corner and saw a small wooden door, open to the meadow behind the castle, and Helen made a strangled noise and darted forward to an opening in the wall, just inside the door.

She ducked under the archway and screamed.

I came up and caught her just as she fell to her knees, still screaming, over the still, blood-soaked body of the nurse, whose throat had been slit.

Of the children, there was no sign, except for a jumble of faint, bloody footprints leading out the door to the meadow.

"Come," I said, "come. Quickly. He can't have gone far."

I pulled her up and we staggered outside, blinking, to a cold, sunlit morning. Ahead, two tall figures bobbed along the path to the stables. We ran after them, all bruises forgotten, all fatigue evaporated by the manic pumping of our hearts. Helen reached them first, taking Magnus by the shoulders as they stood in the stable yard, interrogating a boy of about thirteen years, who scratched his head and pointed down the hill to the village, a mile away.

"Where?" she whispered. "How long ago?"

The boy shrugged, for he hadn't the finely tuned sense of minutes and hours that the modern age stamps upon the human mind.

"It can't be more than half an hour," Silverton said.

"But he took the horses," she said. "The horses I had ready for our escape."

"Can more be saddled?" I asked.

"That will take time," Silverton said. "I'll go on ahead and see if I can catch up."

Magnus laid a hand on his shoulder. "No. I'll go ahead. Keep the women safe."

Silverton nodded, and Magnus went off down the lane at a run. Helen made to run after him, but Silverton stopped her. "It's best if he goes by himself," he said. "You'd only slow him down, at the moment."

She looked at him fiercely and removed his hand from her arm. "Just you damned well try and stop me," she said, and off she went.

Silverton ran a hand through his hair and swore. He turned to the boy and barked an order in Norse, and the boy went running toward the castle gatehouse. Then he pivoted back to me. "Can you ride a horse, do you think?"

"Not very well."

"Then I suppose it's time to learn."

❦

We didn't stop to saddle the horses. Silverton fitted a rope to the headstall of a gray pony, and another to a bay. He chucked me up on top of the gray and swung up behind me, and off we went, leading the bay, until we caught up with Helen.

"Can you ride?" he shouted.

"Yes!"

He tossed her the rope, got down, and helped her scramble on the back of the bay pony. She clapped her heels into the animal's sides and went off at a canter, and I saw at once that she hadn't lied. She stuck to him like a burr, and the two of them raised a cloud of dust all the way into the village, while our gray, burdened by the additional weight, heaved gamely after them. My thighs ached, my bottom bounced against the pony's back. Silverton gripped my waist with one hand and the rope with the other, guiding the pony by I know not what signal. Possibly he wasn't guiding at all, and the poor beast only blindly followed the track and the horse ahead. We reached the first of the stone cottages, and the villagers came out in the lane and watched us, amazed. Silverton shouted a question to one of them, and he pointed to the harbor.

"Damn," Silverton said. "That's what I was afraid of."

We reached the harbor a moment after Helen, who leapt off her pony and ran to the water's edge. "It's gone!" she screamed. "It's gone!"

"What's gone?" I asked as Silverton handed me down from the pony.

"The boat! The boat I had ready!"

Magnus stood at the edge of the wooden quay, firing questions at the fisherman who stood there, quaking, next to his craft. He pointed out to sea. Magnus looked up and shaded his eyes against the bright sun, and a shout escaped him, a noise of fury and despair.

"No!" Helen screamed.

I grabbed Silverton's arm. "Where's he taking them?"

"Damned if I know. Magnus!"

Magnus turned, and I have never seen such an expression on a man's face, as if someone had plunged a claw through his belly and removed his vital organs.

"We'll rig my boat. Come along!"

Silverton was already running along the quay to his own small vessel, bobbing at its mooring. He jumped aboard, discovered the canvas sail folded under the seat at the stern, began to fasten it to the mast. Magnus stepped in after him, making the boat rock violently, and shipped the rudder in place with expert, efficient movements.

Helen and I ran to the water's edge. "For God's sake, hurry!" she said, agonized.

Magnus straightened from his task, just as Silverton gave the sheet a last tug. The sail made a pure white triangle against the blue sky.

"All set?" Silverton asked.

"Go. Get off. I go alone. She will sail faster."

"But—"

Magnus shook his head. "No. I give you command of Hoy. I need you to stay, Fingal. To guard my wife. He wants her."

"*What?*" said Helen. She started forward, and Magnus stepped quickly off the boat and took her in his arms, not to say farewell but to stop her from climbing aboard.

"You must stay," he said to her. "I will bring them back. I swear it."

She swore at him in Norse, and he answered by kissing her. Silverton leapt to the quay and began to untie the rope holding the boat to its mooring. Helen's arms went around Magnus's thick neck. She was sobbing and swearing, both at once, and Magnus put his hand on her head and pressed his cheek against hers. I saw with surprise that his eyes ran with tears. He took her by the shoulders and set her back on her feet, and I shall never forget the way he kissed her a final time, brief and tender, before turning back to the boat and wiping his eyes.

Silverton stepped in and gripped his hand. The sun was bright in his hair.

"She's yours," he said. "Godspeed."

So the Lady slipped her arms and legs into the suit she had worn when she left her old land, and when she was done, her son dragged her into the water and said, 'Go, swim into the bay toward the ship, or I shall go inside the cottage and slaughter the bastard children you have borne this Fisherman, and he will return to find their slain bodies on the floor, and believe you have killed them.' The Lady waited in vain to hear the bells of the church ring three times, but no sound reached her ears, and her son in his impatience took out a knife to prod her ribs, so she drew breath and plunged into the cold water, without looking back at the cottage where she had known all the joys on earth . . .

THE BOOK OF TIME, A. M. HAYWOOD (1921)

Sixteen

❦

Four days later

Winter blew back into Hoy the day after Magnus left, pelting us with sleet and misery, and though we lit braziers and covered the shutters with animal hides to keep out the gales, we could not banish the cold.

"I'm going mad," Helen said, rising once more from her stool to lift the hide from the window and stare at the harbor, or rather the patch of mist where the harbor ought to be. "Something's happened. Can't we send a messenger to Thurso?"

"Not in this weather. Sit down, for heaven's sake. You're letting in a draft."

"I don't care." But she dropped the hide and returned to her seat. Her cheeks were pink, her nose tipped in red. I thought she might have a cold coming on, although she didn't complain, at least about her health. She rubbed her hands before the brazier. On the floor beside her lay a discarded embroidery frame, on which I was attempting to teach her to cross-stitch. Not that I enjoyed embroidery myself— in fact, I detested it—but her mind and her fingers needed occupation.

"He'll be back, Helen," I said quietly. "Didn't he promise you? Hunter's no match for him."

She put her face in her hands. "That's what I'm afraid of."

I bit my lip in remorse. I had forgotten again. I couldn't seem to make my own peace with the notion that Hunter was Helen's son. She was too young to have a fully grown child; she was too good to have a child so utterly lacking in human empathy. I stared at her head, bent at an angle of deep distress, and the whiteness of her hands. What was it like, to know that the child you had carried beneath your heart, into whom you had poured all your love, all your tender hope, had grown into a monster? Had held a pistol to your own temple? And you could not wish him death. Even as he threatened your husband, your children, even as your own happiness and safety depended on his defeat, you could not bear to see him vanquished.

"Shall I call for wine?" I asked gently. "Some other refreshment?"

"No, thank you." She lifted her hands away and found her handkerchief. "I'm sorry. I should be stronger. After everything I've been through, everything I've seen, I really should just buck up, you know?"

"When the weather clears. As soon as the weather clears, Magnus will return with the children."

"Yes," she said tonelessly, wiping her eyes.

I leaned forward. "He won't kill him. He would never kill your son."

"But Hunter would kill him, if he could. God, what happened to my son? I just wish I *knew*. Oh, I can imagine, of course. From his accent, I suppose Tom took him back to America and raised him there, with all the other rich boys. And of course he turned out like Tom. What else could I expect?" She laughed bitterly.

"Was he as terrible as that?"

"He was just an a——hole, that's all. I married an a——hole. It happens. And I deserved it. He was married. He was forty-three years old, he was a Wall Street banker, in Los Angeles for the Olympics, entertaining clients. Mr. Thomas Spillane, managing director for Latin American equities at Sterling Bates and Company. Terribly impressive. He was incredibly polished, like my father. Incredibly rich, like my father. And I was incredibly young and stupid. I was the trophy, don't you see. The pretty blond Olympic diver. Britain's Golden Girl. Oh, I was something, all right. Nineteen years old, can you believe it? He swept me off my feet. I didn't know he had a wife, at first. By the time I did, I didn't care. He told me his marriage was already over, they hadn't slept together in years, the old story. I don't believe I even thought about how she felt. His two kids. How horrible is that? All I remember thinking was that the whole thing was really her own fault, she should have looked after herself better, looked after Tom better. I really thought that. So I expect this is my punishment."

"It's not a punishment. Certainly not a just punishment."

"Karma, then. That's the word we use. Well, the karma kicked right in. I fell pregnant almost immediately. He divorced his wife, married me just before Hunter was born, and while I was still in the hospital I found he was having an affair with somebody else. So it's true what they say. When a man marries his mistress, he creates an open position."

She was staring into the brazier, not at me, and the coals gave a little color to her face. A strand of hair escaped from her headdress to curl against her cheek. This was the first time she had spoken to me of her past, and I hardly dared to say a word, in case she might realize I was listening.

"Anyway," she went on, gathering herself a little, "he took that house in the north of Scotland one summer, when Hunter was six, specifically to get me out of the way so he could freely shag his new girl all over London. I was miserable. I think I might have killed myself if it weren't for Hunter. Tom named him that. I wanted to call him Archie, but Tom said that was a sissy's name. God, he was such a sweet child! I missed him so much. That first year, it was like my own heart had been cut out of my body. I couldn't understand how I was still breathing. I couldn't feel anything. Magnus was so patient, he just waited for me to grieve. I think I learned to love him only because of that. He was so *good*. I couldn't believe a man could be that good, that faithful, day after day, never pushing me, only waiting for me to love him back. Then I looked at him one day and I realized I did. I loved him. So I slept with him." She looked at me at last, and this time there was a little smile at the corner of her mouth. "That went well."

"Hmm."

"Mind you, I'd only ever slept with Tom before. I spent my teens just training, training, training. Trying to please Daddy. I was literally a virgin when I met Tom. Sorry, I don't mean to embarrass you. But you've got to understand how absolutely brilliant it was, going to bed with somebody who actually cared about me. It was the difference between winter and summer. It was—God, it was amazing, it was bloody *amazing*. I already loved Magnus, but after that night I fell *in* love with him, and the best part was that instead of fizzling out, it just kept getting better. Do you know what that's like, to wake up every morning and fall in love with somebody all over again?"

"Yes," I said softly.

"It's like a drug, except it's good for you. No side effects. Oh, but you know that already. He's quite a prince, your Fingal. Your fair-haired stranger. My God, I envy you. No complications, no regrets, no bloody strings holding you to that other world, that horrible world."

"It's not so horrible."

"Yes, it is. I'd rather die here in dirt and chaos, die in child-birth or some stupid infection, than go back to that shallow, awful place. Look what it did to my son. My sweet boy. Tom turned him into a monster." She jumped up from her seat and went to the window again, lifting the hide, peering between the slats of the shutter. The gray light changed her face. I stared at her graceful figure, the slight bulge of her belly beneath the long overdress, almost exactly the shape of mine. She let the hide fall, but she didn't turn. "Night's starting to fall. I miss him most at night. Especially during these frightful gales."

"It won't be long now."

"Oh, stop. You've been saying that for days." She wrapped her arms around her middle. "I want my children back. I want my husband. I want—oh, God, I want our cottage back. Our beautiful, simple life. Those pearls. As soon as Henry brought them in, I knew everything was going to change. A wooden box of priceless pearls, just sitting there, like a test. The way the gods test mortals. Except it wasn't the gods. I suppose it was probably Hunter himself. He planned everything else so well."

"Except that you escaped."

"Yes. When we reached Hoy. He brought me to shore and dragged me into a cave—"

"The cave! In the inlet?"

"Yes, it was an inlet. Not far from here. And I felt this terrible power come over me, just as when I was first hurled into this time, and I—I don't know how—he was holding on to my wet-suit, we were struggling, and somehow I broke free and ran out the cave, and the next thing I knew, I woke up on that same shore in 1906—"

"But that's where I found the sealskin!"

"The sealskin?"

"Yes. The rubber suit. Except it wasn't rubber—"

"My God! You mean my wetsuit? You found it in the cave? When?"

"The day before the feast. I went for a row—"

"Where is it? Did you take it?"

"Yes. I brought it back with me and put it away."

She had turned to face me, and her eyes were bright and large. "Can you show me?"

I hesitated. "I'm not quite sure where it is. The workmen moved our things the next morning—"

A voice interrupted us from the doorway. "Actually, I know exactly where that sealskin lies."

I turned. "Silverton. There you are."

"Where?" asked Helen. "Where did you put it?"

"I found it among our things, as we cleaned up after the night of the feast." He shrugged. "Put it away in a chest and locked it up, so the servants wouldn't discover it."

⌀

That night, I waited for some time after Silverton's breath had lapsed into sleep before I rose from the bed. I wanted to be absolutely sure he wouldn't stir.

As I swung my legs to the floor, the baby moved inside me. He had been restless all day, as if my own unease had communicated itself through the walls of the womb. Nobody else had noticed this disquiet, not even my husband. *Put it away in a chest and locked it up*, he'd said, shrugging, as if the location of the sealskin were nothing more than a curiosity. An innocent coincidence.

The air was still and nearly black. In the neighboring chamber—which was part of our new quarters, connected to this room by means of a doorway recently cut in the stone—slept Helen. In order to reach her, an intruder would have to enter through our bed-chamber first. Once Magnus returned, and Helen was restored to his bed as lady of the castle, her room would become the nursery for our own child. So I told myself, as I sat on the edge of the bed, staring at the dying red light of the brazier in the middle of the room.

But my nerves would not settle. The prickling of my skin seemed to lift each hair. Everywhere I went, these past five days, I had felt it, ebbing and flowing, like a piece of music searching for a climax. Had felt Max. Reaching out for me, just beyond the limits of my perception. Now it found a new pitch, so high and so strong that the baby felt it, too.

I placed my feet on the rug and slid from the bed. Behind me, Silverton made a small, distressed noise. I held myself still, wait-ing for another sound, while the air beat and beat around me, but nothing came.

Softly I walked across the hard floor and found the chest we had brought from our little hut by the sea. I ran my fingers across the beaten wood and found the latch. Opened the lid. Our clothes lay on top, folded neatly. I dug my fingers underneath the layers of woolen cloth until they touched the hard, familiar surface of my notebook. The one Silverton had brought from Edinburgh, the one Hunter had been so desperate to find.

To this day, I don't know what instinct drove me to creep next to the brazier and its faint light, to flip through the pages until I came to the drawing of the cliffs of Naxos. *Put it away in a chest*, Silverton said, shrugging, and in that instant a cold draft went through my veins, and I knew a desperate need to find that notebook, to assure myself that nothing had changed, that the pencil likeness of a woman did not now exist on one of its pages.

I tried now to ignore the electric charge that titillated my palms and the tips of my fingers, originating from somewhere inside the notebook itself. But I could no more ignore that sensation than I could ignore the energetic twitching of the child inside me. I could no more stop myself from turning those pages than I could stop my own heart from beating. And when I flipped a final page and the familiar shape of the Naxos cliffs took shape in the dim, red light, I already knew what I would find.

The pencil drawing of a woman, whose face I now perceived to be mine.

"I hope you don't mind," Silverton said, over my shoulder.

I jumped and turned, nearly oversetting the brazier. Silverton caught my arm and drew me to my feet.

"I drew that the night we were imprisoned here. Couldn't sleep. Saw you lying there in my lap, and I found the pencil inside the portfolio, your pencil, which I kept all those years because your fingers had touched it—hush—"

"Don't let go," I cried, into his chest. "Keep hold of me."

"My God, what's wrong?"

"Let's go back to bed. Take me into bed."

He swung me up and onto the bed, under the covers, and I burrowed myself against him, shaking, clutching, lifting his shirt over his head, lifting away mine, needing his skin, his muscle and bone, a merger of me into him, him and me into one indivisible whole. I don't think I intended copulation, but the two of us had not come together as man and wife since the morning of the feast, the longest abstinence of our marriage, and neither of us could withstand the shock of nakedness. Inevitably he turned me on my back and united us, murmuring words of comfort into my ear. I wrapped my legs and arms around him and told him not to stop, not ever to stop until morning, to keep us joined like this until the sun rose: as if the sun could hold back what was to come. And gamely he sought to obey me, to slow the beat of movement, to regulate the heat and friction as we ground together, while I held on in fury, fighting capitulation with all my strength. I relished the scratch of his beard on my cheek and the weight of his elbows against my sides, for they anchored me to earth. But you cannot resist a tide like that forever. Nature will have her way. Nature created this act for a single, ruthless purpose. At last my own flesh betrayed me, and the sound of my cry forced Silverton's answering shout. We lay panting and tearful, wholly entwined, drained of all strength, and I gasped out, *Don't move, don't leave*, and he promised me he wouldn't, of course he wouldn't ever leave.

But as I held his wet, quivering body with mine, I knew it didn't matter. His promise didn't matter. He wasn't the one who was going to leave.

✍

Possibly we fell asleep, or possibly we only slipped into the demiconsciousness that comes after intense physical passion. I only know we both jolted into alertness at the same instant, by the same sound—a woman's scream penetrating the thick stone walls of the hallway outside our door.

Silverton leapt out of bed and dashed naked through the doorway into Helen's chamber. The door itself was already open, as was the door to our own room. I found my shift, damp and wrinkled beneath me, and I pulled it on and heaved out of bed in the same motion. Silverton emerged from Helen's room, pale and shocked. "She's gone," he said.

I threw him his shirt and ran to the door. Outside, my waiting woman knelt weeping over the body of the soldier who should have been guarding the entrance. A pool of dark blood spread from beneath his head; I could smell it in the air, bright and coppery. She looked up and said in Norse, through her tears, "I knew something wasn't right, I came to see if you were well—"

I fell to my knees next to her. Silverton was right behind me. He touched the man's head, his hands. "Still warm," he said. "Can't have been long. Did you see whether her door was closed, when you woke earlier?"

"It must have been. I never went to sleep."

Our eyes met above the bare, braided head of the waiting woman, and we shared an instant of horror. Had we remained watchful, had we not sunk together into oblivion, we should have heard if anything were amiss.

And the intruder, if he came, must have passed within feet of our joined bodies.

Silverton reached out and took my shoulder. "Stay here. I'll go downstairs and canvass anyone awake."

"No. I must come with you."

"The danger—"

"Silverton," I said, "there is not a chance under heaven I'll stay in that damned room without you."

⁓

Half an hour later, we rode postilion northward across a moonlit meadow. The gale had blown out; the sky was clear and tranquil, though the air remained damp. The stableboy had said he'd seen a man steal into the stable with a woman just before midnight and ready a pony, and the stableboy was too wise to intercede, but he went into the castle and told the waiting woman, who was his sweetheart. They had ridden north along the coast, he said. Wasn't sure where. There was nothing that way for miles. No anchorage except for a small inlet, used occasionally by fishermen as shelter during the sudden gales.

The pony was of that breed native to these shores, short and shaggy and rough-gaited but immensely strong. He bore our weight without complaint. We had eschewed a saddle, and I sat astride in the hollow between Silverton's thighs and the pony's withers, clutching tufts of mane for balance. Silverton had wrapped a cloak around us both, and the heat of his long, ungainly body warmed mine. His chin hovered next to my head; his beard scratched the tender skin of my temple. Perhaps a quarter hour behind us rode half a dozen sleepy guardsmen, fully armed, but I knew we wouldn't need them. Even if they arrived in time, a show of force would accomplish nothing.

The moon was nearly full, gilding the grass and cliffs, the silver-dark sea to our left. The breeze smelled of brine and rain. I felt it whip along my cheeks until my eyes watered. I felt the drumbeat of the horse beneath me, the flex of Silverton's body at my back, and I thought I should always remember them. I should always remember each sensation crowding this particular hour.

The terrain was hilly, and as we descended the last slope, curving down to meet the edge of the little inlet, Silverton slowed the pony to an impatient walk and then swung off. He kissed me briefly. "I'll go have a look. You'll be all right?"

I nodded and watched him turn away to descend the bank in his familiar, loose-limbed gait. The moon touched his shoulders and the top of his head. He reached the bottom of the slope, where the cliffs had crumbled away to form a notch, and disappeared. I heard the faint crunch of his footsteps on the stones, and then nothing.

The pony shifted beneath me and pulled at the bit. I was not accustomed to horses, had scarcely ever ridden one. I slipped to the ground and gripped the animal's headstall. I strained my senses for any sign of what was happening on the beach below, but there was only the rush of the waves, the sporadic hiss of the breeze along the cliffs. Above all, the thump of my pulse as it struck the inner part of my ear. The tick of my nerves, the tingling along my bones. I closed my eyes and leaned against the pony's neck, and the image of a man took shape before me. Not any man I knew. He was tall and gaunt and white-haired, wearing a strangely cut jacket of brown tweed, and his eyes were a deep, melancholy shade of blue as he stared into mine. He seemed to be trying to tell me something.

My eyes flew open. I released the pony's bridle and started down the hill, so quickly that my feet slipped on the damp grass as it gave way into gravel. The soles of my shoes were thin, and the stones dug painfully into my feet, and I couldn't seem to breathe. Though my lungs gasped for air, my chest would not obey. At last I stumbled free of the cliffs to the base of the beach, where the inlet opened up before me like a ghost, and for a moment, spinning one way and the other, I saw only the shingles and the driftwood and the ragged cliffs, the few acres of empty sea shimmering in the moonlight.

Then movement, in the shadows to the left.

I cupped my hands around my mouth and called out Silverton's name. The cliffs echoed back the sound, but no reply came. Only the slapping of the waves, the rustle of wind. I peered into the night, where I had seen the shadows move, and it seemed to me I saw a pair of figures there, like specters, arranged near the fallen tree where Silverton and I had met.

My throat closed in panic. I tried to call out again, but all I could voice was a strangled squeak. *Move*, I told myself. *Move*. But a peculiar paralysis seemed to have seized me, and I had to drive myself forward, one leg and then another, while a series of shocks traveled down my spine and lifted the hairs on my skin. The image of the white-haired man rose again in my mind. The tide was out, and the beach was still wet. I slipped on the shingles, recovered, slipped again. Called out again, and this time my voice engaged, the sound came out, and Silverton's name rang desperately from the rocks.

"Truelove?"

"Yes! Where are you?"

"Here. By the cliffs."

His voice sounded clipped and unnatural. I paused, struggling for breath.

"Is anyone with you?" I called out.

"Yes."

I gathered myself and plunged forward. The shadows grew sharper, and I saw there were not two figures but three. Two of them stood close together, as if embracing. A yard or so apart stood Silverton, taller than either of them by more than half a foot, his hair catching the full force of the moonlight.

Another voice called out. Not Silverton's.

"Prim and Proper! Knew you couldn't be far behind. Damn, I should have brought s'mores."

"Brought *what*?" said Silverton.

"S'mores. S-apostrophe-M-O-R-E-S. You start a fire and make them on a beach at night. Hershey bar and graham cracker and roasted marshmallow. Damn fine. After your time, though. Maybe Mum's heard of them. Mum? S'mores?"

There was a broken-voiced *No*.

"Huh. I guess it's an American thing. Well, come on over, P and P. Don't be shy. We were having a nice little chat, the three of us. Maybe you can help us out. You know, with the female perspective. Plus, you being pregnant and all."

I had been creeping closer during the course of this exchange, until the ghostly figures resolved into human beings, Silverton standing with his back to the sea, Hunter and Helen facing him. I had thought Hunter must be holding her in some way, binding her, but that was only a trick of the darkness. She stood near him but independent, holding her arms around her middle. The moonlight cast deep, frightening shadows on her face, and I thought I saw the glitter of tears beneath her eyes. By now, I was about a dozen feet away from her, and I came to an uncertain stop.

"Closer, closer," said Hunter. "Mum's got a big decision to make. She needs your support. Don't you, Mum?"

Helen shook her head and turned away.

"All right, all right. I'll do the explaining, I guess. I mean, you're probably thinking to yourself, hell, why don't my big, strong hubby just do his commando moves and decapitate that motherf——er? Then we can all go back to our nice, cold castle and snuggle under the blankets together. Right?"

"Don't tempt me," Silverton said.

"Nah, you won't do it. Because it's Mum's decision, ain't it? Big, big decision. A tough one, I'm not going to lie. And I'm sorry for putting you in this position, Mum. I really am. It's just that I had no choice."

"You had all kinds of choices, Hunter," Silverton said. "You've just decided to make the one that places your own mother in a most devastating position."

"Me? Hell, no. Nobody puts Mummy in a corner." He laughed. "Yeah, you won't get that one, either. Shame."

I said icily, "Perhaps, Mr. Spillane, you might have the goodness to enlighten me on the nature of this decision to which you've forced your mother."

"Oh, ho. You know my name, do you? I guess you and Mum had a heart-to-heart or something. That's nice. I'm touched. Poor Mum hasn't had a night out with the girls in years, I'll bet. Cosmos and kale salad and how your man always leaves the milk out on the counter, all that s——. She needs some good girl-friends in her life. So maybe you can help us out here. Asking for a friend. If everyone you loved were living on the other side of a door—the other side of a massively wealthy door, check it, mil-lions of dollars, fancy cars and houses and f——ing kick-ass antibiotics whenever you get a sniffle—everyone you loved except your hot Viking stud, sadly, 'cause he don't come with this deal—would you walk though that door?"

"Helen?" I said. "What does he mean?"

She whispered back, "He means he's got the children. On the other side."

"The other side? The other side of where?"

She lifted her hand and pointed to the rock face, and for a moment I didn't quite understand. Did not comprehend what she meant by this, because how could a pair of young children become somehow imbedded on the other side of a cliff?

And then I remembered. The cave.

"They're inside the cave?" I said, even though I knew that wasn't quite right, that I had missed the point. I had missed it deliberately, because it was too awful to encompass, too terrible a thing for one human being to do to another.

Helen crumpled into the sand, still staring at the faint, shadowed fissure in the rock. "No. Not any longer. Not here, anyway."

"J—— Ch——," said Hunter. "F——ing women. Drama, drama, drama. I mean, get to the point already, right? Here's the story, Prim. That cave, right? I think you know it? That's kind of my own personal portal. My dude, back in my time, who has the same juice as your boy Max. That's where he puts me down and picks me up. You get what I'm saying?"

"Good God." I turned to Silverton. "You're right. There *is* someone else. Someone else with Max's power."

Silverton kept his gaze on Hunter's face. "Who?"

"Doesn't matter who. We'll call him Hollander, okay? I'm not saying it's his real name. Let's just say for the sake of having a name. We have this arrangement, Hollander and me, by which he does his hocus-pocus and gets me out of Dodge, and my friends back home don't f——ing kick his ass into his armpits, right? And that cave is The Spot. That's where it goes down. That's how he finds me. You know the drill, right?"

"And the children—" I began, in horror.

"Yep. The children. Getting to that. Those cute little moppets— and I mean, they are hella cute, no doubt about that, I have thoroughly enjoyed getting to know my little bastard love child half siblings—I put *them* in the cave. You know, like putting a letter in a mailbox? And Hollander opened up *his* mailbox and took them back out on the other side." He brushed his hands together. "Easy peasy, as Mum used to say to me, back when I was a wee lad."

Helen was sobbing quietly, kneeling in the pebbles and dirt. I dropped to her side. "He's lying," I said. "He must be lying. Nobody would do such a thing."

"Yeah, I guess it was pretty harsh, now that you mention it," said Hunter. "But I mean, what choice did I have? And at least it put an end to all this terrible f——ing violence. I mean, who needs that kind of body count? Think of the lives saved. Now we can just stand here in the moonlight and talk it over. Hold hands and sing some Lennon while Mum makes her decision. And I'm sure she'll make the right one. No good mummy would ever abandon her kids in order to have a f——fest with some hot Viking stud. Oh, wait."

"For God's sake, man," Silverton said, "have a little decency."

Hunter sighed. "Come on, mummy dearest. Ticktock."

I wrapped my arm around Helen's shaking shoulders and looked up at Silverton. "Is he telling the truth? Where's Magnus?"

"No sign of him. But I've looked inside Hunter's boat, and I'm afraid it's clear the children were inside." He nodded to the shore. "And footprints. Some kind of struggle."

I followed his gaze and saw the boat dragged up along the beach, just above the line of high tide. I hadn't seen it before because of the darkness and the driftwood. "What about inside the cave?"

"I looked. It was empty. Just footprints."

I turned to Hunter, whose face bore a small, smug smile. The moonlight had a strange effect on his face, bleaching the ginger from his hair, casting his features in a strange, ethereal shadow that gave him the exact look of his mother. The resemblance made me gasp. He cocked his head inquisitively and I rose from Helen's side.

"I'm going to look," I said.

He shrugged and sat down on the fallen tree. "Suit yourself."

I rose, motioned to Silverton to keep watch over Helen, and made my way across the shingles to the cave's entrance. In this darkness, I might have groped my way for some time across the damp, sheer rock, searching for the gap, but in truth I needed neither sight nor touch to find it. I felt its proximity like a hum in my bones, or the way bees find their way to the hive. As I reached the opening, I stretched out my hand, and my fingers felt as if they were stung. I drew back, gasping.

Hunter called out, "Prim feels it. Don't you, Prim? He's right there waiting, isn't he? Waiting by his mailbox. My man Hollander."

"It's not at all like a mailbox," I called back. "Your friend has to do it deliberately. How did he know?"

"Go on. Go inside," said Hunter. "Or are you scared, Prim? Scared he might get you, too?"

"I didn't feel anything," said Silverton.

"Maybe that's because you weren't called, old boy," said Hunter. "Maybe you're supposed to stay right here. It's only us going back who feel the call. What do you think, Prim? Am I right? Maybe those kids were supposed to shoot off into the twenty-first century. Maybe it's all arranged in our stars, like Shakespeare said, nice and pretty."

I couldn't speak. I could scarcely move. The power contained in that cave was like a lure, like a magnetic current that drew upon some substance inside me.

"Truelove?" Silverton said, alarmed.

"It's there. It's there," I whispered.

"What's there?"

"Whatever it is."

A pair of hands closed around my shoulders. He pulled me back roughly, nearly spilling us into the shingles. I saw Helen's white face against the beach nearby, gazing at us in terror.

"Did you see them?" she whispered.

"I don't know, I don't know. But it's there, the power is there."

She made a low, keening noise and bent over her hands.

Hunter rose from the log, brushing his hands. "Let's go, then. Time's a-wasting."

"Wait," I said. "There's no proof. No proof you've sent them through."

"Proof? Proof? What more do you want?" He patted his hips, as if searching for pockets. "I mean, where the hell else are they? Hiding somewhere? They'd have come out by now. We're wasting time."

"Time has no meaning. We could wait a week, and the children wouldn't know the difference. It will be only a minute to them."

"But it won't be a minute to Mummy, now would it? Every minute that goes by is like torture, isn't it, Mum? When someone goes away to another time, and you can't be with them. You can feel them standing next to you, but they're not there. Not that I speak from experience or anything."

"Then at least let her wait until Magnus arrives. Let her say good-bye."

"No!" Helen rose. "I can't face him. Oh, God. His face. I can't."

"Besides," Hunter went on, smiling a little, "he might just be a little bit dead."

"Dead!"

"A little bit." He dug into his cloak. "I know it's here somewhere. Somewhere. Aha! Here we go."

He tossed a shiny metallic object into the air, and Helen reached out reflexively and caught it.

"I think he would have wanted you to have it," said Hunter.

She stared at the object in her hands, and I strained to see it. "How did you get this?" she whispered to Hunter.

"Tore it off his cold, dead body. What else?"

She looked up. "I hate you."

"Ouch. Thanks, Mum. I don't mind telling you the feeling is mutual." He stretched luxuriously. "Well, anyway. I'm out of here. F——ing cold, wet rock. I am going to jump right into a nice hot bath, first thing, and then I'm going to eat an entire jar of peanut butter, straight up. Vodka shots. Get myself a nice hotel suite somewhere, just me and the kiddos, hanging out in our fluffy bathrobes and ordering room service until my dad arrives. And Granddad is going to s—— his pants. I bet he sets up a trust. I play my cards right, and I'm sitting on a gold mine."

"Wait!"

Hunter was strolling across the beach toward the rock, supremely confident. Silverton grasped his arm and snarled, "Over my dead body, you'll reach that cave."

"No!" Helen said. "Let him go."

Hunter turned his head until it was almost touching Silverton's chin. "You heard the lady. Let him go."

"Please, Silverton. I'm going with him."

"Helen—"

"Let him go!"

Silverton gazed at her, and then down the bridge of his nose and into Hunter's face, turned up into the full force of the moonlight. "I ought to thrash you and dump you into the middle of the g——damned North Sea, you miserable bugger."

"But you won't."

Silverton thrust him away, so that he fell onto the shingles, laughing.

"I forgive you, buddy. I had it coming, I admit. I mean, this is a dick move, no doubt about it. I deserve to get my ass kicked." He rose, dusted himself off, and held out his hand. "Come on, Mum. Let's go board our flight. First class all the way."

Helen stared at him, and the expression on her face was not hateful or even angry. It was simply blank, as if she had traveled past emotion, and now felt only shock. She wore no headdress, and the breeze ruffled the hair at her forehead, which shone almost white in the moonlight. She was bathed in silver, and her beauty stunned me. A series of waves hit the shore, more rough than the others, and the sound was like a signal. She turned to me and put her hand on my arm.

"It's the legend, isn't it? You can't fight the old legend."

"What legend?"

"The selkie legend. How the master of Hoy lost his love to the sea, and the castle was never happy again."

"That's only a legend."

"All good legends start with something true." She leaned forward and kissed my cheek. "Take care of him. He loves you terribly."

She turned and took Hunter's hand. In the other hand, she clutched the object he had given her, the relic from Magnus.

I turned into Silverton's chest. My heart was swollen and painful against my ribs. His arm came around me, and he swore into my hair.

"I can't bear it," I said.

Silverton let out an almighty roar, like a beast in a cage. From behind me came the crunch of footsteps on stone, and I closed my eyes and counted the steps. I smelled the sea, the coldness of the air. Crunch, crunch. Then silence, as if the feet had been swallowed up. Silverton's heartbeat pounded under my cheek. My own blood stirred restlessly in my veins. In my head, I heard Magnusson's voice: *She stays by his side for seven years, bearing two children, but at the end of the seventh year she discovers the sealskin and disappears back into the sea.*

The children, I thought. *It doesn't fit. The children stay behind, with their father.*

I opened my eyes and saw a ship.

Silverton must have felt the stiffening of my body. "What is it?" he asked.

I couldn't speak. I pulled free from his arms and pointed my finger. He turned and peered at the water, and I remembered that his eyesight was imperfect, and he didn't have his spectacles, not in this world.

"A ship!" I gasped out, and I started running toward the edge of the water, straining to catch the details in the moonlight. It had already sailed halfway into the inlet. Had Hunter seen it? Was that why he had hurried his mother into the cave?

I turned back to Silverton and yelled, "Get her! Quickly!" Then I cupped my hands around my mouth and hallooed with all my strength.

A faint halloo sounded back. There was a loud splash, as of a boat being lowered into the water, and a voice boomed out, calling my name. Calling Helen's name.

"Magnus!" I screamed. "Hurry!"

But he couldn't hurry. There was no possible way he could reach us in time. In time to do what? Say good-bye? Helen had made her decision. She could not abandon her children to another age, not again.

I started forward, splashing into the water itself, and I don't know what movement caught my notice in that boat. Some shift of the moonlight. I saw them only an instant, fingers curled over the boat's edge, faces illuminated with hope.

Two children.

And I was running back up the beach, flying over the stones, pushing an astonished Silverton aside and plunging into that buzzing, electric cave. The strength of the charge jolted through me. I staggered forward, grasping with my hands in the darkness, grasping whatever I could, grasping at nothing at all, grasping a piece of fine wool.

"Helen!" I screamed. "The children! Magnus! They're here!"

She didn't answer, and my eyes found them, clasped together, huddled on the floor of the cave. Hunter's arms were around her, and his face turned up to me, lit with an almost beatific madness. A madness I recognized, for had I not felt it myself?

I grabbed her shoulders, and instantly the power found me and drew me into its whirling vertigo. I closed my eyes and fought, fought. Pulled at Helen's shoulders with all my strength. Dimly I felt a pair of hands close about my waist, pulling me back. A voice, calling my own name, calling me back. I shouted Helen's name, over and over, locked my fingers together around her chest, and then an even greater force found us, a physical might beyond description. I felt myself ripping, bones snapping, sinews popping.

Release came like a snap of a band. We tumbled free of the cave's mouth in a heap: me, Silverton, Helen, Magnus, to lie still and silent on the rocky shore.

Of Hunter, there was no sign.

So the Lady disappeared with her son into the cold waves, and when the Fisherman returned the next day, laden with rich presents, he discovered only their children, who cried piteously and told him how his Lady had put on her strange suit and swum away with a man who came by the sea. And so great was the Fisherman's grief at these tidings, he never married again, though he ruled as lord of the island and waters he had once plied as a mere fisherman, for he could not bear to see another woman in the bed where he had once known all the joys on earth . . .

THE BOOK OF TIME, A. M. HAYWOOD (1921)

Epilogue

Hoy, Orkney Islands
September 1323

The King now comes to visit us from time to time, but only my daughter sees and hears him. He watches her play with her little brother and talks to her about the games he used to play as a child. Once he addressed me, though not directly. We sat on the floor of the attic, not long ago, practicing letters while an April gale howled outside the window, and Araminta turned to me and said, "His Majesty wishes to know if you are breeding again."

"His Majesty?" I asked, incredulous. (This was the first I had heard of him.)

"Yes. That fat fellow right there, in the strange clothes and the gray beard."

I looked in the direction to which she pointed, and for an instant it seemed to me I could detect a slight shimmer in the air, a faint impression of a pair of familiar blue eyes. Familiar to me, I should say, only from paintings and photographs, for I had never, in my old, twentieth-century life, had the good fortune to meet King Edward in person.

I turned back to Araminta. "You may tell His Majesty that such an intimate subject is none of his business."

There was a little pause, and Araminta sighed. "He says that it *is* his business, Mama. He is passionately concerned in your affairs."

"Then he should ask me directly."

But he never did.

Still, we are a happy lot, the four of us. Araminta, as you see, is a terribly precocious child, and her brother Armand is a cheerful little towheaded chap who rarely complains. Of Hunter, there has been no sign, no breath of news, and we have gradually come to presume he has met some unknown fate elsewhere, and to believe his evil influence gone from our lives. Our only true sadness arrived last spring, when Nature dashed our hopes for a third child—for the King, you see, was correct in his speculation—and I am afraid I have only just begun to emerge from the grief of this loss. My husband has been my chief support. The insatiable carnal appetites of our early days may have moderated somewhat, which is not necessarily a bad thing in the course of everyday life, but our mutual affection seems only to feed upon itself. My great joy still lies in waking up each morning to find some part of my body touching his, and to see the inevitable smile warm his dear face when he opens his own eyes to regard me at his side.

Or perhaps my great joy comes a few moments later, when the door to the nursery flies open, and our children scamper in to land between us in the bed.

Silverton is away just now, visiting Lord Magnus at Thurso to hold council on some recent acts of piracy that have plagued

our fishing and merchant fleets, and the entire household misses
him horribly. When one is accustomed to sunshine, its absence
turns everything gloomy. Araminta, who is the shining red apple of her father's eye and knows it well, has been inconsolable.
She shares his height and his nimble mind and his blue eyes, and
from the hour of her birth, when she nestled in the crook of his
elbow and received her first smile from his overjoyed face, they
have been desperately in love with each other. I'm afraid she
does not take his absences well. The nurse, having put Armand
to bed for his nap, begged me for an hour's relief, so here I sit at
the little table in the attic instead of attending to my own duties
as lady of Hoy, while Araminta tosses her doll on the floor and
sticks her face in the hollow of her folded arms.

"You must pick up your doll, darling. Lady Helen made it for
you with her own hands." (We speak Norse in public and modern English at home, for I have some slight, superstitious fear
that our native language might one day return to our lives.)

Araminta lifts her head and looks at me with her blue eyes
and her stubborn face, and I'm half afraid she'll say cheerfully, as
her father might, *B—— Lady Helen*. But if the idea occurs to her,
she quickly thinks better of it, pressing her cherry lips together
to hold the words back.

"Perhaps we can practice your sums?" I ask.

The look on her face tells me what she thinks of this scheme.

"I have an idea," I say. "Let's go downstairs to Mama's room
and try on the jewels for Lord Magnus and Lady Helen's visit at
Christmas."

Generally speaking, Araminta is not given to such pursuits.
To be perfectly honest, she's what we would have called a tom-
boy, in my own time. But perhaps it's the rain drumming at the
shutters, or the shift of seasons now under way, or the temporary
void in her heart that bears the shape of her adored father. She

tilts her head as she considers my proposal, given in desperation, and then she slides from her stool and takes my hand.

✑

The jewels were presented to me by Lord Magnus, when Silverton was officially invested as the Earl of Orkney's vassal and lord of Hoy, and I as his lady. This occurred perhaps three months after the ordeal on the beach, as Magnus had assumed the titles and lands of his dead father, the earl, and I was nearing my confinement with Araminta and gross with child. I remember feeling generally unimpressed, both with the jewels, which were weighty, and the ceremony itself, which required me to stand upon my aching ankles for rather longer than I would have chosen. After Araminta was born, however, and Silverton added to my collection with a gift of his own, I looked upon the baubles with more affection.

I keep them in a locked chest in my private closet, which was added some years ago to our apartments, on the other side of the bedchamber from the nursery. This is not the chest we brought from our hut in the village, nor is it the chest that occupied the room when I first arrived, which I long ago sent down into the storerooms with its ominous cargo and try not to think about.

No, this chest is more sturdy, weighted at the bottom to make it harder to move, and locked with a key I keep at my wrist. I open the lid now and lift the carved wooden boxes from within, and even Araminta can't hold back a little sigh at their splendor. She tries on the gold circlet, set with pearls, and the emerald ring, both of which are far too large for her. She reaches for the sapphire ring, and I tell her it's the ring Daddy gave me when she was born.

"Why?" she asks, admiring the way it glitters on her finger.

"Because he wanted to thank me for bearing him a precious daughter. Because it's the color of the sea, which he loves, and also your eyes, which he loves even more."

She looks up at me. "He loves your eyes, too."

"Yes. He loves us all very much, darling, and he hates to be away, and he'll be back in two more days, if the winds hold fair."

Araminta nods and turns her attention back to the chest. I adjust the circlet on her head so it won't press the tender skin of her brow, while she rummages about, disturbing the neat folds of velvet that comprise my ceremonial robes.

"Mama," she says, "what's this?"

I look over her arm into the chest, and I notice something I have not perceived before: a small black ribbon wedged in the bottom corner.

A tiny frisson of unease ripples across my skin.

"I don't know, sweetheart. I expect it's nothing—"

But Araminta is her father's child, full of brave, heedless curiosity, and she promptly takes hold of that ribbon and pulls it, causing the wooden board at the bottom of the chest to rise from its place.

"Oh, look!" she exclaims. "It's a dress!"

✆

There's no possible way to explain to Araminta how I came by the items of clothing she pulls from the false bottom of my jewel chest, one by one. I tell her they're like my ceremonial robes, a sort of dress-up for adults, and she begs me to put them on so she can see them properly. I refuse and suggest it's time for dinner.

Araminta knows better than this. Dinner begins at noon, and while the sun might hide behind the clouds at present, she is a native Orcadian, and knows at all times where it lies in the sky. Noon is still some way off. Plenty of time for Mama to try on her dress. Please, Mama.

I stare down at the handfuls of navy wool in my lap, and a waft of sea breeze seems to find my nose. A memory of roses.

But apart from the faint sensation of unease that claimed me when Araminta first made her discovery, I feel no vibration in the air, no familiar electricity. I haven't known these things since that long-ago day on the beach, in the cave where we pulled Helen back from the portal's brink. I have almost forgotten those sensations existed. That desire to return to my own century—*our* century—which fell away and turned into fear after my union with Silverton, has faded into nothing, fed by nothing. Even the grief of missing my dear friend Max—the restless tug of unfinished business and unsolved mysteries—have eased their claims on my heart, over the course of these seven blissful years. I have gotten on with life in Hoy, bearing our children, running the household of a medieval castle, loving my husband with every fiber of my heart. For the past seven years, I have so anchored myself to this world, I scarcely feel those tremors for the other one. I have largely forgotten Magnusson's words, and the legend seeped into the stones of this castle. There are times when I reach into my leather pouch and my fingers discover the smooth, heavy, pointed shape of the bullet I still keep there, and I cannot instantly recall how I came by it.

So I lift up the hem of the blue dress and admire the fineness of the modern weave, and I think to myself, *Why not?* It's part of her heritage, after all. One day I shall have to explain it all to her. How her father and I came to live on this strange shore, and why we speak a language unknown to its inhabitants.

What possible harm could it do, after all this time?

"Very well," I say. "But you'll have to help me with the buttons."

Author's Note

⁓∞⁓

As a recovering anthropology major, I'm endlessly fascinated by the way human beings interpret the world around them and weave their stories into the fabric of cultural myth. Selkie legends abound in the north of Great Britain and elsewhere, and theories as to their true origin are almost as numerous. I read a wide range of both in order to construct the particular selkie tale that forms the backbone of this book, and as with the originals, I'm afraid there is no neat conclusion. That's the nature and the magic of mythmaking—a story's true meaning depends on the active interpretation of the audience.

You may be surprised to learn that the available information on medieval Orkney is rather thin, which delighted me immensely, as I enjoy making things up. While I adhered to the known facts of the islands' history—passing as they did from Picts to Vikings to Norse to Scots—I did invent the castle of Hoy (and its lord) as a vassal possession in order not to disturb the historical succession of Orkney rulers with my shenanigans. Trust me, they're fascinating enough not to require any selkie legends for enhancement. In addition to referencing general histories of the Middle Ages and the Orkneys, I spent many fascinating hours plundering the Orkneyjar website to better understand the chronology, culture, and folklore of the region. Any mistakes, omissions, and other sins (intended or otherwise) are entirely my own.

I'm regularly brought to my knees by the psychic tug of history in historical spaces, and to me, the idea of time travel is as natural as thinking itself. Until we obtain proof of a time traveler more complex than a subatomic particle, however, we can only imagine how this phenomenon might work. In my own head, time makes sense as a kind of river flowing in one direction, and time travel as the ability to jump around to different points along that river. That ability, in the world of these books, flows from a higher power through certain individuals who—for whatever reason—can receive and channel it. Thus far, I've avoided the vexing question of whether a person can exist twice in the same point in time. That, along with many other philosophical problems of time travel, will have to wait for another book.

As always, my deepest thanks are due to my editor, Kate Seaver, and all the hardworking team at Berkley who have believed so passionately in these novels from the beginning. Your enthusiasm for my strange plots, particular voices, complicated protagonists, and ambiguous endings will probably get you into trouble with the Big Bosses one day. I'll happily share my bowl of gruel with you when it does. Until then, I'm just grateful you get me.

No one but Alexandra Machinist knows just how much I rely on her sound advice and unwavering support in this mad career of mine. To my dearest of agents and truest of friends—to her

capable assistant, Hillary Jacobson, and all the team at ICM—
thank you yet again.

As I hurtle past deadlines, I like to complain that I could
write twice as many books if it weren't for the incessant demands
of my husband and four children, which is probably true. But
where's the fun in that? Besides, if they didn't force me to rise
from my laptop in order to make dinner, fold laundry, and clean
the cat litter box at regular intervals, the paramedics would have
to surgically separate me from the armchair after each book. My
dutiful thanks are therefore due to my family for, like, keeping it
real. And for the love that keeps my boat afloat through every
squall.

Finally, my gratitude goes out to all my loyal readers, who
read more deeply, think more carefully, see more keenly, and
laugh more freely than all those sane, boring folk with the un-
cluttered desks and worthy, immaculate bookshelves. You really
do. And no one appreciates your odd taste in books more than
your humble author.

A Strange Scottish Shore

Juliana Gray

Questions for Discussion

1. Emmeline Truelove is a liminal character, having lived most of her life in the space between social classes and gender norms. How do you think this experience is reflected in her personality?

2. Emmeline interacts frequently with characters who do not exist, which she describes as ghosts—of Queen Victoria, of her father, and of King Edward VII. How do you interpret these experiences? Are they really ghosts, or figments of her imagination? Why do they appear in the book, and what role do they play?

3. Emmeline's "father" suggests that she and Silverton are attracted to each other because they both wear masks that hide their true selves. Do you think this is true? What masks do they wear, and why? How would you describe Emmeline's true self, and Silverton's?

4. In effect, there are two "selkie" stories taking place in the book, and two possible "selkies"—Helen and Emmeline. Which character do you think is the basis for the Sinclair

family legend, and which one for the tale in *The Book of Time*?
Or are they both some combination of the two? Why do you
think the author has structured the story in this way?

5. Helen has led an eventful life, both in the modern day and
the past. Do you think her happiness with Magnus is enough
to overcome her grief over losing her son and her familiar
world, to say nothing of modern conveniences? How do you
think you would react to being flung into a previous century?
Setting aside emotional connections, do you think you'd be
happier in the past?

6. How has the treatment of women changed over the years,
from medieval Europe to the early twentieth century to today?
How do you think Emmeline and Helen dealt with these dif-
ferences?

7. Do you believe in time travel? What time period would you
most like to experience if you could? What do you think can
be learned from time travel? How do you think it influences
Emmeline's view of the world?

8. Has Hunter been punished for his bad deeds? What do you
think has happened to him?

9. The author leaves some questions unanswered, and the conclusion of the book suggests a possible new fate for Emmeline. What do you think happens to her when she puts on her
twentieth-century dress? Do you think this is a happy ending for Emmeline?